Rwé

The Whale Spirit

Charles A. Hall

Writers Club Press

New York San Jose Lincoln Shanghai

The Whale Spirit

All Rights Reserved © 2000 by Charles A. Hall

No part of this book may be reproduced or transmitted in any form or by any means, graphic, electronic, or mechanical, including photocopying, recording, taping, or by any information storage retrieval system, without the permission in writing from the publisher.

Writers Club Press
an imprint of iUniverse.com, Inc.

For information address:
iUniverse.com, Inc.
620 North 48th Street, Suite 201
Lincoln, NE 68504-3467
www.iuniverse.com

This is a book of fiction. Some of the names and places are accurate, but some names are figments of the authors imagination-others are used with permission of the individuals.

ISBN: 0-595-12148-9

Printed in the United States of America

Dedication

This novel is fiction. Some of the places are actual, but names of individuals are either fictitious or used with their permission.

I want to thank Hank Searles and Susan Gordon for their help and encouragement to keep me dedicated to this work. Much thanks to my editor, C.J. Stone The Stone Press, Annie Copeland, Designer, and Larry Robinson, Electronics.

Most important, however, are heartfelt thanks to the love of my life and inspiration—my wife and lifelong best friend—Katherine.

This novel is dedicated to the tens of thousands of Native American soldier's, sailors, and airmen who have been treated so disgracefully by their government, yet were the first to answer the call when their country was threatened. They put themselves in harms way and vowed that "It won't happen on my watch!"

And to the ennobled whale, who has sustained the Makah and their culture for centuries.

Introduction

This novel was written for several reasons. In 1998 controversy arose in the state of Washington. After a seventy-year ban on whale hunting, the Makahs resumed a centuries old custom of whale hunting. They received permission from the International Whaling Commission to harvest a few whales. Anti-whaling groups opposed the hunting, arguing that not only would the Makahs eventually take more whales and sell the meat, but also it would open the floodgates for more commercial whaling by other tribes. The Makahs position was that under the Treaty of 1855, they had the authority for the hunt, and their hunt would be for cultural reasons. While national media covered both sides of the controversy, the Makahs primarily responded that the whale was a big part of their culture. On May 17, 1999, the Makahs harvested a whale off the coast of Washington, and enjoyed a religious and cultural celebration.

I have used this forum to attempt to explain in more detail the importance of the whale to the Makah culture. Does the whale protect the Makah warrior in battle? We don't know. We do know that to date, no Makah warrior has ever been killed in battle under the US flag. If I have not done justice to the explanation of the Makah culture, or if I have offended a Makah, I apologize.

In most books and movies the Native American has always been portrayed as a secondary character—sometimes, as an afterthought. In war movies and books, they are stereotyped as "Noble Redmen" that thrive in combat. They don't serve much other purpose than as "characters of war."

Does anyone ever remember Tonto getting the girl? In my own experience as a 20-year career Army officer, with Bachelor and Masters degrees, I felt more respected in combat than in any other assignment. For those reasons I have chosen to make a full-blood Makah the hero.

Vietnam was a controversial war. It was a time when politicians committed the military in a war and did not provide a clear mission or have complete support of the American people. Our armed services are too often sent to countries to do what they are not trained or equipped to do. Even now our military is fast becoming an "international police force." This book is to serve as a reminder to politicians and would-be politicians that the lives of American men and women should be placed at risk only for exceptional reasons, and on missions within their capabilities.

As an educator, I feel and obligation to point out that in order to make this book entertaining, graphic descriptions were necessary. I would classify it as "R" for Language, violence, and sexual explicit scenes. So read at your own peril. If anything in the book offends anyone, for any reason, I apologize. But remember—it's only fiction.

Chapter One

"What I am about to tell you will affect you for the rest of your life. The spirit of the Whale protects our warriors. No one will die! Many Makahs went off to fight in World War I and all of them came home," Adam said as he sat on a big rock on the top of a hill, overlooking a harbor, with his grandson, Johnny Pope.

"How does the whale spirit protect the warriors, Grandfather?" Pope asked, black eyes gazing into his grandfather's.

"You are seven years old and it is time that you learned about our Makah heritage. The Makahs have been here for hundreds of years and have a strong background. We were whalers until the 1920's when the government stopped whaling because the white men had killed too many of them. When the Makahs hunted the whale, we were prosperous. There was plenty of fish, elk, deer, and bear to eat. Since the government stopped our whaling, we have fallen on hard times. The white men have never understood that the spirit of the whale is needed to keep the Makahs alive and growing."

"Did the whales come into our harbor?"

Adam Pope was in his sixties, and like most Makahs, just under 5'7" in height, but very strong, robust, intelligent, and quick with a smile. From all the days in the wind rain and sun, Adam's face was like an old brown suitcase—worn and wrinkled but full of character, and still dependable.

He spent three years in a Bureau of Indian Affairs Tribal school in Oregon—and hated it.

"The spring, summer, and fall village was in Ozette on the other side of the hills where the water is fast and strong. It was an exciting time in the village when the great whales moved along the coast. For days before the hunt, the villagers prepared feasts and talked about the hunts of the past. The hunters went to the creek or river and bathed, and they prayed to the Creator for the spirit of the whale to sacrifice himself to the tribe. The prayer always ended with the whalers forming a circle and facing to the north, then the east, south, west, and back to the north."

"How did you kill the whales?"

"When someone sighted the whales the eight man crew jumped in the canoe and paddled fast into the ocean. While all eight were paddlers, some had other duties. The man that steered was in the back and guided it in the direction that the leader ordered. The 'swimmer' was near the front, and his job was to secure the whale's mouth. The leader was also the 'thrower' and at the front."

"The thrower had a harpoon with a line tied one end to the harpoon and the other to the canoe, with seal skin floats also attached to the line. The leader picked out the best whale and directed the steerer to guide the vessel from the rear of the whale so the big mammal could not see the approach. As they got along the left side of the whale, the 'thrower' hurled the harpoon with great strength into the prey. That started a wild ride because the whale swam very fast, dragging the boat and crew behind him."

"That sounds like fun, Grandfather. Did you ride the whale far?"

"The inflated seal skins helped take the strength from the whale. It died after many hours of swimming in circles. The 'swimmer' dove into the frigid water and tied the whale's mouth shut so that it wouldn't take in water and sink. Sometimes the big creature wouldn't be dead and killed the swimmer. Most of the time the whale was dead, and the hunters attached another line to it and towed it toward the village. As they got closer, more canoes met them, attached lines and helped pull it to shore."

"What did you do with the whale, Grandfather?"

"Everyone in the village cut off their share of the meat, blubber, innards, and bones. Almost every inch of the huge whale served a useful purpose. A few days after the hunt the villagers went to the edge of the water and the leader of the hunt canoe threw a few bones into the water to encourage the spirit of the whale to return. The Makahs had great respect for it. Men in your family were always 'throwers' and were leaders of the tribe because throwing took great skill. I had many kills before the government stopped the hunt. Your father would have been a 'thrower' too, and that is why he spends so much time drinking—to try to forget the taking away of his spirit."

Young Pope thought about his father, William. He knew that he loved his father, but hated it when he drank too much and yelled at him and his mother. When he wasn't drinking, he was a friendly, outgoing man that liked to joke. Everyone thought William was the best fisherman in Neah Bay.

Pope shook the thoughts from his mind. "Did killing the whale make the Makahs warriors?"

"The Makahs were a warrior tribe in the old days, too. For many years they paddled their boats across into Canada, raided villages and returned with slaves. Other tribes attacked the Makah's village as well. Your relatives all fought with spears—like the harpoon. Many Makahs went off to fight in World War I and all came home. I fought with the Infantry in the Ardennes in that war. Most of our young men are fighting in World War II, and they will all come back too. Wars are very difficult, and the strong have a better chance for survival."

Young Pope looked to the west and noticed that the sun was starting it's descent into the ocean. It turned into an orange ball and slowly sank into the water. Pope could almost see the steam rise from the ocean as it devoured the sun.

"Are the sunsets always this beautiful, Grandfather?"

Adam took his old yellow pipe from his mouth, knocked the dead ashes into his hand and carelessly dropped them to the ground. Johnny enjoyed the smell of the smoke coming from the pipe, but loved the familiar smell of tobacco smoke on his grandfather. Adam took his jack knife from his pocket and scraped the ashes from the inside of the pipe.

"Yes. But they are most beautiful when you share them with someone you love."

"What will we do tomorrow?" The boy asked.

He was always concerned about the next day's plans.

"You have been chosen and have the Great Spirit to be a warrior, but you must prepare yourself for it. Preparation is most important in anything you choose to do."

Pope looked at Adam with a confused expression and said, "But how can I do that—I'm too small, Grandfather."

Adam took his cloth tobacco pouch from his shirt pocket and filled the bowl of his pipe. Then he took a wooden match from the same pocket, scratched it against the rock, and lit the tobacco in the bowl. He drew the smoke in slowly, while blowing smoke out the side of his mouth.

"You're never too small to begin preparations. Many years ago, we had bigger men because they took care of their bodies and trained to be warriors. They ate the salmon, deer, elk, bear, and whale to get their spirits into their bodies. They ate herbs and roots from the forest to make their bones bigger and stronger, and didn't get sick."

"But how will I get the herbs, Grandfather?"

"I will show you. Now come, we must go home for dinner. Your mother works hard at the restaurant all day. You should honor her hard work by being at her table on time. We will start your preparations tomorrow."

The two walked down from the hills. At the edge of the village Pope said good night to his grandfather and ran the two miles home.

*   *   *

Johnny Pope was born on a small Indian reservation on the northwest tip of the state of Washington. The ocean lay on the north and west, and a large river ran through the reservation. The village of Neah Bay, where most of the people lived, was in a small harbor. The ground was flat just off the beach where most of the homes were built. Hills protected the village to the north, west, and further south. Due to the warm Japanese current, very little snow fell in the winter. There was over 100 inches of rain every year. The landscape was a rich green year round and the summers a comfortable 70-75 degrees each day. Cedar trees abounded in the area.

One dirt road ran west from Port Angeles, 75 miles away, and ended in Neah Bay. Mudslides caused breaks in the road during the winter months, isolating the village. Outsiders claimed Neah Bay was at the end of the world. Makahs said Neah Bay was at the beginning of the world. It was a beautiful place to live, and young Pope could think of no better place to be.

*   *   *

Pope rushed into his tarpaper and wood house. It had two small bedrooms and a combination living room, kitchen, dining room. His mother, Shirley was putting dinner on the table. Shirley was tall for a Makah, and built for hard work. While in her teens, Shirley was the village beauty, with long straight black hair, that was appealing when worn either down or in braids. She worked as a waitress in the town's only restaurant.

"Hi Mom. What's for supper?"

"Nothing till you wash your hands and face," Shirley said, smiling.

Pope went to the toilet. It was outside and had an old Sears catalog for toilet paper. Young Pope couldn't understand why there were two seats, when he never saw more than one person at a time use the toilet. He quickly relieved himself and ran back into the house. Then he poured water from the pitcher into a metal pan, and washed his hands and face.

Wiping his hands, Pope said excitedly, "Grandfather is going to teach me how to be a warrior. We're going into the hills tomorrow."

"That's nice, son. Now sit down. We're having your favorite dinner. Fried chicken with wild blueberry pie for desert."

Shirley opened the oven of the big, black wood burning stove and displayed a hot pie. The stove heated the entire house. After dinner, Pope took the three lanterns that provided light at night and filled them with oil. It was his job to keep them filled. Then he went outside and brought in wood and kindling for the stove.

*   *   *

Pope woke early, got out of bed and shivered in the morning cold. He slipped into his shoes and put on a heavy jacket. He lifted the lids of the stove and stuffed in paper, kindling and wood. He took a wooden match, struck it on the surface of the stove, and lit the paper. Satisfied the fire was going; Pope scurried back to his bed, took off his shoes, and jumped under the covers, dragging his shirt and pants with him. He dressed himself under the covers where it was warmer. Without washing, Pope left the house and ran to his grandfather's home.

"I'm ready to be a warrior, Grandfather," Pope said as he burst into the small wooden structure on the beach.

Adam looked up from his coffee and picked up his pipe.

"You're just in time, but I bet you haven't had breakfast. I know you haven't washed. There's the basin and water. I'll get you something to eat."

Pope started to argue about washing, but stopped, knowing that quibbling with his grandfather was not a good idea.

He washed and toweled, and said, "I'm not really hungry, Grandfather. Let's get started."

"Here's some hot oatmeal. Now sit down and eat."

Pope wolfed the cereal down and wiped his mouth with his sleeve.

"OK, Grandfather. I'm ready."

"We'll start at the beach," Adam said as he shuffled toward the door.

They walked across the soft sand of the beach, down to where the sand was harder. Adam bent over and picked up a rock and threw it far out into the water.

"Now, you do the same thing, Johnny."

Try as he may, Pope's rock didn't go as far as his grandfathers.

"You must use your entire body when you throw the rock."

The boy took another rock and spun around and hurled it while jumping about six inches in the air. It didn't go any farther than his other rocks.

The old man demonstrated, as he said, "You have to step toward the target. At the same time, rotate the left shoulder back, and step forward, rotating hips and follow through toward the target."

"I think I know now."

Pope took another rock and following Adam's instructions, threw the rock further.

"That's better. Now throw some more rocks."

Pope tossed fifty more rocks. Each time, his instructor gave him words of encouragement. The two gathered several rocks of different sizes and set them on the sand.

"Use the smallest rocks first and throw them as far as you can into the waves. Then throw a bigger rock, until you get to one about the size of a baseball. This will build up your arm strength to throw the spear."

He closely observed Pope's technique, correcting any flaw that his grandson developed.

After Pope tossed the last stone, Adam said, "You must do this every day."

"What's next, Grandfather? This is fun."

"A warrior must have a strong body to sustain him in combat. You do that by running in the sand. I want you to run to that point on the beach where the big rock is," Adam said, pointing at an outcropping with a large black rock, a half-mile away.

Pope took off like a shot. His tiny legs pumping, hair was blowing in the wind.

A few minutes later, Pope arrived back to his grandfather and said, "That's fun too. What's next?"

"I forgot to tell you that you are to run on the soft sand. Because it will make you stronger. Run again, only in the soft sand," smiling at his mistake.

Pope turned and sprinted to the soft sand, then headed for the out-cropping. He had to go around logs and branches that had washed up on the beach. The running was more difficult, and he was out of breath, with beads of sweat on his face when he reached Adam.

"That was good. To get stronger, you are to run to the point and back three times a day. Now, let's walk up to the hills."

As they strolled along, Adam stopped and showed Pope how to identify the roots and herbs that when eaten would make him stronger. As they got deeper in the rain forest, Adam stopped at a small stream.

"Now I will show you the warrior ritual of bathing. Take off your clothes."

"But I don't need a bath, Grandfather. I just had one on Saturday night."

Adam smiled and took his clothes off, setting them in a neat pile. Pope shrugged, took his clothes off, and set them next to his mentor. Adam stood naked next to the stream, bent, and scooped water with his hands, pouring it liberally all over himself.

"You do this every morning to clean your body and build your character. Now you do it, Johnny."

Pope stepped to the stream, put his hand in, and then quickly pulled it back.

"The water's too cold, Grandfather. Can we build a fire and heat it?"

"No. That is how you build character."

Pope bent down, filled his little hands with water, and tossed it on his head.

He shivered immediately but continued to pour water on his body until Adam said, "OK, that's enough."

"Wow. That water is freezing. How do we dry off? With our shirt?"

"No. We let the air dry us. Usually we build a fire before we bathe, but it is too late today. We'll do it next time."

"How about when it's raining. How do we dry then?"

"We find dry wood under the canopy of the trees, and if we can't build a fire, we just put our wet clothes over us. Now we must pray together to the Creator for the return of the whale and for you to take on the warrior spirit."

Adam then faced north. With Pope by his side they both turned and faced the east, south, west, and back to the north.

The old man taught young Pope the warrior chant, and they continued it for about twenty minutes—until Adam was sure young Pope understood. Then the two dressed and strolled back to Adam's home. Neither said a word. Pope thought about the things he had learned that day. He remembered long periods of silence while visiting with his grandfather. It seemed that Adam only talked when he had something important to say.

Every day thereafter the two went through the same ritual.

*   *   *

Young Pope regularly visited the soldiers that camped and trained in the big gun positions that protected the coast from Japanese invasion. The soldiers were friendly and usually gave him candy. Pope asked many questions about how they would fight the Japanese if they came to Neah Bay. It excited Pope to think that he might be able to see a war right there on the reservation.

There were many war films shown in the small movie theater in the village, and Pope saw all of them. *Wake Island, Sands of Iwo Jima, Gung Ho,* and *Guadlecanal Diary* were his favorites, and John Wayne was his hero. He dreamed about the time that he would fight for his country. He would return to the village a hero, with several medals like his grandfather, and everyone would respect him.

Adam took Pope to most of the war movies and one day said, "Johnny, war isn't glamorous like the movies show. I was in a lot of battles, and I never heard a single band. War is like days of boredom, interrupted by a few hours of sheer terror. What I remember about war was the fear, hunger, exhaustion, blood, and sweat. I don't want you to go to war, but I know that you have been chosen to be a warrior and will go. We must do our best to prepare you for that day."

Pope heard what his grandfather said, but he only saw the glamour in the Hollywood stories of war. When he played with his friends it was always a game of "war." He was always the leader, and his side always won.

*   *   *

One night near the end of 1942, Pope's father disappeared. William left no message and didn't tell anyone where he was going. Pope's mother never heard a word from him. Shirley waited until the end of 1944, then went to the tribal judge and divorced William on the grounds of desertion. In November 1945, William returned to the village. He was wearing an army uniform with the rank of sergeant on his sleeves and a chest full of medals.

"I was ashamed of my drinking and joined the army," he explained to Shirley.

"You left Johnny and me to fend for ourselves. You didn't even send us any money."

"I know. I'm sorry. I fought in North Africa, Italy, and was in the invasion of Normandy. I have money saved now."

"It's too late. We're divorced, and that's the way I want to keep it."

William stayed in the village and went back to fishing. He built an indoor bathroom onto the side of Shirley's house. Young Pope spent more time with William, asking him to tell about his adventures in Europe. William agreed with Adam that the war was not very glamorous while he was fighting.

"But I sure did love that ticker tape parade in New York when my unit returned to the United States."

Pope imagined himself leading his soldiers in a parade.

"All the Makah warriors returned from another war," William announced.

Chapter Two

"You are 13 years of age and your grandfather and I are going to have a naming Potlatch for you," Shirley said.

"I already have a name, and I like it," Pope exclaimed with a frown.

"It is tribal custom that when you reach the age of 13, you get another name. We have saved for two years to have this big party."

"Why not just save the money, and I'll keep my name?"

"Your grandfather has already invited friends and relatives from all over Washington state and Canada."

*   *   *

The community hall was decorated with bright red, white, and blue colored paper. Pope's family provided a feast of deer, salmon, and other fish. All the invited tribes sang and danced their family songs, then gave gifts to other guests and to Pope. Unlike the white custom that requires that all the guests bring presents for the host, the Makah custom is that the host gives at least one gift to every guest. The potlatch lasted over twelve hours. About halfway through the party, Adam took young Pope aside.

"Today you are a man, and tomorrow you will learn the ways of hunting and fishing and how to be a warrior."

"OK. **Now** this makes more sense to me, Grandfather."

*   *   *

Waking up, after only two hours sleep, Pope ran the two miles to Adam's house and flew in the door. He was happy to be able to spend more time with his grandfather. It surprised Pope to find Adam dressed and at the kitchen table, drinking a cup of coffee.

Adam looked up and said, "Let's get started. Go out and saddle the two horses."

Pope saddled the horses, went back into the house, and took out a loaf of bread to make sandwiches for lunch.

Adam returned from the bedroom and said, "Today you will learn how to find food in the forest. We won't need the sandwiches."

"O.K., but can I take the sandwiches along, just in case we need them?"

"No."

They rode silently along the trails lined with green ferns and wild grasses, up into the hills, for about two hours before they dismounted.

"The first rule of warfare is to know the land where you fight and use it to your advantage. For that reason, it is important to know all about the hills, trees, valleys, and waterways. If there is a hill near a valley it is wise to be there because you can see your enemy from a greater distance. If there is a river, it can be used in defending against your enemy. Use the bushes and trees to hide behind so your enemy cannot see you."

"The second rule is to know your enemy. The more you know about him, the more chance you have to defeat him. But you should remember to keep your secrets away from him, because he will use his knowledge against you. Just like the Makahs respect the whale during the hunt, you must always respect your enemy. If you don't, you will be defeated. Never show disrespect for your enemy."

"The third rule is to use the darkness to your advantage against your enemy. When he is asleep, you should be moving in for the kill. Use the darkness so he cannot see you as you move toward him. It is hard for your enemy to see when there is fog. Use the fog like you use the darkness."

"The fourth rule is to know yourself. I have tried to teach you about yourself since you were born. The Makahs are about all of the things I have just talked about. We respect the whale, wolf, elk, fish, and bear. We respect the sun, moon, sky, and earth. We respect the trees, waterways, and grass. We respect all of the peoples—our friends and our enemies. This is what you are Grandson, and you will learn this and more all of your life."

Pope looked at his grandfather with pride as he smiled to himself.

Adam showed his grandson the edible leaves, plants, and berries. They shared a lunch of blackberries and salmon berries. Adam pointed at some deer and bears tracks and explained how to estimate how long it had been since the animals had made the tracks. By the time they rode down from the hills, it was almost dark and Pope's head was swimming with the new knowledge.

As they were unsaddling the horses, Adam said, "You can stay overnight because tomorrow we'll get up early and take the boat out and go fishing."

Pope loved to stay over with his grandfather. They slept side by side in the same bed, and Pope felt warm and comfortable. His mother never worried when he didn't come home at night because she knew he was safe at his grandfather's home.

Pope had been fishing many times with his father and grandfather. Today he learned more about where the best fishing spots were for both salmon and bottom fish, and the best time to go to that location. Adam taught him how to spear flounder on the sand bar. While out in the ocean, Adam pointed out the best beaches to land on if the enemy occupied the reservation.

*　*　*

Almost every day that summer Adam and Pope went up into the rain forest and continued young Pope's Makah tribal education. They rode to the top of a foothill and Adam pointed out how the elevation dominated the valley.

"It would be difficult to drive an enemy unit off the top of the hill, or to move in the valley without being shot at from the occupants on the top.

This is the 'military crest' of the hill. It is the highest point on the mound where a soldier can lie down and see all the way to the bottom."

Sometimes they left their encampment after dark and walked to a river or lake and sat quietly through the night. In the morning they waited for a deer or an elk to appear for a drink of water. They didn't shoot any game that summer because Adam told Pope the animal's meat wasn't good to eat at that time of the year.

"If you defend along a river bank, your enemy will be exposed in the middle of the river."

He insisted that Pope continue his daily bath in the stream to cleanse his body and spirit. On those days Pope always ran at least three miles over the hills. Adam made several wooden spears from cedar, all about six feet in length. Pope practiced throwing them at a rise in a hill that looked like a whale.

"Now you must go into the hills by yourself in quest of a *vision*," the old man said as they sat on a log and chewed on a strip of smoked salmon.

"What do I do to have a *vision*, Grandfather?

"You take no food with you and drink only water. You spend all your time praying to The Creator and singing. Build a fire and keep it going. Do not sleep until you have the *vision*."

"How will I know what a *vision* is?

"You will know. There will be no doubt in your mind."

"How long do I have to stay there? Can I come home tomorrow?"

"Do not come home until you have had the *vision*. Be as patient as a warrior and The Creator will send you a sign."

*   *   *

Pope walked up into the hills the next day, worried that he was not worthy and would not get a *vision*. He found a hill with a stream running down the side. He gathered some wood and built a fire. After removing his clothes, he went to the stream and bathed. He stood naked and thought, *OK Grandfather, I'm going to do it. I sure hope I'm worthy enough to have a vision.*

*   *   *

Three days later, Pope burst into his grandfather's house. Adam was sitting at the kitchen table puffing on his old yellow pipe.

"I did it, Grandfather! I did it! I had a *vision!*"

Adam stood, and Pope threw his arms around him and spun him around. "Can you tell me about your *vision*, Johnny?" Adam said, smiling.

Pope was sweating profusely and was out of breath. He put his hands on his knees, took a deep breath, wiped the sweat from his forehead with the sleeve of his shirt, and said, "It was just like you said, Grandfather. I prayed and sang, and The Creator sent me a sign. I'm not just to be a warrior. I am to be a leader, too."

"That is good, Johnny," Adam said softly, nodding his head.

Pope knew his grandfather was as proud as he was, but he also knew that he never got excited about anything. "This is better than I ever dreamed of, Grandfather. I'm going to lead warriors in battle."

"Yes. Now sit down and I'll fix you something to eat. After that you can go to bed."

"I'm not hungry, and I'm too excited to sleep. I have to go tell Mom," Pope yelled as he ran out the door.

*   *   *

The year was a joyous one as Pope spent more time then ever with his grandfather. But his life was to change dramatically.

Two weeks after his 14th birthday, Pope went to Adam's house and found him still in bed.

"Come on lazy bones, it's time to get up," Pope said as he leaned over the bed and shook Adam's shoulder.

Young Pope felt his grandfather's cold skin on his arm, saw Adam's ashen face, and knew that his grandfather was dead. Later, the doctor said Adam had a heart attack in the middle of the night and quietly died.

Since Adam was a whaling chief, people from the entire village and tribes from all over attended the funeral. There was a big dinner and many people stood and told good things about Adam. Pope went through a period of sadness and depression at the loss of his best friend and teacher. Losing his grandfather was hard. The rest of the summer Pope went into the hills and practiced all that he had learned from Adam.

*   *   *

During his high school years, Pope spent all his spare time preparing to be a warrior. Every morning he got up early, ran three miles on the beach, and threw at least one hundred rocks into the waves. Then he went to a stream or river and bathed, prayed, returned home, ate breakfast and went to school.

Pope read books about war that convinced him the best warriors were those in the best physical condition who could fight during periods of reduced visibility. He learned how to move quietly at night and studied how to maintain good night vision. Many nights, he moved about three miles through the thick rain forest to a stream where he knew wild game such as elk or deer went for water. He hid quietly in the bushes until an animal appeared near the water's edge, shot it, dressed it down, constructed a sled and dragged the carcass back to the village.

*   *   *

The small high school on the reservation was well known for its athletic teams. The players were usually smaller than their opponents were, but much faster. Since there were not many boys in the school the team played eight-man football. It was a wide-open game that involved a lot of passing the ball.

As a freshman, Pope played linebacker on defense and loved the contact. By his sophomore year Pope was the starting quarterback on offense and linebacker on defense. Years of throwing rocks and spears had built up his arm so he could throw a football accurately over 60 yards. His team won most of its games over the next three years. It won a state championship in his senior year. Pope set school passing records and earned a spot on the All State team. During the track season, he set a state record hurling the Javelin.

That spring, Pope was called into his coach's office.

"I sent game film to about 25 colleges and universities nationwide. I thought sure you would get a scholarship," his football coach said.

"Did any of them answer?"

"One coach said our high school didn't play against difficult competition and that you are too short for a quarterback."

"Did anyone else answer?"

"No. I even told them that you were not only an exceptional athlete, but you had an inner drive and heart that was impossible to measure."

"Well, I'm really disappointed. I guess I'll just have to prove them wrong."

"What are you going to do?"

"My grandfather had a life insurance policy and made me the beneficiary. He told me that the best way for me to succeed as a warrior is to get a good education. I've decided to enroll in the State University."

Pope decided to major in history, but he also enrolled in the army ROTC. He was a little worried about leaving the reservation because he had only left it to play in high school athletic events. But Pope also realized what he wanted was not on the reservation. It was ultimately several thousand miles away in a foreign country, but he had to complete his warrior education first. He vowed that people would hear about Johnny Pope.

Chapter Three

Pope dropped back to pass, looked to his left, and saw his receiver streaking downfield. A 265-pound defensive tackle closed in fast, reached out with a meaty paw, and grasped Pope's jersey. Spinning away and staggering slightly, the quarterback pulled loose, righted himself, and sprinted to his left. He evaded two more tacklers and galloped into the end zone for a touchdown. A loud screeching whistle stopped the action on the practice field.

"Dammit! Can't any of you guys on defense play this game?" Coach Phillips snorted. "Do I have to remind you that those guy you're playing against aren't even close to Southern Cal caliber players. They're walk-ons. They don't have scholarships. Remember men—you're supposed to eat them for breakfast!" he added. "All right, everyone take ten laps and head for the weight room. Good job, Scout team," Phillips half mumbled as he kicked a clod of dirt. Pope's Scout team let out a cheer and led the 30 scholarship defensive players around the track on their laps.

"Damn Mike, we are really in trouble if we can't stop our Scout squad," Phillips said, shaking his head.

"Yeah, I know Coach, but half our defense is injured. Hell, they spend more time in the training room than on the field," Michaels, the defensive coach, replied as he shuffled along side his boss, toward the locker room.

"What do you think of that quarterback—Pope, I think his name is?"

"The kid's kind of raw, but he has natural instincts for the game."

"Yeah, and he's the fastest Indian I've seen since that Olympic runner, Billy Mills. I wish he were a little bigger though. He looks to be about five foot, nine and weighs about 165 pounds soaking wet."

"If the offensive coach doesn't want him, I'll take him for a defensive back," Michaels said, smiling.

"Nah, I want to see him at quarterback a little longer. He definitely should be playing somewhere," Phillips said and kicked the mud from his cleats before entering the locker room.

* * *

Pope left the locker room and walked across campus to his dormitory. He only had 25 minutes before the dining room closed. He entered the cafeteria, picked up a plate of dried out chicken drumsticks, lumpy mashed potatoes, and shriveled peas. He grabbed a piece of pie and two containers of milk, and handed the bored cashier his meal ticket. Master Sergeant Dennison, Pope's ROTC instructor sat alone at a table near the windows.

Pope sauntered over to the table, set his tray down, pulled out a chair, and said, "Hey Sergeant Dennison, what brings you here? It sure couldn't be the culinary delights."

"Hi, Pope. No, that's for sure. I haven't seen such bad chow since basic training at Fort Leonard Wood," Dennison said, looking up from his tray. "Precision drill team practice starts tonight so I thought I'd eat here. Save going all the way home and coming back," he added.

Pope took to Sergeant Dennison from the first day of class. The big friendly sergeant had retired from the active army after 26 years of service. He had earned a Silver Star, a Bronze Star, and two Purple Hearts, serving in World War II and Korea. He loved Dennison's stories about the 82nd Airborne Division in Normandy and the 187th Airborne Regiment in Korea.

"What's the precision drill team?" Pope asked, picking up a piece of chicken.

"A platoon of 34 cadets do a variety of marching maneuvers. They're the best, and I really enjoy coaching them."

"It sounds like fun. How does one get in the platoon?"

"You've only been in ROTC for about three months, right?"

Pope nodded his head. "Yeah, I'm a lowly frosh, but I really like ROTC."

"What are you majoring in?"

"My major is history for a teaching certificate, but my career choice is the army. I take the history classes to learn more about wars."

The big Sergeant's eyebrows rose. "We don't get many ROTC freshmen who know they want a career in the army. Unfortunately, we only accept sophomores in the drill team. You should work toward becoming a DMS, a 'Distinguished Military Student,' because you can graduate with a regular army commission. You get better assignments and don't have to worry about being discharged involuntarily when the army cuts back forces."

Pope shrugged his shoulders. "It's just as well I can't get in the drill team now because I'm playing football and don't have much time to study. Thanks for the tip about becoming a DMS."

*   *   *

"Glad you could see me, Johnny. Have a seat," Coach Phillips said, looking up from his papers.

Pope looked around and saw the office as a reflection of Coach Phillips personality. A large oak desk was at the wall, away from the door. It contained only the papers Phillips was working on. Pictures of various teams Phillips had coached lined the wall behind his desk. Pope noted a coffee table, leather chair and leather sofa in one corner of the king-size room. Near the chair, a 16-MM movie projector and a cabinet filled with film indicated Phillips watched game films a great deal. Everything in the office represented simplicity and preparation.

Pope pulled out one of the leather-covered oak chairs in front of the desk and sat down nervously. The football season had ended a month before. He was afraid the Coach would cut him from the Scout team.

"How do you like playing football here, Pope?" Phillips asked, leaning back in his chair.

"I like football as much as ROTC, Coach," Pope said, smiling anxiously.

Phillips leaned forward in his chair. "ROTC, huh? How do you keep up with studies, football, **and** ROTC?"

"It isn't easy, but my grades are pretty good so far. I won't know for sure until January."

"Why the interest in ROTC and football? Most students are only able to manage one or the other?"

"I plan to be an army officer some day. Football is the closest thing to combat. You have formations, with plans to attack and defend. You have to make adjustments when your opponents counter or when your players don't follow the plan. Besides, I love football."

Phillips raised his hand to interrupt the young student. "Pope, I've seen you bust your ass every day in practice. You've been hit harder than anyone else has on the field, and you kept coming back. I want to offer you a full scholarship, but I need a commitment from you to the State U football team. Do you think you can make that pledge?"

Pope smiled reassuringly. "Yes Sir, Coach! This scholarship is one of the goals I set for myself and it'll also help me achieve another goal: to prove to a bunch of coaches who didn't offer me a scholarship that they made a big mistake."

Phillips chuckled and stood. "I guess I'm one of those coaches you proved wrong. I'm glad you set goals, Johnny, and I believe in them. My goal is to get this team to the Rose Bowl. I expect you to be a big part of that plan. You can move into the athletic dorm right away," Phillips said, extending his hand to Pope.

"Thanks Coach. You can count on me," Pope replied as he stood, took the outstretched hand, and shook it vigorously. Then he turned and strolled out of the office, leaving the smiling Phillips. Pope exited the building, stopped, took a deep breath of cold air, and exhaled. "Wow! I thought I was getting the boot. Now I can say good bye to the crappy cafeteria food, **and** I get my own tutor!"

*　　*　　*

"First squad to the rear march! Second squad to the rear march! Third squad to the rear march!" Cadet Lieutenant Pope shouted to the precision drill team. Each of the squads reversed directions about three seconds apart and eventually formed a platoon formation going the opposite way. The drill team was practicing for an exhibition at the Coliseum in Spokane, and Pope wanted it to be perfect.

"Platoon halt." All 33 cadets stopped did an automatic left face, and brought their rifles from their shoulders to attention—rifle along their right side, butt on the ground. In the same motion, they kicked the butt of the rifle forward while holding onto the barrel, spinning the weapon in a circle. As the butt landed on the ground next to each man's foot, they thrust the barrel forward, coming to a position of parade rest.

"You looked real good, men. We're finally coming together as a team. Next practice is tomorrow at 1900 hours. Platoon-Atten-Hut! Diss-Missed!" The drill team members in animated conversations, walked to the arms room to turn in their rifles. Pope ambled over to where Sergeant Dennison sat to watch practice.

"If you don't watch out, you're going to get a reputation for being a task master," Dennison snickered.

Pope eased down on the small bleachers next to Dennison. "As you know, Sarge, preparation is important. We're really starting to come together. What do you think?"

"Tell you the truth, this is the best drill team I've had in four years, Pope. How the hell you find time to drill and study is beyond me. Not to mention that you threw three touchdown passes against U Cal Saturday."

"It just takes a little organization, Sarge. Anyway, the football season is over next week, and I'll have more time for ROTC and the drill team."

"You're having a great junior year, Johnny. If the football team wins on Saturday, we'll be five and five. My guess is the Colonel will promote you to Cadet Captain in January."

"Yeah, we've done OK, but the football team will be better next year. I'm really looking forward to going to Ft. Bragg for the summer. Will you be going with us?"

The Sergeant beamed. "Sure. I have to attend ROTC camp every summer. You'll like Bragg. I spent over ten years of my army career there. I always look forward to going back."

Pope grinned mischievously. "Since you're an old paratrooper I expect you to get me a plane ride while we're there." Getting no reaction, he stood, stretched, and added, "Well, I have to turn in my saber and get back to my studies, Sarge."

*   *   *

As the cadets from the northwest got off the airplane at the small airfield in North Carolina, the hot humid air hit them like a blast furnace.

"My God! Is it always this hot here, Sarge?" Pope asked.

"This is good training weather, Johnny. The enemy doesn't just come out to fight on nice, cool, sunny days," Sergeant Dennison said, slapping Pope on the back. "You men wait here, and I'll go check on our ground transportation to Fort Bragg," he shouted to the sweating collegians.

*   *   *

Pope just finished getting a maximum score on the obstacle course, when Dennison approached him. "OK, Pope, you got max points on the squat thrusts, push ups, mile run, and obstacle course. I got a twenty-dollar bet on you to get the highest score of all the five hundred cadets taking the physical training test. Do you need some advice on how to win the grenade throw?"

Taking deep breaths, Pope mopped the sweat from his brow with his bare arm and said, "Thanks a lot Sarge. No pressure on me at all, huh?" He was wearing a white T-shirt, and green fatigue pants bloused into black combat boots. The pants and shirt were soaking wet.

"This is the one time 'close only counts in horse shoes and hand grenades,' doesn't mean crap. You get five grenades. They're worth 20 points apiece. There are about twenty cadets that have 400 points just like you. The only one I'm worried about is the quarterback from The Citadel."

"Do you have any advice for me, based on your decades of experience, oh Great White Sergeant?" Pope joked. He took his hands from his knees, put them on his hips and laughed.

Dennison turned serious, mirrored Pope's hands on hips, and said, "This ain't funny, man. All you got to do is throw five touchdown passes, and I walk away with a grin and a four-hundred-dollar pool. So you just relax and throw. I'll do the worrying for the both of us."

The Citadel cadet competed just ahead of Pope. He stepped out from behind a wall and threw a grenade through an open window twenty yards away. Pope hurled a spiral through the same window. Pope matched The Citadel's toss the second time as well—the Citadel 40, Pope 40. In the second exercise, both men stood in a foxhole and threw grenades into another foxhole thirty yards away twice. The Citadel 80 points, Pope 80 points! The rest of the cadets had missed at least one of the targets.

"All right, this is where the men are separated from the boys, Pope. You lie down in a prone position, facing a circle target forty yards away. Raise up on one knee and throw the grenade," Dennison explained.

Pope squinted against the sun, trying to see a target made from lime in the grass across the field. "How big is the target, Sarge?"

"The entire hub is about twenty yards in diameter, with five inner rings. Each ring is worth four more points until the bulls-eye. The bull is only about a yard in diameter. Hell, just imagine the bulls-eye is a small wide receiver and hit him in stride. Don't worry about missing. You've already done better than 99 percent of the cadets."

Pope knew that Dennison had a lot riding on the throw even though the Sarge appeared relaxed. He strode up to The Citadel, shook his hand, and said, "Good luck."

"Thanks. You, too." The Citadel mumbled, eyes shifting to the ground.

Damn, I've got his spirit! He's psyched out! Pope thought. The Citadel lay down, rose to one knee, and hurled the grenade. Standing right behind the thrower, Pope could see the grenade head straight at the bulls-eye, but it fell short! It landed barely inside the second ring, for 16 points. *OK,* Pope thought, *he choked and came up short. That means I need to add just a little more range with my throw.*

As he lay down on the hot grass, Pope thought, *All right Grandfather, this is for all the rocks we threw into the waves. Imagine that you're driving a harpoon into a whale.* He rose up on one knee, left foot and left hand pointed at the target, cocked his arm, and hurled a perfect spiral. Pope dropped back to the ground and didn't see the grenade land smack in the middle of the bulls-eye.

Dennison collected his bets and caught up with Pope, walking toward the company formation. "Hey, Pope, that was a hell of a toss! I owe you a drink. Let's go to the club tonight, and I'll buy you a beer."

Pope turned and grinned. "Thanks, Sarge but I like to stay as far away from the fire water as I can." Then he added, "You can do me a favor, though."

"Sure. Anything within reason," the happy sergeant replied.

"I want to go through Airborne training eventually, but I'd like to jump from an aircraft here."

The big paratrooper shook his head slowly.

"Damn, I don't know about that. I could get into a lot of trouble. Troops normally train three weeks before they make their first jump. You could get hurt, and the Colonel and the football coach would both pick at my carcass. I tell you what. How about I get you a ride from the 34 foot tower?"

Pope shook his head. "I've seen those towers. They look kind of candy-ass. I want a **real** jump."

"Tell you what. I could lose my job if I got caught letting you jump from an aircraft. You jump from the tower first, and if you insist, I'll get you the jump. What do you say?"

"Deal," Pope, said, shaking the sergeant's hand.

*   *   *

Dennison and Pope pulled up in a jeep at the 34-foot tower where two men stood waiting. They wore tee shirts, caps, fatigue pants, and spit-shined jump boots.

"Pope, these are Master Sergeants Thompson and Hill. Troops shake hands with Cadet Johnny Pope."

As the two tough-looking sergeants shook hands with Pope, Johnny looked up at the wooden structure behind the two men. It looked like a gray room about thirty-five feet up, held by large posts. Four flights of wooden stairs led from the ground to the tower. An open door was in the side of the room, and a steel cable ran from the top of the building past a dirt embankment about 100 yards away.

In a gravelly voice, the shortest sergeant said, as though he had made the comment to thousands of airborne trainees, "The purpose of the 34 foot tower is to teach the trainees to make a proper exit from an aircraft in aerial flight. On the command of 'Hook up,' grasp the metal hook on the end of your static line with your right hand and attach it to the cable above your head. On the command, 'Stand in the door,' shuffle to the edge of the platform, placing one hand on each side of the open door, and look straight ahead. On the command, 'Go,' you will feel a sharp slap on your butt. Pull yourself up, jump out vigorously from the aircraft, and place both feet together. Place your left hand on the large loop, and right hand on the metal handle of your reserve chute hanging from your chest.

You will immediately shout, 'one thousand, two thousand, three thousand.' Then you will look up and check your canopy. Any questions?"

Dennison chuckled after looking at Pope's confused expression and said, "Remember what Sergeant Hill said. I'll demonstrate for you before you go out the door."

The two sergeants strode to the embankment, and Pope and Dennison walked to a nearby bench. Sergeant Dennison picked up a brown harness and showed Pope how to put it on. He put his arm through the right shoulder strap, then the left shoulder strap. Dennison brought long leg straps, from his crotch to a large metal ring at his stomach and clicked them in place. After tightening the leg straps snugly, Dennison fastened the reserve chute across the top of the metal ring.

After repeating the process with Pope, Dennison said, "Does that feel OK?"

"Yeah, except the harness is so tight it feels like it's trying to pull my crotch up to my shoulder blades."

"That's the way it's supposed to feel. Once the chute opens the pressure releases. Be sure you've checked your balls so they're clear of the straps. Otherwise you'll have a squeaky voice for months," Dennison said, laughing.

The two men walked up the stairs, and when they reached the top, Pope walked to the edge of the "room" and peered out the door.

"It looks a lot higher than 34 feet," Pope said, suddenly wondering why he asked to make the jump.

"No sweat. Just watch me go out the door, then you wait until I get back, and I'll walk you through it."

Dennison hooked himself up, shuffled to the door, leaped out, placed his feet together, and grasped his reserve chute, all in one motion. He slid along the steel cable to the embankment, and the two sergeants caught him and unhooked the static line.

"You make it look easy, Sarge," Pope said as Dennison got to the top of the stairs.

"The exit was easy. It's the run back and walk up the stairs that's tough on this out of shape old trooper," Dennison said between deep breaths.

"I think I got it. You give the commands, and I'll follow them," Pope suggested.

"OK. Here we go," Dennison said. Then he said loudly, "Hook Up." Pope took the hook and fastened it onto the cable.

"Stand in the door." Pope shuffled to the door, placing each hand on the outside, and looked straight ahead.

"Go!" As Dennison slapped him on the rump, Pope reacted with a quick bolt out the door. The exit was clumsy as Pope found himself reaching, but never finding the ring on the reserve chute. When he reached the end of the line connected to the cable, the force created great discomfort in the groin area.

Pope was so happy that he didn't fall to his death that he enjoyed the slide down the cable to the embankment. The sergeants stopped Pope's slide and unhooked him. Both laughed when he bent over and checked his groin area to convince himself that his family jewels were still intact. Pope thought that he could wait until airborne training to jump from an aircraft.

Pope found out where the drop zones were and spent Saturdays watching parachute jumps. He envisioned himself some day making a night jump into a combat zone.

*　　*　　*

On the flight back to Washington, Pope thought the summer camp was the most exciting two months of his life. While he enjoyed learning about leadership, communications, and weapons, his favorite subject was small unit tactics. He excelled on the physical side of the training as well, particularly during the long-range patrols. It amazed Pope how much what he learned from his grandfather in the rain forests of the Pacific Northwest, was part of Army doctrine. He was looking forward to his senior year in college.

Chapter Four

On the day that Pope arrived back at State U, the football team started fall practice. The team was very enthusiastic because league coaches picked State U to finish in the top three in the conference. That meant that they might be able to go to the Rose Bowl. The team had set the conference championship as their goal!

After practice, Pope went to the office of the Professor of Military Science and Tactics for ROTC. The Army Colonel told him that he was designated a "Distinguished Military Student." The Colonel appointed him Commandant of the Corps of Cadets, with the rank of Cadet Colonel. Pope knew that it was going to be a great year—but he could hardly wait for graduation so that he could go back to Ft. Bragg for airborne training.

After starting the season with a heartbreaking loss to Northwestern University, the State U football team reeled off ten straight wins. They won the conference championship by beating their cross-state rivals, The U, in the final game.

The weeks leading up to the Rose Bowl game were hectic for Pope because he was the center of media attention. Not only had he set school passing records but also because he was an Indian. To complicate matters, he took three history classes and one literature class, and finals were two weeks before Christmas. Between attending classes and team meetings during the day, Pope spent most of the nights reading and studying.

They completed finals and moved to a motel in Pasadena to prepare for Illinois, the Big Ten Champion. State U was a twelve-point underdog against the undefeated and number one ranked "fighting Illini." Some experts predicted an upset because of Pope's mobility and passing ability. The media also made a big play about him being an Indian and Illinois having an Indian mascot.

*   *   *

On January 1, over 100,000 spectators filled the Rose Bowl. Pope stood on the sidelines with the team, listening to someone sing the *Star Spangled Banner*. The sun was shining brightly, and a few wisps of fluffy clouds moved slowly in the sky. There was a slight warm breeze, and he had the familiar smell of crushed grass in his nostrils. Pope looked around the packed stadium and he couldn't imagine he would be playing in front of so many people. It was going to be a big day, and he would seize the moment!

After an eighty yard opening drive touchdown for Illinois, it was clear to Pope his team was in for a tough game. At the beginning of the second quarter, State U had third down, seven yards to go for a first down on its 45. Pope dropped back to pass and two blitzing linebackers hit him at the same time, driving him to the turf. He felt a sharp pain in his left wrist as his hand twisted under the crush of the other two. Pope heard a roar go up from the crowd as an Illinois lineman pounced on his fumble.

Pope screamed with pain as the enemy tacklers jumped up to go after the loose ball. The referee blew his whistle, ran to the quarterback, and said, "Don't move son, we'll get you some help."

He waved to the sidelines for the trainer.

After examining the arm, the trainer said, "It's starting to swell. We'll get some ice on it right away."

He helped Pope to his feet, holding Pope's arm across his stomach while both walked off the field.

"How bad is it, Doc?" Coach Phillips asked as they arrived on the sidelines.

"I can't tell if it's broken. I'll take him into the training room for a x-ray. If it isn't broken we can give him some pain killer."

"I'm sorry, Coach," Pope said as the trainer led him to the training room.

20 minutes later, the X-rays showed no fracture. The trainer taped the injury and put ice on it. He gave Pope some aspirin and a shot of painkiller in the wrist. Pope immediately felt better, and the two ran back onto the sidelines. He looked up at the scoreboard and saw that Illinois led 10-0 with six minutes left in the second quarter.

He picked up a football and motioned for a teammate to play catch. As the player threw Pope the ball, he tried to catch it, and it dropped at his feet.

"Well, I don't have to catch any passes anyway. Snap the ball to me."

Pope got behind the center and received a couple snaps, dropping the second. Coach Phillips walked up to Pope with a worried expression, and said, "How do you feel, Johnny?"

Pope shrugged his shoulders and said, "I think it's OK, Coach. It doesn't hurt, but it's dead so I don't have much feeling in the wrist. Let me give it a try?"

"I don't want to take a chance. Our defense is keeping us in the game, and O'Brien is doing OK at quarterback. You just take it easy, and we'll reconsider in the second half."

"Let me at least try, Coach? We need to take advantage of every chance we get," Pope pleaded.

Without answering, Phillips turned on his heel and made his way back to his place on the sidelines. For the remaining minutes of the first half, Pope sat by himself with an ice bag on his wrist; depressed he was letting the team down. He told himself *an injured warrior would not give up the hunt. He would figure out a way to continue to stalk the whale.* State U trailed at half time by a score of 10-0.

It was a subdued State U locker room at half time. The coaches talked to the players about adjustments they were to make during the second half.

"We need you, Johnny. Can you go in the second half?" Phillips asked with hand on Pope's shoulder.

"You know I'll give it my best, Coach," Pope said with a smile.

"I can't ask for anything more. You'll do fine," Phillips said, patting Pope on the back.

"The guys really look like they're down. Do you mind if I say something to them?"

"I don't think it can hurt. Go ahead."

Holding a football in his hand, Pope made his way to the front of the assembled team. They sat on long benches in front of lockers, their heads bowed. Pope tossed the ball a couple feet in the air and caught it with both hands.

"For the past two seasons, people have counted State U out, and the team has overcome adversity time after time. I've learned a great deal from Coach, but the most important thing I learned—and I'm sure that this lesson will last me a lifetime—is that I should never give up. That I'm not beat until I think I am. Things are never as bad as they seem, and if you keep thinking and working, good things will happen. Well, I believe that things are not as bad as some of you think. We've held the number one team in the nation to 10 points in a half, and we're only two passes away from leading them. I'm not finished, and I hope you aren't either." Dead silence hung in the air in the locker room, and Pope shouted, "Lets go have some fun."

He slapped the football with both hands and threw it out the door leading to the field. The players, as one, erupted in yells and cheers and ran out onto the field. As he watched his teammates screaming, slapping each other on the backs and jostle each other, Pope knew he had breathed new life into his team—but he hoped his wrist would meet the test.

State U received the second half kick-off and promptly drove eighty yards, as Pope scored on a 25 yard run around end. The defense held Illinois to three downs and a punt. The second time State U had the ball Pope tossed a 50-yard scoring pass to his halfback. As he ran to the sidelines, he started to feel a slight pain in his wrist. *Great, the painkiller is starting to wear off,* he worried.

To the surprise of most of the spectators in the stands and the television audience around the country, State U led 14-10 at the end of the third quarter. Two minutes into the fourth quarter, an Illinois end got behind a State U defensive back and scored on a 75-yard "flea flicker" bomb.

Pope answered, with another 50-yard touchdown aerial. With just over eight minutes to play, State U led, 21-17. By now, the painkiller had worn off and he had a better feel for the ball. Unfortunately, each time the center snapped the ball to him, pain shot up his arm. The defense held Illinois to four downs, and the State U offense took over.

As pope started out on the field, Phillips grabbed him and said, "Don't take any chances. No passes, just run time off the clock."

With just under two minutes left in the game the State U halfback tried to fight his way forward for a first down when the ball was knocked from his hands. An Illinois lineman scooped it up and ran 45 yards to put Illinois ahead, 24-21.

State U had first and ten on their own 25-yard line with one minute and 35 seconds to go in the game. The Illini fans were screaming "Defense! Defense! Defense!" The State U band frantically played the fight song.

In the huddle Pope said in a calm, steady voice, "OK, just give us some good blocking, and we're going to get this ball into the end zone."

He connected on three straight tosses to move the ball to the Illini 45-yard line. After three incomplete passes, State U had fourth down, ten yards to go for a first down with 42 seconds remaining in the game.

Pope went back to pass, couldn't find a receiver open, and darted to his left. An Illini tackler pushed him out of bounds on the Illinois 32-yard line. As he was knocked to his left he instinctively dropped his left had to break his fall. When he hit the ground, excruciating pain shot from his wrist, up his arm, across his shoulder, and exploded in his head. He jumped up immediately, shaking his head and wrist at the same time as he jogged to the huddle. *I picked up a first down, and there's still magic to be made. Block the pain from your mind*, he thought. The entire crowd was on its feet screaming.

Three plays later, State U had the ball on the Illinois 25, fourth down and three yards to go for a first down. With four seconds remaining in the game Pope called time out and ran to the sidelines. The noise in the stadium was so loud that the coaches and Pope had to shout to hear each other. Kicking a field goal for a tie was the first option discussed by the coaches.

Pope waved both hands, interrupting them.

"Coach, I think I can speak for the team. We didn't come all the way here for a tie. Let's go for it?"

"Yeah, but a tie would be like a win for us, Johnny. This is the number one team in the country. No one expects us to win," Phillips said.

"We can get a **moral** victory by losing by the score we have now. But right now we know we're better than those other guys are. You may be in this position again in your career—or maybe not. But this is our last chance. Just give us a chance, Coach. We won't let you down."

The tone of Pope's voice and his look of determination convinced Phillips.

"All right, let's do it! Send four receivers into the end zone and find one open," Phillips shouted as he slapped Pope on the butt.

He ran onto the field to his teammates in the huddle. A strange hush came over the stadium as the crowd suddenly stopped shouting and the bands stopped playing. It was as though the spectators were either praying silently or resting their voices.

"OK. We only have one play left, and we're going for the whole thing."

Every player smiled and nodded at their leader.

"Linemen, block till you drop. Receivers, get into the end zone and keep moving to get open. We'll snap the ball when the center decides. No one move until the ball moves. We don't want any penalties. Now let's get this ball into the end zone and go home smiling," Pope said.

He gave the team the formation and play. They broke from the huddle and ran to the line of scrimmage.

Suddenly the entire stadium erupted in noise. It was louder than at any time in the game. It was as though each spectator knew that the louder he or she yelled, the more successful their team would be. Pope walked to the line of scrimmage. The team lined up in a formation with two receivers on each side of the center and split out wide on both sides. He noticed the middle was open, with only one defender. Pope decided to check off the play called in the huddle and run a quarterback draw.

The crowd was so loud that Pope knew that his teammates would not be able to hear the new play. He quickly turned to his halfback and told him the new play and to tell it to each player on the left side of the center. Then Pope sprinted to each of his teammates on the right side of the center and told them the new play.

He got behind the center and barked out the signals. The center snapped the ball and Pope dropped back as if to pass. All four receivers ran straight down the field ten yards and broke to the sidelines, taking their defenders with them. Pope stopped, cocked the ball back to fake a pass, tucked the ball under his arm, and sprinted straight ahead.

He saw his blockers open a huge hole, with only one defender between him and the goal line. Pope dashed straight toward the Illinois safety, faked to his left, and cut to his right. The safety leaned slightly in the direction of the fake. When Pope cut back, the safety was a half step out of position for a clean tackle. He lunged at Pope and had one arm around the quarterback's leg. Pope broke the tackle and darted into the end zone as time expired. State U fans flooded the field as the winning players triumphantly jumped on each other.

After the media had finished interviewing him, Pope sat near his locker with an ice bag on his wrist. He looked at his teammates happy faces. He knew he had never felt closer to them, and he would always remember how much their friendship meant.

He would not forget the important lessons he learned by playing football. How much the tactics of war and football were alike. The most important were the "never give up" attitude, preparation, and the ability to adjust to the opponent's changes.

*   *   *

Pope graduated with a teaching degree and a Regular Army commission in the Infantry. He asked Coach Phillips to pin second lieutenant bars on his shoulders on graduation day. After the ceremony Pope stepped outside the fieldhouse and scanned the crowd. Hundreds of parents, relatives and other graduates stood talking, laughing, and taking pictures.

He finally caught the eye of the man he was looking for. Sergeant Dennison marched up and saluted him. Pope reached into his pocket for the traditional dollar bill. It's given to the first enlisted man that salutes a newly commissioned officer. He returned Dennison's salute and handed him the bill.

The Sergeant took the cash and put it in his pocket.

"Take good care of those young men America is going to give you to command, Lieutenant. Good luck, Johnny!"

"Thanks Sarge, I'm going to miss you."

The two men shook hands and hugged each other, oblivious to the crowd that surrounded them.

*   *   *

Pope had his choice of duty assignments and chose the 82nd Airborne Division at Fort Bragg. He only had a month before he had to report to Ft. Benning, Georgia, for training.

Pope stopped in the city and spent two days looking for a car, and finally bought a brand new forest green Ford convertible. He transferred his meager belongings into his new wheels and pointed it toward the reservation.

It was a bright sunny day. Not a single cloud in the sky. Unusual for late June, Pope thought. He put the top down on his convertible. Several people he knew and had grown up with waved and yelled greetings to him as he drove through town to his grandfather's house. He decided to stay in the house he had inherited from Adam—not because he didn't want to stay with Shirley, but because here he felt closer to Grandfather.

When he entered the house, the faint smell of his grandfather's tobacco lingered. Pope felt good being back home. After unpacking, he showered, put on his class A khaki uniform with blouse and drove to his mother's home.

He pulled into her driveway, and Shirley ran out of the house to give him a big hug. She stepped back, held him at arm's length, and looked at him. Her son had filled out to180 muscular pounds. His big, coal-black eyes and strong chin emphasized his black hair, and round, handsome face. His tan made his straight teeth appear whiter when he smiled the engaging smile inherited from his father and grandfather.

"You really look good, Johnny, but I don't know whether to spank you or salute you. Everyone has been calling me for the past hour, telling me they saw you driving through town!"

"Yeah. Well, I had to go home, unpack, shower, and change into my uniform before seeing you," he said with a big smile.

"Your grandfather would be proud of you, Johnny. How long before you have to report for duty?" She asked. Shirley put both arms around his arm and led him into the house.

"I have to report to Ft. Benning, Georgia, on the twentieth. I plan to take a few days to drive there, so I should be here for over two weeks."

"That works out just right because your father and I are planning a pot-latch for you next week. It's going to be one of the biggest this town has ever seen!"

"I really wish you hadn't, but I understand. What's for dinner? I'm starved for your cooking," he said, and he flopped down in the familiar easy chair in the living room.

*   *   *

Pope spent the long summer days running on the beach and going up in the hills to take morning baths and to pray. Almost every evening, he went to the hill at the northwest tip of the state and watched the sunset. Pope thought about Grandfather and how much he missed him.

The potlatch was bigger than Pope's mother had expected. The tribal council was proud of Pope and told the media about the party. Several reporters and television crews were in the community hall with the guests. Pope's father surprised him by making a speech. William was never one for saying much in private, much less in public.

"I'm proud Johnny graduated from college. He's the first commissioned officer of all the Makahs that have served in the U.S. military. No Makah has ever been killed in combat. My father spent seven years teaching Johnny the warrior tradition. Today Adam is looking down at his grandson with great pride!"

After the potlatch, Pope went back to his home, took off his uniform, looked at it, and thought, *Well Grandfather, this is what you've trained me for. I just hope I don't let you or anyone else down. I think I could use more training. I hope the army gives it to me before I lead warriors in combat.*

Chapter Five

Pope loaded his belongings into his convertible, said good-bye to his mother, father and friends, and started his new adventure. He drove south through Oregon and California and headed east into Arizona. Four days later he pulled up at the front gate to Ft. Benning.

"Good morning, sir, if you're planning to report for duty, you'll need a post sticker for your car. If you're just visiting, you'll need a temporary sticker," the young gate guard said after rendering a snappy salute.

"I'm reporting for duty, so which line is mine?" Pope asked, motioning in the direction where two long lines led to two tables outside a small concrete building.

"Sorry, sir, but you get the longest line on the right. I guess this is just the start of your career of hurry up and wait."

"Yeah, I guess you're right," Pope said as he returned the MP's salute and pulled into the parking lot near the line of people.

He stood in line and thought about how he was glad that he drove to Ft. Benning instead of flying and buying a car in Georgia. It was nice to see so much of the United States. He had traveled around the country with the football team, but only saw airports, motels, and football stadiums. This time he got to see how the people lived. He had no idea that his country was so big!

Lieutenant Pope spent 12 weeks with 200 other second lieutenants attending the Infantry Officers Basic Course. His favorite classes were small unit tactics, weapons, and supporting firepower. His least favorites were supply, transportation, communication, and medical support. For the most part, the students went to class eight hours a day, five days a week and had the evenings to themselves. It was a very relaxed atmosphere with a minimum of physical training and no harassment by the cadre.

*   *   *

The last three weeks the company spent in the field, living in tents. During the first week, the students fired the rifle, pistol, and machine gun. The following two weeks, they learned about platoon offensive and defensive tactics, map reading, and terrain appreciation. The last three days in the field, he learned an important lesson about himself.

After Pope's training company took seats in large bleachers, a captain gave them a lecture about escape and evasion techniques. He showed them their current location on a map and told them they had to travel to an assembly area eight miles away. After the instructor finished answering questions, there were explosions behind the bleachers and someone threw several smoke grenades in front of it. Fifty screaming armed soldiers dressed in aggressor uniforms exited the smoke and pointed their weapons menacingly at the students in the grandstands.

The aggressor leader shouted, "You are all prisoners of war. Remove your helmets and web gear and leave them at your feet. Move!" The class of second lieutenants removed their equipment as quickly as they could.

Within a minute the leader screamed, "Get out of those bleachers and form a double line in front of me. Now!" Several aggressors fired their weapons in the air. The students scrambled out of the bleachers, several lieutenants falling as they formed two lines. With their hands on the top of their heads, they marched a mile north to a large fenced in area that had a large building in the center.

Pope was in a group of fifty men who were herded into a room so small the men were crammed into the room. They stood cramped together, and an aggressor in an officer's uniform screamed, "Sit!" All of the prisoners tried to sit at the same time, and there was not enough room, so some were half-standing and half-sitting.

Two aggressor soldiers pushed their way into the mob, grabbed Pope by each arm and dragged him out of the room. In the hallway, one of them gave him a red plastic capsule.

"Put this in your mouth between your teeth. Don't worry, we're not going to hurt you."

"What are you going to do?" Pope asked nervously.

"We're going to interrogate you so that the other students can watch."

"What do you expect me to do?"

"Every question we ask, you just answer with your name, rank, and service number. When my partner loses his temper, he'll act like he is punching you in the mouth. When he swings, bite down on the capsule, and red food coloring will fly out of your mouth. It looks like real blood. That's all. No sweat, Lieutenant."

They dragged him into a small room adjoining the large room where the "prisoners" were sitting. There was a large window between the rooms so the students could watch the interrogation. The aggressors threw him onto a chair near a table. One sat on a chair across the table, and the other stood, menacing to the side.

"What is your unit, Lieutenant?" the interrogator asked.

"Pope, John A., Second Lieutenant, United States Army, 088541."

"I didn't ask for that information. I said, 'What is your unit?'"

"Pope, John A., Second Lieutenant, United States Army, 088541."

"God damn Yankee Imperialist! If you don't answer my questions, we'll kill you!" the aggressor shouted. He looked at Pope for 20 seconds, then added, "What nationality are you? Indian? Are you a fucken Redskin?"

"Pope, John A…"

"Listen you fucken blanket ass. I don't know why you should want to fight for the United States. They killed your ancestors and took over your land. They used you to make a name for their college by using your football skills. They don't care anything for you. We want to help you. All you have to do is cooperate. Now, what is your unit?" the interrogator said quietly.

Oh shit, Pope thought. *I don't like the way this is going. I wasn't just pulled out at random. They want to make an example of me. I damn sure don't like the racial epithets. Well, let's get on with it…*

"Pope, John…"

The mean looking guard screamed, "Damn it, Sarge, let me take care of him! I'm tired of wasting time. I'll get him to talk!"

"Now, take it easy, Corporal, the Lieutenant is going to cooperate with us. Aren't you Lieutenant? All you have to do is tell us what unit you belong to, and we'll let you have a nice, warm room. What do you say, Lieutenant?"

"Pope, Jo…"

Before he could finish, the big guard took two steps forward and grabbed Pope by the front of his fatigue shirt. He yanked him to his feet and screamed, "Maybe this will loosen your tongue!"

With a sweeping upper cut, he caught Pope squarely under the jaw with a right fist. Food coloring mixed with the blood from the inside of his mouth went flying across the room, as he fell backwards. The lights went out in the interrogation room as the students next door first groaned, then yelled.

He got to his knees as the room spun around. The big guard tried to help him. "I'm sorry, sir. I didn't mean to hit you. Are you OK?"

Pulling his arm away from him, Pope glared at him and said, "You son of a bitch, don't let me catch you off post!"

The aggressor captain entered the room. "Move the prisoner into the other room," he ordered.

When they opened the door the students still yelled.

"All right, knock it off. Take a look. He's OK," the aggressor captain shouted.

The red stained Pope was shoved into the mob as the yelling stopped.

"Now, everyone take off all your clothes and go outside. You have one minute. Move!" The commander screamed.

As he removed his uniform, Pope's jaw and head ached. He felt himself panic as he had never felt before. He thought the walls were closing in on him and breathing was difficult. After two hours of doing exercises in the rain outside the building, the aggressor commander told the prisoners to get dressed.

The commander ordered his men, "Open the gates." Then he turned to the prisoners and yelled, "We're allowing you to escape, but if we catch you, we'll drag you back here, and you'll be interrogated again. Now get out of here!"

Pope knocked over two men as he darted for an opening and was one of the first men out the gate. He ran about two hundred yards into the Georgia pine forest and stopped to catch his breath. As he sat on a large fallen tree he noticed several men run by him in a southerly direction.

Now I know how the whale feels when the painted men in the wooden canoe are stalking him, he thought. Pope also learned he had a weakness— he would not be able to withstand captivity. He made a conscious decision to not let the aggressors capture him. He decided to hole up until dark and travel at night. He sat in the opening of a large stump and listened to shooting and shouting and knew the aggressors had captured several of his classmates. He fell asleep and an hour later awoke with a start, soaked to the skin.

A storm centered directly over the training area. Heavy rain, thunder, and lightning made the forest a macabre scene. He stretched his legs, got a bearing and moved out in a southeasterly direction.

He had gone about a half mile when he stopped to get his bearings. A bolt of lightning revealed a shadowy figure from behind a tree.

"God damn! Son of a bitch! Christ! How do I get out of here?" The voice whimpered.

"Are you a student?" Pope asked.

"What? Who's that? Are you aggressors? I give up. I've got my hands raised."

Pope stepped to the student and said, "Put your hands down. I'm a student, too."

"Oh, man. Am I glad to see you. Do you know where you are? I'm lost. All I want to do is get in out of the rain. I'm freezing my ass off."

"You're heading for the eastern boundary of the exercise area. I know where I am and where I'm going."

"Good. Can I go with you?"

Pope hesitated, "I don't intend to get captured. If you want to give up, head southwest, and you'll run into aggressors. What's your name?"

"Jennings—Bill. All I want to do is get in out of the rain," he said, teeth chattering.

"I'm John Pope. They'll think we'll head due south or take the western boundary because there is a road there to guide on. That's where all the aggressors should be. I'm planning to head to the eastern boundary and fol-low it south to the assembly area. So take your pick, Bill. I'm moving out."

"Hey, you're the guy the aggressors punched out during the interroga-tion. Are you OK?"

"Yeah, I'm fine, and I'm not going to be captured. See you around," Pope said, as he turned and headed southeast.

"I'm right behind you, John."

The two men moved slowly through thick pine forest and bushes. The rain continued to pelt them. They stopped to rest for short periods, prima-rily because they immediately became cold. Shortly after 0400 hours Pope stopped as he saw a cigarette glowing to his front, twenty-five yards away.

"Wait here, Bill. Someone is smoking straight ahead of us. I'm going to move forward and check it out. I'll be back in ten minutes," Pope whispered.

"Be sure to come back for me, John," Bill said to the black shadow as it disappeared into the darkness.

He crept forward about twenty yards and a bolt of lightning cracked overhead revealing two aggressors sitting under a poncho lean-to. They were both looking straight at Pope, but neither saw him.

"Man, I'm freezing. I'll be glad when morning comes, and it warms up," Aggressor number one said.

"Yeah, me, too. I almost wish we were over by the western boundary. At least those guys are keeping warm capturing students. We just sit here and freeze," Aggressor number two replied.

Pope turned and ran in a crouch back to his waiting partner.

"OK, Bill, there are two aggressors up ahead. All we have to do is go around them to the left."

"How far do you think it is to the assembly area?"

"Not far. About two miles. Let's get home and change clothes," Pope said as he turned to bypass the sentries.

At 0700 hours the two men reached the objective and were safe. Their legs, knees and hands were skinned and bruised, because they had fallen down two hills and tripped over six fallen trees. They were the first students to finish the escape and evasion course. The sergeant in charge of the trucks told them that his orders were to wait until 20 students showed up before sending a load back to camp.

After the lieutenants waited an hour the sergeant told a driver to take them to the bivouac area. By noon all of the students had returned to the camp. Pope found out that he was only one of three students that had successfully escaped and evaded to the pick up area.

*   *   *

Pope spent eight weeks after graduation in Ranger school. The first week of Ranger school was a marked contrast to the Basic Course. There was physical training galore, and the cadre screamed at the candidates continually. Their screaming vocabulary always seemed to end with "Give me ten push ups!" The school commandant told the Ranger candidates there was a large attrition rate for every class.

He was right—the cadre pushed the candidates to the limit of their endurance. Those that survived not only learned what their strengths were but their weaknesses as well. The surviving students experienced the closest thing to actual combat that the army had to offer.

He loved Ranger training because its doctrine was exactly what Adam had taught him. To travel light, at dark, and strike where the enemy least expects. The Rangers trained by patrolling the mountains of Georgia then went to the swamps of Florida. The training took its toll on Pope and the rest of the graduates. On graduation day, he put his khaki uniform on and found that it was too large for him. He had lost 15 pounds!

*   *   *

Ranger Pope took two days off and relaxed at the officers' club swimming pool before reporting to the airborne school at Ft. Benning. Although he was still weak from Ranger school, he adapted to airborne school and his body recovered fast. There were 100 students in his class—five graduates of his Ranger class. The Rangers, to the chagrin and disapproval of the other students, antagonized the airborne cadre, resulting in more push-ups for everybody. There was absolutely no night training, and the day ended by 1600 hours.

The last week of training the class reported each day to the parachute shed, picked up a parachute and made one jump from an aircraft. Pope had a feeling like no other when his parachute opened, and he looked around as he descended.

By 1000 hours each day, the students lounged around the swimming pool. It was like one big game for Pope, but all good things come to an end, and graduation day arrived. It was time to stop being a student and go to work!

*   *   *

Pope was stationed at Fort Bragg's 82nd Airborne Division for about six months when he decided to telephone Sergeant Dennison.

"Hi, Sarge, How are things in the great Northwest?"

"Well, we've got a pretty good precision drill team this year, but not as good as yours. What's new with you, Johnny?"

"I've really been busy. My first command in the 82nd Airborne Division was a rifle platoon of 40 men. It's better than I ever imagined, Sarge. As the only officer platoon leader in the airborne Rifle Company, I present all of the instruction to the entire company. Our rifle company trains five and a half days a week, sometimes 12 hours a day. When I'm not training the troops, I'm writing lesson plans for the next day's training. Since the normal training day starts at 0600 hours, I only get about four hours sleep a night."

"That all sounds familiar. It reminds me of my days at Bragg."

"I went to the US Army Jungle Warfare school in Panama for training and returned to train personnel in our Battle Group to be jungle fighters. I really learned a great deal about jungle fighting. I had some arguments with instructors there because Army doctrine dictates soldiers do not travel in the jungle at night due to reduced visibility and risk of accidents. I believe the risk is worth it because the enemy won't expect troops to move at night. I proved my point during several patrols, when my patrol was able to move with stealth at night and accomplish every objective."

"It sounds like you haven't changed, Johnny. Remember though that army doctrine isn't cast in stone. It changes every day."

"Our Battle Group just finished its Expert Infantryman's Badge testing. It isn't the Combat Infantryman's Badge, like you wear, Sarge, but it's the next best thing to it."

"Yeah. We call the CIB the dumb infantryman's badge, because all you have to do is be a member of an infantry unit for a month, in a combat zone, and get shot at. The EIB is called the smart infantryman's badge because you have to pass some tough tests to qualify."

"Yeah, Sarge. To qualify for the EIB, we were tested in several categories including, weapons firing, first aid, camouflage, map reading, road march, physical training, grenade throw, and Atomic, Biological, and Chemical warfare techniques. I gave classes to my platoon, and most of them made it through to the end of the competition. In the entire Battle Group, only 23 officers and enlisted men received the EIB. Me and three of my platoon members wear it now!"

"That's great, Johnny. You should be real proud of yourself and your men. I know that the EIB is a big thing all over the army."

"Thanks, Sarge. I hope everything is going OK for you. I have to go now. My regards to Mrs. Dennison."

*   *   *

Pope pinned on new first lieutenant bars, and the same day took over his new duties as executive officer of Headquarters and Headquarters Company. He didn't care for the assignment because it was strictly administrative in nature, and there was absolutely no field duty. He missed being in the field with the troops.

The assignment didn't last long. Three months later, the Battle Group Commander called Pope into his office and told him that he was relieving an airborne company commander for cause and replacing him with the young first lieutenant. Pope smiled at his good luck. He not only got to be back with the troops but would also command an airborne rifle company as a first lieutenant—a coveted assignment usually reserved for senior captains.

Pope trained his troops in night movement extensively. The company pulled off a flawless night attack during its Army Training Test (ATT). Pope had his attacking platoons crawl the final three hundred yards to the objective. The aggressors didn't detect the attackers and were completely surrounded. The controllers had to call an administrative halt to the test so the aggressors could move their armored vehicles away for the next stage of the test. Pope's company received the highest score in the division. Pope's unit was part of the Strategic Army Command, and he wanted it ready for any kind of combat!

*   *   *

Pope telephoned Dennison with exciting news.

"Hey, Sarge. I'm out of purgatory and on my way," Pope exclaimed

"Well, lets not waste a lot of time on small talk, Johnny. Mrs. Dennison and me are fine. What's the big news?" Dennison replied, laughing.

"I'm on my way to Vietnam."

"That's great, I guess. If that's what you want. I haven't heard from you in about three years. What have you been doing?"

"After only two years at Bragg, I received orders assigning me to work in the Detroit Field Office of the Army Counterintelligence Corps. The Commanding General of the Division and the Battle Group Commander called the Pentagon to try to get the orders changed—to no avail. The officer in the pentagon told them that the Counterintelligence Corps received officers from the combat arms branches for a three-year detail. Further, the Counterintelligence Corps selected the officers! I spent four months learning about intelligence procedures at Ft. Holabird, Maryland."

"It sure doesn't sound like your kind of work."

"I did learn more about the importance of intelligence. I learned many techniques to develop intelligence and use it against an enemy force. Just as importantly, I learned techniques to keep our secrets away from the enemy. But it got worse."

"How is that possible?"

"I worked in civilian clothes as a counterintelligence special agent in downtown Detroit. Most of the work involved doing background investigations for security clearances, but our unit also monitors communist party USA organizations. Three months after arrival, I was promoted to captain and named Special Agent in Charge of the Detroit Field Office— the largest in Fifth Army. Most of my time has been spent supervising agents and coordinating with the Detroit Police Department, the Wayne County Sheriff's Office, the FBI, and the other two branches of military counterintelligence—Office of Naval Intelligence, and the Air Force's Office of Special Investigation. I hate the boring, mundane office work."

"I can't imagine that kind of job. Especially for an airborne-ranger infantryman!"

"I know! Well, the war was picking up in Vietnam and I volunteered a week after my arrival in Detroit, but was rejected. They told me I had just arrived in Detroit. I volunteered for Vietnam six months later, and the army rejected me again. After almost two years in Detroit, I was thoroughly depressed and volunteered for Vietnam for a third time. Anyway, I just received orders to report to the J-2 Order of Battle Section of Military Assistance Command, with four months TDY at Bragg. I'm supposed to attend the Military Assistance Training Academy, to learn about jungle warfare, the Viet Cong, and the Vietnamese language."

"That sounds great. I still can't see you in a headquarters assignment though."

"That is my next problem. As soon as I get to Bragg, I'm going to start working on getting a field assignment. Obviously, it won't be a command because the Army's role is to advise the Vietnamese commanders. Anything to get me out of Detroit and into Vietnam."

After he hung up the telephone, Pope thought that *he was finally ready to do what he had prepared for his entire life. Many questions remained unanswered: Had he prepared himself enough for the rigors of combat? Did he have the heart of a warrior? Could he lead men in combat? And the most important question of all: Was Grandfather right when he said, "The spirit of the whale will protect you?"*

Chapter Six

Pope thought it was very strange to board a commercial airline for the flight from San Francisco to Saigon, Vietnam. The big jet landed at Tan Son Nhut Air Base just outside Saigon and taxied next to a large metal hanger. As Pope got off the plane with the other uniformed passengers, the heat and humidity hit him and he immediately sweated through his tropical worsted class A uniform.

"Damn! It's hotter here than North Carolina," he said to no one in particular. Eighteen hours in the air and twenty-two hours since take-off from San Francisco, he thought. *Man, I'm so tired I can barely move. What a way to start a war!*

A sweat-soaked master sergeant ushered the entire planeload into the adjacent hanger. There were about 250 wooden chairs in front of a small stage containing a speaker's lectern. The new arrivals sat in the uncomfortable heat talking and smoking for what seemed like hours, but it was actually only a few minutes.

The sergeant, standing in the rear shouted "Gentlemen, the Commanding General!"

Chairs scraped the floor loudly as everyone jumped to attention.

A ramrod straight, middle aged man with short-cropped graying hair entered the hangar. He wore a heavily starched short-sleeve khaki uniform, pistol and holster, and four stars on his collar.

He shouted, "As you were, men. Please take your seats," and marched to the podium.

There was more screeching of chairs as the men sat. The General stood at the lectern gazing at the 200-plus soldiers, sailors, and airmen for several seconds.

"Welcome to Vietnam and the Military Assistance Command, Vietnam. You are the first team! There are only two reasons that you are here: Because you volunteered; and because you are among the best in the military! Your job is simple. Teach the Vietnamese how to win their war. This is the Vietnamese people's war. Your job is not to lead, but to give them advice. You will credit them with the victories, and take blame for the defeats. There is no room for pessimists in this command. If you're a pessimist, catch the next plane out of country. Good luck, good hunting, and God speed!" He turned on his heel and marched off the stage.

"Atten-Hut!" the sergeant screamed.

Another loud noise as the men leaped from their chairs and stood at attention. As fast as the general had arrived, he left, leaving the assembled group standing and looking at each other in wonderment. The general impressed Pope. Not just what he said, but that the commander would take time from his busy schedule to meet every arriving airplane. The sergeant moved to the lectern.

"Gentlemen, your transportation will be here in about five minutes. They will take you to your temporary quarters. Drop off your gear there, and you will spend the remainder of the day inprocessing. Officers load on the first four buses and enlisted men on the last four."

Eight gray buses pulled up outside the hanger, and the groups loaded aboard. Pope saw the vehicles had metal screens on the windows but no glass. The longhaired US Navy enlisted driver saw Pope eyeing the windows.

"Sir, the screens are there so VC terrorists can't throw grenades in the windows."

"I think I can figure out why there's no glass. I don't know how anyone can live in this kind of heat," Pope said, wiping his face and neck with his handkerchief.

"You get used to it. I been here seven months, and I don't hardly notice it. I still sweat like a hog, but I don't pay it no mind."

About the time the bus exited the big air base, a smell hit Pope like a punch in the nose. It was a combination of diesel smoke and other exhaust, garbage, food cooking and human excrement. Together it smelled as though the country was decaying.

Pope noted Saigon was a huge city with traffic bumper to bumper. It had a strange mixture of vehicles. Most were olive drab painted military trucks. There were numerous small Renault taxicabs, mopeds, bicycles, and cycalo—a bicycle that pushed a small two-passenger cart.

"Sir, you have to be careful in Saigon, cause there are a lot of terrorists. The VC don't wear uniforms, so civilians go around throwing grenades in bars, blowing up restaurants—hell, they even blew up a movie theater last month." the driver explained to Pope.

After an hour ride through crowded downtown Saigon, the driver pulled the bus to the curb of a large French-style hotel.

"Sirs, this here is the Majestic Hotel. You officers have one hour to check into your quarters here and meet me back in the lobby. I'll take you to the MACV compound for inprocessing," he announced loudly.

Pope was the first one to exit and led the other officers into the old hotel. It had sand bags piled five feet high around the front door, and two US Army sentries alertly eye-balled the passing vehicles. The Vietnamese receptionist at the desk told Pope in broken English that he already had a room assignment. Pope took the key and rode an ancient, slow elevator to the fifth floor.

He walked down a dark, narrow hallway to his room. It was a rather stark room, with one bed, a nightstand, a small desk, and a chair. There was no toilet bowl in the bathroom. Next to the sink was a three-foot square porcelain platform, about four inches in height. There was a hole, about two inches in diameter in the center, and on each side of the hole were foot-shaped platforms two inches high. A pail next to the faucet was the "flush system." He had never been to France, but it looked like people there didn't sit down when they used the toilet.

"Well, I guess it's not much different from taking a crap in the field," he said aloud.

The room was air-conditioned but smelled musty. He took a quick shower and changed into a short sleeved khaki uniform. Then he picked up his orders and records and went down to the lobby to wait for the bus.

The bus reappeared, and the passengers loaded for the fifteen-minute ride to the MACV compound. A big brick wall topped with rolls of concertina wire surrounded the entire city block of buildings. Piled sandbags protected the entrance, and armed US Army sentries operated a gate. The guards inspected the driver and vehicle for identification and for bombs. After about five minutes, the bus moved into the compound and stopped near a brick building. A lieutenant ushered the newly arrived officers into an air-conditioned theater for an orientation.

Pope noticed an old friend from Ft. Bragg talking to a sergeant in the back of the auditorium. The captain was an average-built 27-year-old with blond hair and blue eyes. While Pope was stationed at Ft. Bragg, they shared a room. Just as Pope approached them, the conversation ended and the sergeant walked past him and out the door.

"Bill Jamison! What in the hell is an Adjutant General Corps officer doing in Vietnam?" Pope said as he took the young captain's hand and shook it firmly.

"Battles can't be won without paper, Johnny, you know that. I'm sure not surprised to see **you** here, though. This isn't much of a war, but it's all we've got. So you think you've found your fight?" Jamison said with a smile.

"I'm sure glad to see you, Bill. You're an answer to this warrior's prayers. I've been assigned to J-2, MACV here in Saigon."

"That's great! I'll get you a room in my BOQ."

"Thanks for the offer, but what I'd really like is a field assignment. I have been pushing papers in the Counterintelligence Corps in Detroit the last two years, and I'm sick of staff work. Besides, I didn't come all the way to Vietnam to sit behind a desk."

"Well, I just happen to be the officers assignment officer for the entire country. If you want to go to the field, I'm sure it can be arranged. Step into my office," Jamison said as he led his friend out the door and into an adjacent building. In the AG office, Jamison leafed through some papers on his desk.

"Look, Bill, I have a lot of friends from the 82nd Airborne advising the Vietnamese Airborne Brigade. Can you find me a slot there?"

"The Airborne Brigade is stationed in Saigon, Johnny, and while it's called the strategic reserve unit, in reality it's the Vietnamese president's own counter-coup force. They don't get out in the field very often."

"They are bound to get out in the field more than a headquarters type."

Jamison looked through more papers and said, "It looks like all the captain slots in the Airborne Brigade are filled now. I can leave you in your current assignment until a slot opens up there. I have an immediate opening for a Sector intelligence advisor in Binh Tuy Province—looks like the kind of job you might like. You can use your intelligence and infantry training together. If a job opens up in the Airborne Brigade, I can transfer you."

"I think I'll take the Binh Tuy job. There's too much brass in J-2, MACV. They see a 'gopher' doing a good job, I might not be able to get myself out of there."

"A wise choice, my friend. I can have the orders cut this afternoon. Stop by and pick them up after 1600 hours."

"Thanks a heap, Bill. I owe you."

"Damn right! And I intend to collect. Now we better get back to the theater for your orientation and in-processing."

"I really appreciate this, old friend. Hell, it's late 1963 and I know there are damn few army advisors in the field."

*   *   *

A knock woke Pope from a sound sleep. He picked up his watch from the nightstand—it was just after 0800 hours. Pope slipped into his fatigue pants and shuffled to the door, rubbing the sleep from his eyes. He opened the door. A sergeant dressed in combat fatigues held a Thompson sub machine gun. About 240 pounds were well distributed over a six-five frame that filled the doorway. A long hooknose was the most prominent part of his face. *Damn! This guy looks just like John Wayne,* Pope thought.

"Morning, sir. Are you Captain John Pope?" the hulk bellowed, the noise shaking Pope awake.

"Yeah, I am, Sarge. You don't have to yell."

"Sorry, Captain. I'm SFC Bill Waters, assistant Regional Force advisor for Binh Tuy Province. I'm here to get you to your new home," he said without lowering his voice.

"I just found out yesterday I was assigned to Binh Tuy. How did you find out so fast?"

"The advisory team got a radio message from MACV yesterday afternoon. I've been in Saigon for a supply run. We're required to let the advisory team know where we're staying in Saigon. I got a message last night to get you on a Caribou at 1400 hours today. So, here I am."

"Well I'll be damned. Don't stand in the doorway all day, Sarge. Come on in and make yourself at home."

Pope shook the big man's paw and ushered him to the only chair in the room. Waters plopped his big frame in the chair.

"What kind of processing do you need to do, Captain?"

"The only place I have left to do is the supply center. Do you know where it is?"

"Does a monkey shit in the jungle? I was there just yesterday."

Pope went into the bathroom, shaved, showered, and dressed in fatigues. After packing, he hooked the rucksack over his left shoulder and picked up his duffel bag.

"Here, let me help you with the duffel, sir."

"No, thanks, Sarge. I hump my own ruck."

"A man after my own heart."

They caught a taxi to the MACV compound. Pope put his gear in the front seat. Before entering, Waters moved the front seat as far forward as it could go. When he sat his knees still met the back of the seat. As the two men entered the supply center, Pope noticed that it was empty except for an army staff sergeant.

"Morning, Sarge. I wasn't able to get jungle boots when I was at Ft. Bragg. They told me if I was assigned to the field in Vietnam, they would be issued here," Pope said.

Jungle boots have a cleated rubber sole and heel, but has a steel plate in the sole and the top and sides are canvas. Holes just above the sole allow water to drain.

"What size do you wear, sir?" The sergeant asked, with an air of authority.

"Size ten."

"Sorry, sir, all we have is a size nine or eleven. Will either of those do?"

"I wear a size ten, Sarge. All I have with me are Corcoran jump boots, and I'm told that they wear out after about three weeks in the field here. I'm heading for the boonies this afternoon." Corcoran jump boots look like regulation combat boots, but are expensive, high gloss leather.

"Can't help you, sir. Why don't you come back in about a month when we have a new shipment?" the sergeant said, as he began casually leafing through a catalog.

"Hey, Sarge. The Captain needs some boondockers. I've had these jungles and another pair for three months and look how they are worn. His jump boots won't last a month in the bush. Now give him some God damn boots, and we'll get out of your life!" Waters boomed, in his usual loud voice.

The supply sergeant appeared to back up from the sheer force of the volume, but recovered quickly.

"Look, Sarge, I don't have any. I can't manufacture the Goddamn things. Maybe the Captain can get some on the black market."

Waters rubbed the side of the sub machine gun cradled in his left arm and glared menacingly at the supply sergeant.

"Yeah, and I wonder how they got on the black market?" He leaned over the counter and looked down, and the supply sergeant jumped back. "I see a damn Saigon Commando like you has jungle boots. What size are they?" Waters growled.

"I wear a size ten, but what difference does that make?" the sergeant replied.

"Do you ever get out in the field, Sarge?"

Seeing the direction of the conversation, the supply sergeant replied defensively, "I've never been out of Saigon. But I signed for these jungles."

"OK. Take them off, and the Captain will sign for them." Then he turned to Pope and said, "You'll sign for the boots won't you, sir?"

"Be happy to, Sergeant," Pope answered.

"But what am I supposed to wear the rest of the day?" The supply sergeant pleaded.

"You look like an enterprising guy. I'm sure you'll think of something," Pope said, showing his teeth.

As the supply sergeant unlaced the footwear, Pope asked, "I need a weapon. Can I get a CAR 15 issued?"

"Sir, advisors in the field get their weapons from the unit they are advising. The Vietnamese don't have CAR 15s." He smirked and handed a form and pen for Pope to sign for the boots.

"Thanks, Sarge. It's a pleasure doing business with you." Pope signed the form, picked up the footwear, and sauntered out of the supply room.

"Well, I guess it was a stand-off, Captain. You got the boots, but the supply sergeant got to keep the weapon."

"He hasn't seen the last of us, Waters." *I wonder if Grandfather's hunters had trouble getting the proper clothes when whale hunting,* he thought.

They stopped at the snack bar, had some lunch, took a taxi to II Corps air operations at Tan Son Nhut and caught their flight to Binh Tuy. They boarded through the tail of an aircraft that Pope had never seen before.

The advisors moved near the front of the aircraft and nestled into canvas seats on the left side of the big transport.

"What kind of aircraft is this?" Pope asked.

"It's an Australian transport plane but manufactured by DeHaviland in Canada. The Caribou can take off and land on a short runway. The Aussies have a reputation for going into areas the US Air Force won't." The engines roared as the pilot ran them up to taxi. "The Aussies are popular with the advisors in the field. They're our life line," Waters shouted.

The aircraft took off, circled over Saigon, and headed east. Pope looked down and saw Saigon a-sprawl, with the Saigon River running through the center. A boulevard separated rows of beautiful French villas and the sheet metal roofed shanties in other parts of the city. As they flew east, Pope watched the colorful countryside, rich with vegetation and miles of quilt-like rice paddies. Families of farmers worked in the fields.

An hour after take-off, the crew chief, a heavy featured, muscular, and friendly man leaned toward the window near Pope and said, "We're about to land, mates. There's the airfield below us now."

He pointed at a small airstrip, cleared of vegetation for four hundred yards around it.

"That looks like a pretty short strip for this big an aircraft," Pope answered.

"It's not a problem, mate. We land here every week."

Out over the ocean, the Caribou banked to the left and lost altitude as it headed west toward the airstrip. The aircraft approached the field and touched down with a bump. The engines reversed, emitting a loud roar. Pope felt himself leaning far to the right in his seat as the craft suddenly slowed. The crew chief shrugged his shoulders and grinned at Pope and Waters as the Caribou taxied up to a covered concrete pad. A sleepy-eyed first lieutenant sat waiting in a jeep parked nearby. *Well, that was some landing. It looks like the beginning of an interesting relationship,* Pope thought.

Chapter Seven

"Good afternoon, I'm Captain John Pope, new Sector Intelligence Advisor."

"Afternoon, Captain Pope, I'm Lieutenant Jack Jutte, assistant Regional Force/Popular Force advisor. Welcome to Binh Tuy. Excuse me for not saluting, Sir. The Major thinks a terrorist might target officers." Then he turned to Waters and said, "Hi, Sarge. Did you get your ashes hauled in Sin City?"

"You know I don't mingle with the local riff-raff, Ell-Tee," Waters said with a smirk.

Pope looked Jutte over. The lieutenant went about 5'10" tall and weighed over 200 pounds—a little on the "soft" side. His brown eyes seemed to twinkle with the wise crack. Pope saw no other soldiers near the airport except the portly lieutenant.

"Isn't there any security for this airstrip?"

"The Major doesn't think we need security here because the province is the most pacified in Vietnam," Waters deadpanned. "Let's get the supplies loaded into your trailer and get the man home, Lieutenant. You get to ride shot-gun in the jeep, Captain."

"What kind of CO is the Major?" Pope asked, throwing his gear in the back seat of the jeep.

"A smart professional officer," Jutte said as he loaded boxes of supplies in the trailer.

"He doesn't rock any boats," Waters added, tossing mail sacks in the back seat.

The three waved at the crew of the Caribou and mounted the jeep. They rode silently down a winding, two-lane dirt road for about six kilometers. Pope thought *the two responses about the Major were strange. One noncommittal and the other critical in a respectful way.*

Pope noticed that the road was cleared of vegetation for about three hundred yards on both sides. There was no sign of life until they reached the outskirts of Lai Gi, the Province City. The smell was as bad as Saigon but different. The town reeked of a combination of cook stoves and open sewers.

They drove through the city of small shops and houses; some made completely of straw and others of dirt bricks and metal and thatched roofs. Each time the jeep slowed, small, happy children yelled, "Hey, GI," and "OK."

"I don't know where the kids learned their English, but that's about the extent of it around here," Jutte said, as he waved at the kids.

The children all seemed to wear the same clothing—short sleeve buttoned shirt, shorts, and no footwear. They were handsome kids and reminded Pope of kids in his village.

They entered a boulevard with larger lots and nicer homes, and Jutte pointed out the Regional Force Battalion compound.

Waters slowed the jeep and prepared to make a left turn into a fenced complex. Jutte said, "That's the chopper pad, sir. It's right across the street from our headquarters."

Pope glance at the helipad then looked where the jeep was headed. It was a small, rectangular compound, about 100 yards by 50 yards, enclosed with barbed wire. A yoke on top of the fence cradled a row of concertina wire. On one side was the boulevard leading to the military province headquarters. On the edge of the multiplex, away from the road, was the top of a sand dune.

They drove up and stopped, and a Vietnamese soldier exited a small building. He opened the large, wooden gate, saluted the jeep, and closed the gate after the jeep pulled forward. Pope saw a volleyball court near a small building that was probably the guard shed.

"That long row of rooms on the road side is the sleeping wing," Jutte said. "It has twelve identical rooms, one for each of us ten advisors. In the center is a latrine with five sinks and five toilet stalls and a shower with three showerheads. That other long structure nearest the minefield is the kitchen, dining room, offices, and dayroom. That small shed near the guard house is where our maids wash our clothes."

A concrete walk connected the two main buildings. Waters parked the jeep near the corner of the building.

"What's on the other side of the sand dune?"

"That's no man's land. There is barbed wire and a minefield. The trees have been cut down and flora cleared for about 300 yards."

"Are there fighting positions up there?"

"Nah. The Major doesn't think we need them. The end room nearest the volleyball court is yours. It isn't any different than any of the other rooms. This is your home away from home, Captain, and we don't stand on formalities here."

Pope picked up his duffel bag and rucksack from the jeep and entered the room. It was about 12 feet square. The bed had a thin mosquito net draped over four tall bedposts. There was a desk, a chair, a footlocker, and a wooden wardrobe. A ceiling fan circulated the air and cooled the small room.

"We'll leave you to unpack. Chow is at 1800 hours, and if you need anything, I'm in room nine."

Pope did not expect this type of living quarters in a combat zone. He pulled a copy of his orders from his notebook, picked up his rucksack, and walked toward the dayroom and office to find the Commanding Officer. Between the buildings, he saw two soldiers with shirts off, digging in the sand.

One stopped working and rubbed the sweat from his forehead with his arm. He wiped his hand on his pant leg, turned to Pope, and extended his hand.

"Hey Dai Uy, A'm speck fow Ah-Chie Ban-eh-stuh, the rad-yo telphone op-rator. The slow digg-uh heah is the team clerk, speck fow Jim Maw-tin. Welcome to Add-visry Team 96." Bannister flashed a boyish, grin. His pants hung loosely on his skinny butt. The drawl identified him as being from somewhere below the Mason-Dixon Line.

Pope shook their hands and sized up Martin. He was a blond, tanned, good looking young man. *Looks like a surfer or football player,* Pope thought.

"I've really been looking forward to meeting you, sir, if you're the ex-State U quarterback—I'm from Los Angeles. When I was a young kid, my dad took me to Pasadena, and we saw you break the heart of Illinois in the Rose Bowl."

"That was a long time ago. You look like a football player Martin—did you play?"

"In high school I quarterbacked the team to the city championship my senior year."

"We'll have to get a football and play some catch when we find time."

"I just happen to have one in my room," Martin said.

"Where are you from, Bannister?"

The radio operator leaned on the handle of his shovel.

"Lonesome Hill, Texas, Suh. Have yuh-ahl heard of it?"

"Sorry. But you probably never heard of my hometown either. Would you men mind telling me what you're digging?"

"It's our idea, sir. It's a duck pond for our two guard geese," Martin said pointing his thumb toward two white geese rooting in the sand nearby. "Some pentagon genius figured that geese will make noise by honking when an intruder appears. Now every advisory team in the country has a pair."

"I heard about that when I went through the advisors school at Ft. Bragg. Are they any good?"

"Not really, sir," Martin said. "They're like government bureaucrats. All they do is eat, shit and squawk—and they're protected by the government," and he threw his head back and shook with laughter.

"They's act-chully become pets for us, and they give us a laugh cus when we have Vet-neese vis-turs the geese chase 'em," Bannister added. He poked his buddy in the ribs and both diggers chuckled.

"So I guess the pond will be a play pen for your geese."

"They not are geese, suh. They belong to the May-ger. If we had are way, we'd uv ett em months ago."

"We're building the pond so the fowl spend more time in the water and less time walking and crapping on our sidewalk. As the lowest ranking enlisted men, Bannister and I have the shit detail. That is, we have to clean up after them," Martin said, spitting in the unfinished hole.

"Well, good luck. I hope your plan works. Can you tell me where I can find the Major?"

"Just inside the dayroom to the right is his desk," Martin replied as he went back to his digging.

Pope entered the building and looked around. On the far left was a kitchen with a wall separating it from the dining area. In the center, a dozen chairs surrounded a long rectangular table. The far right corner contained a couch, a couple easy chairs, a wooden bar with five stools, and a refrigerator. To the right was a corner office area with three desks, chairs, and storage cabinets.

Working on paperwork at one of the desks was a heavy set, forty-ish man with a receding hair line and wearing only fatigue pants, soiled white tee shirt, and rubber shower shoes.

Pope marched up to the desk, stopped, placed a copy of his orders and personnel file on the desk, and saluted.

"Sir, Captain John Pope, Sector Intelligence Advisor, reporting for duty."

The seated man looked up, returned the salute casually, stood, and extended his hand.

"Welcome to the team, John. I'm Major Tom Sullivan. We've been expecting you. We heard yesterday via radio that you were on your way. It doesn't appear you hung around Saigon very long."

Pope took the limp, soft hand and shook it vigorously.

"No, sir, Saigon is too dangerous and confusing a place for me. Besides, I didn't think I had any choice. Your bouncer, Sergeant Waters, escorted me here."

"Yeah, we were lucky to have Waters in Saigon when the message came through. I hope he was able to help you during inprocessing. The Caribou makes a run out here once a week to bring our mail, movies, and chow. I guess you're a bonus this week."

Sullivan skimmed the orders and Pope's records and thought that Pope could be Mexican, Hawaiian, or even Japanese. He leaned back in his chair and scratched his abundant belly.

"We're really glad to have you here. We've never had an intelligence advisor, and it appears by your records you have some good training."

"Thank you, sir. My original assignment was to J-2, MACV, but a friend of mine in assignment got my orders changed."

"You look like you could pass for Vietnamese. What's your origin?" Sullivan said as he rubbed his stomach.

Oh shit! Pope thought. *I should have known I would have to explain to him. It seems like the only ones that ask my nationality are those that it matters to. I hope this guy isn't a racist.*

"Sir, I'm full blood Indian. I'm a registered Makah."

"I'm from Kalispell, Montana. We have the Flathead tribe nearby. I don't think I've heard of your tribe. Where is it located?" Sullivan sniffed.

"It's on the northwest tip of the state of Washington. My ancestors were whale hunters and warriors. They are primarily fishermen and loggers now."

"If they were warriors, who did they fight?"

"Other Indian tribes and some Russian fur trappers. More recently, we have fought in both world wars and Korea. As a matter of fact, there is a belief in our tribe that the spirit of the whale protects our warriors. No Makah has ever been killed in combat under the US flag."

"Well, that's all very interesting. You won't get much chance to test that conviction here. I'm proud to say that Binh Tuy is the most pacified province in the country. No US advisor has been shot at in anger since I've been here. I expect to keep it that way. Anyway, I'm glad you had the orders changed. It's hard telling when we would get an intelligence advisor if you hadn't. It's fairly close to dinnertime, so why don't you just relax and I'll introduce you to the entire team then. They should all be here."

Pope shrugged his shoulders, looked around, and said, "I'm pretty much rested, sir. If you don't mind, can you just take a few minutes now to fill me in on the team and our responsibilities?"

Damn, Sullivan thought. *It looks like this guy is going to be pain in the ass, Gung Ho.*

"Sure," the major said sniffing again as he shuffled to a cloth covering a map on the wall. He moved the fabric aside and exposed a map of South Vietnam.

"Binh Tuy is a Province—that's like a state in the United States, except a South Vietnamese Army Major is the Province chief, who is kind of like a governor, except he also has military responsibilities. There are three districts, run by ARVN captains." Sullivan pointed at the map and said, "Hoi Duc to the north, Tanh Linh in the middle, and Ham Tan in the south. We're located in Ham Tan. The military and civilian offices are located at province headquarters, three hundred yards east of here."

"Excuse the interruption, sir, but where do 'Sectors' fit in?"

"In our vocabulary, sector is a synonym for province and sub-sector is a synonym for district. Your counterpart is the Deputy Province Chief for Security. Captain Dang is responsible for gathering intelligence information and planning combat operations against the Viet Cong. He is one of the bravest men I know and is always looking for better ways of killing Charlie. You have a helper, SFC Doug White, who is the assistant sector intelligence advisor. He used to be a medic in Special Forces, so his medical knowledge is valuable in recruiting agents—but you'll figure that out when you meet him. As you can see by the map, Binh Tuy is on the southeastern part of II Corps and is due east of Saigon. It is part of the Central Highlands, and there are not only mountains but hills, plains, and rice paddies, and the southern portion is on the South China Sea."

"So we are directly subordinate to II Corps?"

"No, we have Binh Lam Special Zone headquarters in Phan Thiet that we report to. Above them is the 23rd ARVN Infantry Division in Ban Me Thuot, then II Corps."

"You mentioned the pacification program. What's the status?" he said as he shifted his weight from one foot to the other.

"If you want combat, you won't see much here. Most of our efforts go toward the pacification program. It involves working with USAID and their pigs and Bulgar wheat project and training of Rif Pif forces. We've moved people from their farms into the hamlets for their protection. They can leave the hamlets during the day to work their farms or chop wood. We have some incidents with Viet Cong, but the largest size VC units we've seen are squad size."

"I stopped by J-2, MACV and got a commitment from them for unlimited funds for intelligence gathering."

He took the rucksack from his shoulder, opened it, and poured a stack of Vietnamese paper money on a nearby desk. Sullivan's eyes opened wide as he stared at the cash.

"That looks like a lot of money. How much is it?"

"They gave me five thousand dollars in Vietnamese Piastres to start. I can get more with a radio message. They will send a courier with the cash"

"We have a safe here for you to store it."

"I had some ideas, and I ran them by the J-2 people. They said they were OK, pending your approval. I'd like permission to organize and train a Reconnaissance and Intelligence platoon, advertise rewards for reporting of Viet Cong, and also a weapons bounty."

"Sounds like a couple fairly good ideas. We'll need to get them approved by the province chief. Captain James, the RF/PF advisor can help you with the R & I platoon organization."

As if on cue, a balding, blue eyed captain entered carrying two boxes of food.

"Hi, Rick James, Rif Pif senior advisor and resident short timer," he said as he set the cartons near the cash and shook hands with Pope.

"How many days do you have before you go home, Rick?"

"Ninety one days and a wake up. How about you?"

"I've been in country three days, so I guess its 362."

"God, if I had that many days left I'd slit my wrists. I'm so short I have to unlace my boots to pee," James said, laughing at his own humor.

"Captain Pope has the funds to create a Reconnaissance and Intelligence platoon in the RF battalion, Rick. I'd like you to give him all the help you can."

"No sweat, sir. Welcome again, Johnny. I have to check on the cooks to see how dinner is coming," Rick said over his shoulder as he carried the boxes into the kitchen.

"This is only a ten man advisory team, John, and we all have extra duties. James is the mess and supply officer—you'll inherit those jobs when he leaves."

"I noticed we have Vietnamese soldiers guarding our compound. Do they do a good job?"

"Not really. We all pull two-hour walking internal security details during periods of darkness. Basically we stay up to be sure our guards remain awake and alert. You get tonight off, but you have a shift tomorrow night."

Martin and Bannister entered the room wearing shorts and jungle boots and carrying a volleyball.

"So, are we playing, sir?" Martin asked the major.

"Does a tiger live in the jungle? Round em up, and let's play. You've got five minutes to change into your in-country athletic uniform, John,"

Sullivan said, clapping his hands together. It did not escape Pope that this was the first time that Sullivan had exhibited any enthusiasm.

"Sir, I think I'll pass on volleyball," Pope said, thinking that he had more important things to do than play games.

"I don't want to hear it. This is not a voluntary sport. **Everyone** plays volleyball. It's not only our way of getting exercise, but we can blow off some steam. We have what we call jungle rules. There are just two of them—you can only hit three times on one side of the net, and the ball must stay inside the marked lines. The game gets a little physical at times, but with your experience in football, I'm sure you can take care of yourself."

"Well, since you put it that way, how can I refuse?" Pope grinned, sheepishly.

Pope changed into shorts and T-shirt and made the short walk to the volleyball court. Nine Americans and two Vietnamese guards were practicing. They all stopped and clapped their hands and cheered as Pope joined them.

"Well, Captain Pope, the All-American jock that doesn't like to play volleyball. You'll like this game, sir. It's more like football," Jutte shouted and the others laughed.

"John, I want to introduce you to the rest of the advisory team. You've already met Jutte, Waters, Martin, Bannister, and James. This is SFC Doug White, your Intel assistant," Sullivan said.

A black man with a very serious face and about the same size and build as Pope extended his hand.

"Pleased to meet you, sir. I'm looking forward to serving with you."

"Thanks, Sergeant, I've already heard about you, and I'm anxious to get started working with you, too."

Sullivan interrupted, "And this is Lieutenant Larry Granger, the Civil Affairs advisor. He's our resident ladies' man and West Pointer."

An athletic built; square-jawed man stepped forward and extended his hand.

"Sir, I'm glad you're here. Now I'm not the newest guy on the team."

"Thanks, and I hope I don't have that distinction long."

"Captain Wayne Bishop, the Psychological Warfare advisor."

Bishop stepped forward. "You don't know me, but I saw you maxing the PT test at Bragg during rotcy summer camp in '57. You didn't get much competition from me at Bragg, and you won't get much athletic competition around here either."

Everyone guffawed as Pope shook Bishop's outstretched hand.

"Well, so which team is stuck with me?" Pope asked.

"We do it the playground way," Sullivan said. "The two lowest ranking EM are captains and they choose their teams."

Bannister "won" the coin toss and, with a loud sigh, selected Sullivan first. The winner of the toss always won the privilege of having the major on his team, even though Sullivan was not the best player. Martin laughed, chose Pope, and gave him a high five. The two Vietnamese guards were the last ones picked. It became obvious why as the game progressed. The guards were willing, smiled a lot, but were not very athletic. The most that could be said for them was that the Americans didn't get physical with them.

It didn't take Pope long to figure out that jungle rules were practically no rules. On the first serve, Martin set the ball perfect for Pope to kill. As he leaped to spike the ball, the mammoth Sergeant Waters drove a step through the net, beat Pope to the ball, and spiked it inside Martin's court.

The startled Pope fell backwards to the ground as he heard Waters bellow, "Welcome to Binh Tuy, Captain!"

Everyone roared—even Pope's teammates. As Pope glanced at Sullivan, he detected a look of satisfaction—or even a smirk. After Martin's team regained the serve, Jutte served a line drive that was headed for the center of the net. Pope grabbed the top of the webbing and pulled it down. The ball cleared the barrier and bounced off the stomach of the surprised Waters.

"Touché and olé, Sarge!" Pope shouted to the glee of both teams.

Just then a big dark cloud settled over them, and rain drenched the players within seconds.

"Are games called on accounta rain, Major?" Pope shouted hopefully.

"Nah, in Binh Tuy we play volleyball like football. No games are called off for weather reasons. Besides, this way I'm sure you get a shower today!"

Cold rain soaked the players for the rest of the game. Pope held his own with the physical play. It was a pretty even contest, but Martin's team won, and he went bounding around the court yelling and giving all his teammates high fives.

The volleyball game ended, and the advisors went to their rooms, took showers, and reappeared in the dining room. Each had an assigned seat; so Pope asked Jutte, which chair was unassigned and sat in the one Jutte designated.

Everyone waited and chatted until the major appeared. Two small Vietnamese women brought food in from the kitchen and set it on the table. Pope was surprised to find the food not only cooked American style but also very tasty.

After dinner, White set up the movie projector and announced the movie would start at 2000 hours. All the team members were lounging around the day room drinking beer and soda while talking when there was a loud boom. The walls shook and the windows rattled. Pope broke into a cold sweat and instinctively dove to the floor. The other team members laughed and slapped each other on the back.

Granger sauntered over to Pope and helped him up.

"That's the Regional Force 105 Howitzer artillery battery firing Harassment & Interdiction. It's down by province headquarters, and they do it every night. You'll get used to it and be able to sleep through it. Sorry, but they did the same thing to me. You'll find that there isn't much to laugh about around here, so we have to take it when we can."

"Well, I'm happy to be able to bring some humor into your otherwise humdrum lives," Pope said, shaking his head.

Pope returned to his room after the movie, sat on his bunk and thought—*I really have some negative vibes about this place, Grandfather. A racist senior advisor that's convinced that there are no enemy in his province.*

The team sits around the compound and plays volleyball every day. We have all the comforts of home. It's not the war you described to me, Grandfather.

Chapter Eight

Pope was unpacking when Captain James strutted through the open door.

"Hey, Newby, a Regional Force Company is going on a search and destroy operation today. It should be a nature walk. Would you like to go with me and get a feel for what's ahead?"

"What's a nature walk?" Pope asked, closing his footlocker.

"It's a walk in the woods and no contact with Victor Charlie. We send RF units out occasionally. Not necessarily based on intelligence but to make sure the enemy doesn't start massing too close to province headquarters."

"Sounds fine to me. By the way, what sort of intelligence apparatus do you have here?"

"Not much, really. Your counterpart, Captain Dang, looks like a brown Lou Costello, but spits bullets. Captain Trang is the Chief of Staff, and he doesn't put much effort into intelligence gathering. Most of our Rif Pif operations are not based on intelligence. They are just search and destroy operations."

"Looks like I've got my work cut out for me. Where do I meet you, and how long is the operation?"

"It's an over-nighter. Don't worry about chow. We eat with the Vietnamese. We'll pick up weapons, grenades and ammo from the Regional Force supply. It's kind of peculiar because Uncle Sam provides all the weapons. They are issued to the South Vietnamese, and we have to go to their supply for our needs. Sometimes it's a pain in the ass because supply sergeants in Vietnam are not always honest, and weapons get on the black market."

"Where can I get a map of the operational area?"

"See Sergeant White. We'll get an overlay from the Regional Force commander. I have to pack my gear. I'll pick you up in a half hour." James turned on his heal and disappeared out the door.

Pope packed toilet articles and clean socks in his rucksack, went to the office, and found White working at a desk.

"I'm going on an operation with Captain James, and he said you have a map for me."

"Sure. What part of the sector would you like, sir?"

"I don't really know where we're going, but it's a two day operation, and we're leaving from here."

"You'll only need a map of Ham Tan District then, sir. About half the district is 'Indian Country'…oh, excuse me, sir," White stammered. "That's not my term. It's one used by everyone around here, though. It means land that is not under the control of the government."

"That's OK, Sarge. I heard the same phrase at the advisors school at Bragg."

Ironic that a black NCO would repeat a racial slur, Pope thought.

Waters drove the jeep and the two captains the short distance down the boulevard to the Regional Force battalion headquarters. It appeared odd to Pope that thatched roofed homes were constructed right up to the barbed wire fence that surrounded the military complex. Inside the compound were several long, one-story structures.

"What is the purpose of all the buildings, Rick?"

"Some billet unmarried soldiers, others are housing for married personnel, supply and maintenance, and offices."

The parade grounds were a beehive of activity—soldiers hurried about carrying packs and weapons. They were barely five feet tall and slightly built. It appeared to Pope that the infantrymen would not be able to carry their loads. And if they did, they would not be able to carry them very far.

They went to the supply room in a building near the edge of the compound. Pope picked up a 45-caliber pistol, three magazines, a 45 caliber Thompson sub machine gun, an ammo vest containing eight magazines, 200 rounds of ammo, and three smoke and four fragmentation grenades. Before leaving, he borrowed cleaning equipment from the supply sergeant and field stripped and cleaned both weapons.

James led the way to the Regional Force commanders' headquarters. Captain Thanh, a short, slight, light-skinned Vietnamese was seated at an empty desk. Pope loaded ammo into his weapon's magazines while listening to Thanh brief James on the operation.

Thanh stood near a large wall map and pointed at a line marked on the map overlay. He held an ornate pipe, and as he pointed at the route, he followed the line with his pipe.

"First Company, commanded by Lt. Diem, will move out by truck in one hour and go just past the airstrip, where they will dismount and move by tactical formation in a westerly direction for six kilometers. They will establish an ambush position before dark on a well-used trail. The following morning, they move in a northeasterly direction, in a half circle. Then finish on the opposite side of province headquarters before nightfall of the second day."

A long pull on the pipe—inhale and very slow exhale. Pope thought *Thanh might be using the pipe for long pauses and dramatic effect, much like Grandfather did.*

"I have contacted Special Zone headquarters in Binh Thuan and we should have a medevac chopper available. Due to the short notice, we have no air cover," James said.

"That should be no problem because we will have 105 artillery support on call from here." A long drag on his pipe. This time he appeared to be trying to swallow the smoke after inhaling.

He was surprised that Captain Thanh appeared to be in his forties, while commanding a battalion. In the US army forty-year-olds were usually lieutenant colonels. The Vietnamese must have a different rank structure, with more time in grade before promotion—much like the US cavalry in the old west.

"You speak very good English," Pope said to Thanh in his best Ft. Bragg Vietnamese, as he rammed cartridges into the pistol magazine.

"Thank you, Captain Pope. You speak very good Vietnamese. Have you been to Vietnam before?"

"I don't really speak the language very good. Thank you for the compliment. I want to practice so that I can really speak and understand it. And no, I have never been to this country before." It suddenly dawned on Pope that Thanh was about half drunk.

"Well, it appears the troops are being loaded on the trucks. Lt. Diem will be waiting for you. Good luck," Thanh said in English, staggering to his chair.

Four two and half-ton trucks were parked in front of the headquarters building. About a hundred small soldiers with packs that appeared too large for them to carry talked fast and climbed into the vehicles. Pope counted over twenty soldiers per truck.

"Say, Rick, is it my imagination, or is Captain Thanh drunk?"

"Hell, no, he's stoned! Didn't you notice the smoke that smelled like burning horse shit? It's opium. Quite a few officers puff it like we smoke cigarettes. In fact, it's socially acceptable around here."

"Do they use that crap on field operations?"

"I've never seen Thanh on a combat mission. The largest unit sent out is company size. Thanh's duties are primarily administrative. I've never seen Vietnamese commanders smoke dope in the field."

"What can you tell me about Diem?"

"He looks like a soldier, but like Thanh and other officers, he tries to walk the fine line between pleasing us and staying alive."

Lieutenant Diem pulled up with his jeep and driver and dismounted, and James made the introductions. Pope slipped into his fully loaded ammo vest and packed the grenades, extra ammo, and magazines into his rucksack. He carefully inserted magazines into both his pistol and sub machine gun and placed them on safe. Pope and James crammed into the back seat of the jeep.

Lieutenant Diem got back in the vehicle, turned, smiled, and said in broken, halting English, "Welcome Captain Pope, I think we kill many VC on this operation.

"Thanks, Lieutenant Diem, I'm glad to be here."

Pope wondered if he really was glad to be on this excursion.

The Jeep headed out of the compound, followed by the trucks. The convoy made its way past the airstrip, stopped along side the road, and let the troops dismount. In minutes, five soldiers appeared near the vehicle.

"Those men are the company RTO and four cooks that are also the personal security for the commander and advisors," James said.

One platoon of about twenty men disappeared into the jungle, and the command group and the remainder of the company fell in behind them. With the added weight of his rucksack, ammo vest, and weapons, Pope sweated through his uniform immediately. The additional burden of uncertainty created more perspiration. The column seemed to move like a spring—coiling and uncoiling. After walking on a trail through the thick jungle for about an hour, the unit halted.

The soldiers sat in place, reached into their packs, and brought out pots containing rice and meat. The four chefs set their packs down. In about 20 minutes, they served a bowl of rice with cold chicken soup to the commander and advisors. Pope found the food fairly tasty but was surprised by the way the company seemed to be taking an "administrative meal" in a "tactical zone." No local security had been sent out by any of the platoon leaders. *This looks like the beginning of a bad operation,* he thought.

Pope walked off the trail into the jungle about ten yards to relieve himself. As he buttoned his pants and turned around, two soldiers watched and smiled at him.

Pope found James and said, "When I went to take a leak, two cooks followed and watched me pee. What's the deal?"

James laughed and said, "They aren't queer, they're bodyguards. The commander would lose face if an American advisor was killed while with his unit."

"I noticed no local security is sent out during chow, and there is no flank security for the column on the move. Don't you think that it's kind of dangerous?"

"I used to worry, but that's the way they operate. We have not had any problems in the nine months I've been in country."

"But there's always the first time. Do you think it would do any good for me to talk to Diem?"

James frowned. "Not really. And besides, that's my job. You're just here as an observer."

The column resumed movement on the trail, interrupting the advisors discussion. After walking for three hours a single shot rang out from the rear. The soldiers dropped to the ground pointing their weapons off the trail. Pope lay in the brush scanning the bushes and trees. He thought it must have been a lone sniper. He wondered if there were any more close by. Diem talked on the radio for a couple minutes and turned to James.

"One soldier WIA. We need medevac. You can get?"

Without answering, James took the handset from his radio and talked with Binh Lam Special Zone air. He gave them the information and the coordinates of his location on the ground.

"Chopper on the way. Should be here in thirty minutes."

Diem nodded, turned and strolled in the direction of the gunshot, James and Pope following. About a hundred yards away, a group of soldiers stood around a man who was lying on his back with his shirt off and a large bandage on his shoulder. The commanding officer questioned a sergeant.

"The sergeant say, the soldier following the wounded man did not have the safety of his rifle on. He tripped and shot the man to his front."

Pope looked at the wounded man and saw that the bleeding had stopped. He wondered why Diem didn't appear concerned about the lack of discipline.

In a small clearing, just off the trail, it appeared that a campfire had been built earlier. Pope walked to the area and looked carefully around. He yelled at James to have a look.

"Are civilians allowed this far out in the jungle to cut wood?"

"No. This is a 'free fire zone.' This is what we call contested land."

"According to the signs, about six VC built a fire, cooked a meal, and did not try to hide the fact they had been there. It rained at about 1700 hours yesterday. My guess is we missed a squad of enemy by a day," Pope said with a sigh, rubbing ashes from the fire through his fingers absently.

"How do you know all that from just looking at the area? They didn't teach us that in the advisors course at Ft. Bragg," James said.

"I learned tracking from my grandfather, on the reservation. He taught me signs to look for. There's no doubt in my military mind that six people were here yesterday."

They both returned to the command group and sat on the trail. About a half-hour later Pope heard a chopper approaching, poked James in the arm, and pointed to the sky.

James picked up the hand set from his radio.

"Army helicopter, this is American advisor on the ground, over."

"Advisor, this is Dust-off one two delta. Are here for transport, do you have passenger?"

"Affirmative, one two delta. We have passenger. Make your approach from the north. I throw smoke. Please identify, over."

Pope pulled the pin and threw a green smoke grenade in the open field.

"This is one two delta, I identify green smoke. We will make our approach from the north."

The chopper landed took the wounded man, and the column resumed its movement.

By the time the company arrived at the planned ambush site it was almost dark. The sun had already set. Twilight was fading. The night would soon squeeze in on them. Lightning illuminated the jungle. The flashes gave the trees a grotesque form. The thunder boomed like artillery.

Rain hit the forest like a wet sheet. Ten minutes later, it penetrated the jungle canopy and soaked the troopers. It took about an hour for the chefs to build fires and cook rice and soup for dinner. Darkness enveloped the unit. Diem announced through the noise of the storm that the company would form the ambush position: he would set up a machine gun pointing down the trail.

Diem said proudly, "I will be near the machine gun to activate the ambush."

James took Pope aside and said, "We'll sack out next to Diem to make sure we know what's going on."

"Christ, I would have thought Diem would set up the ambush before chow and before it got too dark. Shouldn't we help the lieutenant set up the ambush, now?"

"No, it's too dark. They know what they're doing. We would just get in the way. Don't sweat it. Try to get some sleep."

Rain slackened and Mosquitoes buzzed around Pope's head. He removed a small plastic bottle of insect repellent from his rucksack and rubbed it over his head, neck, and arms. He removed his pancho and pancho liner, wrapped them around himself and positioned himself behind the machine gun. He looked down the trail over the barrel of his Thompson. As he lay there he heard very loud noises of movement in the jungle all around him and he guessed that it was the men settling in. Within an hour, everything was quiet. The rain stopped, leaving him cold and wet.

Pope stayed awake the entire night, and all he heard was the nocturnal sounds of the jungle and James breathing quietly near him. He thought about what had happened during the previous day: *the VC traveled their trail and made no effort to hide it. James showed too little concern: worst, the RF Company stayed on the trail and made no attempt to hide their presence. It was like the unit was trying to stay away from the VC. If the enemy used this trail earlier, they might use it tonight. In the middle of 100 men, he felt isolated.* He saw shadows on the trail throughout the night, but no Charlie.

*   *   *

When the sunlight appeared through the jungle canopy, Pope sat up and looked around. The machine gun crew was asleep and so was Diem. He got to his feet, men slept in cloth hammocks tied to trees for as far as he could see. He kicked James lightly on the leg.

"What's going on, Johnny?"

"Nothing but a lot of sleeping. The whole God damn Viet Cong army could have come down this trail last night and I think I would have been the only one awake to greet them."

"Don't sweat the small stuff. There was no contact, and no one got hurt," James said, as he got up and rolled his pancho and liner.

Pope shook his head and wondered how any war could be won like this. Within minutes, the entire company had taken down their hammocks and ate the same meal they had prepared the day before, only cold. Pope and two bodyguards crept down the trail a hundred yards. There were several footprints of people wearing rubber-soled sandals made of truck tires. He decided that it was a heavily traveled trail, but not in the last 24 hours. The rain the previous night obliterated most of the tracks and made it impossible to estimate when the footprints were made. The point squad of the company interrupted his inspection.

*   *   *

About three hours later there was a loud explosion from the rear of the column, followed by sporadic small arms fire. The soldiers hit the ground while the commander got on the radio. *Damn, this sounds like it,* Pope thought. *My first battle. I hope these soldiers show me more in a fight.* He switched the safety off on his Thompson, stuck his head up, and looked around, trying to spot the enemy. The firing stopped as fast as it had started.

Diem gave the hand set to his radio operator and said to James, "We have two wounded, can get chopper?"

"Wait one," James replied as he reached nonchalantly for his radio hand set.

Pope followed Diem to the rear of the column. Two soldiers were seriously wounded. One had metal fragments in his back and the back of his legs. He was lying on his stomach in severe pain. The other was lying on his back with a sucking chest wound, and part of his jaw was hanging down from his face. The medic covered their injuries with dressings.

"One of the soldiers must have foolishly clipped a hand grenade to his suspenders by the pin ring," Diem said quietly. "The weight of the grenade worked the pin loose. It fell from his belt and exploded, wounding him and the soldier walking behind him. The shooting was from a few soldiers that thought that the explosion was caused by attacking VC."

Pope shrugged his shoulders and shook his head. *Sloppy soldiering, and the commander doesn't give a damn. It's like he thinks a medevac chopper is the solution to his problems, he thought. Hell, we don't have to worry about the enemy killing us. We're doing that ourselves.*

James arrived and said, "The chopper will be here in one hour."

"There is a river about one hundred meters from here. We'll move the wounded there and have lunch."

At the river, twenty soldiers had fashioned makeshift fishing poles and cast their lines into the water. The rest of the unit had removed their packs and uniforms, and were swimming in the river. Pope removed his rucksack and ammo vest and set them down on the trail and wiped his brow with the back of his hand.

"Damn, I haven't been this hot since I left the Jungle Warfare school in Panama."

"Yeah, the temperature in the sun here is usually above a hundred and humidity about 98%—but you'll get used to it," James said.

"Well, I'm going to take a bath," Pope said and pulled a bar of soap in a plastic wrap, and a towel out of his rucksack. He took off his boots and all his web gear and placed them carefully on the ground. Then he stood and lathered himself all over with the bar of soap. His uniform was already wet with sweat. He removed his sox and lathered his feet. With sox in one hand and soap in the other, he dove into the river. As he stood, chest deep in water, Pope washed and rinsed the sox, and put them in his pocket. Then he lathered his face and hair, rinsed the soap off, waded to the bank, and climbed out.

He sat, wrung out the wet sox, put them on, and then put his boots on. He took the towel and wiped his face and hair.

"That's the damnest bath I've ever seen. You learn that on the reservation too?" James asked.

"No, Jungle Warfare school in Panama. It saves time and I'm not 'vulnerable' as long."

"Say, I hear your Indian tribe is good at fishing. What do you think, Lieutenant Diem, shall we ask Captain Pope to teach us how to fish?"

"Captain Pope, it would be helpful to catch fish fast so we can cook our meal and get moving."

Pope looked around the troops still in the river. He thought, *it looks like James is either trying to ridicule me or put me on the spot.*

"OK, Lt. Diem, but you'll have to move your men out of the river and back from the bank about 15 meters."

Diem shouted orders to the men, and they moved back from the waters edge. Pope walked to the bank, took two hand grenades from the pouch on his harness, pulled the pins, threw them about ten meters into the river, and dropped to the ground.

The two grenades exploded under the surface, throwing up huge geysers. Seconds later about twenty fish floated to the top.

"You can have your men get the fish now."

A shocked Diem shouted instructions to his men and several swam out and brought the dead fish to shore.

"Hardly seems traditional, Johnny. Where did you learn that?" James asked.

"I got it from my grandfather. He learned it from commercial loggers on the reservation, but they used dynamite."

Diem smiled broadly, "Thank you Captain Pope," he said, and shouted orders to his men. Twenty explosions along the river rocked the calm, Diem announced the company had enough fish. The medevac chopper arrived and departed with the two wounded soldiers. The unit finished it's meal and was on the move.

After two more hours in the jungle, the troops arrived in the Province City of Lai Gi and marched down the street and into the battalion compound. The soldiers laughed and seemed to be having a good time when the commander dismissed them. As Pope, James, and Diem walked toward the jeep driven by Waters, Diem smiled.

"It was a good operation. I hope you and Captain Pope will come to the company party tonight."

He saluted and walked away without waiting for a response. The advisors got into the jeep.

"I don't get it—Diem said it was a good operation and mentioned a party. I don't know about you, but I thought the whole operation was a rat fuck. They took a stroll down a trail in the woods with complete disregard for simple security. They set up on a trail and everyone but me slept all night. Three soldiers were wounded by 'friendly fire,' and we had no contact with Charlie. What's to celebrate?" Pope said, voice rising.

James glanced at Waters, and flushed.

"Johnny, after you've been here a while, you'll understand better. They have been fighting wars in Vietnam for decades. They consider an operation to be successful when no contact is made with the enemy. The commander had a pretty good idea there were no VC in the area, that's why there was no security out."

"But it's almost like they have an agreement with Charlie to stay out of each others' way. It's also teaching bad habits. You know they could have used this as a training mission so when they go into dangerous territory, security is second nature. For two days those soldiers were sauntering around at the 'route step.'"

"The South Vietnamese are good soldiers. They just lack good leadership. You'll see that when they get into a fight."

"I'm not so sure I want to get into a fight with them. Frankly, I'm surprised you put up with this shit. You learned from the same book I did—you either engage the enemy, or you get the hell off the battlefield."

The two-minute ride to the advisors' compound was in silence.

As the jeep pulled up to the parking lot, Waters said enthusiastically, "Hey, captains, turn the frowns upside down, we've got a good movie tonight."

Thunder sounded in the distance and lightning smashed through a big black cloud moving in from the hills. The cold, drenching rain splashed against pope's face, but he didn't feel himself cooling off.

Pope stomped into his room, threw his rucksack on the bed, sat down at his desk and thought: *No one will die. I really need the spirit of the Whale to help me. This is going to be a long year, Grandfather. How can we win a war without establishing a sound intelligence network, then use that intelligence to seek out the enemy and destroy him in detail? How can an officer be sent out with a foreign unit and not have any say in what's happening? It's as if we're nothing more than high priced aircraft coordinators. All the Vietnamese really want from us is to be able to provide choppers for them when needed. How do people survive this kind of soldiering? These Vietnamese are like little children, playing a deadly game. And what of my vision to lead warriors in battle?*

Chapter Nine

"What makes you think you know more than an officer that has been serving in Vietnam more than nine months?"

Pope looked up from his desk in his room, and gazed at the red-faced senior advisor. He rose slowly to his feet, and wondered how to react. The only sound in the room was the whir of the ceiling fan.

He cleared his throat, quietly.

"I'm not quite sure what you mean, Major?"

"You know damn well what I mean. James told me that you criticized his action on the search and destroy mission in front of Sergeant Waters. Do you deny that?"

"No sir. You're correct. I owe Rick an apology for the confrontation in front of Waters. I also disapproved of him in private, for which I won't apologize. I don't think he tried to exert necessary influence on his Vietnamese commander."

"It's not your place to reprove him. That's my responsibility."

"Does that also mean that I'm not allowed to express my opinion, sir?"

"Hell, no. You know better than that."

"Then I would like to express a difference of opinion with you if I may."

Sullivan started to say something, stopped, face flushed and stormed out of the room, slamming the door behind him.

*   *   *

Sergeant Nguyen Duc, a nineteen-year-old interpreter knocked on Pope's door a few minutes later.

"Sir, my name is Sergeant Duc and I have been assigned as your interpreter."

"I wasn't aware that I would have an interpreter. Have a seat on the bed," Pope said, gesturing with his hand.

"Thank you. Yes, sir, I am also able to translate documents for you."

"Well, that's fine, Duc. Where are you from?"

"Sir, I was born and raised in Saigon. I joined the army to be an interpreter so I would not be drafted into the fighting forces."

"You speak very good English. Maybe you can teach me some Vietnamese."

"I would like you to correct my English when necessary, sir. I would prefer not to teach you Vietnamese because then you would have no use for an interpreter. The army may then need me more in the infantry." Duc said, shifting nervously on the bed. "If you insist, I will teach you our language," he quickly added.

Pope laughed and said, "I don't want you to do anything you don't want to do. This is your country. I'm just here to help."

"Thank you, sir. I will do my best."

"Us Americans have come half way around the world to help the South Vietnamese fight communism."

Duc thought for several moments and replied, "I see sir, what you mean is that if your neighbor's house is on fire you better help him extinguish it or your house will also catch fire."

"That's a very good analogy, Duc. Perhaps you can tell me why each time I want to visit a Vietnamese officer between 1200 and 1430 hours, they are not available?"

"Sir, because of the hot weather, the officers go to their quarters and take a nap and have a meal."

"Why rest in the middle of the day? I'll bet the Viet Cong don't take a siesta."

"I don't really know, sir. Maybe if the officers didn't want to take a nap they would join the communists."

Pope laughed uncontrollably for a few moments, then said, "You're probably right, Duc. These are strange times we live in."

"Sir, I have been asked to take you to meet your counterpart, Captain Dang."

"Great! Let's go," Pope said, as he strapped on his pistol, and hustled out the door.

*   *   *

A pretty Vietnamese secretary ushered Duc and Pope into a stark office in province headquarters. Captain Dang was seated behind his desk, working on papers. The large room looked even bigger due to the absence of furniture. There were two fabric chairs, a straight-backed chair, and a coffee table positioned in front of the desk. Two large pots containing palms occupied two corners of the room. *This place is almost as big as the community hall on the reservation,* Pope thought.

Dang looked up and said in English, "Ah, Captain Pope. I have been looking forward to meeting you."

He hurried around the big desk and shook hands, grasping Pope's outstretched hand with both of his.

"Please have a seat," he said, waving Pope toward a chair.

"Thank you, Captain Dang. This is Sergeant Duc, my interpreter. He is here to help us if we have problems with our languages. I don't speak very good Vietnamese, but I intend to learn."

Dang nodded at Duc, who came to attention and waited until both officers sat in easy chairs across from each other. Then he took a seat near the American.

"Major Sullivan told me that you are an American Indian. You look like a Vietnamese officer," Dang said, his round, soft face breaking into a smile.

"Yes, I have been mistaken for several nationalities: Japanese, Spanish, Hawaiian, and now, Vietnamese. Have you visited the United States?"

"Oh yes, twice. I attended the Infantry officer's career course in Fort Benning. Then I went to the Command and General Staff College in Fort Leavenworth, Kansas."

"What sort of assignments have you had, Captain Dang?"

"I am from the north and fought with the Viet Minh against the French, but I hate the North Vietnamese communists. I was a battalion commander for eight years and have been deputy province chief for about six years."

"You have a very impressive background. I am anxious to work with you."

"Thank you. I am sure we will have success together. Now let me tell you about our little organization. You and I are responsible for the security of the province. Through our Sector Operations and Intelligence Center, we collect information and plan combat operations against the VC."

"Do you run the SOIC?"

"No. That is the responsibility of Captain Trang, the Chief of Staff. I believe you might be able to help him improve intelligence gathering."

"That wouldn't be hard," Pope muttered.

"Excuse me?" Dang said.

"Nothing. Are the Popular and Regional force troops effective in providing security?"

"Since we don't have many VC in our province, they are adequate. If more communist activity occurs, we will need help. Our Regional Force personnel are draftees, wear green uniforms, but are not regular ARVN soldiers. They are paid by province headquarters and comparable to the US National Guard. Most of the soldiers are long-time residents of Binh Tuy. About half are married, and their families live either on the military compound or in the village close by."

"I understand people are moved into villages to protect them from the VC. This could create a 'bunker' mentality like the great defensive positions of World War I and II. Soldiers can develop a false sense of invincibility. They become lazy while sitting around waiting for the enemy."

Dang shifted his weight in his chair and grimaced.

"Yes. I think that happens here, but our orders from Saigon require us to operate in this manner."

"I recall a general who said that 'bunkers are monuments to a commanders stupidity'."

"I agree with you and him. I believe officers who seize the initiative and take the battle to the enemy win wars. Maybe we can figure out how to provide security to the villagers while seeking out and destroying the communists."

"Would you be surprised if I told you I believe that there are more VC in our province than we think?"

Dang leaned back, folded his arms across his plump chest and grinned.

"Finally I have someone that thinks as I do. I have been a minority of one against Major Nhia, Major Sullivan, and Captain Trang. I believe as you do that there are many communists here. Do you have any ideas for operations against them?"

Pope leaned forward in his chair, eyebrows raised.

"I have a suggestion for a start. I have US funds to hire and train a Reconnaissance and Intelligence platoon. These soldiers can be used to scout deep into enemy territory to gain information."

Dang nodded and thought *this captain is willing to provide more than worthless advice.* He rose to his feet.

"Yes, I like the idea of that kind of platoon. I will talk with the Regional Force Battalion commander so he will cooperate with you. Come, let me show you around the SOIC so you have a better idea of the way we operate."

The trio toured the small office building. Pope was not impressed with Captain Trang. A thin, older officer with small eyes and a scraggly goatee. He seemed indifferent to both Pope and Dang. Pope noticed that the operation did not have many intelligence agents. What sources they had did not appear to be protected from the enemy.

*   *   *

Pope and Duc visited Captain Thanh at Regional Force headquarters the next day. They discussed the commander's family for a few minutes, and then Thanh abruptly changed the subject.

"Captain Pope, I have been talking with Captain Dang, and he said you have some ideas about forming a Reconnaissance and Intelligence platoon with soldiers from my unit. There might be some difficulty because we have no funds to pay them."

"That should not be a problem, Captain. I have adequate funds."

"Maybe you can tell me more about what you had in mind."

"What I want is a platoon of hand-picked, unmarried men that can be trained to travel at night and perform reconnaissance operations that will gather intelligence to help other units. They will be trained in information gathering as individuals and in small teams. Do you have soldiers like that Captain Thanh?"

"Yes, we do, but what would be the command structure?"

"I will pick, pay and train the men. I will purchase weapons and equipment for them. We will conduct combat operations for the sector, just like your other units.

"It is the custom in Vietnam for the battalion commander to pay the troops. Perhaps you can give me the funds, and I can make the proper dispersal to the men?"

Pope was aware of the rumors that Vietnamese commanders rake off US dollars provided to pay the troops.

"That is very kind of you, Captain Thanh, but since these are special intelligence funds, I must personally make the payment and get signatures."

Thanh's face flushed, but just as quickly, he smiled and said, "You will need an officer to command the troops, but sadly, I have none available at this time," then he lowered his eyes to his desk.

"I will require four corporals and a platoon sergeant. Since they will operate for the most part in teams, no officer will be needed to command them."

"Well," Thanh said wryly, "There must be an accountable officer. I will volunteer to be the officer responsible for commanding them. Naturally, you will have operational control, and you can just check with me when you need something. How much do you think the unit commander should be paid monthly?" Thanh added, as he carefully examined his fingernails.

This guy is a real piece of work, Pope thought. *He'll give me his worst soldiers in return for a kick back. This is some army.*

"I think you have a good plan, Captain. Each of the soldiers should get three times as much as their regular pay, and you will receive the same. Are you agreeable to that?"

"You are most generous, Captain Pope. Please come back at this time tomorrow, and I will have your volunteers."

Waters met Pope and Duc as they left the headquarters.

"Excuse me, sir, but can I have a word with you in private?"

"Sure, Sergeant. Duc, why don't you take the jeep back to the compound, and I'll catch a ride with Sergeant Waters."

The two of them got into Water's jeep, but the sergeant didn't start the engine.

"Sir, I'd like to talk with you in confidence and speak freely. OK?"

"What is it, Sergeant?"

"Sir, I've been in the army 16 years, and I've never been a part of such a screwed up mess as this battalion. I think you saw that when you went out with First Company on a search and destroy operation. The other companies aren't any different. Nothing seems to work in getting them shaped up. I believe the soldiers could do the job if they had good leadership. I've tried to help them, but they don't take advice from sergeants—only officers."

Pope noticed for the first time that Waters was speaking as quietly as everyone else was.

"What's your point, Waters?"

"Major Sullivan told me you're forming an all volunteer R & I platoon from the Regional Force Battalion. I want in. I want to be part of a unit that I can influence. I think you can use me because I've trained units in the states. I know the RF troopers, and I can help you find the best recon soldiers."

"What does Captain James think of your idea?"

"Not much. He thinks you're pushing too hard. But I convinced him to approve it because we'll still be working with RF troops. Besides, he knows how helpless I feel about giving advice and the Vietnamese not taking it because I'm just a sergeant."

"What do you think of James?"

"He's preoccupied with counting the days till he goes home. I think it best if I just say I agree with what you think of him."

"OK, Waters, you're in. The first thing I want you to do is take a requisition to MACV in Saigon and pick up thirty CAR 15 rifles, complete with spare parts, magazines, and training and combat ammo. You'll have to go through J-2, MACV because they are funding the platoon."

"That's great, sir. I'll do my best. But, why the CAR 15, sir? I thought that was an Air Force weapon."

"It is, but we'll be traveling at night in the jungle, and we need the packs and equipment to be as light as possible for these smallish soldiers. The old M-2 carbine is light, but the magazine is not big enough, it is unreliable, and lacks knock down strength. The CAR 15 is a perfect weapon for a small unit that needs to put out a lot of firepower fast. This outfit will be mobile, agile, and hostile." Pope noticed that Water's voice was back at *his* normal level.

"Gotcha, Captain! You can count on me."

"I just bought a Vietnamese platoon and paid dearly for it. Tomorrow, we'll come back and get our volunteers. I want you to be sure we don't get the crap of the outfit."

As the jeep headed toward the compound, Waters chuckled. "Hot damn, sir. It is a pleasure to work for a captain who isn't afraid to take chances and step on toes. Now maybe we can do something worthwhile!"

*   *   *

The next day, Pope, Waters, and Duc were met at battalion headquarters by a small but husky, dark-faced sergeant. He smiled easily and had a gold cap on his front tooth that glistened in the sun.

In Vietnamese, he said, "Sir, I am Sergeant Ma, your new R & I platoon sergeant."

Pope replied in Vietnamese, "Nice to meet you, Sergeant, but you are a **candidate**. I will pick the platoon sergeant based on ability. Where are the other men?"

The little sergeant made no effort to hide his disappointment.

"The other volunteers are in the end barracks."

"Good. Lets have a look."

Ma led them to one of the long one-story structures and into a room that had no furniture. It had a musty smell mixed with strong tobacco smoke. About two dozen dark-faced soldiers sat on the floor, smoking and talking. As the command group entered, the volunteers jumped to their feet and snapped to attention.

In Vietnamese, Pope said, "Have a seat and continue to smoke." He turned to Duc and added in English, "Please interpret for me because I don't want any misunderstanding."

"I am looking for volunteers to form a fighting platoon. You have to be unmarried and physically able to stand the rigors of long range patrolling. You must be able to learn to gather information, and be willing to be in the jungle for extended periods. The men selected will receive three times as much pay as you now receive and stand a good chance of fighting communists. If you do not want to be part of the platoon, you can leave now."

The soldiers smiled, looked at each other, nodded, and all of them remained in place.

Duc helped Pope review all of the men's service records, and Waters talked with each soldier. Pope interviewed each volunteer privately. He determined that of the thirty volunteers, 24 were Montagnards and six were Vietnamese.

"Damn, sir, it looks like we got mostly Montagnards. You want to go back to the battalion CO?"

"Wait a minute. Let's talk about it. I learned about the highland people from the Green Berets when I studied at Bragg. The Montagnard is a French word meaning 'mountain people.' They're the largest minority population in country and are treated by the Vietnamese as 'second class citizens.' They belong to tribes from the Central Highlands, but many had been moved from the hills to the hamlets for their own protection."

"Yeah, I heard most Montagnards would rather stay in the hills, but the government was scared that if they stayed there, they would be influenced by the Cong."

"Green Berets call them 'Yards' and claim that they are more at home in the jungle than in the villages and hamlets. You say you know these soldiers. Have they performed their duties OK?"

"I've never seen any of them get in trouble. They are enthusiastic and work harder then the Vietnamese. I heard they are supposed to be damn good fighters. But remember I haven't seen any of them fight here."

"It looks to me that our friend Captain Thanh offered up what he considers second class soldiers."

"Shit, yes. The records of the six Vietnamese show that they are malcontents and malingerers. Did you expect anything different?"

"Well, I think he sent just the kind of fighters that we're looking for."

"What the fuck, over?"

"The Yards are like the American Indians. They live in the mountains and are accustomed to hardship. They are a hard working and honest people by nature."

"I know they hate the Viets. Do they like us?"

"They don't have any allegiance to the government of Vietnam or to the Viet Cong. My job is to buy their allegiance first and we earn their loyalty second."

*   *   *

Pope received permission from Dang to move the unit to the airstrip. There he had an open area for marching, battle drill, and quick reaction exercises. He also had the surrounding hills and jungle for other training. He drew up plans for a month of intensive individual and small unit instruction. The first three days were spent in individual indoctrination— primarily close order drill and testing.

*   *   *

Within four days, Waters returned from Saigon with the CAR 15's.

"I've got a surprise for you, sir," Waters said, pointing at three large cardboard crates that were unloaded with the rifles.

"Well, lets take a look, Sarge," Pope said, taking his K bar from it's sheath and cutting open a container.

"I've got a buddy in J-4, supply and he gave me material for uniforms for our platoon. Now all we have to do is find a seamstress to make them."

"Tiger skin. Like the ARVN rangers. This is great, Sarge!"

"My wife is very good with her sewing machine. I'm sure she would be happy to make the uniforms, sir," Duc volunteered.

"Outstanding! I'll pay her to do the job," he said, clearly pleased with the idea of having a distinctive uniform for the handpicked soldiers.

"Got something else for you, sir," Waters said, removing a new pair of jungle boots from his rucksack and tossing them to Pope. "Size ten, wasn't it?"

*   *   *

Pope learned quickly that the Yards were not very well educated, and it was necessary to keep the training short and simple.

"They learn from constant repetitive drills and primarily from rote. They especially liked being out of the compound and in the jungle," Pope said.

"I really like training them because they're so damn eager to learn," Waters said.

"Yeah, they seem to follow instructions to the letter."

Duc's wife arrived at the airstrip and took the measurements of all of the trainees.

By the seventh training day, Pope instructed the Yards in movement in the jungle at night.

"These guys not only have the aptitude but the interest in moving under periods of darkness."

"Yes, sir. The only problem is that every one of them smoke and like to bullshit—especially when they're happy. Light and noise discipline are hard for them to get."

"Why don't you put it in terms of stalking wild game?"

"Good idea. I'll try it. The Yards are really willing soldiers and "ass chewings" aren't needed."

"Yeah, I've found that usually, when a mistake is made, just bring it to the attention of the man, and a reminder of the correct way is all it takes."

"They've picked up on the CAR 15 rifle, too. I was amazed. Within 24 hours of training on care and cleaning, every one of them could field strip and put the weapon back together in the dark."

"Great. We don't have to teach map reading or compass training because the Yards grew up in and traveled about the province all of their lives. We can use that time for me to give them the same kind of tracking training that my grandfather gave me on the reservation."

By the end of the second week, five of the soldiers were dropped from the platoon, not for disciplinary reasons but because they were physically unable to do the training. Pope, Waters, and Duc trained with the CAR

15 and all three were armed with it. Pope was glad to return the heavy, awkward submachine gun and ammunition to the supply sergeant.

*   *   *

Duc's wife brought the first set of uniforms to Sgt. Ma at the airstrip camp. Sergeant Ma was pleased and had the men change into them immediately. From the amount of smiling, laughing, and talking, Pope knew the soldiers were also happy with their new uniforms. Ma formed them into a platoon formation and made a show of inspecting every man. Then he put on a demonstration for the advisors, Duc, and Mrs. Duc as he took the platoon through close order drill.

"Sergeant Ma, it is with great pleasure that I appoint you official platoon sergeant," Pope said in front of the formation of troops.

"You will not be sorry, Captain," Ma said, gold tooth shining brightly in the sun.

The advisors met with Ma to organize the platoon.

"I want to have a 21 man element—a platoon sergeant and four teams of five men each. Since we are not organized for prolonged battle, they will not carry crew-served weapons."

"How will they be armed?" Waters asked.

"Each soldier will carry the CAR 15, a basic load of ammo, four hand grenades, a K bar knife, and 45."

"I still have 25 men. Shall I send four back to the battalion?" Ma queried.

"Hell, no. We're training them. We'll keep them as replacements."

*   *   *

In the middle of the third week, Pope and Waters accompanied a team that was in training for a night ambush. They had rehearsed the plan in the training area twice, and he was satisfied. *With this outfit, I don't have to advise,* Pope thought. *I can lead them. This is almost as good as commanding a US outfit.*

They waited until the sun dropped behind the hills, and darkness enveloped them. With a point man and machete assistant in the front, they broke trail as quietly as possible. The seven man patrol made more noise than he liked, but it couldn't be helped. They traveled about two kilometers when the point man stopped. Pope silently walked forward in a crouch.

"This is the trail," the point man whispered.

"Go back and bring the rest of the patrol forward."

As they arrived, he motioned them into their position in the L shaped ambush.

"Your men are talking too much, corporal. Get them quiet," Pope hissed.

The team leader crept into the darkness toward his men. Pope and Waters took up their position, one on each side of the "L." Everything was quiet except animals moving in the jungle. As he looked down the path, Pope thought about how *he had sat in ambush on the reservation all night waiting for an elk or deer to enter his kill zone.* He sweated through his uniform and felt the moisture leave his mouth. He strained his eyes down the lane. *Is that movement? I think it's two men. Yes, it is. They are carrying rifles. This is it. O whale spirit, be with me now!*

The two communists were talking and smoking, as though they were sure they would not run into government forces. The moon broke through the clouds and he could clearly see they were the enemy. He wondered if this was what it was like for his grandfather as their canoe moved in on the whale. He took careful aim with his CAR 15 and squeezed the trigger. The tiny weapon recoiled slightly and the rest of the ambushing force opened fire an instant later. He saw one enemy soldier crumple to the ground and the other fall backward as if kicked in the chest by a horse. Within three seconds it was over; two dead VC, no friendly casualties.

Pope had just killed his first man, and he wasn't sure how he felt about it. *The man wasn't trying to kill me. But he would if the positions were reversed. Isn't that what war is all about? The killing is justified, and the ambush is successful. I came here to put my training to use. Now I am a warrior!*

Waters jumped to his feet, ran to the men, and checked to see if they were dead. He turned and signaled thumbs down that they had not survived the fusillade.

"All right, corporal, move your men two hundred yards down the trail. We'll set up another ambush there."

No more VC entered the kill zone that night. Just as the sun provided the slightest light, Pope sent one man back to the first ambush site to check the bodies again. Within minutes he returned and said that nothing was any different. The team returned to the area, cut two long poles, tied the bodies on them like dead deer and took turns carrying them back to the airstrip.

Training was halted for the day for a celebration. Pope took the old French Mas 36 rifles taken from the bodies to Captain Dang and briefed him on the results of the operation. At noon the entire RF battalion arrived at the airstrip and walked by and viewed the corpses that had been laid out on the tarmac. Three nights later another team ambushed and killed a VC paymaster and guard and split 3,000 Piastres that was confiscated.

*   *   *

At the start of the fourth week of instruction Pope sat in the training area considering different ways to get information from the enemy. He wanted to plan a method to either capture or silently wound a VC so that he could be interrogated. He approached Ma with the idea.

Ma smiled and said, "All Montagnard soldiers are just as good shooting the cross bow as they are the US rifle, sir. The bow is silent and more likely to wound the VC."

He went to his tent and brought out a crudely constructed cross bow and a quiver of arrows. He took an arrow and rubbed the tip with his stubby finger.

"The tip is hardened with fire. It is strong enough to bring down a wild boar."

"How does it work?"

Ma, with his bare foot, stood on the bow and pulled on the twine to cock it. Then he placed an arrow in the seat that went perpendicular with the bow. He aimed at a tree twenty yards away and fired, and the arrow zinged straight into the target. Ma turned and smiled broadly.

"It is a number one weapon, sir."

"That's very impressive, Ma. Let's try it."

Each of the next three nights, a six-man ambush team was dispatched. The extra man in each team was armed with the crossbow. Their instructions were to shoot the bow to wound the VC. When the enemy soldier fell, the others were to subdue him. The advisors accompanied the teams the first two nights, but made no contact with communists.

On the third night Pope decided he and Waters would remain in camp. The following morning the team returned carrying two dead VC.

Ma explained, "The team established the ambush, and the VC came into the 'kill zone.' Then they shot and killed one of the VC. The bow man hit the other with one arrow, but was off his mark and killed the enemy."

The team leader was disappointed, but Pope explained they learned a method of silently killing VC. They still needed to figure a way to capture them.

Later, Pope had some of his scout's manufacture the cross bows, and the team sold them to visiting dignitaries and aircraft pilots at the advisory compound.

*   *   *

The next night Pope and Waters accompanied a team on an ambush along a well-traveled trail, six kilometers from province headquarters. Pope lay on the ground next to Waters, thinking how *the cross bows compared favorably with the spears and bow and arrows of his tribe.*

A screaming artillery shell passed over their heads and landed about one hundred yards to their left. Ca-rump! It exploded, shaking the ground.

Startled, two team members stood and backed away from the sound. *Artillery H & I firing*, Pope thought. A few seconds later a second round went screaming over their head and landed about fifty yards closer.

"It seems like the artillery is shooting at us," Waters shouted.

"Corporal, get your team and withdraw. Now." Pope shouted.

The ambushers moved quickly through the forest, when a third round landed almost directly on the site where they had been positioned minutes earlier. *Damn!* Pope thought. *Something's got to be done about this!*

*   *   *

"Captain Dang, we almost got hit by our own artillery last night," Pope said, clearly agitated.

"What time did it happen?"

"We had only been in position about thirty minutes when three shells landed. Who is responsible for location of artillery firing?"

"The artillery officer for the RF battalion plots them, with recommendations from the artillery officer at province headquarters. The chief of staff makes the final approval."

"I think we have a spy in our midst. We stayed away from areas in which H & I firing had taken place. None had been fired before in that area."

"It does seem like more than a coincidence."

"I would like to stop sending overlays of our ambushes to higher headquarters a week in advance. Is that possible?"

"I will check with Special Zone and get back to you, Captain Pope."

The following day Dang told him that the Chief of Staff said overlays were still required, but ambush plans would not be sent. Dang would personally check each evening to be sure H & I firing did not take place near ambush sites.

*   *   *

On the last night of training all four teams went out on separate ambushes. The following morning, two teams came back with a total of four dead VC and four captured rifles. Pope was happy with the results of the platoon's training. He declared the remainder of the day a holiday, with a feast and party that lasted half the night.

The next day, there was a graduation ceremony at sector headquarters, and the platoon stood in formation in their tailor-made ranger uniforms while many local civilians and soldiers from the RF battalion attended. Major Nhia decorated 16 of the platoon members, Pope, and Waters.

While everyone was in a good mood, Pope made good on a request by Ma that the R & I platoon be permanently encamped at the airstrip. He convinced Captain Thanh the platoon could provide security for the important field. Pope saw a none-too-happy expression on Major Sullivan's face.

Pope thought: *Great, no matter what I do there is no pleasing my boss. We've still put together a hell of a group of fighting men. I'm convinced of two things. First, the South Vietnamese soldiers can close with the enemy and kill him. And second, there is a lot more communist wandering around loose than Sullivan wants to think. Now I wonder if the whale spirit can not only save my ass, but my career.*

Chapter Ten

"We've figured out how to ambush and kill VC, but not how to capture them. If we can get prisoners, maybe we can get into the VC infrastructure," Pope said, interrupting Sullivan, as he worked at his desk.

Sullivan looked up, frowned, and tossed some papers forward on his desk.

"The Vietnamese have not really had any success capturing VC agents. Why do you think you can show up and immediately solve the mystery?"

"I've checked the sector intelligence gathering apparatus. I find they have an inadequate one at best. They seem to pay lip service to it, sir."

Sullivan leaned forward in his chair and glared at Pope.

"You've killed a few VC, and now you have all the answers. OK, what do you want?"

"I've got a couple ideas I'd like to run by you."

Sullivan sighed, leaned back in his chair, and folded his arms across his chest. "All right. Let's hear them."

"Captain Dang told me he has a double agent working with a group of VC from our village of Lai Gi. They meet every other week, and our man provides them with food as they discuss their information and plans. We get some sleeping powder and put it into the food that the agent gives them. The VC eat the food, take a nap, and we move in, tie them up, and bring them home."

"Sounds simple. Have you considered that a double agent can betray you as fast as he can betray the VC?"

"Of course I have, sir. We'll use proper counter-ambush procedures."

"OK. Maybe Dang can get the sleeping powder from the local hospital."

"We talked about that, sir. They may ask too many questions. We don't want to endanger our agent and plan. The fewer people that know about our plot, the better chance for success."

"So where do you expect to get the sleeping powder?"

"I'd like your permission to get an aircraft to take me to Saigon. I'll get a prescription from a US doctor. If that doesn't work, I'll go to J-2, MACV and get a written order for a prescription."

"All right, permission granted. You said you had another scheme."

"Not really a 'scheme,' but a proposal. I'm told we haven't had any 'cordon and search' operations in the province. I think we should start them."

"Now what the hell is a 'cordon and search' operation?"

"A unit of the RF battalion goes out after midnight, and cordons off a village. The police and intelligence people wake up the villagers, search for contraband, and check to be sure everyone has ID cards. Those that don't have proper identification are arrested and interrogated. If any VC hiding in the village try to escape, the RF force shoots them."

"I don't know about that. You'll be stirring up the pot. Major Nhia may not want his RF companies away from province headquarters."

Pope shifted his weight from one foot to the other, crossing his arms.

"Sir, we should be checking for these little peckerwoods that go out and collect taxes, and disappear. I've discussed this with Captain Dang and he agrees. Maybe you could tell Major Nhia that if the province is as pacified as he thinks, headquarters will not be endangered with the RF battalion units away."

"All right. I'll try to sell Nhia on your plans. In the future, I would appreciate it if you discussed these proposals with me **before** talking with Dang. You stir up a hornet's nest, and I'll have your ass, Captain. Now lay on your aircraft, and I'll see Nhia.

*   *   *

Sullivan received approval from Major Nhia for both of Pope's proposals. The following morning a UHIB chopper landed at the helipad and picked up Pope. An hour later, it landed on the roof of the US military hospital in Saigon. Pope walked down the stairs and entered a long corridor. The smell of antiseptic, medicines, and illness filled the air.

He found the registration desk and got directions to the chief medical officer's office. He walked around the corner of the clean, white corridor and saw a door with a glazed window. "Captain Horatio Wellington, Chief Medical Officer," was painted in black letters on the door. A pretty, petite Vietnamese woman sat at the desk in the office. She glanced up and smiled at him.

"Good morning. I'm Captain Pope. I don't have an appointment. I would like to talk with Captain Wellington."

"Let me see if he is available, sir. Please have a seat."

As she opened the door to an inner office, he considered the soft chair in the corner near a magazine rack and chose a straight chair near her desk. *I don't expect to be here long*, he thought. The cute receptionist returned almost as soon as he sat.

"Captain Wellington had a cancellation. He will see you now, sir."

Pope entered a large office. It had certificates and diplomas hanging on two walls and paintings of New England scenes on the others. A large tank filled with tropical fish was near a window. Bright white, matching overstuffed living room chairs and a sofa neatly surrounded a black teak coffee table. On the far wall was a large desk. The surface had an ornate wooden desk plate with "Captain Wellington, USN," carved on it—and nothing else.

Behind it sat a gray-haired, distinguished looking man. The most prominent part of his face was a long nose that seemed to point to the ceiling whenever he spoke. Pope felt a twinge of anxiety through his combat uniform that contrasted with the furnishings of the office and the white uniform of the seated officer.

"Is there something I can do for you, Captain…Pope is it?" He said leaning forward, squinting to read the nametag on Pope's shirt.

From his tone of voice, Pope felt that Wellington was letting him know that there was a great chasm between Navy and Army captains. He thought he should remain standing at a formal parade rest.

"Sir, I'm the sector intelligence advisor for Binh Tuy province. I have a rather unusual request of you."

"Get on with it, Pope," Wellington sniffed.

"I have an intelligence agent that has weekly meetings with communist soldiers. He provides them with a meal. I would like to place sleeping powder in the food. We capture the VC as they sleep, so that I can interrogate them."

"Yes, but what does that have to do with me?"

"I respectfully request that you write a prescription for a sleeping powder that will temporarily disable the guerrillas, sir."

"In case you didn't realize it, Pope, the medical corps is in the business of saving lives."

"I realize that, sir, but this would be a humane way of bringing the VC soldiers career to an end. If we don't bring them in sleeping, we'll have to shoot them."

Wellington snorted an angry sound, intentionally loud.

"We prescribe medicines for sick and wounded people. That is our responsibility. Do you realize that dispensing medicine like this is against regulations? It might even be against the Geneva Convention."

For Christ's sake, Pope thought. *I didn't come here for a damn lecture. I'm not going to get anywhere with this prick. Now how do I get away from here gracefully?*

"Sir, this war in Vietnam is fought unconventionally. We know how to kill VC. Now I'm trying to take them out of the war without killing them. I would think that would be what you would want, sir."

"What I want is to follow written regulations. Permission refused. Will there be anything else?"

"No, sir. Thank you for taking the time for me."

Pope snapped to attention, Wellington nodded, and Pope marched out the door. Thoroughly depressed, he thought *Wellington probably wonders why he's been passed over to admiral twice.* He decided to go to J-2, MACV for help.

*   *   *

On the way to the roof, he asked a corpsman for directions to the latrine.

"The latrine on this floor is closed for repair, sir, but I guess it would be OK for you to use the one in the doctor's lounge. It's down the hall, third door on the right."

"Thanks. I appreciate it."

He entered the room where two doctors sat on a couch arguing about which baseball team was better, the New York Yankees or the Boston Red Sox. Pope nodded to them and went into the latrine. As he exited the bathroom, he decided to make one last attempt to get the sleeping powder prescription.

"How you doing guys? I'm Johnny Pope, a Sector Intelligence Advisor in Binh Tuy Province. I'm not a baseball fan, but I've got a proposal for you," he said, giving his most engaging smile.

"If it's not about baseball, why do you think we'd be interested?" The shorter of the two medical men queried.

"I'm guessing you guys don't get out of Saigon much. How would you like some VC souvenirs? The kind of stuff that we capture from Communist soldiers in battle."

"You've got **my** attention!" the taller of the two answered excitedly. "But what's the catch?"

"Very simple. It's pretty easy to ambush and kill communist soldiers. I want to capture VC so we can interrogate them and try to get intelligence information so we can get into their infrastructure. If you gentlemen give me a sleeping powder prescription that can be mixed undetected in food, we'll give it to the VC. After they fall asleep, we tie them up and take them off to the poky. Plenty of gain—no pain."

"What's an infrastructure?" Asked the tall one.

"An infrastructure is the organization or apparatus of the communist force or unit."

"Man, I'd love to have a set of those black pajamas," the shorter one exclaimed.

"How about a weapon? Can you get me a weapon?" the taller one asked.

Pope laughed to himself as he thought that *most weapons captured were of US origin. Black pajamas are bought on the street because most civilian peasants wear them.*

"Hey, whatever you guys want. I have to tell you, though; I tried going through channels by talking with your boss, Captain Wellington. He not only turned me down but gave me a mini-lecture on the laws of land warfare and where the medical corps fit into it."

Both medicos looked at each other and laughed.

"We don't worry about that overblown asshole," the short one said.

"OK, Just thought you should know. Now what about the prescription?"

The two went into a discussion about sleeping medicines, a language unknown to him. They exited the huddle, and the shorter of the two scribbled out a prescription and handed it to him.

"By the way, I'm Phil Donner and this is Tom Villone." He hesitated and added, "Incidentally, this is probably not the first time you've heard this, but you look like a Vietnamese—would you be offended if I asked to see your ID card?"

Pope laughed, reached into his back pocket, opened his wallet, removed his identification, and handed it to Donner.

"No, it isn't the first time. It happens all the time. I'm Indian—from the state of Washington."

"Hey, I thought I knew you! Aren't you the same Johnny Pope that won the Rose Bowl game against Illinois?" Donner asked.

"Guilty, but I had a bunch of help."

"Well, I'll be damned! The stakes just went up. If I get a football, will you autograph it for me on your return trip?"

"Be glad to. By the way, can you double this prescription? We want to run a test before using it."

"That's easy," Donner said, taking the prescription, scribbling on the paper and returning it to Pope.

"Thanks again, guys, and you can count on seeing me the next time I'm in Saigon."

Pope hurried to the pharmacy, got the prescription filled, ran up to the waiting chopper, and headed back to Binh Tuy. Since the aircraft traveled slower and lower, he got a better look at the countryside. When they crossed the border of Binh Tuy, he noticed several smoking fires in "no man's land." Since he knew that there were no government operations, they could only be either VC or civilians that didn't belong there.

When they arrived in Binh Tuy, he went to the kitchen and had the cook prepare a Vietnamese soup. He emptied six capsules of the sleeping powder into the meal. After it had cooled, Pope took it to where two dogs slept in the sun. The dogs, Co Van Me (Vietnamese, for "American advisor"), and Charlie, were long time mascots of the advisory team. Both eagerly lapped up the concoction with tails wagging. Within five minutes, they fell away from the large pot, and were sound asleep again. He tried unsuccessfully for forty minutes to awaken them, then pronounced the experiment a success.

*   *   *

Pope and Dang planned the operation with the sleeping powder for the following week, during a regularly scheduled visit between some VC soldiers and the double agent. The deputy province chief's cook prepared a meal for the four VC and the double agent. Dang doctored the food with the sleeping powder and gave it to the agent handler, who gave it to the double agent. The spy was not told about the sleeping powder, for fear that he might act differently. They didn't tell him about the second part of the plan, either.

Pope and Waters, without telling anyone else, took two teams from the R & I platoon for the ambush. The night before the double agent was to meet the four VC; they led the team to an ambush position at the meeting site. The other team remained about a kilometer away and in radio communication. They were to be either a quick reaction force to help the team if they got in trouble, or if the plan developed properly, they would help carry the sleeping prisoners.

They were in position by 0200 hours. Pope told Waters to get some sleep. They had gotten wet with sweat, moving to the ambush site in the dark. He was awake in the prone position, and the cold, damp night was almost unbearable. He wondered if he had thought of everything. *Will the medicine work as good with humans as it did with dogs? If it's a trap, can the reaction force get here in time? I better keep my eyes and ears peeled to our rear in case the enemy tries to come up on us in the dark.*

The morning sun made it's way into the clearing, turning the jungle hot and humid. The smell of rotting vegetation permeated the area. The wide, green plants surrounding them seemed to suck out the clean air. Pope found himself laboring to breathe even though he wasn't exerting himself. The ants found the humans within five minutes after they lay on the jungle floor. It seemed as though half of them drank the sweat, making the skin itch: and the other half bit the flesh, causing pain. He wondered what kind of insects or weather hindered Grandfather's whale hunters as they stalked their prey.

Shortly after noon and just before Waters was about to scream with discomfort, the double agent appeared in the clearing. He removed some pots from his pack, set them on the ground and sat next to them on a log. Within minutes, four-armed VC entered the clearing. They wore black pajamas, conical straw hats, and carried Mas 36 rifles. The enemy soldiers shook hands with the agent, and the five squatted, talked, and ate the prepared meal.

After a few minutes the men fell asleep, one by one. Within forty-five minutes, all were snoozing. Pope and Waters stood up, weapons drawn, and crept into the clearing. They picked up the slumbering communists' weapons and tried to wake them. Pope signaled the rest of the team to take up a perimeter defensive position, then had the leader radio the other team to move to the meet location. By then Waters had all of the POW's hands tied behind their backs.

Within a half-hour, the other team arrived and the two groups picked up the four sleeping prisoners and carried them about five hundred yards from the site. They left the napping double agent there, not knowing he had betrayed his comrades. Pope figured that by not compromising the plan, the spy could still be useful as an intelligence informant. They waited for a half-hour for the sleeping powder to wear off. When the prisoners were awake enough to move on their own, they marched them back to the compound.

They were questioned by Dang. After the interrogation the deputy province chief told Pope one of the prisoners was a district leader and another a paymaster. The POW's gave the names of over fifty VC that lived within Lai Gi. The next night, the entire RF battalion was awakened from their sleep, received orders, and executed a complete encirclement of Lai Gi. The R & I platoon and the police went into the homes of the sleeping VC, arrested them, and took them off to jail. It was the biggest round-up of VC using intelligence agents in the history of the war to date.

*   *   *

A correspondent from one of the wire services picked up the report through Vietnamese channels, and he called Dang for an interview. Dang chose to tell more about Pope and the R & I platoon. The story highlighted Pope as an Indian with his own "tribe" of Yards. The reporter emphasized that Pope looked like a Vietnamese and used his Indian heritage to lead Montagnard tribesmen in jungle warfare. The Montagnards were similar to the Indian tribes in the United States, and were treated like second class citizens. The story was picked up and published in *The Stars and Stripes.*

*   *   *

A week later, Pope, Dang, and Sullivan met for dinner with Major Nhia. The province chief wanted to use the meeting to personally thank Pope for the successful operation.

"Captain Dang had the double agent, and he planned the operation, sir. All I had was the idea for the sleeping powder. Dang deserves the credit."

"There's plenty of credit to go around, Captain Pope. You and Captain Dang make a good team," Nhia concluded.

"We have been very fortunate in not having many incidents in the sector the past several months. But I'm not really sure that we have been very effective in keeping the VC from controlling the people," Pope said.

"What do you mean, Captain? The VC is not attacking our villages. We control the roads," Nhia said, defensively.

"Major Nhia is right, Captain. I think you're making too much of an isolated incident," Sullivan exclaimed.

"Excuse me, sir, but not just one incident. With the killing of all the VC soldiers and capturing of two paymasters, and over 50 Viet Cong living in our province town of Lai Gi—don't you think our pacification program needs some help?" Pope queried.

"What do you mean by help?" asked Dang.

"What we have discovered is that the VC are in fact all around us. They are working within our ranks. They don't have to attack the villages. They can spread their propaganda, threaten villagers, and win the hearts and minds of the people."

"Tell the Major what you suspect about Viet Cong spies, Captain Pope," Dang added.

"Sir, the only time we conduct successful operations against the enemy, the only ones that know about it in advance are Captain Dang and I. When we plan an operation with units of the RF battalion, there is no contact with the enemy. It's almost as though they know where we are going and avoid us."

"Maybe they don't want to engage a unit of company strength," Nhia countered.

"That may be true, but we may also have spies among us, sir."

Sullivan scowled and said, "I really think you're making too much of it, Captain Pope."

"Maybe so. In any case, sir, we need to get out to the villages more often."

"What are you proposing, Captain?" Nhia asked.

"Cordon and search operations, using parts of the entire RF Battalion every single night for the next two weeks. Not just in this district, but Hoi Duc and Tanh Linh as well. We would also establish a US MedCap team to go into the villages throughout the sector and provide medical services to people while simultaneously recruiting intelligence agents." Pope looked at Captain Dang and added, "I would like to accompany the MedCap team to establish my own agent network. That way I am assured that government spies will not have access to them."

"You have given me a great deal to think about. You'll have my answer tomorrow. Now, will you gentlemen join me in a fine meal?" Nhia said, as he gestured toward the dining room.

*   *   *

The next day Sullivan returned from a visit to province headquarters with the news Pope wanted. It was a go for both plans.

"I want you to know I don't appreciate the way you handled the proposals with Nhia last night. I still think you're witch-hunting. Don't think you can wave a newspaper article at me and get whatever you want."

"Sir, I apologize if I offended you. There was certainly no intent. I assumed that in a meeting such as that, I could express my opinion. Now that I know better, it won't happen again."

"Well, I'm keeping an eye on you, and you better not screw up what I've spent seven months developing here," Sullivan warned. "You will coordinate the entire operation with our advisory team and Captain Dang. I'm holding you responsible."

"I really believe that we're moving in the right direction, sir, but we have to keep our operations under wraps."

Pope went to his room to draw up plans. As he worked, he thought: *Christ, not only do I have to fight the VC, but a senior advisor with his head in the sand. We have really opened Pandora's box. Have we bitten off more than we can chew?* Then he thought again what his grandfather said. *"The whale spirit protects us. No one will die." We're taking the fight to the enemy. We're making it difficult for him to sleep. This is a start in not only taking back the province, but also taking back the night from the enemy. But how will the Communist react? Can we force him into consolidating his forces and come out of the woods to fight us on our terms? It's not a gamble. It's something we must do!*

Chapter Eleven

Captain Dang's office was a beehive of activity. Vietnamese officers and US advisors worked for three days on the new plan, "Operation Win." It was an all-encompassing offensive operation to rid the sector of communist guerrillas and "win the hearts and minds of the people" by providing them protection.

Pope spent the morning at the airstrip and had just waved good-bye to the last Caribou transporting the two RF companies to Tanh Linh and Hoi Duc Districts. A lone single-engine civilian aircraft circled above.

Pope's jeep radio crackled, "Binh Tuy, this is State-24 alpha, over."

"State, this is Binh Tuy, over," Pope answered.

"This is State-24 alpha. I have an American female USAID representative aboard. Request landing instructions, over."

"Roger, State, what is the mission of the rep, over?"

"Have no idea, Binh Tuy. She will remain at your location several days, over."

"This is Binh Tuy, I am located at the strip and have you in sight. Land from the west, out."

The tiny plane made its approach, landed, and taxied to the covered concrete platform where Pope stood waiting. When it came to a stop, Pope walked to the aircraft and opened the small door. Before he could say anything, a smiling female stepped out with an outstretched hand.

"Hello, I'm Kathryn Williams, USAID representative. I'm here to check on our programs in the province."

The most beautiful woman he had ever seen stood in front of him. She was about 5' 4" tall, with long red hair drawn back and held with a simple gold clip. She had ocean blue eyes that seemed to look right through him. Her face was porcelain-like, but slightly tanned. It was radiant and beamed with friendliness. She was dressed in tan slacks, and a yellow blouse that appeared tailor-made for her hour glass body. He smelled a scent of Chanel No. 5.

"I'm Captain John Pope, sector intelligence advisor," he said, taking her soft hand and shaking it gently.

"I'm only human, Captain Pope. I won't break," she said squeezing his hand firmly, and smiling.

She seems to read my mind, he thought. *I hope I can keep my cool with her.*

"Let's get your bags and we'll take you to team headquarters," Pope said, blood rushing to his head. He thought, *she's so beautiful and confident, I don't stand a chance with her. As fine as she is, she has her pick of any field grade officer or high ranking civilian in a country where there are practically no American women—so relax, John—she is not only out of your league, but out of your universe!*

"If I insist that you call me Kathryn, can I call you Johnny?"

"Yes you can Miss Wil...I mean Kathryn." *Oh you're really doing great, John-boy. How long has it been since you left the reservation?*

The pilot came around from the other side of the aircraft and introduced himself. "Hi, I'm Jack Dauber. Is there any place I can get something to eat before I head back to Saigon?"

"You're just in time for lunch. Hop in the back of the vehicle," he said handing Kathryn's lone bag to him. Pope thought, *this guy is so good-looking, gets all kinds of flight pay, and fly's her all over the country—they are probably a couple.*

As they rode down the dirt road in the jeep, Kathryn explained, "I've been sent to see how the Bulgar wheat and pigs have been distributed by the Vietnamese government. We also received a rather large request for blankets from a Lieutenant Granger. Do you know him?"

"Yes. Now I'm starting to see why you're out here in the boonies. Larry is our resident ladies' man. He must have heard about you and asked for the blankets, expecting you in the bargain. He's a pretty resourceful guy," Pope said, laughing.

"No. Actually I got this trip from a CO-worker who went home on an emergency leave."

"You'll like Larry. Everyone does." *Now why in the hell did I say that?* Pope thought.

"Where are you from, Johnny?"

"A small Indian reservation in the state of Washington. You've probably never heard of it."

"I'm a small town girl myself. A little place just outside Hillsdale, Michigan."

"Sorry, I never heard of it. Where did you go to school, University of Michigan?

Kathryn couldn't help thinking; *this guy is drop dead handsome. I hope my excitement isn't showing too much.*

"University of Illinois. How about you?"

"State U in Washington."

"I **thought** I recognized you! You're the Indian quarterback that played football against us. It was the Rose Bowl. I was a cheerleader—and **you** ruined my vacation!" she said, voice raising as she playfully poked Pope in the ribs with her elbow. The jeep veered to the left, and pope righted it and laughed.

Archie Bannister monitored the radio transmission between the pilot and Pope. When the jeep pulled into the compound the entire team stood by the volleyball court waiting to meet the **female** USAID representative. As Kathryn dismounted the jeep, Larry Granger stepped forward. He stuck out his hand and smiled.

"Hi, I'm Larry Granger, Civil Affairs advisor, and head of the welcoming committee. Welcome to Binh Tuy."

"Thank you. I've heard all about you, Lieutenant," Kathryn said, smiling. While shaking his hand, she looked over her shoulder at Pope.

The rest of the welcoming committee laughed and introduced themselves, and they all went into the dining room.

Pope took Kathryn to the guestroom located next to his room and set her bag on the footlocker.

"This is your room. It isn't much, but we call it home. We're not used to having women guests, as you can probably already tell. We have only one latrine, but we'll work something out. I'll get you some towels."

"Thanks Johnny. Can I get cleaned up before lunch?" *Christ, is this guy for real. Doesn't he have a clue that lieutenant doesn't hold a candle to him?* She thought.

"Sure. I'll get the latrine cleared for you and stand outside the door."

Pope got Kathryn a towel, returned, and escorted her to the latrine. After about five minutes, Kathryn exited, and they both went into the day room, where everyone was already seated at the table. Pope noted that his seat was empty as expected but Bannister was not seated in his assigned chair next to Granger. He was in one of the guest chairs and wore a Cheshire grin.

Pope led Kathryn to the table and pulled out his chair for her, and as she sat, the entire group erupted in laughter. He went around to the opposite side of the table, sat next to Granger, put his arm around him, and gave him a big hug. This caused more giggles around the table at the expense of the "Don Juan." Granger smiled and took the ribbing good-naturedly.

"Are there any Civil Affairs operational plans this week, Major?" Kathryn asked, after the laughter subsided.

"As it happens, you're in luck. Tomorrow we're sending a team out by helicopter on a day trip to Tanh Linh. You're welcome to go along. We'll be sending a MedCap, Civil Affairs and PsyOps team. The group keeps getting bigger, so it looks like we'll have to request an additional chopper. Captain James, will you take care of the request?"

"What time do you want the choppers, sir?" James asked.

"The other one was laid on for 0700 hours, so the same time would be fine. You may want to invite the pilots for breakfast. They always like our cooking. Let's say 0600 if they'll be here for breakfast."

"Roger that, sir, I'll take care of it right after lunch."

"Do you send these teams out very often, Major?" asked Kathryn.

"Not really. This is a project initiated by Captain Pope. He thinks it will be a way to win the hearts and minds of the people while providing more security for the general population. Now, enough talk about business—how long have you been in country Kathryn?"

"I've been here less than two months—but Captain Pope and I are old friends." She smiled, turned to Pope and said, "Aren't we, Johnny?"

This evoked catcalls and laughing at Pope's expense.

Blushing noticeably, he answered, "We just met today, but I played football against her school when we were in college."

"That may be true, but we can still brag that we went to different schools together," she said, evoking more guffaws from the men.

"Well, if it was the Rose Bowl, I was at the same game. So that means all three of us went to different schools together—although mine was a junior high school," Martin added.

"God, doesn't that make me feel old though," Kathryn exclaimed to even more laughter.

*   *   *

After lunch, Pope and Kathryn took the pilot back to the airstrip and loaded the jeep trailer with Granger's blankets. After watching the plane take off, Pope took Kathryn on a tour of the R & I platoon encampment, Lai Gi, sector headquarters, and the RF Battalion headquarters. Pope noticed how "together" Kathryn was around everyone. But his confidence grew at every stop. By late afternoon, they returned to the advisory team headquarters, where there was a great deal of activity, preparing for the following day's operation.

After dinner, Pope excused himself to Kathryn.

"I think I'll skip the movie tonight. I have the 2400-0200 watch, and I have a busy day tomorrow."

"What are you watching in the middle of the night?"

"We all pull shifts of guard duty. We have Vietnamese guards, but the Major thinks we should have an American awake while the others sleep."

* * *

Pope was seated on a kitchen chair, his CAR 15 slung over his shoulder. His feet were on another chair, on the sidewalk between the sleeping quarters and the dining room. There, he could observe both buildings, the fence near the minefield, and the gate to the compound. The sky was filled with stars, and the full moon reflected off the goose pond. The geese were curled up next to each other near the pool. One of the dogs, Co Van Me, lay sleeping next to Pope.

He had only been on duty for about 15 minutes when Kathryn exited her room. Clad only in a white cotton nightshirt that reached half way up her thighs, she approached him. The second thing he noticed was that she had well-constructed athletic thighs and calves.

"I don't see how anyone can sleep with all the artillery firing," Kathryn said.

"I forgot to tell you about the H & I before I went to bed. I hope it didn't scare you too much."

"Luckily, Larry Granger warned me ahead of time. Although I about fell out of my chair after the first shot during the movie."

"They didn't warn me, and I did the snake thing under the desk the first night. It gave everyone a chuckle. You get used to it after a few weeks."

"Do you mind if I keep you company, Johnny?"

"No, I don't mind. Here, have a seat," he said taking his feet from the other chair and pushing it in Kathryn's direction. Co Van Me stood, stretched, shook herself, and disappeared around the corner of the kitchen. It was as if the dog knew that someone else was there to keep Pope company.

Kathryn situated the chair so that she sat facing him and said, "So this is what you meant by watch."

She is confident and self-assured in every breath, he thought.

"This isn't very formal, so we don't follow all the rules of guard mount. I agree with the Major. We should keep one American awake during the hours of darkness in case of a VC attack."

"Then why do you have the two walking Vietnamese sentries?" she motioned with her head in the direction of two Vietnamese soldiers standing by the front gate.

"Their job is to guard us. My job for my two-hour shift is to be sure that they are awake and alert. This is a very strange place.

"It's the strangest place **I've** ever been"

"As a matter of fact this is the only place that I've ever seen where people wear shorts and T-shirts during the day and wear complete uniform, with jungle boots at night."

"I guess I'm not really dressed for night duty, am I?" She asked, stroking her hair back from her face with her hand.

"No, but not for day duty either." He chortled, noticing that she didn't have anything on under her nightshirt. *She's even more beautiful by moonlight, and she's flirting with me,* he thought.

"I've been talking with Larry Granger. He reminded me of an article I read in *The Stars and Stripes* about you. Do you mind if I ask you some personal questions, Johnny?"

"I don't mind as long as you don't mind if I don't answer all of them."

"That's fair," she said, smiling. "Is it true that you're full blooded Indian and the grandson of a chief?"

"Yes, it's true, but you have to understand that in most tribes there are a lot of chiefs."

"And you grew up on an Indian reservation and hunted whales?"

"I grew up on a reservation, but our tribe hasn't hunted whale since the 1920s. We had to stop when the government put them on the endangered species list. It's too bad, because the whale is a big part of our tribal culture. It's about what we are. Young people growing up shouldn't lose their culture."

"You mean that your tribe killed too many whales?"

"No, we only killed what we needed for subsistence. The commercial whalers all over the world killed them. Indians are the original conservationists, you know. We only kill what we can use, and the animals and earth are all a part of our circle of life."

"Why did you decide to join the army?"

"I didn't join the army. The army is my career. As a descendent of whale hunters, I was meant to be a warrior. We have a strong spirit to be warriors. It's really hard to describe. It's our culture. I don't expect you to understand."

"You meant to say **you people**, and I do understand, because I don't think I'm part of **those** people."

"Anyway, what are your plans when you leave Vietnam, Kathryn?" Pope asked, trying to change the subject.

"I don't really have any specific plans. I wanted to get into the Peace Corps, but the timing wasn't right. I majored in economics, and I heard about USAID, and I thought there might be a career in the State Department."

"You're not one of those bleeding heart liberals, are you, Kathryn? Those people have been keeping the Indians down for decades with their good intentions."

"Are you kidding? My family has been Republicans for generations. Although I have to confess that I vote pretty independently. That is, I vote for the man I think will do the best job. Not just for any Republican. Why, would you ignore me if I was a liberal, Johnny?"

Kathryn moved her chair closer to him. She was so close he could feel the warmth of her body. She tipped her head to the side and looked into his eyes longingly. He set his rifle on the sidewalk, took her face in his hands, and kissed her on the mouth, as they both stood. She moved her body against his and put her arms around him. In that instant, he confirmed that she had nothing on under the cotton nightshirt.

After a long kiss, he pulled away and said, "It's pretty hard to ignore someone as beautiful and sensitive as you."

"I've been waiting all day for you to kiss me, Johnny," she said, rubbing his cheek with the tips of her fingers. "I'm not really this forward. I just feel so different when I'm with you."

"I feel the same way. But you're so beautiful, I never thought I had a chance with you."

"Don't ever sell yourself short, Johnny, you have a lot going for you." *Yeah, and especially that animal magnetism,* she thought, as she kissed him again.

After about ten seconds, he took a step backwards and knocked the chair over. The geese awakened, flapped their wings, and honked loudly.

"Don't get me wrong, it's not that I don't like kissing you. It's just that I don't think I can concentrate on my duties at the same time."

Kathryn giggled and said, "OK, I can't think of anything else either when you kiss me. But you have to promise me a date when you're in Saigon."

"It's a date. As a matter of fact I have to make a trip to Saigon in the next couple weeks to take some war trophies to a couple doctors at the hospital. Can you do me a favor now and either go back to bed or put a jacket on? I'm afraid one of the team members will get up to use the latrine and get the wrong idea."

She laughed and replied, "that's probably a good idea. Besides, the artillery has stopped. Maybe I can get some sleep."

She made an exaggerated yawn, raising her nightshirt all the way up to heaven, kissed Pope on the mouth again, and promenaded to her room.

I've got to keep my mind on business. I have to remember what I learned at Fort Bragg. That is, to keep a "combat area psychology." No matter where I am

I have to keep my guard up. Now I better spend the next hour thinking about our plans for the next two weeks.

Chapter Twelve

The MedCap team consisting of Pope, White, Granger, Bishop, Kathryn, Duc, and three Vietnamese army officers boarded choppers for the twenty-minute flight to Tanh Linh. When they landed, the village chief met them and showed the house that would be used as an examining room. There was already a line of over fifty women, children and old men patiently waiting.

White, Duc, and Pope went into the house. It was made of wooden poles with a straw roof and sides. It had one large room, with a small table near a fire, some wooden shelves, a wooden bed with no mattress, and two wooden chairs. Someone had dug a round hole large enough for three or four Vietnamese. To the rear were two straw mats on the dirt floor.

"The hole is where the civilians go in case of a battle in the village, sir," White explained.

While White examined and treated the illnesses or injuries, Pope and Duc recruited the patients to be spies. The process was very simple. After White examined and treated the patients, Pope talked with them—Duc translated.

"If you know anything about the communists, let us know, and we'll pay for the information. Give us the information through the village chief, and if you don't trust him, come to the advisory compound near province headquarters or show up at the next MedCap visit."

Duc was surprised by how much information about VC's that the sick villagers provided. He was even more surprised by the amount of information the children gave Pope.

"Captain, why do you try to enlist children in your ring of spies?"

"It's simple Duc, children are the best sources of information: Number one, the enemy doesn't pay attention to children, so kids can go everywhere without suspicion. Number two, children are truthful. They won't lie to us."

*   *   *

After examining thirty people, it was lunchtime and the team had agreed to meet at the market place to eat C rations together. As Pope, Duc, and White approached the market place, they could see that Kathryn, Granger, and Bishop were already there waiting.

"So, have we won any hearts or minds this morning?" Pope joked.

"We've played a lot of music, handed out a bunch of your reward posters, and talked to a lot of people. How effective it will be remains to be seen," Bishop said.

"We handed out about half the blankets we came with and discussed some public works projects with the village chief. The people seem pretty happy," added Granger.

"I found about what I expected. The Bulgar wheat is not being eaten. It's being used for sandbags for fortifications. Somehow we have to come up with a meal made from wheat that they'll like," Kathryn reported.

"What genius thought people that have lived on rice for generations would take to wheat just because we give it to them?" Pope asked rhetorically. "It's like the US government did to the plains Indians in the1800's. They took nomadic tribesmen, put them on a reservation in the middle of the desert, and tried to make farmers out of them. We don't seem to learn from history," he added.

"I know. We're finding the same thing all over the country. They just don't like wheat. They seem to be doing OK with the pigs, though. In some of the provinces, the villagers were given a pair of pigs with no explanation that they were to be used for breeding. Some of the owners ate one pig and saved the other for later," Kathryn said, evoking laughter from the advisors.

"I see quite a few pigs running the streets here," Pope replied.

"I've found only a couple cases where the family ate one of them. I think they have the idea about breeding them," Kathryn added.

"There are plenty of sick people to administer to," White said.

"I'm happy with the intelligence contacts I've made," Pope said.

*   *   *

The team spent the remainder of the day at Tanh Linh and returned to sector headquarters in time for dinner. Pope remained on the chopper as Waters and five R & I platoon members boarded for the trip to Hoi Duc. When they got to the district headquarters, Dang was waiting.

"The RF Company and national policemen are ready to move. Departure time is scheduled for 2000 hours as you requested, Captain Pope."

"That's great. Thank you, Captain Dang."

"Are you sure we can be in position by 2400 hours by moving during darkness?"

"Yes, the Yard scouts that I brought along know this area very well. The village is only four kilometers from here, and we should be able to make the move through the jungle and be in position in plenty of time."

"I am concerned because our soldiers are not used to moving at night."

"I know. Charlie has owned the night too long. It's time we took it from him."

At exactly 2000 hours the reinforced company departed district headquarters in a modified column formation with the five Yard scouts in the lead. There was a full moon, and they broke trail as they went along. By 2300 hours the entire company had encircled the village.

The policemen, scouts, Pope, Dang, and Waters walked up to the barricaded entrance to the village. The popular force guards at the gate halted them, and after Dang identified himself, let the group enter. They went in and woke the village chief. With a portable loudspeaker, Dang ordered the villagers to report to the market place with their identification cards. He also warned them that if anyone tried to leave the village soldiers that had encircled the village would shoot them.

Within minutes about a hundred women, children and old men stood sleepy-eyed on the street. As he stood in the darkness, Pope thought it unusual that the villagers did not seem upset about being rousted from their homes in the middle of the night. They must feel like the whale does as the canoe of hunters wake him from dozing in the sun.

After the chief told Dang that all the villagers were present in the market place, the scouts, with flashlights, searched the houses for anyone hiding. The policemen lined the villagers up and checked their ID cards.

The police arrested four men and two women that didn't have ID cards. The rest of the villagers were allowed to return to their homes. Pope was clearly disappointed in the results. He expected to find more communists. The six people arrested were long-time residents of the village and claimed to have lost their ID cards.

The six prisoners were taken to the chief's house for further interrogation. While Pope watched the ID check at the market place, a slight built man who appeared to be in his late forties approached him.

"Are you the American advisor that gives reward money?" The man whispered in Vietnamese.

"Yes, I am. Do you think it's safe for you to talk to me in front of everyone here?" Pope replied in Vietnamese.

"Yes, as long as you question about ten other people when we finish."

"OK, what information do you have for me?"

"I work in the forest. I go to cut wood every day. I have been meeting every week with a tall man who is very intelligent and well dressed. Four armed guards always escort him. He says he is communist. I think he is a very important man. Today I saw a picture of him on a poster that was given to me by the village chief. Is it true that you will give 30,000 Piastres for information leading to the death or capture of this man?"

"Are you saying that you have been meeting every week with Colonel Khanh, the VC province chief?"

"I have been meeting with the man in the poster with a reward of 30,000 Piastres. Yes. He has asked me for information about the village and district headquarters. I have told him that I am just a poor woodsman and know nothing about the defenses."

"When will you see him again?"

"In three days we have a planned meeting."

"If I gave you information, do you think you could gain his confidence by giving it to him?"

"Yes, but when will I be paid. I'm a poor man, and I have a large family."

"You have to prove to me that you can get me good information before you are paid anything. But I promise you that if we kill or capture Colonel Khanh you will be a rich man. I will meet you alone two hundred yards north of the village at 10:00 tomorrow morning."

"Will you give me money for other information I give you now?"

"It depends on the information. What can you tell me?"

"There were about thirty less villagers here tonight then there were yesterday."

"Why did they leave, and where did they go?"

"I don't know the answer to either of the questions. But they must be VC, or why would they leave?"

"I'll give you some money when I meet with you tomorrow."

The man departed, and Pope called ten more people and asked them questions about whether or not they had seen any VC in the village.

*   *   *

The following morning at 0800 hours, Pope and his five Yard scouts left the village and went into the jungle 200 yards north. The scouts were hidden in areas that could cover him if the freshly-recruited agent betrayed him. Then he sat on a log and waited. At 1015 hours the same man appeared carrying an ax and shook hands with Pope.

"Do you have a plan, sir?"

"Yes. You meet with Colonel Khanh and tell him you would like to be a spy, but you need money. If paid, you will try to find out information for him. In one week, I will be back with a MedCap team. You will stand in line to get medical treatment. Once in the house, I will discuss our next part of the plan. Do you have any questions?"

"No. I am ready."

"Here is some money for the information you gave me last night. Do not discuss our conversation with anyone. Your life depends on it."

Pope arose from his seat on the log and gave the man some Piastres. When he raised his hand five scouts appeared from their hiding places and followed the American into the jungle.

*   *   *

When Pope returned from the meeting, he went to Dang.

"I have reason to believe that the Viet Cong were tipped off before our Cordon and Search operation last night."

"What makes you think so, Captain Pope?"

"I thought we should have made more arrests. Then a new spy told me that there were about thirty fewer villagers gathered in the Market Square than usually live in the village. I confirmed it by questioning other villagers."

"Yes, I was disappointed in the number of arrests myself."

"I believe that somehow the VC got hold of our plans and tipped the communists off, and they got out of our net."

"Do you have any ideas?"

"Yes, we can confirm the report by coming back to this same village in about a week and see if we catch any more communists."

"We will come back in a week. The only ones that will know about future Cordon and Search operations will be you and me, Captain Pope."

*   *   *

In the next two weeks Pope got little rest as the MedCap teams went to a different village every day, and the RF Company did a C&S operation every night. They went back to the village in Hoi Duc a week later and conducted another C&S operation. This time they arrested 21 communists, and killed five armed Viet Cong trying to escape. Pope was elated with the results. Pope thought to himself *maybe the best way to win the hearts and minds of the people might be to grab them by the balls and their hearts and minds would follow.*

*   *   *

Pope walked into Captain Dang's office. The little captain, seated at his desk, rose and shook Pope's hand.

"I have recruited a spy that might be able to set a communist colonel up for an ambush."

Dang's eyebrows raised. "Do you think the agent is reliable?"

"Only time will tell. His information about the guerrillas leaving the Hoi Duc village before our C&S operation was reliable."

"What is your plan?"

"This is really a sensitive area. We need to give the VC colonel enough worthless information to gain his confidence for a short period. If we wait too long, he may catch on, or get impatient and kill our agent." Pope thought for a minute and said, "Can you provide a trustworthy agent handler that can give the agent the worthless information?"

"I know just the man. I'll take care of it today," Dang said, visibly pleased.

*   *   *

Pope and the Yard scouts met again with the agent from Hoi Duc. He gave the spy more money, and the code name "Lau." He established a four-week schedule to work with Dang's agent handler. The handler would give Lau information about the district headquarters that could be checked by the VC colonel but was not detrimental to the security of the district. The idea was to gain the confidence of the colonel while Pope developed a plan to kill him.

*   *   *

During the two weeks of Operation Win, Pope saw Kathryn only at lunchtime. They took their lunches and moved away from the other advisors for some privacy. They spent most of their time talking about their own backgrounds, families, and dreams of the future. It was the highlight of the day for both of them.

After the two-week non-stop operation, Pope met in Dang's office and discussed the results of Operation Win.

"We have really developed a large sector-wide network of agents as a result of the MedCap visits. If you don't mind, since I'm paying for the operatives, and because I feel it's safer for them, Sergeant White and I will handle the spies and provide reports only to you," Pope proposed.

"I agree with you. There may be spies in the SOIC, and we don't want to lose agents."

"Based on the results of the two C&S operations in the one Hoi Duc village, I'm convinced there are spies among us. We must be extra careful until we ferret them out."

"Yes. I am conducting an investigation of the SOIC on my own."

"How many total arrests did we make during the C&S operations?"

"Over 200 people with no ID, and we killed 17 guerrillas that tried to escape. We had no friendly casualties."

"Have we received any information about VC base camps?"

"No. Most of the VC live in the villages and organize in the jungle. I did find out some information that you'll find interesting."

"What's that?"

"We captured a cell leader who told us that the reason there are few violent incidents in Binh Tuy is because our province is used by the Viet Cong as a rest area."

"That explains why our province is so pacified. Will you please pass that information on to Major Nhia? This may give us leverage for more combat operations and reinforcements."

"I have already told him. He didn't take it as good news."

"No, and I don't think Major Sullivan will either. They are both convinced the province is well pacified. What will happen to the villagers with no ID cards?" Pope asked.

"They will be treated like VC, and they will be required to go through the 'Chieu Hoi' program. It is a process where they get four weeks of government indoctrination and are given new ID cards. Unfortunately, some of them will still be VC—and they will have genuine ID cards."

"Doesn't that make the Chieu Hoi a bad program?"

"Yes, but there is no good alternative. The only other choice is to kill them. Remember that our responsibility is to provide security for the people. Some of them really do lose their ID cards or are AWOL from government units."

"Do you think the Civic Action and PsyOps operations were effective, Captain Dang?"

"Yes. I was very happy with those results. In fact, the province chief told me that he was pleased with the results of Operation Win and thinks we should repeat it in about six months."

"I agree, but I think we discovered that we need to increase our search and destroy operations. There are a hell of a lot more VC in this province than we both dreamed."

"Yes. Your agent network should be giving us the information to mount those operations."

"I'm going to Saigon for the week-end. When I get back, I want to start making plans to zap that VC colonel in Hoi Duc."

"I hope you have a restful week-end in Saigon. Will you have a chance to visit with Miss Williams?"

"I wouldn't be at all surprised," Pope said, and he grinned shook hands with his smiling Vietnamese friend, and headed out the door.

*   *   *

Pope returned to his room in the advisory compound and thought, *we've got to figure out some way of finding out who the spies are in our own ranks. Christ, I'm sure not looking forward to tell Sullivan about the VC taking R and R in his pacified province. But enough about combat operations— now its time to start thinking about the weekend with Kathryn.*

Chapter Thirteen

Saturday morning Pope packed his war souvenirs, toilet articles, and some slacks and sport shirt in his rucksack, and caught a helicopter to Tan Son Nhut Air Base. After exiting the helicopter he went into II Corps air operations to sign up for a return trip. The operations sergeant was reading a Playboy magazine.

"Morning, Sarge, I need a trip back to Binh Tuy province Sunday night. Can do?"

The Sergeant looked up from his magazine and said, "Well, let's take a look at the schedule, sir."

He looked at some papers on his clipboard and said, "We don't have anything scheduled, but I've got a chopper coming in Sunday evening that's dropping off some passengers and heading back north. Be here at 2100 hours, and you've got a ride."

"Outstanding. Do you happen to have transportation available to get me downtown?"

"Sure, sir, you can use Bombach there," the sergeant said, pointing to an army Sp4 lounging on a couch reading another Playboy magazine.

"Bombach, take the captain wherever he wants to go, and get your ass back here without any intermediate stops," the sergeant shouted to the soldier.

As the soldier got up and walked out to the jeep, the sergeant said, "Sir, it's Corps policy that all personnel coming in from the field are required to check their weapons here and pick them up on their return flight."

Pope stopped, looked at the floor, thought for a few moments and replied, "I notice that you wear a side arm sergeant. Do you leave it here when you return to your quarters downtown."

"No, sir."

"Then you understand when I tell you that I'll take care of my own weapons," Pope said over his shoulder as he sauntered out of the building.

"Yes sir, suit yourself," the sergeant said as he shrugged his shoulders and picked up his Playboy.

As the jeep made its way through the traffic in Saigon, Pope was amazed by how people went about their business as though the country was not at war.

"I didn't catch your name, soldier."

"Tom Bombach, sir."

"Been in country long, Bombach?"

"Got 78 days and a wake up, sir, and I'll be back home in Detroit."

"I was stationed in Detroit in the Counter Intelligence Corps. It's a nice place," Pope lied.

"Yes, sir. It'll be nice to see my wife again. It's been a long time."

"What are your plans when you get home?"

"Well, first thing, I'll ring the doorbell, and my wife will meet me at the front door. Third thing, I'll set down my duffel bag sir," the young soldier said with a big grin.

"I've got this vision of you and your wife at your front door, Bombach," Pope said, laughing.

"Yes, sir. Then I'm going to take a trip to the bathroom and see if the toilet seat is up."

Pope shook his head and chuckled. "You're quite a character, Bombach."

They passed several off-duty US soldiers escorting beautiful wasp-waisted young Vietnamese women wearing traditional Oai Dai, a flowing dress-pants set. While he noticed many "white mice," the nickname given the Vietnamese national policemen who wore white uniforms, and carried weapons, the Americans he saw were unarmed.

As though reading Pope's mind, Bombach patted his pistol.

"Sir, you're right in keeping your weapons. Saigon is no place to be unarmed. Hell, I heard last week a sailor was just walking down Tu Do Street, minding his own business, and he was shot by a Saigon 'cowboy' riding a motorcycle. I carry mine everywhere I go."

"Thanks, Bombach. I'll keep that in mind."

The jeep stopped abruptly in front of a modern, white, multi story hotel, with steel bars on the windows of the first four floors. Armed US guards were stationed behind sandbags stacked in the front entrance.

"This is it sir, Brinks Hotel."

"Doesn't look too shabby. Thanks a lot for the lift Bombach," Pope said and went to the front desk to register.

*   *   *

The Brinks was like any five-star hotel in the United States. Three immaculately dressed Vietnamese employees staffed a large reception desk. They didn't seem to have anything to do. Pope completed the registration form, paid the $2.00 per night fee, and picked up his key. He took the elevator to the seventh floor and went to his room.

It was large. A queen size four-poster bed with a large mosquito net took only a small part of the chamber. The furniture was almost brand new and looked as if it had been shipped from the United States.

He emptied his rucksack and put the contents in the closet. Then he carefully placed his CAR 15 under the bed. After taking off his clothes he carried his toilet articles and pistol into the bathroom. He was glad to see the toilet with seat.

After a fifteen-minute shower, he shaved and dressed in civilian slacks and sport shirt with the tails untucked. It was still a half-hour before he was to meet Kathryn in the lobby, so he called the desk.

"This is Captain John Pope. I'm supposed to meet an American woman named Kathryn Williams in the lobby at 12:00 noon."

"No American woman has arrived yet, sir." The Vietnamese desk clerk interrupted.

"OK, thanks. When she does, will you please tell her I'll be waiting for her at the bar on the top floor?"

"Yes, of course, sir."

Pope placed his pistol in the back waistband of his slacks and caught the elevator to the top floor. The entire rooftop was a combination restaurant and nightclub. The left half was an open seating area with about fifty tables, and six GI's were seated at three different tables. There was an adjoining bandstand but no band. The other half of the rooftop contained an enclosed room with glass doors.

He entered the room and saw a huge restaurant, with a bar off to the side, next to the entrance. The restaurant was beginning to fill up with uniformed military personnel. There were a few people at the bar and very few women customers in either. The restaurant was air-conditioned.

"Hey, boonie rat! Was the field all you wanted it to be?" A man seated at the bar yelled at Pope.

Pope turned toward the familiar voice and recognized Captain Bill Jamison, the assignment officer that had changed his orders to the field.

"Bill! How the hell are you? Yes. It's all that I imagined, and then some."

"You're a real celebrity. I've been reading your press clippings. The big news is you're dragging Victor Charlie out of the woods in droves in the most pacified province in-country. Doesn't that bring you at odds with your counterpart? Not to mention, your boss?"

"Surprisingly, my counterpart seems to understand. My boss isn't real happy with me disrupting his tranquil life. Dang and I think there's something big building and we've been lucky to find it out just as they're starting. Say, this is quite a place." Pope said as he waved his hand in a semi circle.

"Yeah, this is the home away from home for many of us 'Saigon commandos.' The hotel was built a few years ago, then taken over by the US government and modernized. It's used as a combination bachelor officers quarters and hotel for transient US personnel."

"Why are so many people in here at this time of day?"

"It's also the dining facility for officers and civilians stationed in Saigon. It's a rough life—and you had a chance to be a part of it, my friend. Say, if you don't have any plans tonight, I can get us a couple Vietnamese women for dates and come back here tonight. They have a live band with singers and comedians, and dancing is allowed."

"Thanks anyway, Bill, but I'm supposed to meet someone for a date tonight. She's a real nice girl from Michigan that works for USAID."

"Man, you don't want one of those homely round eyed broads, buddy. If they could get a date in the States, they wouldn't be here. I can get you a Vietnamese beauty—and for free. She works in an office in my building."

"This one is different, Bill. And she's real pretty."

"Oh bullshit! You've already been in the boonies too long, when the USAID gals start looking good to you. They're all pigs and think they're God's gift to the lonely GI. If she was pretty, she would be at home, raising kids," Jamison said in disgust.

Just then, the door opened and Kathryn appeared in the portal. Her long, red hair was curled and flowed across her shoulders. She wore a powder blue silk dress that was skin tight with a spread bottom that ended just above the knees. In high heels, her legs had a perfect form. The wind from the air conditioner blew her dress and made it even tighter. She was carrying an overnight case and a big smile as her eyes caught Pope's.

He got up from his stool, and she ran over to him. She dropped her bag, threw her arms around Pope and kissed him long and hard on the mouth. He stepped back and looked Kathryn up and down.

"Wow, that's the best greeting I have **ever** had!"

Everyone had stopped eating and talking and looked at them. He glanced at Jamison who was sitting with his mouth wide open. Kathryn was completely oblivious to the attention she was receiving from the other guests.

"You sure know how to stir up a room," he added.

"Johnny, it's so good to see you!" She exclaimed.

"I guess I overstated my case a minute ago," Jamison mumbled.

Pope chuckled and said, "Kathryn, we were just talking about you. I'd like you to meet an old friend, Bill Jamison."

"Any friend of Johnny's is a friend of mine," Kathryn said, smiling and shaking Bill's hand firmly and vigorously.

"I shouldn't be surprised that Pope would find the only beautiful American woman in Vietnam. When we were stationed at Ft. Bragg, we would go to Myrtle Beach for the weekend. I just put old Johnny out on a blanket in his bathing suit and trolled for women," Jamison said, laughing.

"And you told me you had no experience with women," Kathryn joked, as she had both arms around Pope's arm.

"Well, let's eat. Will you join us for lunch, Bill?" Pope said, desperately changing the subject.

"Ha! You couldn't pry me away now. Look around, Johnny. We're the envy of every guy in the room."

The waiter seated them, and Kathryn asked, "How many days will you be in Saigon, Johnny?"

"I have a chopper scheduled to pick me up at 2100 hours tomorrow."

"That's great. I'm off until Monday myself," Kathryn said.

"Swell. We're all off until tomorrow night." Jamison said with a laugh.

"Sorry about that, old friend, but after lunch, you're not part of this group. You understand, I'm sure," Pope said with a grin.

"Shot down again. But not without a fight. Kathryn, don't you have any friends almost as pretty as you that you can fix me up with?"

"Yes, I do, Bill. One in particular that's prettier than I am, but I don't think she's available on such short notice. Maybe another time?"

"I can't believe she's prettier than you. Hell, you're a knockout! But you've got a deal," Jamison exclaimed. "May I suggest the T-bone steak? It's delicious," he added.

They all ordered steaks and made small talk, mostly about each other's background and how many days they had left in-country.

"The steak was as good as you said, Bill" Pope said as he finished. "But I feel kind of funny. Life in Saigon seems decadent. Especially since people are getting killed and maimed every day in the field."

"I know what you mean." Kathryn said, taking Pope's hand. "The people are so poor, and here we are."

They were all quiet for a minute.

"Say Bill," Pope said lightly. "I'm trying to locate a couple American army doctors. They helped me capture a few VC, and I promised them some souvenirs. They may not be working at the hospital where I met them. Any idea how I can find out where they are?"

"As usual, you've got the right man. Just write their names on a piece of paper, I'll check it out and leave a message at the desk for you. I'm sure you and Kathryn will be out visiting the museums and libraries all afternoon."

Pope pulled out pen and paper and started writing.

"Well, thank you for being so considerate. You're a real gentleman, Mr. Jamison," Kathryn cooed.

"With that compliment, I can only take as a signal for me to beg my leave," Jamison said as he arose. "Don't get up, I can find my own way to the door. By the way, Johnny you can buy my lunch. Kathryn, I'm really glad to meet you and look forward to seeing you—and a friend—again, real soon."

"Thanks again, Bill, for the assignment and for tracking down the doctors," Pope said as he handed the paper to Jamison.

"Nice to meet you, Bill. We'll get together real soon," she stood and hugged him.

They sat at the table drinking iced tea for about forty-five minutes. Pope stared at her and marveled at her beauty. He wondered how he was going to make it through the day until night fell on the romantic city of Saigon.

Chapter Fourteen

As though reading Pope's mind, his thoughts were interrupted, "Well, I don't expect to sit here and drink tea all day, Mr. Pope. Is your room close by?" Kathryn said in a falsetto voice.

Pope jumped to his feet, knocking his chair over.

"Its just a few flights down."

Inside his room, Pope set Kathryn's bag on the chair near the door, reached to his back waistband for his pistol, placed it on the bag, and turned to meet Kathryn's warm, moist lips. Her body was pressed against his, and she trembled as her tongue darted into his mouth. After the long kiss, he took Kathryn's long hair in his hands, smelled its flowery fragrance, and kissed it.

He whispered softly, "I've been waiting so long for this."

"Don't talk now, Johnny. Later." She took his head in her hands and kissed his chin, right cheek, left cheek, and forehead. Pope reached up her back and lowered the zipper on her dress. He unbuckled her belt. Kathryn unbuttoned his shirt and unbuckled his belt. He pushed the dress off her shoulders, and she wiggled—his slacks and her dress dropped to the floor at the same time.

The telephone on the nightstand rang loudly. He stepped back, and she pulled him toward her.

"Don't answer it. It's probably a wrong number."

He breathed deeply to regain his composure.

"I better answer it. It might be my boss. You know I'm not exactly one of his favorites."

"Oh, hell! Go ahead" she said, still panting.

He rushed to the phone and quickly picked it up.

"Hi, Johnny, Bill Jamison. I'm not interrupting anything am I?"

"What's so important?"

"Nothing. I just want to show you how efficient I am. Both doctors are on duty at the hospital until 1900 hours. If you miss them, they stay at the Embassy Hotel."

"Thanks a lot. You could have given the message to the desk clerk," Pope growled.

"Yeah, I could have, but I'm trying to impress Kathryn," he laughed

"You're impressing her all right! See ya."

He dropped the phone into its cradle and turned to Kathryn. "Let's see now, where were we?"

She ran across the room and threw her arms around him. He kissed her and reached behind her and unfastened her bra. She wriggled out of it, and it dropped to the floor. He picked up Kathryn and set her on the bed. He pulled her panties down over her legs and feet and kissed her firm, heaving, breasts, rubbing his tongue over her firm nipples. He reached down between her legs and felt her—warm, moist, and soft, as her hips moved rhythmically.

She pulled away from a long hard kiss and gasped, "Now, Johnny, please."

She pulled him toward her and as his head moved above hers on the bed, she reached down and took him and put him inside her. She heaved her pelvis forward and wrapped her legs around his hips to take all of him. She groaned in ecstasy as he thrust in and out until she cried out with pleasure. He reached a climax shortly afterward.

They made love two more times before they fell asleep, exhausted but content in each other's arms.

*   *   *

He was still asleep when Kathryn awakened and went into the bathroom. She came out and sat in the chair next to the bed and looked at his naked body. She thought *how handsome he is, with his dark skin, black hair, coal black eyes, and his muscular 170-pound body. At that moment, she was sure that she was in love with him and had been from the minute that she first saw him.*

Pope opened his eyes and looked at Kathryn sitting in the chair.

"What a great life, to find a naked lady in my bedroom when I wake up."

She walked to the bed, sat next to him, and bent to kiss him on the mouth.

"Hi, handsome. Are you going to sleep all day?"

"Do you know you are the most gorgeous woman that I have ever seen?" Pope said, as he kissed her cheek and forehead, smelling the sweet musk of lovemaking.

"I bet you say that to all the ladies. But I'll still take it as a compliment."

"Do you have anything planned for today?"

"We've already done what I had planned for the day."

Pope laughed said, "Well, my week-end is open except for delivering the souvenirs. If you don't mind, I'd like to make the delivery as soon as possible. I still have time to meet them at the hospital. Will you go there with me?"

"Let's go," Kathryn said and stood up.

"I didn't mean to go **immediately**. Why don't we take a nice long shower and get dressed **before** we go?"

*   *   *

At the hospital, they were directed to the same lounge where Pope had met the doctors before. The doctors were on the same couch, talking and eating donuts.

"Don't you guys do anything but hang around the lounge?" Pope asked, laughing.

"Hey, It's the sleeping powder guy! But who cares, **who's** the gorgeous red head?" Phil Donner shouted.

"I'm here bearing gifts, and the girl isn't one of them. Kathryn Williams, these are Doctors Phil Donner and Tom Villone—my CO-conspirators."

"Where have you been hiding, Miss Williams?" asked Villone as he shook Kathryn's hand.

"I'm from a long line of huggers, do you mind?" Donner said, as he stood with open arms.

"I don't usually hug everyone, but I'll make an exception because you're a friend of Johnny's." Kathryn smiled as she moved into Donner's arms for a short hug.

Pope took a few minutes to explain how the sleeping powder was used and the results.

"We read about the arrests of several VC in Binh Tuy and were wondering if you used our sleeping powder on that operation," Villone said.

"Why didn't they mention our sleeping powder in the article?" Donner asked.

"We don't want the VC to know about it. We didn't even tell the agent that delivered the tainted food. We may want to do it again."

"Yeah, so don't you have something in your little bag for us?" Donner asked, pointing at Pope's rucksack.

"OK, let's get to the goodies," Pope said as he set his rucksack on the table and opened it. He pulled out a set of well-worn black pajamas and a pair of sandals. He handed them to Donner.

"These were taken off one of the VC we captured using your sleeping powder. Here's a pair of 'Ho Chi Minh boots' that goes with the suit. They appear to be about your size."

The "boots," were a pair of sandals with the soles made from a truck tire.

"Man, this is really great. I can hardly wait to show these to my old man. By the time I get home, I'll have concocted some story that I stripped them off a VC that I killed in hand-to-hand combat," Donner said as he accepted the gifts and laughed.

"And for you, Tom, I brought a Mas 36, French rifle." Pope pulled out a rifle that had been field stripped to fit in the ruck. "I'll put it together for you now."

As Pope worked on the weapon Donner left the room and moments later, returned with a football.

"Thanks for the suit, but remember that you promised to autograph a football for me. Just write, 'To my buddy, Phil. The man with the golden arm.' And sign it."

He tossed the ball to Pope. Pope caught it, took out a pen, and wrote on it.

"We read in *The Stars and Stripes* that you really caught a big bag of VC," Villone said.

"He's caught a lot of VC since he started working in Binh Tuy," Kathryn bragged.

"Well, another fan heard from. Where do you fit in here, Kathryn?" Phil said.

"I work for USAID and worked with Johnny in Binh Tuy, and now I'm **with** him," she cooed as she wrapped her arms around Pope's arm.

"Damn. The field grunts always get the glory and the beautiful girls!" Donner said as he put his hand to his chest and fell backward on the couch.

"Are you going to need anymore sleeping powder, Johnny?" Villone asked.

"No. Not right now. But if I do, you guys will be seeing me again. Listen, we've only got the weekend, and it's almost half gone. If you need a favor, let me know."

"Yes. Do you have a friend as beautiful as you?" Phil asked, looking at Kathryn.

"Yes, I do. And his name is Captain Pope." she said firmly while smiling.

"Well, friend, let's get out of here and start seeing the bright lights. See you guys." Pope tossed the football to Donner, shook hands with the two doctors, and left the lounge with Kathryn.

*   *   *

They caught a taxi back to the Brinks Hotel, changed clothes for dinner, and rode the elevator to the dining room. Kathryn wore a red brocade knee length dress with a pearl necklace, red pumps, and bare legs. As they entered the dining room, all eyes were on Kathryn again. There was only a handful of Caucasian women but several Vietnamese women escorted by American men in civilian clothes.

Both had a Filet Mignon with red wine. The band was set up in the open part of the roof, so they moved their drinks out to the terrace, and Pope got a table close to the band. While they were playing, it would be impossible to conduct a conversation, and all he really wanted to do was look at Kathryn while the music played.

The sun went down, and the city cooled. A man approached the table and asked Kathryn to dance. She put her hand on Pope's and smiled.

"No thanks, I'm sitting this one out."

About five minutes later, another man asked her to dance and got the same response. After five uncomfortable minutes, Pope said, "Kathryn, would you like to dance?"

"I thought you'd never ask," Kathryn said as she stood and moved toward the dance floor.

"I guess I was being selfish. I like to dance, but I prefer to just look at you now," he said in her ear.

"I love to dance, too, but if we stay seated, I may have to fend off more requests during the evening," she said, kissing his ear.

"Then let's dance. We've got all night to look at each other."

They danced until 1:00 and went back to Pope's room. When they were inside she put her arms around his waist, kissed him, and patted the pistol in his waistband.

"Why do you carry that around with you all the time?"

"For protection."

"But, no one carries weapons in Saigon when they're off duty."

"You have to build good habits. Ones that you maintain no matter where you are. No matter what anyone says, Vietnam is a combat zone wherever you go. Those who forget that don't get a second chance. I keep my pistol under the pillow at night, everywhere I go."

He took it from his waistband, crossed the room to the bed, and placed it under the pillow.

"Well, I want to see all your weapons!" Kathryn shouted. She kicked off her heels, ran across the room, and jumped into his arms, and they both fell on the bed.

This time, their lovemaking was torrid. She tore at his shirt with trembling hands. She needed his help to undress her and him as well. As he lay on his back, she kissed him all over his body and sat straddling him. She reached down and put him inside her and moved up and down. She started slowly, with long strokes, then moved faster and faster. Her moans and whimpers became shrieks of pleasure. Pope screamed aloud as he reached the height of his lovemaking emotions. Kathryn kissed him on both eyes, rolled over and held him in her arms, and they lay together for several minutes.

"That was pretty loud. I hope we didn't wake someone that has duty tomorrow."

Kathryn laughed and said, "I wouldn't worry about keeping anyone awake in Saigon on Saturday night."

"I can't think of a better place to be than with you on a Saturday night." Pope said, stretching and putting his hands behind his head.

"Say, why do you suppose the other men in your team have nicknamed you 'IceMan?' You've never seemed cold to me," Kathryn said, laughing.

"I have no idea. That's the first I've heard of that nickname. No one has ever said it in front of me. Did anyone tell you why?" Pope wasn't stupid enough to think people didn't talk about him behind his back, but hanging a name on him was serious.

"No. I was talking with Sp4 Martin one day, and he referred to you as IceMan. I asked him where he heard it from and he said Sgt. Waters."

"Well, that's interesting. It's a puzzle I expect to solve after I've had some sleep," Pope said, and he rolled over and cradled Kathryn's head in his arm and smelled the sweetness of the perfume behind her ear.

*   *   *

Kathryn opened her eyes at 0900 hours and saw Pope sitting in the chair next to the bed with a blanket wrapped around him, looking at her.

"I never get tired of looking at you and your beautiful body."

"Yeah. I bet I really look gorgeous, with my hair all messed up and no make-up on. Come on over here, and let's make love," she said, with an outstretched arm.

"I'm an early breakfast guy. Let's get some energy, then come back?"

"Party-pooper," she groaned as she rolled over and faced the wall.

Pope went into the bathroom and adjusted the water in the shower. He stepped in and began lathering his body with soap, then he felt Kathryn scratching his back gently with her fingernails. She took the soap from his hand and began lathering his body. As she got to the hairy part between his legs, he became aroused. He turned around, faced Kathryn, and she kissed him on the lips as the water poured down on their heads. She reached down and put him between her legs and squeezed. Pope picked her up, and she wrapped her legs around his hips. He reached down and put himself inside of her, and she sighed. Pope moved her against the wall in the shower and began moving rhythmically inside her. Both moaned together in pleasure, and he gently lowered Kathryn to the floor of the shower and sat with her. With the water still cascading down on them, Pope held her.

"You seduced me anyway, didn't you?"

Kathryn laughed and said, "Let's get something straight O great warrior. You don't have the last word in everything!"

After the "shower," they dressed and took the elevator to the roof and enjoyed a big breakfast. They spent the rest of the day touring Saigon in a taxi. She showed him the presidential palace, the American Embassy and the "river people" that lived along the Mekong River. They stopped at a tailor shop, and Pope was fitted for a gray silk suit. He also picked out some material for a dress for Kathryn. After dinner at the Majestic Hotel dining room, they went to Pope's room at the Brinks Hotel and made love again.

Pope held Kathryn in his arms and said, "I've never been in love before. But I have this feeling for you that I've never felt for anyone else except my grandfather. I just feel so great when I'm with you. I think it must be love."

"Wow, I've never been compared to anyone's grandfather before, but I know what you mean. I'm glad, Johnny, because I've loved you from the moment I saw you at that little dirt airstrip when you were stumbling, fumbling, and mumbling," she said seriously, but couldn't help laughing at her own joke.

"I was pretty bad, wasn't I?"

"Not that bad. But I can't see you then or ever as this 'IceMan' that Sergeant Waters hung on you."

"OK, OK. Seriously, my grandfather was a special man, and you're a special woman. I'll have to tell you about him some day. But now, it's time to pack up and head for Tan Son Nhut," Pope said. He kissed her and got out of bed.

"I don't want to take a shower now, Johnny. I want to smell you on me as long as I can," Kathryn said, and she began dressing.

They packed, checked out of the hotel, and caught a taxi. He dropped Kathryn at her hotel in Cholon, the Chinese section of Saigon, and caught his scheduled helicopter.

As Pope sat in the darkened chopper, listening to the rhythmic thumping of the chopper blades, he thought: *So much has happened in the last couple days. I do know for certain though that I love Kathryn. Will Grandfather be right when he said, no one will die?*

Chapter Fifteen

More of Pope's agents reported VC units in the area—and alarming number had moved south from Darlac Province. While White examined and treated the civilians, Pope, Duc and Waters talked with the recruited agents at Hoi Duc. By late morning the agent, (code name Lau) in contact with the VC colonel arrived in the house.

"Have you anything to report, Lau?" Pope asked in Vietnamese.

"Yes, Captain, the VC colonel has met with me every week for the last three weeks."

"Do you think he believes the information you have been giving him?"

"I think he does, sir, because once he told me that he had someone check the information I gave him."

"So, what have you seen or heard?"

"The last time I saw him, he said things would be changing in Binh Tuy very soon."

"Do you know what he meant by that?"

"No. I am just reporting what he said, sir."

"What else?" Pope asked, noticeably irritated, because he wished he had time to train his agents to ask questions that would clarify off-handed comments.

"When I have gone out to cut wood, I have seen more VC soldiers moving in the forest."

"How many, and how were they armed?"

"In a week, I have seen three groups of six or seven. And they are different men. They are armed with rifles and ammunition belts. But the guns are different. They are not the old long French ones, but shorter, new weapons. Each group stopped me and asked if I had any information about government troops or if I could get food for them."

"And what did you tell them?"

"That I am just a poor wood-cutter and know nothing of government soldiers, nor did I have any food."

"Can you lead me to the place that you always meet the colonel?"

"Yes, Captain, but why?"

"That is not your business. How long would it take for you and me to travel to that place?"

"About two hours."

"Good. You will take me there tonight after it gets dark."

"But what of the curfew, Captain?

"You have never been out after curfew?"

"I have to say yes, sir," Lau said as he looked at the ground."

"Good. I want you to stay here with the American sergeant and don't leave the house until you and I leave together."

"I will do that, Captain."

Pope turned to Waters and said, "Your job is to baby-sit him until we leave. He's not to leave the house, and he's to have no contact with anyone. Clear?"

"Crystal. Are we going into the jungle with him on recon, sir?"

"No, **I'm** going with him on recon. You're too big and ugly to pass for a Vietnamese peasant. Sgt. Duc, I want you to get a pair of black pajamas, sandals, and straw hat. You and I are close to the same size—Just say you need to borrow them for yourself. Be sure they are not new. I want to look like a friend of Lau's."

"Sir, it is very dangerous for you to go into the jungle by yourself," Duc answered, clearly concerned. "Besides, maybe you can't trust Lau. I will go with you," he added.

"No thanks Duc. You're right I can't trust Lau, but we'll be traveling at night, and I want to move quietly. We'll be coming back during the day, and three people together would look suspicious to any VC we may encounter. This is to be a one-man recon patrol. I plan to avoid contact with Charlie. If we meet, I'll try to talk my way out of trouble."

"Sir, the Major isn't going to like this. Not only that, but being out after curfew, you might get shot by government troops," Waters said.

"The Major isn't crazy about anything I do, and I hate to say this but I don't think the government troops are alert enough to catch anything, but Zs."

*   *   *

The rest of the day they worked with agents at the MedCap location. Pope, Duc, and White had dinner with Captain Khoa, the district chief. Afterward they took a meal to Waters and Lau.

Pope lay on the hard wooden bed, with no mattress, next to Lau and slept for about an hour. Waters woke him at 2400 hours.

"Sir, did you tell Captain Khoa you were heading out alone?"

"Hell, no. I don't trust any Vietnamese. And don't you either, Sergeant," Pope said.

He shook the sleep from his head and changed into the black pajamas, sandals, and hat. He took his pistol, placed it in a leather belt inside his pajama pants, put the cone shaped straw hat on his head, and hooked the cloth loop under his chin.

"I don't plan to use this on anyone except myself, Sergeant. Since you'll be going out on operations with me, you should know that I don't ever plan to be captured. I'll either fight my way out or use this on myself. It has nothing to do with protecting secrets or heroism. I just don't think I would be very good at being a POW."

"Damn, sir. You never cease to amaze me. But I understand. I know I couldn't stand captivity either. When I was a kid my step dad used to lock me in a closet when I was bad. Since then I don't like closed-in places. Why don't we make a pact that if either of us is wounded and capture is inevitable, that the other finishes him off?"

"Do you mean that if one of us is wounded the other is obligated to shoot him in the head so he isn't captured?"

"Yes, sir. I know it won't be easy, but I'd rather that you killed me then and there than dying in captivity."

"I think we understand each other, Sergeant," he said extending his hand to seal the agreement.

Waters took the outstretched hand, shook it firmly, and said, "Now that we've made the deal, don't go out and get your ass shot off tonight."

"Never happen, GI," he said light-heartedly, glad to have the morbid agreement made and finished.

"Why don't I take a five man RF patrol and trail you as security, Captain? Just in case our buddy here is a rat."

"It's too risky. You people would make too much noise and might jeopardize our plans for the colonel."

*   *   *

To Lau, Pope said in Vietnamese, "lead the way, Lau, and remember that we have to avoid the guards as we leave."

"That is no problem, sir. I know the way."

Lau led Pope past a darkened thatch-roofed house and to a bamboo fence that enclosed the village. The agent carefully removed a cut out section of the fence that was large enough for a man to crawl through. After both exited the wooden structure, Lau carefully replaced the hole cover.

"Be careful to follow in my footsteps because we are going through a minefield, sir," Lau whispered.

Pope nodded, and the two crossed the minefield outside the hamlet and melted into the jungle. As Pope tripped over a rotting log and vines, he thought about the possibility of Lau betraying him. He second-guessed himself about the wisdom of going into the jungle alone.

Pope followed closely a few steps behind the spy. He noticed they were on a trail and tapped Lau on the shoulder.

"This is a trail we're on. We may run into communist soldiers in the dark."

"Sir, I travel on this trail many nights, and I have never seen any communists. They use the trail only during the daytime."

Pope nodded and patted Lau on the shoulder, signaling him to move forward. They followed a pattern of moving for 15 minutes, then stop. He set landmarks in his mind on the move. When they stopped, he put his head under his shirt, and with a small penlight and pencil, made notes on a pad.

They repeated this for three and a half hours, until Lau stopped and whispered, "This is the place, sir."

"Good. Now we stop here until daylight. And stop calling me, sir. Someone might hear you."

Pope spent the rest of the night awake, going over the landmarks in his head and memorizing them. Lau lay curled up against pope's side and slept the rest of the night.

*   *   *

Back at Hoi Duc, Waters and White awakened, washed, and waited for Duc to return with their breakfast.

White said sarcastically, "I wonder how The IceMan is doing on his one man reconnaissance?" White respected Pope's courage and tenacity, but thought of him as somewhat of a pain in the ass, because he was such a hard charger and brought everyone with him.

"Don't you worry about IceMan, Whitey. He's in his element now. He'll be back, grinning like a shit eating dog," Waters said as both laughed.

Duc returned with a sad face, interrupting their joking.

"Captain Khoa, the district chief asked us to eat breakfast at his head-quarters, and I had to tell him that Captain Pope went on a reconnaissance mission. He is very angry and wants us to report to him now. Sorry about that, sir."

"Oh shit, I'm not looking forward to this Vietnamese breakfast," Waters said, motioning the others to follow him to district headquarters.

* * *

When the sun broke through the jungle canopy, Pope saw that they were in a clearing, about 40 yards long and about 20 yards wide. The opening had a thick growth of ferns and bushes all around it. He scanned the area, drew a diagram, made several notes in his pad, closed it, and placed it in his pocket.

"That's all I need. Let's go, Lau."

They paralleled the same trail back to Hoi Duc, and moved slowly, stopping occasionally so Pope could check his notes. They stopped to avoid two groups of two unarmed men each that appeared on the trail. Lau recognized that they were woodcutters, but Pope did not want to meet them, so they hid until the woodcutters passed by. When they were about 200 yards from the village, he placed a hand on Lau's shoulder.

"This is where we part company. I don't want anyone to see us together."

"When will I see you again?"

"You will be told by your agent handler," Pope said as he sauntered away, leaving the double agent squatting on the trail.

Pope walked in the front entrance of the village. The two Popular Force guards simply nodded at him as he shuffled by. He wondered if the soldiers ever stopped any strangers for identification. Hell, he could have been a VC assassin.

The MedCap team waited by the chopper. He could tell by the expression on Duc's face that there was some explaining to be done. A slightly irritated Captain Khoa stood nearby with his hands on his hips.

The district chief said, "Sgt. Waters took your uniform to my office. May I speak with you there, Captain Pope?"

"Yes, of course. Waters, tell the pilot that I'll be back in thirty minutes, ready to go."

Pope and Khoa made the five-minute walk to headquarters in silence. They entered Khoa's office, and he closed the door.

"Captain Pope, you did a very foolish thing by dressing like a peasant and sneaking out of the village last night. May I ask why you did not tell me in advance?"

"I went on an intelligence mission I felt was not only important, but for my own safety, I didn't want anyone to know about. I'm sorry I couldn't tell you, Captain."

"But I am responsible for what happens in the district, and I should be told what goes on. I would be seriously disciplined if an American advisor were to be killed in my district, especially if I didn't know that he was out of a village at night with no security," Khoa said, only this time with a little pleading in his voice.

"I have reason to believe there are spies in government offices in Binh Tuy. I have been told that no one can be trusted here, Captain. I am also concerned about my safety," he replied, echoing Khoa's concern in an attempt to strengthen his argument.

"Please believe me, I can be trusted. Ask Captain Dang. He will vouch for me. If he does not, then you will have to be under an armed guard while in Hoi Duc District."

There was no point in arguing further. Pope said, "I'm very sorry for any inconvenience to you. Thank you for your hospitality, Captain Khoa."

Pope changed into his tiger skin uniform, picked up the peasant garb, said his good-byes to the upset district chief, and headed back to the chopper. When Pope arrived, he handed the clothes to Duc.

"Please return these to whoever you borrowed them from."

"I bought them from someone in the market, sir."

Pope reached into his pocket, gave Duc some Piastres, and the group boarded the chopper for province headquarters.

*   *   *

After reporting the results of his recon to Sullivan, Pope and Waters went to the airstrip and inspected the adjacent region for a rehearsal site. About 200 yards from the airstrip, they found an opening in the jungle about the same size as the agent meeting place he had reconnoitered in Hoi Duc. They found Sgt. Ma and explained the plans.

"Our next operation is an ambush. I will hand pick four of our best men to accompany Sergeant Waters and me."

"I think you should use our number one team, sir. They are used to working together."

"This is an important job, and I want the top scouts, Sergeant Ma. Besides, we trained the platoon to operate in all different configurations."

"Very well, sir. Let me know who you would like to use."

When Pope handpicked the four best Yards, it happened that he selected one from each of the four teams. Ma knew better than to ask him the details of the mission. He figured the American would tell him if and when he wanted to. The six-man team, Waters included, worked together in marksmanship training, ambush discipline, and immediate action drills each day for two weeks. Every other night they made six-kilometer trips in different areas of the jungle to practice night movement.

*   *   *

During the second week, Pope brought the team together at the rehearsal site. "Men, you have been selected to go with Sergeant Waters and me to ambush a five man VC patrol. That is what you have been training for."

He gave each of them a number from two through five.

"Sgt. Waters and I will shoot the lead man or the first man from our right. The number two man will shoot the second man to the left, the number three man will shoot the third man to the left, and so forth."

He placed each of them into their ambush positions at the practice area. In the middle of the ambush site, Waters built and emplaced five dummies, complete with black pajamas. He methodically took each man and walked to the mannequin he was assigned to shoot so that there could be no mistakes. Waters placed a sixth dummy, sitting on a log. Pope told the soldiers that no one was to shoot him because he was working with them.

Each afternoon for a week the team rehearsed the ambush. Pope triggered the ambush by shooting the lead man, and Waters shot the same man. Then a split second later, the entire team opened up on their individual targets on full automatic with their CAR 15's. He had the team lie in ambush for at least four hours to train them in self-discipline. There would be distractions from insects, animals, and heat—but the soldiers had to put that out of their minds and concentrate on their targets.

*   *   *

Satisfied the team was ready, Pope went to Captain Dang with his plan.

After explaining the concept, Pope said, "We will go to Hoi Duc with a MedCap team tomorrow so it looks like a regularly scheduled visit. At 2400 hours, the assault team will depart Hoi Duc and make a night move to the ambush site. No one except Major Sullivan, Sgt. Waters, and me know that our target is the VC colonel. The members of the R & I platoon going with us believe we are going to ambush a Viet Cong patrol."

"It sounds like a well thought out operation, Captain Pope. Do you mean you do not plan to tell the District Chief?"

"I'm glad you brought that up. I had forgotten about that incident. When I went on my recon of the ambush site, Captain Khoa got pretty put out because I didn't tell him. I wasn't sure whether he had a genuine concern for me or if he wanted to warn VC compatriots."

"You are absolutely right in not trusting all Vietnamese, Captain Pope, but Captain Khoa is an old friend. He can be trusted. I would trust him with my life."

"Then I prefer you go with me, and you tell him just a few minutes before we depart. You can stay overnight with him. Once we have made the kill, I will radio you, and both of you can take the MedCap choppers to our location to pick up the bodies. But I want your word that no one else knows about the plan."

"You have my word, and I will be happy to go with you. Would you like me to go with you on the ambush?"

"No, I think your presence at district headquarters is important, especially to bring a quick reaction force to my assistance if Lau betrays us."

"Does Lau know you are going to kill Colonel Khanh?"

"No. I thought it best if I don't tell him. That way he won't get nervous and give away the ambush."

"Good idea. Well, I think you have thought of everything, Captain Pope. By this time two days from now we will make history by killing the highest ranking communist of the war."

*   *   *

Pope briefed the details of the plan to kill the VC colonel to Sullivan. The senior advisor couldn't hide his excitement.

"This will be a major setback for the VC in this sector if you pull this off."

Pope went to his room and inspected his gear for the operation. While packing he thought: *This is the biggest thing to happen in this Province or this country during this war. Even Sullivan approves of the mission. Have I thought of everything? Will the agent betray us? Will the Spirit of the Whale be with me during this important operation?*

Chapter Sixteen

The MedCap team consisting of Pope, Waters, White, Duc, Granger, Bishop, Dang, and the four Yards loaded up on two Huey choppers and flew to Hoi Duc. White treated the sick and wounded while Pope questioned the agents. He received reports of more and better armed communist guerrillas moving about in the area. He wondered why there was so much enemy movement, yet there were no additional acts of terrorism or tax collecting. He had difficulty concentrating, because the thoughts of his primary mission kept forcing their way into his head.

During the afternoon he caught about two hours of sleep on the hard, wooden bed. He awoke from a bad dream sweating profusely. Waters was seated on a chair next to the bed reading a paperback novel.

"We better get the Yards together and check their equipment and weapons, Sarge," he said, looking at his watch.

"I did that while you were working with your agents this morning, sir."

"Have you checked the radio and put an extra battery in your rucksack?"

"Already did that, sir, while you were asleep."

"I can't think of anything else to do. I sure hate this waiting though. Some bad thoughts keep entering my mind. What if the VC isn't there? What if Lau doesn't show up? What if there's a larger VC unit not far from the meeting place? What if Lau is setting us up for an ambush?"

"I hear you, sir. Shit happens. You have a good plan, and it has been well rehearsed. You've made alternate plans if any of those things occur. I think you've got everything covered. Everything is going to work just fine."

All of the American advisors joined Dang for dinner at Khoa's headquarters. They were all seated around a circular table in a large dining room, and served Chinese soup, chicken, beef, and rice. They had their choice of soft drinks or Biere Larue, the Vietnamese beer. Pope was not a beer drinker, so he sipped a Coke to help him ingest a couple of the entrees he didn't like. He thought it was the perfect atmosphere to keep his mind off the mission. The meal was pleasant, with a great deal of joking, bantering, and laughing.

Near the end of the dinner, a waiter brought a dish in a rectangular aluminum-baking pan. It appeared to be a dessert because it looked like a Jello type mix, dark red with crushed nuts sprinkled on the top.

"What is in the pan, Captain Dang?" Pope asked.

Dang picked up a tablespoon, scooped out a large portion and ate it. He gave a Vietnamese name for the dish, and said, "It's number one, Captain Pope. You try."

He handed the empty spoon to Pope, who took it, scooped out a large portion, and put the spoonful in his mouth. His eyes shot wide open, and he leaped from his chair, grabbed a bottle of Biere Larue and drank the entire quart bottle. Not satisfied, he grabbed another bottle and gulped down about half of it. Then he sat in his chair and drank some soup to try to get the taste out of his mouth. During Pope's demonstration of chug-a-lugging beer, all of his friends at the table were in hysterics.

"I'm really sorry. That was the bitterest food I have ever tasted. I expected something sweet. What is in the pan?" Pope said, as he wiped his face with his napkin and the advisors wiped the tears from their faces with their napkins.

"I'm sorry you didn't like it. It is a Vietnamese delicacy. It is coagulated chicken blood with peanuts on top."

Which brought another uproar from the advisors.

* * *

After dinner, Pope and Waters went to the house where the four Yards were waiting and resting.

He had them form a little circle around him and explained to them in Vietnamese, "We are going to ambush a VC colonel. If we get him, he will be the highest-ranking enemy killed in the war. He is easily identified because he is tall for a Vietnamese, wears brown clothing and carries a pistol. Sergeant Waters and I will kill him, and you four will kill his guards. There is a 30,000 Piastres reward for the colonel, and we expect to get about five weapons. The four of you should get about 33,000 Piastres to split up."

The Yards looked around, smiled, nodded, and said encouraging words to each other. Pope thought that even though he knew that all of the Yards were expert sharpshooters, he trusted himself and Waters more to take out the colonel.

After the briefing, five of them took a nap while Waters stood guard duty. He woke them shortly before 2400 hours. It didn't take them long to get ready. They carried only their CAR 15, ammo belt and ammo, four hand grenades, and two full canteens of water. Waters carried the radio.

The team crept out the back of the house with Pope in the lead. They used the same hole in the fence that Lau had shown him on their last excursion. The group moved in a file formation quietly into the jungle, Pope at the point. He stopped every 15 minutes to check for landmarks and got under his pancho with a penlight to check his map and notes. During the entire two and a half-hour movement, no one said a word, and there was a minimum of noise. What little noise they made was covered up by the night sounds of the jungle, which included the sounds of the nocturnal animals.

Pope found the ambush site an hour earlier than planned, and he placed each team member into position individually. Part of their ambush discipline was no noise and no movement, no eating, and no relieving themselves. They had not been allowed to drink from their canteens on the move because of the sloshing around noise from partially-filled canteens.

In the ambush positions they were allowed to drink slowly and quietly from their canteens to replace perspiration fluid loss. If they had to go to the toilet, they simply did it in their pants and cleaned up in a stream after the ambush. Waters was lying next to Pope and was ordered via sign language to take a nap. Within minutes Waters was asleep and snoring lightly.

Pope kept his eyes on the "killing zone," and had no difficulty staying awake. He had spread out his poncho to lie on but didn't cover himself, thinking he would not doze off if he stayed chilly. He was alone with his thoughts and the croaking of the frogs.

In the gray early morning light, he crawled to each team member, pointed out approximately where their target would be and had them crawl forward and cut vegetation to clear fields of fire. By mid-morning his uniform had dried, and his lips became parched. By noon, the red ants had become well acquainted with both Waters and Pope. The mosquito repellent had kept the gnats away, but the ants were attracted by it, as though they liked the taste. The two men kept reminding each other with their eyes that they couldn't kill the ants that ate at their bodies. Pope chanted the ceremonial whale hunting song in his head.

*   *   *

At 1300 hours, Lau arrived at the right end of the clearing and sat on a log. A few minutes later a VC soldier dressed in black pajamas and carrying an AK 47 rifle appeared in the clearing to the left. He walked cautiously to Lau, and they talked for a couple minutes. They were too far away for Pope to hear the conversation. The scout turned and signaled back to the jungle with his right hand. Three more VC emerged in the opening led by a man about Pope's height, wearing a tan uniform with a holster and pistol on his belt.

Pope grinned, tossed a stone at Waters and pointed at the colonel. Waters smiled back and nodded. Pope's excitement mounted as he thought that his plan just might work. The communist guerrillas walked forward to meet the two waiting men. The colonel shook hands with Lau and sat on a large tree stump next to him as they talked.

Pope had sighted in on the colonel with his CAR 15 from the moment Khanh had entered the clearing. Khanh walked with an air of confidence. It was apparent the communist leader knew who he was and that he was safe. Pope could see the wrinkles on the leader's face. He did not think he would ever be able to get this close to his enemy.

The sweat rolled down Pope's face, but he refused to wipe it off. He simply cleared the sweat from his eyes by blinking, took a deep breath, let half of it out, and slowly squeezed the trigger. As he felt the slight recoil of his weapon, he heard the firing of Waters beside him, then a split second later, the rest of the killer team. The noise of the weapons on automatic was deafening.

When Colonel Khanh was hit, he fell abruptly to his left, away from the ambushing soldiers. His body fell against a large tangle of creeping green vines. Lau, face frozen in terror, his eyeballs white, jumped backwards, tripping over the log and fell to the ground. The other four VC without firing a shot retraced their steps, sprinting into the jungle. Pope turned his weapon on the fleeing guards, but it was too late. They had already disappeared into the jungle before he could get off a shot.

He leaped to his feet and screamed, "God damn it, attack!"

He sprinted after the fleeing enemy, with Waters and the four Yards in hot pursuit. They ran about 100 yards into the tangle of bushes and vines. He realized that they had lost the initiative, and could be rushing into an ambush of their own. He halted the team, and they moved quickly back into the clearing.

"Form a defensive perimeter," he shouted in Vietnamese to the Yards. They scurried in four different directions.

"Army air, this is American advisor, over," Waters transmitted to the helicopter that had been orbiting over Hoi Duc since 1200 hours. Pope had them in the air to be sure they could be contacted by radio in case a quick reaction force would be needed to help them.

"This is Army helicopter. Are you ready for assistance? Over"

"Affirmative. Mission completed. We got the son-of-a-bitch. LZ secure. Report to our location.

"Wilco. Estimated arrival one zero minutes. Out."

Lau had gotten up from the ground and was white as a sheet and shaking, as he said, "Sir, the colonel is dead. Did the others get away?"

"Yes, damn it. Don't worry, choppers are on the way to pick us up. You'll get your reward, but we'll have to relocate you because your life is worthless if you stay here."

"I would like to stay with you, sir, until I am relocated."

Pope looked down at the dead VC leader and saw that there were about twelve bullet holes in the body. Waters interrupted his thoughts.

"The choppers are airborne and will be here in ten minutes. How in the hell could all of the Yards have missed their targets?"

"Shit, I don't know, Sarge but I'm damn sure going to find out. "

They heard the thump-a-thump-a-thump of the incoming choppers.

"Army helicopter, this is Army advisor. Change in plans. Keep one bird airborne and bring the other one in for a quick pick up of the team and dead colonel. We have to get out of here fast. I pop smoke. Please identify, over."

Pope pulled a green smoke canister from his belt, pulled the pin and threw it into the clearing.

"I identify green smoke, over."

"Roger, land from the northwest, out."

When the helicopter landed, Pope, Waters, and a door gunner loaded the colonel's body on the chopper. The four Yards jumped aboard as the pilot "pulled pitch" to gain altitude. The door gunner next to Pope wrinkled up his nose.

"What the hell did you guys do, sleep in the God damn sewer?"

Waters noticed an embarrassed expression on the Yard next to him and asked him in Vietnamese if he shit his pants. The embarrassed Yard nodded and looked down.

Waters yelled over the engine noise to the crew chief.

The Whale Spirit

"Soldier, if you lie in an ambush position for eleven hours and have to take a crap, you don't just get up and walk to the nearest latrine."

"Sorry, Sarge. I didn't know."

*   *   *

Word must have been passed to the citizens of Hoi Duc, because when the choppers landed, the MedCap team, Dang, Khoa and about 150 civilians waited at the helipad. As the chopper shut down, Pope took the team aside to question them about the screwed up mission.

"How could all of you have possibly missed the VC guards?"

The team members looked at each other then looked at the ground. One of the Yards stepped forward.

"Sir, we are very sorry. We did not plan against you. Each of us thought that we were better marksmen than you were. We were afraid that you would miss the colonel, and we would not get the reward. All of us shot at the colonel. I'm sorry. I thought that the VC would stay and fight and we would still kill them all."

As Waters turned away to stifle a laugh, Pope said, "OK, I understand. I have to admit that I wanted to shoot the VC colonel because I thought you might miss him, too. You'll get to split 31,000 Piastres for the colonel and his weapon. But damn it, in the future, you just do as I say!"

"Yes, sir! We will follow your orders."

The Yards all came to attention and gave their best hand salutes.

"Now go change your uniforms and be back in twenty minutes. I want to get a picture of you with the dead colonel."

They all scurried off toward the market place together, like chastised children.

"Hey, sir, remember what I said last night. Shit happens. We got the colonel, and we didn't get ambushed. It was a successful mission," Waters said as he laughed again.

Pope shook his head, smiled and walked back to where the people were crowded around the body of the dead colonel. The chopper crew chief already had the colonel's belt and pistol strapped around his waist. Pope walked over to him and reached out his hand.

"Thanks for securing the weapon for me, Sergeant. I'll take it now."

The soldier dutifully unbuckled the belt and handed it to him. Dang approached with a big grin and shook hands with him.

"Congratulations, but what happened? Didn't the colonel have any guards?"

"Yes, but my Yard team didn't trust Waters or my marksmanship, so we all shot at the colonel, and no one shot at the guards," Pope said shaking his head in disgust.

"Well, the important thing is that we killed Khanh. I would like to have a chopper take the dead colonel, Major Nhia, and me to Saigon to identify the body and report to higher headquarters. Will you come with us?"

"No, thanks, Captain Dang. Someone should stay here. Besides, I have to write a report that goes through US channels. But you can have the chopper. I would like you to take Lau and his wife and baby with you because they should be relocated to the Mekong Delta for their own protection."

Pope thought he *didn't want to be lost in Saigon waiting around and watching the province chief and deputy province chief take bows for the Yard's kill. He would rather throw a party for the R & I platoon tonight.*

"Of course. But we will need to give him the reward."

"The funds are in the safe at the advisory compound. I'll get it when we go to Binh Tuy."

After taking several pictures of Colonel Khanh and the team, he had them wrap the colonel in a poncho and load him back on the chopper. The MedCap and R & I teams loaded on the other chopper, and they returned to sector headquarters. Someone must have radioed province headquarters because by the time they had arrived in Binh Tuy, a crowd had formed, and several officials from the headquarters were there as well as Major Nhia, Major Sullivan and the rest of the advisory team.

*   *   *

Shortly after their arrival, a fixed wing aircraft landed, carrying a US army Brigadier General from MACV headquarters—**the** J2,—and a reporter from *The Stars and Stripes*. There was also a reporter from the major Saigon newspaper. Sullivan had contacted MACV and reported the kill. He anticipated the need for the reward money and had it with him when he met the chopper.

The general shook hands with Pope and said, "Congratulations on killing the highest-ranking VC in the war. You did an outstanding job. We need enterprising young officers like you in J-2. How would you like to come and work for me?"

"Thank you, sir, but there is still a lot to do here in the field. We have just started building our team, and I don't think now is a good time to leave them," Pope said, hoping that the General did not know that he was originally assigned to J-2.

"That's OK, son, I understand how you feel. We need officers like you in the field, too. I just wish to hell I could get out of Saigon and into the field."

After about two hours of answering questions and picture taking, Sullivan, Major Nhia, Dang, Lau, and the General took off in a chopper to Saigon with "their" trophy. The fixed wing aircraft that brought the general took Lau's family and possessions.

"Sergeant Waters, how about contacting Ma and have him set up a party for the R & I platoon?" Pope said.

"Roger that, sir. I took the liberty of already doing that for you. We're to be there at 2000 hours," he said with a grin.

"There you go, reading my mind again! Thanks. I don't know about you, but I'm still jumping around with these damn red ants in my pants. I'm heading home for a shower. You coming?"

"I'm with you Dai Uy. I feel like I've been beat in the ass with a wet rabbit!"

*   *   *

While they were in the shower Pope lathered himself with soap.

"Say, Sarge, I heard the team calls me 'IceMan,' and it came from you. Is that right?"

The sergeant took his time lathering up his body with soap. He said, slowly and sheepishly, "Well, yes sir, but there was never any disrespect meant. It's just that nothing seems to rattle you. It seems that the deeper you get in shit, the cooler you get. I really believe that your eleventh commandment is, 'Thou shalt not sweat'."

"I get rattled, Sarge, but I just don't like to show it. It makes people nervous."

"I hear you, sir. But I meant no disrespect. Hell, I think you know that I'll follow you anywhere."

"Well, there may be a limit to that, too, Waters. But while we're on the subject of nicknames. I can't let you get away with hanging one on me without me giving you one."

"OK, sir, but go easy on me," Waters said, clearly worried.

"A week or so ago Jutte and I were talking and I said that you reminded me of someone. He asked me whom, and I said John Wayne. You're big, and you're ugly. So now I dub you, Duke Waters." He tapped the naked 'Duke' on both shoulders with his bar of soap and laughed.

"All right sir, it could have been a hell of a lot worse. I was worried that you might call me candy ass or something."

*   *   *

That night almost the entire advisory team went to the airstrip for the party with the R & I platoon. There was plenty to eat and drink, and the story about the killing of Colonel Khanh was repeated. Ma stepped to the platform and asked Pope and Duke to join him as he made a speech in Vietnamese.

"We want to thank Captain Pope and Sergeant Waters for all they have done for us. I give them the traditional Montagnard copper bracelets. They are only given by the tribesmen to outsiders they respect."

He placed one on the right wrist of each advisor. The other soldiers nodded and clapped their hands.

"Captain Pope came to our country and helped give the soldiers pride in themselves and their families. Together, we will build a legend of the American that looks like Vietnamese and built a fighting group of tribesman just like his Indian tribe at home. And Sergeant Waters is our Montagnard 'Duke Wayne'."

The tribesmen nodded and applauded, but the Americans laughed loud and long. Even those that couldn't speak Vietnamese understood the joke about Duke Waters.

Since the platoon had been formed, Pope had transported the Yards to the advisory compound to watch the nightly movies and their favorite was John Wayne. Pope presented the reward money to the killer team and gave them two days off because they wanted to take the money to their families.

*   *   *

Pope and White spent the following week working with Dang and the SOIC, planning more search and destroy operations for the RF battalion. The R & I platoon sent out two ambush teams each night around villages in Ham Tan District. Pope felt that with the killing of Colonel Khanh, terrorist activity would pick up a bit. He did not have to wait long. Four days after the killing, a villager brought in a poster to the Hoi Duc district chief that was issued by the Viet Cong. It offered a 5,000 Piastre reward for the "killing of the enemy of the people, Captain John Pope, American advisor." When it reached the advisory compound Pope took some good-natured ribbing from the team, particularly Jutte.

"This must be an insult to only offer a sixth of what Captain Pope had placed on the colonel's head."

"Yeah. I am offended by the amount, but I had to expect that Charlie would do the same thing to me. It doesn't mean much because they want to kill advisors anyway. It's not as though they'll make a concerted effort."

Privately, his thoughts *ran back to what his grandfather had said many times: No one will die! People die in combat, but he had never heard of the enemy putting a price on the head of an infantry captain before. Instead of being intimidated, he would have to be even more active against the Viet Cong. Besides, if Grandfather was right, the spirit of the whale that had protected all the Makah warriors protected Pope.*

Chapter Seventeen

"You men are to go to Saigon and have medals pinned on you," Sullivan informed Pope and Waters. "Report to MACV headquarters at 0900 hours on Friday in class A uniforms."

"With your permission, I would like to stay the week-end, sir?" Waters asked.

"That's fine sergeant. You've earned it. Captain Pope, you'll need to be back early Saturday for the planned search and destroy operation."

"Damn, I forgot about that. I guess I'll be back Saturday, too," Waters said.

"Go ahead and stay, Sarge. I can take Lieutenant Jutte in your place," Pope said.

"OK, I'll let Captain James know about the change," Sullivan said.

*　　*　　*

Pope telephoned Kathryn's office in Saigon and made contact.

"Hi, Honey, I have to be at MACV at 0900 hours tomorrow morning for a ceremony. Can you meet me at 1200 hours at the Brinks Hotel bar?"

"Oh Johnny, it's so good to hear your voice. I'm sure I can get the day off."

"That's great. Do you think you can get your friend for a date with Bill Jamison? Remember that we both owe him."

"I told my friend about Captain Jamison. She's sitting right here, Johnny, but that means I'll have to find someone else to take my duty on

Friday—but I think so. Yes—she's nodding to me now. Do you want me to contact Captain Jamison for you?"

"Hey, that would really be a big help. It shouldn't be hard for you to locate him. He's in the MACV assignment office."

"All right. I'm really anxious to see you."

"Me too—It won't be long." He hung up and turned to Waters.

"I hope you can find something to do in Saigon, Duke. As you heard, I'm busy all day."

"Sir, I've been in the army for 16 years and have had worldwide assignments from Korea to Germany. I think I can find my way to the bright lights."

*   *   *

Early the next morning, Pope and Waters got into their Class A khaki uniforms and a helicopter picked them up at 0800 hours. The flight to Saigon took 45 minutes.

"You guys must really be VIP's, Captain," the lieutenant pilot said to Pope over the intercom.

"Hell, no. We're just ordinary grunts."

"Oh yeah? I radioed Tan Son Nhut for landing instructions and they told me that I had been ordered to land at the pad at MACV headquarters. Only VIP's land there."

The helicopter slowed as they landed in the fenced in MACV compound. A major met them and escorted them into a building. He told them they were going to the office of the Commander of United States forces, MACV (COMUSMACV).

A security sergeant at the office door took their weapons and baggage. When they entered the outer office, Pope was surprised to see Kathryn and Bill Jamison seated there. Kathryn jumped up, ran into his arms, and gave him a big kiss.

"Johnny! I'm so proud of you! I read in *The Stars and Stripes* about you killing the VC colonel, but I didn't know they were going to give you a medal. Why didn't you tell me when we spoke yesterday?" Without hesitating, she turned to Waters and stood on tiptoes as she hugged him and kissed his cheek. "It's good to see that you're taking good care of my guy, Sergeant Waters. Thanks."

"My pleasure, ma'am," Waters said, grinning.

Pope looked around the office and saw several secretaries and army officers watching them, smiling. He became visibly embarrassed. Waters covered his laugh with a big paw.

"Well, I didn't think it was going to be such a big deal, and besides, I had help from Waters and some Yards." He turned to Jamison and said, "Good to see you, Bill. I guess you're the one that located the place and told Kathryn."

"It's a small price to pay for the double date we're going on tonight, old buddy." He extended his right hand and said "Hi, Sergeant Waters, I'm Captain Jamison. I'm glad to meet you. I've heard a lot about you."

"Thanks, Captain. The pleasure is all mine."

The major returned and ushered the four people into the general's office. Inside the large room, standing at attention in front of his desk, was the same general officer that talked with the planeload of new personnel the day Pope arrived in-country. He wore a starched, short sleeve khaki uniform that had four silver stars on each side of the collar. He had a black leather belt and holster with a pearl handled revolver strapped to his hip. Behind the desk were an American flag and a red flag with four white stars. Several field grade officers stood to the rear of the room.

As Kathryn and Jamison joined the group of observers, Pope and Waters marched up to the general and together rendered their best hand salutes. An army captain read from a citation that both men were awarded the Silver Star medal for actions that resulted in the killing of the highest-ranking Viet Cong officer in the war. When the captain finished, the general took a medal from a sergeant and pinned it on Pope's breast pocket, shook hands and saluted. He repeated the process with Waters.

"Stand at ease," The general said and he paused. "I am very proud of both of you men. Killing a high ranking Viet Cong officer will indeed help the Vietnamese in their war. I expect even bigger things from you in the future. Captain Pope, I hope this doesn't backfire on you, because I heard there's a price on your head," he added, with a smile.

Laughter filled the room, but Kathryn wasn't smiling. After having coffee and cake with the guests, the general turned to the major.

"Sam, I know these soldiers need a ride to their quarters. Can you lay on my car for them?"

"Of course, sir."

Outside the office, the two men picked up their weapons and rucksacks. Pope turned to Waters and asked, "Where are you staying, Duke?"

"I've already made arrangements to meet an old running mate that works here in J-4 and stay with him. I don't need a ride. Besides, if I rode in a general's sedan, all I would do is worry that some MP would arrest me for car theft. I guess I'll see you when I get back on Sunday night. Lt. Jutte should be fine on that operation with you tomorrow, sir."

The major escorted Pope and Kathryn to a waiting staff car and removed the red flag with the four stars from it.

"Drop the couple off wherever they want to go and return."

When they were seated in the back seat, Pope said, "Brinks Hotel, driver."

"You're getting to be quite a celebrity. You get a medal and a ride in the Commanding General's car. You really know how to impress a girl," Kathryn said.

She kissed him on the mouth.

"Yeah, I guess I **have** come a long way from Neah Bay. I just wish my grandfather was still alive to see this."

"What operation was Sergeant Waters talking about?"

"Just a little search and destroy mission in Tanh Linh District that I'm going on with an RF company. There seems to be more VC activity in the sector, and we have to get more units moving around to make contact."

"But why do you have to go? Why not the battalion advisors?"

"The senior advisor has been so short that he stays in the compound. If the advisors don't go, then the battalion will just sit on their ass in the contonement area. The VC will have the run of the sector. We're all taking our turns."

"Well, you be careful. I heard about that reward on your head, and there just might be a smart VC out there that's scheming to bring you down."

"Nah. The bullet hasn't been made to kill me. Besides, I have the spirit of the whale going for me. But let's change the subject. What else do you have planned for me today?"

Kathryn's face twisted slightly, and then she smiled.

"First, let's get you out of that uniform, then go do some shopping. I want to pick up your suit and my dress and buy some accessories. Bill Jamison and I have a big night planned for the four of us. We're to meet him at 1900 hours at your hotel bar, and we'll go to dinner and dancing."

*   *   *

The car stopped in front of the Brinks Hotel, and the driver got out and opened the door for the couple. Pope thanked the driver, and they entered the hotel. Jamison had already made room reservations for them. In their room, Kathryn put her arms around him and kissed him on the mouth.

"Now, let me help you out of that uniform."

"Sounds like a good plan, but can I put my weapons and our luggage down first?"

"You're such a spoilsport. I guess so," Kathryn said and she walked to the bathroom with an exaggerated strut.

Pope unpacked his civilian clothes, put his CAR 15 under the bed, and set his pistol on the nightstand. He was just taking off his shoes when

Kathryn returned wearing nothing but a beautiful smile. She tiptoed to Pope as he stood. Then she looked down below his belt and saw the bulge in his pants.

"Well, it looks like you're ready, too."

"I'm always ready for you, Sweetheart."

Pope put his arms around her. He kissed her and felt her naked body against his. She unbuttoned his shirt and unbuckled his belt. She unbuttoned his trousers, and as his pants fell to the floor, she helped him remove his shirt. Pope fell backward on the bed with her on top of him, and they rolled over. He kissed her heaving breasts as she moaned quietly and reached down to stroke him. She pulled him toward her and put him inside her. Pope moved up and down as he felt her—soft, and moist. Her hips heaved, and her head bobbed as she made animal sounds. Kathryn and Pope suddenly screamed as they both climaxed at the same time.

He rolled over and continued to hug her. Kathryn whispered in his ear, "That was the best ever, Johnny."

"You know, when we're 'coupled' I feel we're actually connected."

"What do you mean?"

"It's like we're not just together physically, but spiritually, too."

"I know what you mean. It's like we're a part of each other."

"Yeah. It's the most wonderful feeling in the world. I wish it could last forever," Pope said with a chuckle, visualizing a perpetual erection.

"So do I, Johnny."

Within minutes, both were asleep in each other's arms.

*   *   *

He awakened first and looked at Kathryn, sleeping peacefully, for about ten minutes.

She opened her eyes and saw him.

"Hey, there's a soldier in my bed, and he's staring at me."

"I've already told you that I never get tired of looking at you." He kissed her lightly on both eyes and added, "It's after noon. Shall we get something to eat?"

"I don't feel like leaving this bed, but I know we only have the day."

They showered together, dressed, and went to the restaurant on the roof to eat. After a leisurely lunch, they caught a taxi to the tailor shop and picked up Pope's suit and Kathryn's dress. They did some sightseeing in Cholon because Kathryn wanted to stop by her room for a minute, then they went shopping at the big Post Exchange in Saigon. He thought how strange it was to lie in ambush and kill a man one-day, and a few days later, be a tourist in downtown Saigon.

On the way back to the hotel, they stopped and picked up some snake skin shoes Kathryn had ordered earlier. Above his complaints, Kathryn insisted he wear his new suit that evening. He wore a blue opened neck sport shirt, drawing the line at wearing the necktie Kathryn had bought for him at the Post Exchange. Kathryn wore the emerald green silk dress he bought for her, and her new snake skin pumps. As the garment was tailor made, it showed off every curve in her body.

They went downstairs and caught a cab back to Cholon to Kathryn's quarters to pick up Bill's date. Waiting in the lobby was a pretty, twenty-something woman, blond hair, blue eyes—a little taller than Kathryn, and with an impish grin. She was wearing a red dress that accented her attractive figure.

"Well, you must be Barbara Justice. Kathryn has told me a great deal about you. I'm Johnny Pope, and I'm sure glad to meet you."

"I've been looking forward to meeting you, too, Johnny. To hear Kathryn talk, you're some where between Superman and Jimmy Stewart." She laughed, and Kathryn beamed.

*   *   *

The trio went back to the taxi and returned to the Brinks Hotel.

Pope entered the restaurant with a woman on each arm. Within seconds, Jamison approached them from the bar, shook hands with Pope, kissed Kathryn lightly on the cheek, and turned to Barbara.

"Hi, I'm Bill Jamison, I've been looking forward to meeting you."

"I'm Barbara Justice, and I'm pleased to meet you, too, Bill. Kathryn has told me a lot about you," Barbara said flashing her white teeth.

"Well, folks, we can either stand here and stop all traffic and activity while everyone stares and envies, or we can go to a restaurant of my choice for dinner," Jamison said.

"Dinner gets my vote," Kathryn said and pulled Pope toward the exit.

Jamison said, "I have reservations at the Mekong floating restaurant. Has anyone been there before?"

Barbara had been there once before and liked it. The others had not.

A taxi took them to a beautiful restaurant on a barge on the Mekong River. When they entered the crowded restaurant, Pope noticed most of the clientele were GI's escorting Vietnamese women, but there were a large number of Vietnamese and Chinese couples. They all showed the same interest in Kathryn and Barbara.

After they were seated, Jamison said, "They have Chinese, Vietnamese, and French food here. All of it good. Don't you think, Barbara?"

"I really like the French food here."

Jamison ordered a before-meal wine, then all of them ordered from the French menu. Jamison good-naturedly tried to talk Pope into ordering the Escargot—snails, steam-cooked in butter, but he stayed with the more conventional Filet Mignon.

"I thought your people liked stuff with hard shells, Johnny." Jamison kidded.

"Some of **my people** do, some don't. I like clams, but I don't care for oysters—or snails—fancy name or not."

"Kathryn told me that you're from an Indian tribe in Washington State, Johnny. That's interesting. I was a history major, and I'm fascinated by Indian history," Barbara said.

"I'm fascinated with **one** Indian in particular," Kathryn said, rubbing Pope's hand to the laughter of the others.

"I read where some Washington State tribes were whalers centuries ago. Did your tribe hunt for whales?" Barbara asked.

"Yes. I had promised to tell you about my grandfather, Kathryn. Now is as good a time as any. He was a tribal chief. He was a whale hunter until 1927, when the US government put the whales on the endangered species list."

"But the Indians didn't kill too many whales. I read that white commercial whalers over-harvested them," Barbara interrupted.

"Yeah. It was devastating to our tribe because whales were not only something our tribe needed to live, but they were a big part of our culture."

"What do you mean by 'your culture'?" Kathryn asked.

"My grandfather told me the Makahs have been a warrior people for centuries, and they got their strength from the spirit of the whale. The whale is part of all our art work."

"Has the whaling ban had any effect on people in your tribe now?" Jamison queried.

"Yeah, it's affected the spirit of the people. They fish for salmon and halibut like they always have, but the spirit of the whale is missing. It seems the prosperity of the tribe dissipated soon after the whaling ban. But they have continued to be warriors. On a per capita basis the Makahs have sent more young men and women off to war than any other community in the Olympic Peninsula, and no Makah has been killed. Some of the elders have said it has been because of the spirit of the whale."

"So you're saying that the Makahs have powerful medicine. The spirit of the whale will keep you from getting killed in war?" Jamison questioned.

"I'm just saying many Makah people believe it. I'm not really convinced, but I'll tell you when I rotate back to the states," Pope said, and they all laughed.

"So you don't really believe you have a 'spirit' shield that keeps something from killing you in Vietnam?" asked Barbara.

"There's more to it than that. My grandfather encouraged me to be a warrior since I was a small child. He said I should prepare myself for war. I went into the hills and came back with a vision that I was to be a warrior leader. I've spent my entire life grooming myself for just that. From throwing rocks into the waves and throwing a whaling harpoon to throwing a football and hand grenades. From taking cold baths in the stream every morning and running 3 to 5 miles every day when I was in high school to being in good physical condition now. From living and moving at night in the Olympic forest, to going to Ranger and Jungle Warfare schools to learn how to fight this kind of war. I even played football because I believe the game is a minor form of war."

Jamison let out a deep breath and said, "That's really interesting. You gals are pretty good. Johnny and I lived together for two years at Bragg, and he never told me all this stuff. I hear you saying you have trained your whole life to be a soldier, and that it's possible you're protected from harm by a whale spirit."

"What I heard is the Makahs may be protected by a whale spirit, but they can hedge their bet by being better soldiers," Kathryn added.

"But what about the artillery shell that kills someone five feet away from a Makah, and the Indian survives? That's just luck, not skill," Jamison retorted.

"So my argument stands up. In that case, he is protected by the whale spirit," Kathryn replied.

"Oh, that reminds me. I've got that opening in the Vietnamese Airborne Brigade you were waiting for. Are you still interested?" Jamison asked

"No, thanks. My system wouldn't be able to handle it. I've started some programs in Binh Tuy that I want to finish. Besides, I'm just a plain old reservation Indian with simple tastes."

"Don't bull shit a bull shitter, Johnny, you've come a long way from the reservation. But I was pretty sure you were happy where you are."

"This discussion could go on all night. Let's talk about something more interesting. Where is this place we're going for dancing, Bill?" Pope said.

"It's called Francois, and is owned by a Frenchman. I think you'll like it, Johnny, because it's so loud you can't hold a conversation there."

They finished their meal and caught a taxi to Francois. It was a single story nightclub about the size of the club on the roof of the Brinks Hotel, but it was enclosed and air-conditioned. It had a bandstand and stage near a dance floor, with tables all the way to a bar on the other side of the room. The floorshow was in progress as they entered. There were four Vietnamese women dancing to an American song sung by a male Vietnamese vocalist.

As they waited for a table, Jamison leaned toward the trio and shouted, "I've been told most of the Vietnamese singers can't understand or speak English. They learn the lyrics of the songs by listening to American recordings."

"If that's true, he sure does a terrific job with 'I Left My Heart in San Francisco,'" Kathryn shouted back.

A waitress led them to a table about four rows from the dance floor. A Vietnamese comedian told some pretty raunchy jokes. After the show, the band played dance music, and the two couples moved to the floor. Their discussions were limited to talking in each other's ear while dancing. The comedian appeared again and announced it was 11:30 PM—there would only be one more number before closing.

"We have a 2400 hours curfew in Saigon, Johnny," Jamison said after the last dance. "We should take separate taxis because I have to get Barbara home," he added with a wink.

"Sounds fine to me. It's really been a great night. I hope you enjoyed yourself, Barbara. It would be nice if the four of us can get together again," Pope replied.

"I'd like that, Johnny. Kathryn and I don't socialize with each other enough. And I'm really pleased to be able to spend some time with you and Bill."

"I think that can be arranged. Don't you, Bill?"

"Roger that! We'll see you folks real soon," Jamison said, shaking Pope's hand and kissing Kathryn on the cheek. He turned and took Barbara by the elbow and led her out the door to a taxi.

Pope and Kathryn got in their own taxi. He put his arm around her, and she put her head on his shoulder.

"This has really been a super day, Johnny," Kathryn said with a sigh.

"Yeah, it's really been special being with you."

"What I especially enjoyed is that I learned so much more about you."

"I talked a whole lot more than I wanted to. I hope I didn't monopolize the conversation."

"No, you just answered questions, and the others were interested in your heritage."

"Well, next time we talk less about me and more about you," Pope said, and he pulled her closer to him.

When they got to the hotel room, Kathryn said, "I meant to ask you, Johnny, why did you call Sergeant Waters, 'Duke'?"

Pope laughed. "The mystery is solved, and that's my pay back. I found out Waters gave me the nickname of IceMan because he thinks I'm cool under fire. I told him that I didn't have any hard feelings, but I had to give him a nickname. He reminds me of John Wayne because he's so big and ugly, so I dubbed him Duke."

"That's so funny. When I first met him, he reminded me of John Wayne, too." Kathryn frowned. "Bill Jamison mentioned the Airborne Brigade. Does he have an assignment for you in Saigon, Johnny?"

"When I first arrived in country, I tried to get in the Airborne Brigade to be with some friends from Fort Bragg. I also thought that it was a good outfit. I found out that it is nothing more than a palace guard and rarely gets to the field. There were no vacancies, so Bill got me reassigned from Saigon to Binh Tuy."

"But if you took the airborne assignment, you would be stationed here in Saigon with me."

"Don't you have to go out in the field quite often?

"Yes, but we would still be able to see each other more often," Kathryn responded, clearly irritated.

"I thought about that, Kathryn, but I wasn't meant to be a Saigon commando. I'd love to be stationed close to you so I could see you more often. I'm just happy in the field."

"I think you're being selfish about this, Johnny. I have plenty of opportunity for dates here, but I turn them down because of you. I'd like you to reconsider," she said, voice rising.

"There's nothing to reconsider. I've made my decision. I'm sorry we don't agree. You have to make your own decisions about your life."

"Then maybe *I* should do some reconsidering," she pouted.

Pope waited, watching her face, giving her a chance to say more. She just sat and looked down at her hands.

"I have to be up at 0-dark-thirty to go to Tan Son Nhut and catch a chopper back to Binh Tuy. Why don't I call the desk for a wake up call for 0500? Since tomorrow is a day off for you, just stay here until you're ready to head home. There's no point in you getting up that early just to say good-bye to me. Besides, the curfew ends at 0600, and I have to be at the airfield then."

"Fine."

They both sat in silence for what seemed like an eternity and Kathryn quietly stood and walked to the bathroom and closed the door behind her. Pope picked up the phone and made the call to the front desk. He packed everything except what he planned to wear in the morning, and slipped under the covers. Kathryn came out of the bathroom and quietly got into bed.

As she lay in bed, facing away from Pope, Kathryn thought: *Why does Johnny have to just think of himself? He's had plenty of action. Why not take an easier job in Saigon? The Airborne Brigade is prestigious, and might even get into combat. He would be with his friends. We could even get an apartment together. Sure, I would have to go up-country sometimes, but it's not as though I would be in danger—like he is. God, why does he have to spoil things by being so pig-headed. He said, I would have to make my decision about myself. Well, how would he like it if I cut him loose and found someone else? There's plenty of fish in the sea. And more men then women in Vietnam—yeah!*

Who am I trying to kid? If there were, I would have found him before I met Johnny. He's so perfect compared to all the others. I know he loves me. And he makes me feel good. I can't think of anything else but him when he's not around. Part of why I love him is because he's a warrior. That's why I'm so proud of him.

Why is it that whenever a woman finds a man, she tries to change the very things about him that she found attractive in the first place? If I forced him to transfer to Saigon he may never forgive me. Hey lady—you're kidding yourself again. You're not going to change his mind. He's made his decision and told you to make yours. Hell, I don't want him to change. I love him the way he is.

I just hate to give in to him. Daddy was right, he said I always get my own way, and someday I was going to be in for a rude awakening. I guess this is it. But how do I give in gracefully?

Kathryn turned over to her other side, and saw Johnny, on his side, facing her. "Johnny? Johnny?" she whispered. He snored quietly.

Well, I'll have to wake up when he does in the morning, and apologize to him. She kissed him softly on the forehead and lie there thinking what a fool she had been to ruin the perfect day and risk losing him. *I'm not going to take that chance again,* she thought as she drifted off into a deep sleep.

*　　*　　*

At 0500 the phone rang, and Pope picked it up quickly, hoping not to awaken Kathryn, set it in the cradle gently, and got up. He went into the bathroom, shaved, and dressed. Then went back to the bedroom, took his pistol from under the pillow and kissed the still sleeping Kathryn on the forehead. He reached under the bed, picked up the CAR 15 and his rucksack.

Pope had made arrangements for a jeep to pick him up at the hotel to take him to II Corps air ops. The jeep was parked at the curb in front of the hotel. The driver was talking to one of the guards. Pope threw his gear in the back seat and mounted the vehicle. The driver got in, started the engine, pulled away, and drove silently down the deserted street.

When they arrived at the corrugated steel building, the ops sergeant said "Good morning, Captain Pope, you're just in time. The chopper will be taking off in 15 minutes. Would you like a cup of coffee and a donut?"

"I'd love one of each, Sarge. You're a lifesaver."

After his breakfast, Pope ran out to the waiting chopper and sat quietly during the flight to Binh Tuy, thinking about how great the previous day and evening had been. *I just wish it hadn't ended the way it did. Did I make the right decision about staying in Binh Tuy? I hope that Kathryn cools off and sees things differently.*

His reflections turned back to his little war. *There has to be a spy or spies among us. But who are they? Where are they? What can we do to stop them? We have enjoyed some success with combat operations, but too many had turned out to be just "nature walks." Was the next one going to be just another walk in the sun? Or am I going to need the whale spirit?*

Chapter Eighteen

When the chopper settled down at the helipad in Binh Tuy, Jutte sat waiting in a jeep. Pope thanked the pilot for the lift, jumped from the chopper, and walked to the jeep.

"Morning, sir, First Company is scheduled to leave by fixed wing to Tanh Linh in one hour. I'll brief you as we go," Jutte said. He started the engine of the jeep, and shifted it into gear.

"Damn, Jack, I hate going out with Diem and his outfit. He not only doesn't know what he's doing but doesn't show much interest in learning."

"I know, sir, but his company was the only one available."

The vehicle entered the advisory compound and braked to a halt.

"Well, what bothers me is that we'll be searching an area that we haven't occupied for several months."

"What sort of intelligence have you gotten from your spies, sir?" Jutte asked as they walked to Pope's room.

"The good news is: the sightings have been no larger than two or three-armed VC together. The bad news: is if we run across a good size unit, Diem may not be up to the job."

"We don't have artillery support because we're out of range from Tanh Linh, and US air support is one hour away. We have medevac choppers available on call. I'll carry the radio. I asked Sgt. Duc to stand by in case you want him."

Pope re-packed his rucksack for the patrol and said, "Damn, I hate not having artillery support. I would like Duc to go with us. If we get into deep shit, I want to communicate with Diem fast, and I'm afraid I won't be able to think in Vietnamese quickly enough."

"I've laid on the best scout from the R & I platoon, sir."

"That's good news. I have some real bad vibes about this operation. Take a couple extra smoke grenades this time, just in case we have more medevacs than usual," Pope said, and he hooked two extra red smoke grenades on his own harness. "Now, let's go see the Major," he added.

"OK, sir, I'll meet you in his office. I have to stop by my room and pick up my gear and the extra smoke grenades."

Pope laughed as Jutte's big body lumbered at an exaggerated double time to the ammo bunker on the opposite side of the volleyball court.

"Well, the celebrity has returned. How was the ceremony, Johnny?" Sullivan smirked as he looked up from his desk.

"Just fine, sir. And thank you for putting us in for the awards," Pope answered, knowing Sullivan had not recommended the awards. They had come from COMUSMACV—which was why it didn't take so long.

"I didn't have anything to do with it. That came straight from COMUSMACV."

"Anyway, thanks. Did Sergeant White give you the maps covering our operational area? He was to prepare them for Jutte and me."

"Here they are. By the way, right after you left yesterday, we got word Captain James got a four-day drop because his replacement was in country. Three hours later, Rick was on a chopper to Saigon. He said to tell you that he was sorry he wasn't able to see you before he left but was sure that you'd understand."

"I wonder what the hell the short timer will have to talk about now? Yeah, I'm sorry I missed him. When is his replacement supposed to be here?"

"Monday. And he's bringing a medic we've been waiting a long time for."

"Outstanding. Maybe I can get a little more Intel work from White now."

"Did you get any sleep last night?"

Before Pope could answer, White, Duc, and Jutte walked in.

"Sir, I'll be taking you to the airstrip. Are you ready?" White said,

"Roger that, White." Pope turned to Sullivan and said, "I got plenty of sleep. I'll see you in three days, sir."

They all packed into the jeep and rode silently to the airstrip. Two US Air Force C-123 transports were parked on the tarmac near the covered pad. The First Company had not arrived yet. Forty-five minutes after scheduled lift off, the unit was airborne. Pope fumed because it was typical of the way Diem didn't pay attention to details. They landed at Tanh Linh, about thirty-five miles north of sector headquarters. When the aircraft were off-loaded, he took Diem aside and spread his map on the ground to review the operations order.

They both squatted on the ground; Pope pointed at a spot on the map and said in Vietnamese, "We are here. Now, as Captain Dang explained to me, we are to move out on a search and destroy operation due west for 10 kilometers today and set up in a night perimeter defense. The second day, we travel 18 kilometers in a southeasterly direction and set up another night perimeter. On the third day, we head back to our current location to be picked up and taken by air back to sector headquarters." He followed the map with his fingers as he talked.

Lt. Diem nodded several times and responded, "Yes, sir. That is my understanding. I think today we will kill many VC, sir."

"Since we have not operated in this area in force for many months, I suggest we move slowly and with caution. We don't know if there are any VC units located in this area. Where is the quick reaction force located?"

"Second Company is located here and will come to help if we need them."

"Good. They will need choppers to deploy to our location. Let's hit the trail, Lieutenant." Pope said. He stood and folded his map.

"Sir, I have already ordered the men to take their noon meal before we leave. We should depart in about an hour."

Pope didn't answer but was clearly irritated by the lieutenant's dallying around.

*   *   *

An hour and a half later, the company departed the airstrip—Pope steaming. The Yard scout was at the point followed by the lead rifle platoon the command group—Pope, Duc, and Jutte: and the other two rifle platoons. The weapons platoon's 30-cal. Machine guns and 60 mm mortars were attached to the rifle platoons. As they walked in column, Pope thought *there was no way that they would be able to cover the planned ten kilometers today.*

It was the dry season, and the heat was almost unbearable as the troops cut their way through the jungle brush and vines. Pope noticed that they were walking on a trail.

"We have orders to stay off trails, Lieutenant."

Diem took the radio handset and talked to the platoon leader ahead, then turned to him and said, "We are getting off the trail now, sir."

An hour later, Pope noticed that the pace had quickened because the lead platoon was back on a trail. Followed by Diem, Duc, and Jutte, Pope hurried past the lead platoon to his Yard scout grabbed his shoulder and spun him around.

"You have been told to stay off trails. Why are we on one again?"

"I am sorry, Captain. The platoon leader told me to take the trails both times."

Diem spun on his heel and walked to the platoon leader and screamed at him in Vietnamese.

"You are to stay off trails forever!"

The rest of the day was a nature walk with no contact or casualties. When they stopped at 1800 hours to establish a night perimeter, they had traveled about six kilometers. After dinner, Jutte made a commo check to be sure he could call the medevac choppers.

He walked to where Pope was lying on his poncho liner checking his map. "We have commo with medevac, sir."

"Thanks, Jack. At least **something** isn't fucked up today."

"I'd be a damn sight happier if someone else was commanding this unit, sir."

"You and me both. I'm not just pissed off; I'm worried about this guy. Stick real close to me tomorrow in case something happens."

They were in a triple canopy, so darkness enveloped them early. Pope told Jutte to get some sleep, and he would remain on watch all night.

*   *   *

It was still dark in their encampment, but the morning sun strained to penetrate the jungle canopy.

Pope shook the sleeping Diem and said, "We'll have to depart early to make up the four kilometers lost yesterday."

"Yes, sir, that should not be a problem. But the men drank all the water from their canteens yesterday, and there are no wells, creeks, or rivers in our operational area."

"Damn, lieutenant, this is the dry season." Frustrated, Pope turned and shook Duc awake. "I need your help to translate because I'm pissed off."

Duc stood and stretched.

"Yes, sir."

"Tell Diem that heat and thirst can be just as deadly as the enemy. Didn't you make plans for aerial delivery of water?"

Duc nodded and translated in a singsong voice, smiling. Then Diem answered in Vietnamese. Duc turned to Pope and translated

"Sir, the Lieutenant says he did not. He thought you would be able to radio Special Zone and have water delivered by chopper."

"God damn it, Duc! I understand some Vietnamese. I heard you say something like, 'The Captain respectfully wants to know if you requested water resupply.' I want you to not only translate verbatim what I say, but in the same tone of voice I use."

"Sir, I cannot be disrespectful to the Vietnamese officer. No matter that I am translating for you. He will lose face in front of his men."

"For Christ sake," Pope said, perturbed at the interpreter's attitude and the commander's lack of planning. "All right. I'll do my own communicating now."

Duc bowed his head and backed up a few steps.

"Look, Lieutenant, water delivery is a goddamn supply mission and should have been requested in advance. We can only get choppers **immediately** for tactical reasons. I don't know if we can get air support for that on such short notice," Pope said in the best Vietnamese he could muster. He turned and left the Lieutenant staring at the ground.

He turned and walked to where Jutte was making a commo check.

"Jack, I just found out…"

"Yes, sir, I heard. I'm trying to get with Special Zone for a supply of water," Jutte interrupted.

Pope thought about how the operation was already a screwed up mess, and it was only a day old. Jutte got through to Special Zone, but they would not deliver the water resupply until the afternoon. Diem grudgingly hurried the troops through breakfast, and they were on the move by 0700 hours. The sun burned off the morning mist and broiled First Company. They traveled through thick elephant grass without incident and made their planned southeasterly turn.

Water became a problem as the thirsty column slowed to a crawl. By noon the blistering afternoon sun offered no mercy. The troops drank from stagnant pools covered with scum. Pope and the advisory group carried two canteens each, so they were not drinking from mud puddles yet.

"Sir, we don't have any food for the men because it takes water to cook rice and soup. How soon can we expect the water supply?" Diem asked.

"Not until some time this afternoon. I noticed that your men are drinking from stagnant water holes. That water is contaminated. Don't you have water purification tablets?"

"No. We've never been this far from water before," Diem said in a slight whimper.

"Jack, get on the radio and find out where the hell the water resupply choppers are and tell them to bring in a supply of iodine tablets as well."

*   *   *

The column trudged through the sweltering heat. At 1600 hours, a single helicopter circled overhead. The unit stopped in an open area of saw grass and scrub brush and provided security for a landing zone. When the chopper settled down, Pope and Jutte ran to the Huey, and the door gunner handed a single five-gallon can of water to the advisors. Then he reached into his pocket and brought out three small bottles of iodine pills.

The stunned advisor poked the pilot in the shoulder and said, "Where is this unit's requested resupply of water?"

"That's it, Captain. Water for three advisors and water purification pills."

"Well, something got fucked up in the translation, because I heard my lieutenant call Special Zone and request water for a Regional Force infantry company."

"I don't know about that. I just did what I was told. Shit happens, sir."

"This outfit is combat ineffective now and needs water immediately. I'm going to call Special Zone again and request another water resupply. Will you take a written message so there are no more screw-ups?"

"Sorry about that, sir. I'll be glad to take the message."

Pope wrote a note in his tablet, tore off the sheet of paper, and slapped it in the hand of the pilot.

"You can count on me sir, You **will** get at least one chopper filled with water delivered to this location before sundown," the pilot said as he put the message in his flack jacket pocket.

Pope went to a dejected Diem and squatted next to him.

"We will get a water supply sometime later today. To avoid heat exhaustion and prostration, we should remain in place until the water is delivered. What water we have should be issued only to the most needy soldiers."

"Thank you. I agree, Captain. I will give the orders to the platoon leaders."

The company formed a night perimeter defense, and the water was given to several soldiers that were sick. Pope scoured the area to find vegetation that held moisture and was consumable. He found some sprouts like the ba-aksh grown on the reservation. He showed Diem how to cut, strip, and suck the moisture from the plant. Diem relayed the information to the platoon leaders.

Soon, several soldiers were dispatched to cut the stalks. Within an hour, every soldier sucked on the moist plants. *Well, Grandfather, it looks like your training in the forest came in handy again*, he thought.

Just before sundown, the Huey returned, followed by a Chinook helicopter with a large rubber bladder sling loaded. The Huey orbited above until the bladder was lowered to the waiting troops. He noticed there was absolutely no discipline as the thirsty mob pushed and jostled to get to the water. Pope, Jutte, and Duc provided security while the troops emptied the bladder. They filled their canteens from it, then drank the water until the canteen was empty, then filled them again. The Chinook returned. Jutte reattached the bladder, and the chopper flew away to the north. The Huey landed in the small landing zone, and Pope ran to greet the pilot.

"Hey, thanks a lot guys. I knew you wouldn't let me down," he shouted over the noise of the aircraft engines.

"We've got twenty-four five gallon cans of water, sir. Can you get some help off loading?"

"Roger that." Pope turned and signaled Jutte, and Jack and six soldiers immediately unloaded the chopper.

"This should last us the night. Will you need a written request to have the same thing delivered at noon tomorrow?"

"No written message is necessary. I told the people in Special Zone there was one pissed-off Airborne-Ranger Captain out here. You'll get the resupply tomorrow. By the way, here's a gross of iodine pills," the pilot said, handing him a large cardboard box.

"Thanks again. I owe you. We'll see you tomorrow."

As the advisory team filled their canteens, Jutte said, "This has really been a screwed up operation. I can't see what else can possibly go wrong."

"I don't either. But you know what Waters says? Shit happens! I'll be glad when we're back in the compound."

The other cans of water were used to prepare dinner, breakfast, and lunch for the troops. The company stayed in the perimeter defense with fifty-percent alert during the night.

"You go ahead and sleep, Jack."

"No, sir. You didn't get any sleep last night."

"I'm OK. I wouldn't be able to sleep anyway."

"If you get real tired, promise me you'll wake me, sir."

"I will, Jack. If we stop tomorrow, I'll try to grab some Zs."

It was more difficult for Pope to stay awake, because he had not had any sleep in forty-eight hours, and not much before that. He had plenty of time to review the operation, and consider what might happen tomorrow. He thought, *we started late and the lead platoon leader tried to make up for it by getting on a trail. Diem forgot to request water delivery in advance. Special Zone screwed up our water resupply request. We're way behind in our operational plan. My interpreter doesn't want to hurt the feelings of a screwed up Vietnamese officer.*

I don't think Makah warriors in other wars had these kinds of problems. At least they were in US units and had the US armed forces behind them. In this war I have to depend on incompetent commanders that I have little influence over. I'm really beginning to wonder if you are going to be right about the whale spirit keeping me alive during this war, Grandfather.

Chapter Nineteen

Pope woke Diem at daybreak, and the troops ate breakfast. Within an hour, they were cutting their way through the jungle. The thick triple canopy kept out the sunlight, stunting the growth of plants underneath, making it easier to move. Pope felt good because they had made up lost ground in the past four hours.

A single shot rang out from the front of the column, followed by several rounds from friendly forces and the column took cover. As they lie on the ground, Diem talked on the radio and turned to Pope.

"The scout has been killed by a sniper, and the VC got away."

"Damn. Do you have someone familiar with the area to lead the column?"

"No, sir, we will have to do it from here, giving directions to the lead platoon leader."

"I guess that will have to do."

The company was on the move again. Pope took a deep breath and kept walking, hoping luck would catch up to the hapless unit. More small arms fire crackled from the front of the column. The force didn't stop, and he asked Diem what was going on. Diem talked on the radio while running and yelled to Pope.

"Sir, the lead platoon has made contact with two VC, and we are chasing them. Today we kill VC."

The entire column moved at a slow trot through the underbrush for about two hundred yards with sporadic firing from the front of the column. Pope really felt nervous about the strung out unit.

Pope said to the panting Diem, "Lieutenant, we need to stop and deploy our forces to attack the VC. We can't just run after them with a hundred men in column."

"No, sir, we kill VC," the sweating Vietnamese commander answered, eyes ablaze.

About ten minutes later, the command group broke out of the jungle into an open area. Pope squinted through the bright sunlight and saw that the lead platoon was running up a ravine. It was 200 yards long and the top of the sides were 100 yards apart. There was only scrub brush and brown saw grass, about knee high. The snipers were leading them into an ambush!

As they reached the ravine where the rise extended 100 yards, he shouted at Diem.

"Stop this God damn column, Lieutenant! This is a perfect place for an ambush and your outfit is spread out all over hell and dead tired."

*   *   *

Diem repeated, "No, sir, we kill VC," and hand grenades exploded around them. Enemy rifle and machine gun fire raked through the ranks of the rag tag mob. One of the cooks next to Pope took machine gun fire in the chest, knocking him against Duc, and they both went sprawling. Everyone immediately hit the ground.

Pope could see that they were in the middle of a perfect L shaped ambush. Two RPD machine guns formed the horizontal part of the L and shot down the long axis of the ravine directly on the column. The green tracers spit out deadly fire on the panting victims hugging the ground. The hail of fire tore through the long, dead grass around them.

Pope saw eight enemy riflemen dug in on the military crest of the rise to his left—the vertical part of the L. He could see the bullets kicking up dirt all around the command group, but couldn't spot any more of the prone RF infantrymen. Pope stuck his head up, but still couldn't see any government soldiers because of the knee-high grass. Diem had his ear to the ground and his eyes closed. Pope could tell Diem was alive because his face was fixed in a grimace.

Jutte was on the ground-to-air radio frequency, calmly repeating, "Any aircraft in the vicinity, this is US advisor on the ground, urgent, come in, over." He turned to Pope and shouted, "Well, sir, we're really in the toilet now, and Charlie is pulling the chain!"

Pope closed his eyes tightly to regain his confidence. *All right, remember what my football coach at State U said—things are never as bad as they seem,* he thought. *Simple solution—attack or die!*

With bullets still hitting all around him Pope crawled to Diem and shouted above the explosions and weapons, "We're in the middle of a kill zone. The only way we can get out is to attack. Now give the order to your platoons."

The cowering Diem replied, "No, we stay here and fight. I will radio for the quick reaction force."

"Shit, we'll all be dead before they hold the first formation. Now give the order, or I will."

Just then one of the cooks lying next to the company commander screamed as two rounds of small arms fire went through his back, killing him instantly. Two rounds hit another cook in the back and leg two yards away. He cried out and lay on his stomach, jerking spasmodically.

"No, we stay here and fight," Diem whimpered.

"Well, then at least fire your goddamn weapon. I'll pass the order."

He motioned to Duc and Diem's radio operator to move closer to him. The two soldiers crawled about ten feet to the frightened commander and Pope.

"Tell the RTO that all soldiers are to drop everything but their weapons and ammo. I am going to throw some smoke grenades to conceal us. Exactly one minute later the lead platoon is to attack at 11 o'clock to 2 o'clock, or straight up to the point of this ravine. The other two platoons will attack from 6 o'clock to 12 o'clock, or up the left side of the ravine. You got it?" Pope shouted to the interpreter, and he turned over on his back and shook his own rucksack off.

For a split second he looked in Duc's eyes and was surprised he couldn't see any fear in them. Duc nodded and passed the message to the RTO, who sent it to the platoons. The RTO shouted he could not reach the last platoon in column, but the others got the message. The crackle of rifle and machine gun fire continued to rain death on the frozen column.

"Jutte, drop your radio and throw all of your smoke grenades down the ravine to give us concealment."

Pope threw smoke grenades up the ravine to cover the lead platoon. The entire hollow looked strange in yellow and red smoke. There was very little breeze, and the depression trapped the smoke, making it difficult for the enemy to pick up targets. Pope took two fragmentation hand grenades from his harness and set them down next to him. He estimated the distance and location of the two machine guns at the top of the rise to his front. *Whale spirit; please let me be accurate with these throws.*

He put one grenade in each hand, pulled both pins and rose to one knee. He looked at the machine gun to the left, 50 yards away, and threw a spiral. He switched the other grenade to his right hand, took aim at the machine gun to his right, and tossed another spiral.

*   *   *

Pope stood, He could see the yellow and red smoke was still covering the RF troops. Pope fired his weapon at the machine guns and sprinted toward them, Jutte, Duc, and the company RTO right behind. Bullets whistled by Pope's head. Not a single soldier from the lead platoon rose to attack. The grenades exploded, and the machine guns stopped. Pope stumbled over two dead RF soldiers, but caught himself and sprinted ahead. He reached the crest of the ravine in seconds and sprayed the prone bodies of three machine gunners hit by grenade fragments.

Pope was far ahead of the small attacking force. He ran about twenty-five yards into the jungle, firing his CAR 15 at the VC at the top of the ravine to his left. Some enemy directed their fire toward him, and he heard the bullets hit the branches of the trees.

When Pope stopped and turned, he could see Duc and Jutte running toward him. The Vietnamese RTO had been killed before he could crest the hill. Jutte fell to the ground, and Duc hesitated momentarily, then ran into the jungle toward Pope. Pope stopped his covering fire and ran to Jutte. Duc turned and followed closely behind. Jutte fired his Thompson at the VC near the crest of the ravine.

"Where are you hit, Jack?"

"The left arm, but I'm OK, sir," Jutte replied. He dropped an empty magazine and inserted a full one in his weapon.

"Good. We've knocked out the machine guns and broken the horizontal part of the L in the ambush. Let's flank the enemy fast. I'm going to lob a couple more grenades along the crest of the hill, and we'll attack."

The VC continued firing down into the ravine, but there were no sounds of returning friendly fire. Pope rose on one knee, threw one grenade about 40 yards and another about 25 yards. The grenades exploded. The three men got to their feet, and ran toward the VC, firing their weapons from the hip and screaming at the top of their lungs. One guerrilla rose from his foxhole to fire and was hit in the face and killed. Another VC rose to fire from another foxhole, and Jutte knocked him backward with a burst from his Thompson.

The three attackers emptied their magazines at almost the same time and dropped to the ground to reload. Within seconds, all firing stopped. The VC were sprinting for the trees. Pope took a grenade from Jutte and lobbed it fifty yards toward the fleeing communists.

*   *   *

Pope, Duc, and Jutte stood where the enemy had stood only minutes earlier, and looked into the ravine. The smoke dissipated. They could see the carnage of the VC ambush. Silence surrounded the three. The smell of cordite, smoke, and death hung in the air.

"It's great to be alive, isn't it?" Pope said.

"I don't see how anyone could have gotten out of that," Jutte said, shaking his head.

"Vietnamese soldiers, this is Sergeant Duc, interpreter for the American advisor," he shouted in Vietnamese. "We are on the top of the hill, and the enemy has fled. If you are injured make some noise or movement if you can." A few moans: some wounded soldiers moved.

"Duc, go pick up Lt. Jutte's radio and bring it up here. Jack, let's have a look at that arm," Pope said, and took Jutte's first aid packet from his belt.

As Duc started down the hill, Pope tore Jutte's sleeve, exposing a bloodied bullet wound on both sides of the lieutenant's arm.

"You're lucky, Jack, the bullet went clear through. There isn't much bleeding, meaning it missed a vessel. You have pretty good movement, meaning it missed the bone. I'll just bandage it for you."

He removed the gauze bandage from the packet, wrapped it around Jutte's beefy arm, and tied it off.

"It hasn't even started hurting yet. When Duc gets back with my radio, I'll start calling for the medevac. Sir, does your foot hurt?"

Pope looked down and saw a hole above the heel of the boot on his right foot. He sat and quickly unlaced his boot, exposing a sock with a small amount of blood around a hole. He removed the sock and breathed a sigh of relief as he wiped the blood away and saw a small wound that barely opened the surface of the skin.

"Got lucky today, Jack. The bleeding has even stopped," he said. He slipped the sock and boot on his foot, smiling.

"As fast as you were moving, I don't see how the fuck a bullet could have found one of your feet," Jutte said, laughing.

Pope could see a couple wounded RF soldiers crawling in the ravine. He looked down near the bottom of the clearing and saw some RF soldiers emerging from the woodline. He waved at them, and they waved back.

Pope walked to the two enemy emplacements and found three dead VC around an RPD machine gun at each position—all killed by the fragmentation grenades. *Damn,* he thought. *Those were some lucky grenade tosses.* He walked the crest of the ravine and found five more dead VC with AK 47s instead of Mas 36s. RPDs, AK 47s—Charlie was raising the stakes. At the end of the woodline he met eleven RF soldiers.

"Do any of you have any medical training?" Pope asked in Vietnamese. They all shook their heads.

He pointed at the two nearest him and said, "You two go identify the wounded men. Put their bayonets on their rifles and stick the bayonet into the ground next to them. Try to make them comfortable until the chopper arrives. You other men take up defensive positions here toward that wood line, in case the VC come back."

Pope walked down into the killing zone for a closer look at the damage done in the ambush. It was clear not many soldiers followed him in the counterattack. It was just as clear not many of them returned fire once they were caught in the open. Several weapons had not been fired at all, but they could have been cut down before they had a chance to use their weapons. Most of the bodies had multiple bullet and grenade fragment wounds. He found Diem's body where he had left him. The lieutenant had a bullet hole in his head and two in his back.

It seemed ironic that on the first operation that he had accompanied Diem, he questioned the officer's aggressiveness. On the second operation the dead Lieutenant's offensiveness cost him his life and command.

He walked the length of the carnage, returned to Jutte's location, and had a pretty complete report. First Regional Force company: forty-four KIA, including three officers, twenty-one WIA; one US advisor WIA—he didn't count his own heel wound. Enemy: Eleven KIA and two machine guns, and nine rifles captured. Counting some more stragglers that joined the group, what was left of First Company was one warrant officer and twenty-five enlisted men.

"Medevac choppers are on the way, sir. Major Sullivan is on his way from sector headquarters."

Great. That's all I need is another lecture from our fearless leader, Pope thought.

"Thanks, Jack. I'm going to get our stragglers together and form a perimeter defense. The choppers can't land in that ravine, so we'll have to carry the wounded to the top. You bring the choppers in here."

A warrant officer was the platoon leader of the last unit in column. Only a small part of his platoon had gotten into the ambush. When he had received Pope's radio message to attack to their left, he did so, but there was no enemy. He didn't think to try to turn the flank of the VC ambush, and he could get no one on the radio for further orders. After telling him to form the perimeter and send some men down to move the wounded to the chopper pick-up point, Pope heard the familiar thump, thump, thump, of the choppers in the distance.

He turned and looked into the sad face of his young interpreter, "Come on Duc, let's go down and see what we can do for the wounded."

*   *   *

When Sullivan got off the Huey, Jutte shook hands with him and said, "Sir, a while ago I never thought I would see you again."

"You've been wounded, Jack. Sit down and fill me in."

Jutte explained how the company commander had led the unit into the ambush and refused to attack to get out.

"The IceMan really took over in a hurry. He commanded the company to attack and led the assault. He even got up on one knee and looked down the muzzles of two machine guns and threw two grenades that were direct hits that knocked them out. The crazy Indian was way out in front of Duc and me when I got hit. He saw it happen and ran back to help me.

Then he decided to turn the flank of the ambush and led a three man assault that saved the lives of the rest of the RF Company."

"You did great, Jack. I'm going to recommend a decoration for you."

"Hell, all I did was follow Ice. Waters was right. Captain Pope doesn't know what fear is."

"Great job, Jack! Now you get on the first chopper out, and we'll visit you as soon as we can," Sullivan said, leading Jutte to a waiting Huey.

Pope and Duc carried the last wounded man to the chopper point where Sullivan and Dang were waiting. Sullivan's attitude changed immediately upon seeing Pope.

"How the hell did you let the company commander lead his unit into this ambush, Captain?"

"I had no control over him, and he had no control over his troops."

"It's good you got the company out, but we lost a lot of good men, John."

"I know that, and I take responsibility for getting us into the ambush as well," Pope replied. He suddenly felt very tired.

"Sir, Captain Pope tried to get Lieutenant Diem to stop the company from chasing the snipers. Then he threw many smoke grenades to conceal us when we attacked the VC." Duc said to Dang in English.

Dang nodded and said, "Yes, Sergeant, Lieutenant Jutte already told us that. I don't think you could have done any more than you did, Captain Pope."

"We have a QRF battalion from the 23rd ARVN Division enroute to reinforce, pursue the enemy, and move the dead out. I want you to come back with us on the chopper, Pope." Sullivan said.

"I'd rather stay here and finish my job."

"I can't leave one American advisor in the field by himself. It's against MACV policy."

"I've been in the field alone before."

"Yes, but I didn't know it, God damn it. Now, no more arguing."

"Captain Dang, we have some counterintelligence work to do. The VC had to know the exact route of our search and destroy operation. This was not a hasty ambush. They were dug in," Pope said. "We've captured some communist machine guns and assault rifles. The first of their kind in Binh Tuy. Some unusual things are happening here," he added.

"I agree with you, Captain Pope, and I have some ideas we can discuss later. But where did you ever get the idea to use smoke grenades for concealment in an ambush? I've been to the US Army infantry school, and I never heard of it."

Pope shrugged his shoulders and said, "It just came to me because I believe very strongly a unit can be more successful if it can maneuver against the enemy under periods of reduced visibility."

"I'd like to discuss that theory with you at length, Captain Pope."

"Let's head for home," Sullivan interrupted.

The four men got on the waiting chopper and flew to sector headquarters.

Pope was sleepy, and bone weary. The adrenaline rush had deserted him. Depression at losing most of the company took over and consumed him. He thought: *Well, Grandfather, so far you were right. I'm still alive, but we lost so many men today. I still think I could have done more to avoid the ambush. I don't think Sullivan thought much of my action today. Hell, how would he know? In all his months in Vietnam, he's never been shot at! He flies over the problems on the ground. This is a different war than other Makahs had to fight. Spies in our own ranks that can betray us in minutes. We lost so many men.*

Chapter Twenty

The day after the ambush, Rick James replacement arrived on the regularly scheduled Australian Caribou. Pope wanted to talk to him alone, so he volunteered to take the jeep to the airstrip to meet the plane. Still depressed, he sat in the vehicle near the covered pad and watched the Caribou taxi up to him.

The first man out was Waters, with an armload of mail pouches. He was followed by two men, both about the same size—medium built. The captain was a studious-looking man, wearing black rimmed GI glasses. The other had dark-skin, black hair, and a bad barber. When he bent over to set his duffel bag on the ground, Pope saw his hair was cut too high in the back. It looked like someone put a bowl on his head and cut the hair around it.

Waters looked at Pope and thought that something was wrong. It looked like Pope had shrunk about six inches!

"Morning. I'm John Pope. Welcome to Binh Tuy. Hi, Duke—welcome home."

They all shook hands with Pope, and the aircraft crew loaded packages of food into the jeep trailer.

"Glad to meet you, John, I'm Bob Cox, Rick James's replacement. This is SFC Ramon Gomez, the new medic."

"Nice to meet you, sir. Son of a bitch it's hot here. Even hotter than San Antone," Gomez said, wiping the sweat from his face with the sleeve of his shirt.

Pope figured Gomez was a Tex Mex, and said to Cox, "I'm from Washington—the state, where are you from?"

"I'm a cowboy from Montana! But the closest I got to a horse was the parade animals when I was at West Point," he said with enthusiasm.

"Captain Cox and Lt. Granger will be able to knock their rings together, sir!" Waters said with a smile.

"Yeah. And I think the Major is from Montana, too. Duke, I'm really sorry, but I got your First Company shot up yesterday. Lt. Jutte is wounded and was evacuated to Ban Me Thuot."

"Son of a bitch, sir. I knew I should have come home with you. I **thought** you looked different. How is the El Tee?"

"He's OK. One clean bullet through the arm. It got more fat than muscle," Pope said in a lame attempt at some levity.

"That God damn asshole Diem probably screwed up the operation, sir."

"We all share the blame, Duke. Diem was killed in the ambush. The Major will brief you all when you get to the compound. How was the week end?"

Before Waters could answer, Gomez interrupted and said, "Shit, sir, this man knows how to act! He and another NCO picked me up Saturday night at the replacement depot, and we invested our money in 'houses and lots.' Whore houses and lots of whiskey!"

They all laughed and Waters said, "Yeah, and I'm still hung over."

On the ride to the compound, both new men enthusiastically asked numerous questions—Gomez's questions, liberally laced with profanity. Pope already liked the comic relief provided by the Tex-Mex sergeant with the bad haircut.

*   *   *

When they arrived Pope said, "Bob, can I talk to you in my room for a minute?"

"Sure, John."

Pope motioned Cox to the only chair in his room, and sat on his bunk.

"You may hear a lot of things about Rick James and the RF battalion. You'll have to sort them out yourself"

"Did you have a problem with James?"

"Yes, I did. I don't blame him entirely, but the RF battalion never got off its ass the entire year James was here. I don't believe Rick made much of an effort to get them moving."

"Do you have any suggestions?"

"The battalion has some good soldiers who need better leadership and training. Just look around and make your own decision."

"Well, Waters didn't think much of James either. He sure thinks the world of you, though. Thanks, John. I'm sure I'll be asking your advice."

"I'm sorry I got First Company shot up. Why don't you and Waters get a briefing from the Major? If you have any other questions, get back to me. I'm glad you're here. Good luck."

*   *   *

Pope spent the next three weeks working with Dang, trying to find the spy in the SOIC, the RF battalion, and Tanh Linh District. They kept running into walls. Sullivan told the team that with so much VC activity in the area they needed to shore up their own defenses. He ordered several hundred sandbags from Saigon.

They dug a bunker, 16' X 16' square in the center of the compound, near the "geese pond," and put steel airfield decking and sandbags on the top. There would be room for the entire team to take refuge when a mortar or rocket attack occurred. Each day every available man, officers included, worked on the hole and filled sand bags. Since the compound was built on a sand dune, there was plenty of sand. When the bunker was completed, Pope and Sullivan carried supplies for storage.

"Sir, this is a solid bunker for a rocket or mortar attack, but what happens if there is a ground attack? Who defends us?"

"That'll be the responsibility of the RF battalion."

"I'm concerned because I don't see any positions being dug by them, either near our compound, or between here and province headquarters."

"Why the hell do you think you have the answer for everyone's problems?"

"I think this one is **our** problem. Stand at the top of the sand dune behind the dayroom and you can see we're sitting in the middle of the best avenue of approach to the province capitol."

"I don't think the VC would muster the manpower to attack a province headquarters."

"You didn't think there were many VC in the province, either," Pope said, sorry as soon as the words left his mouth.

"That's insubordination, asshole."

"I apologize, sir," Pope interrupted, raising both hands. "For our own reasons, we don't like each other. We both know that. Why don't we just agree with that and do what's best for the advisory team?" He added.

"Fine, I don't really give a shit. Do whatever you want," Sullivan said as he stomped out of the bunker.

Pope had a meeting with the advisory team—minus Sullivan, who was busy at province headquarters. They all agreed to dig fighting emplacements throughout the compound.

Standard foxholes were impossible because the sand kept sifting back into the hole as fast as they dug it out. They had to dig huge holes and pile sandbags inside to form the walls of the foxhole. The team dug three large machine gun emplacements on the crest of the hill near the minefield and one foxhole between them and the dining room building.

When they finished that project, they dug foxholes on the side of the compound near the street, in case they had to fall back into supplementary positions. There was a great deal of good-natured complaining, but

the job was completed faster than any of them expected. Not coinciden-
tally, the RF battalion started digging emplacements on both sides of the
advisory compound a week after the Americans started their project.

"Do you still have the contact in J-4, supply, Duke?" Pope asked.

"Yes, sir."

"Catch a flight and bring back three .30 caliber machine guns, with
spare parts and barrels for each."

"How about ammo?"

"You should be able to get that at RF headquarters. Check there before
you go to Saigon."

"Roger that, sir."

*   *   *

The advisory team continued routine MedCap operations. SFC
Gomez fit in well with White. Now they could treat the sick civilians
twice as fast. Pope made more contact with agents and expanded his intelligence network.

Captain Cox brought new enthusiasm to the RF battalion, and
Captain Thanh seemed to like him. They worked closely together to refit
First Company and provide better training for the entire battalion.

Two weeks after the ambush, Jutte returned to duty from the hospital.
He gave Cox and Waters an entirely different version of the Tanh Linh
battle than the one provided by Major Sullivan.

Two days after Jutte's return the senior advisor of II Corps and his
Vietnamese counterpart flew into Binh Tuy. They pinned a second Silver
Star on Pope and a Bronze Star with "V" device, Purple Heart, and
Combat Infantryman's Badge on Jutte for their actions in the Tanh Linh
ambush. Sgt. Duc received a Vietnamese Cross of Gallantry from the
Vietnamese Commanding General. Pope wondered why Sullivan had put
him in for the Silver Star. He found out later that Sullivan had put Jutte in

for the awards. Jutte had made the recommendation for Pope when he was in the hospital—and pissed Sullivan off.

*   *   *

An army L-19 fixed wing observation aircraft was allocated for Pope to fly over the province every day to locate VC activity. The warrant officer pilot was a slim man with flaming red hair. He had been in country over two and a half years. His daring flying and risks earned him the nickname "Red Baron."

The L-19 is a very thin skinned, slow flying, unarmed aircraft. Red jerry rigged two rocket pods below each wing with an igniter that was activated by wires that led across the bottom of the wing to the cockpit. He painted a makeshift sight on the windshield of the cockpit so that he could sight through the aiming device to the target. When he pulled on one of the wires, the rocket ignited and sailed in the direction the aircraft was pointed. The observer sat directly behind the pilot and had foot pedals and a "Joy stick" for steering. There was no instrument panel in the back seat.

Red always carried about a half dozen peanut butter jars that he had collected from various mess halls. Next to them was a bag of fragmentation hand grenades. The observer placed the hand grenade in the peanut butter jar, pulled the pin of the grenade and threw the jar out the window in the direction of fleeing Viet Cong. When the jar hit the ground and broke, the handle separated, igniting the fuse and the grenade exploded. This was Red's "mini bomb."

Each day Pope and Red took off in the L-19 and toured the entire province, using a different route every day so that they could observe the ground from different angles. If they saw Viet Cong soldiers in an open area, they flew in very low and Red fired at them with his rockets. As they got closer Pope dropped the "mini bombs," then held his CAR 15 out the window and fired at the enemy.

*   *   *

After this little air-to-ground war had gone on for about three weeks, the duo were on a routine mission, fairly close to Tanh Linh village. Red spotted two armed VC sauntering along in the middle of a rice paddy. When the enemy soldiers saw the airplane, they fell in the sucking mud. Red maneuvered the aircraft for the run with the sun to their back; Pope spotted the soldiers slogging along in the direction of a woodline near a hillside. Red fired a rocket that hit behind the fleeing enemy. Pope dropped two mini bombs that exploded between the communists and knocked them in opposite directions.

Within seconds, Red pulled the aircraft in a steep climb to gain altitude and come around to be sure the enemy was dead. An RPD machine gun opened fire from the hillside and stitched the bottom and side of the aircraft. One of the rounds hit the joystick between Pope's legs, knocking the stick askew and the round deflected into the ceiling of the cabin. The ricocheting bullet distracted Pope, and Red was too busy flying to pinpoint the location of the automatic weapon. Red flew the aircraft in a big circle, returning to the hillside and fired three rockets into the general vicinity of the machine gun.

As the tiny aircraft gained altitude, Red said, "Damn! That was pretty close, Captain. Are you all right?"

"Yeah, but we've got some holes in the fuselage and the tip of the joy stick got shot off. I think we got two Victor Charlie's KIA."

"My instruments look OK, so I guess nothing vital was hit."

"We better mark that spot and check it from different angles in the future, Red. A machine gun usually means there's at least an enemy company close by."

"Roger that. Well, let's head for the barn and check the damage."

They flew along quietly for about 30 minutes.

Pope said, "Say, Red, what happens to me and the aircraft if you get shot?"

"For Christ sake! Do you mean you don't know how to land this thing?"

"Hell no. I'm just a plain old infantryman. I'd never even rode in one of these planes before I met you."

"Well, let's give you some lessons before we call it a day, and let's make this business of teaching you how to fly the plane **after** the shooting our little secret. OK?"

"That's fine with me. I don't want anyone else to know how stupid I am."

Red showed Pope how to fly and land the little craft, and Pope made several touch-and-go maneuvers at the airstrip.

Gomez was waiting at the airport with a jeep to drive Pope back to the advisory compound and noticed the take off and landings. When they taxied to the covered pad, Gomez saw the bullet holes in the fuselage. Red shut off the engine, and the two aviators climbed out of the plane as the sergeant approached.

"Where the fuck did the bullet holes come from, sir?"

"Charlie got off a few lucky shots. No sweat, Sarge," Red replied nonchalantly, trying to low-key the operation.

"Yeah. Just a little argument, Sarge. No big deal," Pope added.

"So you decided to learn how to land that plane **after** your pilot damn near got his ass shot off, huh, Captain?"

"Yes, and wipe that shit-eating grin off your face, Sergeant," Pope said.

"Yes, sir, but you can bet your sweet ass I'm not keeping this quiet," Gomez laughed.

He shifted the jeep into gear, and they sped off. Within minutes of their arrival at the compound the story was told and retold, and Pope took a great deal of ribbing at the dinner table.

*   *   *

On Sunday morning, the advisory team were lounging around the day room, reading and shooting the breeze, when Cox and Gomez burst into the room.

"We just got shot at when we were coming back from the airfield," Cox exclaimed.

Pope looked up from his paperback and said, "Here we go again. You guys are the fifth or sixth to report being shot at coming back from the airstrip. Did you hear the rifle report?"

The two men looked at each other and shook their heads.

"That's really weird, now that I think of it, sir. I didn't hear any shot, but I damn sure heard the round go by my head. It damn near give me a new part in my hair," Gomez replied.

"I don't see how you can be shot at by a sniper and not hear a gunshot. I've never heard of a sniper rifle with a silencer on it. It doesn't make sense because the silencer would reduce the accuracy of the rifle," Pope said.

"I don't know about that, but I know when I hear a round go by my head," Cox added.

"How many times have you guys been shot at?" Pope asked sarcastically.

They both looked at each other and replied, at the same time, "Once."

"OK, let's put this crap to bed once and for all. Granger, Duke, get your weapons and ammo. All five of us meet at the jeep in five minutes. We're going hunting," Pope said.

"You guys point out where you were shot at," Pope said as he drove down the dirt road toward the airstrip.

"It was about two kilometers this side of the airfield," Cox said.

Pope stopped the vehicle in a dried out creek bed that crossed the dirt road. It ran perpendicular to the woodline and the road. The depression was deep enough that the jeep's top was not visible from the woodline. The trees had been cut back from the road, and the vegetation killed with a defoliant for about 150 yards. There were good fields of fire from the tree line to the dirt road.

They dismounted, and Pope said, "OK, if there is a sniper, he'll be in that woodline and about 50 yards from this creek bed. You four crawl up the creek towards the jungle, about a hundred yards. When you're in position, I'll drive up to the airstrip, sit for a couple minutes, and then high tail it back here to pick you up. If he draws down on me, you drop him."

The four men looked at each other, nodded, and crawled up the creek bed. Pope sat in the jeep and watched them. When they stopped, he started the engine, and drove toward the airstrip. He'd gone about thirty yards and had just shifted into third when a bullet ricocheted off the top of the windshield and past his head. He pushed the accelerator to the floor and heard automatic weapons firing from the direction of the four advisors.

He sped to the airstrip, spun the jeep around, and roared back to the creek bed, dust flying behind him. When he arrived, he could see the four advisors about 75 yards from the road. Cox and Gomez were grinning and dragging a VC body, and Duke waved a rifle at Pope.

"Well, I guess you know we weren't giving you a line of bullshit, sir," a panting, sweating Gomez said as he dropped the foot of the dead VC soldier near the jeep.

"I guess we've been right all along, sir. Look at this silencer," Duke said as he handed the Mas 36 to Pope.

The old Mas 36 had a hand-made silencer that looked like it had been fabricated from a tin can. Steel wool was stuffed into the opening between the barrel and the tin.

"It's pretty ingenious all right," Pope said as he examined the rifle.

"Charlie surprised us by shooting at you on the way to the air strip instead of on the way back like he had done before," Duke said.

"Yeah, surprised me, too. He probably saw a slower moving target. It was a pretty fair shot, too," Pope said and he pointed at the dent in the top of the windshield cover on the jeep.

"Jesus Christ, Sir. I think you're pushing that 'spirit of the whale' shit a little too far. You wouldn't get me to put my Mexican ass out there as no decoy!" Gomez said; shaking his head. The others laughed.

"Whale spirit nothing. I didn't believe you guys got shot at. And if you were right, I figured Charlie would follow his habit of shooting at us on the way back from the airstrip when I would be going like hell!"

"Well, since I was the first one to report getting shot at by a sniper out here, I get to tell the rest of the team about this when we get back."

Granger said. "I've already got a name for Charlie here—Elmer, after Elmer Fudd, the duck hunter," The others cackled.

During the next few weeks, Pope was the butt of jokes about being a decoy, and he took them all with a smile. He eventually got the last laugh though.

After Gomez cracked a joke, Pope said, "You know, I've been giving this a lot of thought. Maybe we should have left Elmer out there alive, because he was such a lousy shot. What if Elmer's replacement is a crack shot? What'll we call him, Sergeant York?"

*   *   *

They got reports of more communist sightings in the area. Small guerrilla units stopped traffic on Highway 1 and collected taxes. Two small hamlets were occupied by a handful of VC. The enemy chased the Popular Force squad away and occupied the hamlets, spreading fear and intimidation. They murdered the village chief, severed his head, and placed it on a post near the flagpole. Then they took down the South Vietnamese flag and ran up the National Liberation Front flag.

The leader told the villagers that anyone who took the flag down or touched the head would be killed. After remaining a day, the VC left the villages and disappeared into the jungle. Dang and Pope flew into the hamlets after the enemy departed. They took two R & I platoon teams with them. When the choppers touched down, Pope and Dang walked quickly to the flagpole. The crowd got bigger as they followed the two officers.

Pope was shocked at the sight of the grotesque figure on the pole. It was black, and unrecognizable. The hair had fallen to the ground. The smell of decaying flesh was overpowering.

"You can read about a hundred different atrocities and feel badly, but you only have to **see** one to appreciate the horror."

"Yes. I'll take care of the head if you'll take down the flag, Captain Pope."

Dang removed a Vietnamese flag from his belt and walked to the post, wrapped the head with it and handed it to a wailing woman standing by.

He whispered something in Vietnamese to her. They walked to her home together. She cradled the foul-smelling remains of her beloved spouse: he put his arm around her shoulder and comforted her.

Pope walked to the flag pole grasped the rope and lowered the VC flag. He unfastened it from the rope, spit on it and wiped his feet with it. Then he picked it up and placed it in his belt. He removed another Vietnamese flag from his belt and ran it up the flagpole. When it reached the top, he tied it off, took a step back and saluted it.

An hour later the two officers were on the chopper riding back to Binh Tuy.

"I left the two teams there temporarily for security."

"Good, We should send civil affairs/psyops teams with a company of soldiers in tomorrow," Dang said.

They rode in silence the rest of the way.

* * *

A few days later, Pope showed the flag to the advisory team in the day room.

"Say, our wooden junks and cross bow sales to pilots and visitors are going good. Why don't we replicate this flag and sell them as authentic?" Granger asked.

Yeah, I can have Duc's wife sew them for us," Waters added.

Within a week, Duc produced a tattered VC flag, complete with chicken blood splattered to add authenticity. The flags proved to be the biggest sales item.

During one of the sales, Waters explained to a friend, "Hey, our interpreter's wife sewed the flag and sprinkled chicken blood on it."

"I don't give a shit. When I get back to the States, I'm the only one that will know that."

* * *

There seemed to be a great deal of VC movement near Bo Ninh, the small hamlet where Pope and Red Baron had almost been shot down. The village had been built about 100 yards from the base of a heavily vegetated hill complex. Civilians had been sniped at from the woodline, and a platoon of VC occupied the hamlet for three days. Just as an RF company from Tanh Linh was dispatched to drive them out, the VC retreated to the hilly jungle. Pope told Dang the hamlet and its inhabitants could not be adequately protected.

"Why don't we close down Bo Ninh and move the civilians to Tanh Linh?" Pope asked.

"There is not enough room for them in Tanh Linh village complex."

"There are less than 100 civilians. We can move the fence out to the west and expand the complex."

"The civilians don't like moving their homes. If we forced them to move, it would just be proof to them that the VC are right. That we cannot provide our citizens with protection."

"I sure hope the communists don't decide to fight over the hamlet, because it could be a bloody battleground."

*   *   *

Pope's agents reported the Viet Cong planned to split South Vietnam in two. Binh Tuy Province landed square in the middle of the split.

Pope wondered if the Regional Force battalion would be large enough to repel the invaders. *The war in this little province is expanding, and we still have a spy or two in our midst,* he thought.

Chapter Twenty One

"A platoon of VC have just captured Tuy An, a hamlet, about 10 kilometers west of Hoi Duc District headquarters. I am planning to have the Second RF Company from Hoi Duc make a night move and attack the enemy at the village the following morning," Dang said as he pointed at the map on the wall.

"Do we know how many VC have occupied the village?" Pope asked.

"Three different villagers report twenty-two soldiers armed only with individual weapons."

"Since there are no automatic weapons, you don't suspect a company sized force?"

"That is correct, Captain Pope. I can't go on the operation because Major Nhia and Sullivan are in Saigon for pacification program conferences all week. Will you go?"

"Yes. We won't have any artillery support because it is out of range of the 105 howitzer at Hoi Duc. I'll lay on a slick and gunship for first light, during the attack, so we'll have some kind of support."

As Dang departed, Pope went to Captain Cox's room and explained the operation. The short, stocky man looked up at Pope over the top of his GI glasses.

"I think I'll go on the mission with Granger, and you stay here."

Pope raised his hand.

"We can't do that, Bob. The Major has a policy that two inexperienced people don't go out on a combat operation."

"But Larry has been here for over three months."

"He's been on MedCap missions, but no combat operation. This one will break his cherry."

"Remember, Johnny, I have date of rank on you, and I'm the acting team leader in the Major's absence. It's my decision!"

"Don't pull date of rank on me, God damn it. You know as well as I do that date of rank among captains is like virginity among whores. If you really want to go, you have to go with someone with experience. I can't go with you because one of us should stay here. Duke and Jutte are in Tanh Linh on an operation. Let's take Granger and switch him for Jutte, and you take Jack with you."

"No. Granger and I have already talked about going on an operation together. We want to earn our Combat Infantryman Badges together. So my decision is: we're going on this one. It looks pretty simple."

"Yeah. But things aren't always the way they appear. I don't want to see you earn your CIB posthumously. The Major is always looking for a reason to have my ass. If you insist, I'll lay on a slick and gun ship escort for this afternoon. Dang and I will fly to Hoi Duc with you and Granger," Pope said with a sigh of resignation.

"OK. I'll brief Larry, and we'll be ready to go at 1600 hours," Cox replied with boyish enthusiasm.

*   *   *

After the choppers dropped the officers at Hoi Duc, Dang went to visit the Second Company commander. Pope sat near the helipad with Granger and Cox.

"Second Company only has about 100 men. The company commander is pretty new, so try to exert influence on him right away," Pope emphasized.

"Why are we traveling at night? Isn't it dangerous?" Granger asked.

"The VC don't expect you to travel at night. So you have the element of surprise in your favor. There's a road that leads directly from here to the village. The commander will try to get on the road. Don't let him. Stay close to the machine gun crews. Make sure they don't throw away their ammo. It gets heavy and cumbersome in the jungle, and they like to ease their burden.

"Once you get about 200 yards from the village, maneuver into position to attack just as the sun comes up. Once you assault with the lead platoons, sweep through the entire village aggressively until you get to the opposite end. Then reorganize and establish a perimeter defense, in case of a counterattack."

"Sounds pretty simple to me," Cox said, grinning.

"Stop saying that, Bob. It makes me nervous."

Dang and the commanding officer of Second Company approached the US advisors. "Second Company is ready to go at 2000 hours. It will be a difficult move at night, but it should be OK."

"Fine, Captain Dang. I've briefed Captain Cox and Lieutenant Granger on the operation."

*   *   *

They all had dinner with the district chief. Dang and pope flew back to province headquarters in the chopper before dark. On the way back, he confirmed with the pilot that the two aircraft were on strip alert at their base in Phan Thiet, effective 0400 hours the following day. They would return to support the operation if needed.

*   *   *

At 0600 the next morning, Martin awakened Pope.

"Sir, Captain Dang called and said Second Company is inside the village, but has six WIA and needs a chopper."

"Get hold of Phan Thiet flight operations and get those choppers here to pick up Captain Dang and me right away. Tell Sergeant Gomez to put his medical aid kit together to come with us. I'm going down to sector headquarters."

He leaped out of bed, fully clothed. He took his pistol from under his pillow, slipped it into his holster, and fastened the belt around his waist, then grabbed his CAR 15 and disappeared out the door.

When Pope got to sector headquarters, it was a beehive of activity.

Dang turned from the wall map and said, "Second Company has secured the village, but they have taken casualties. There is no report of enemy casualties. I have requested Vietnamese medevac choppers for the wounded. Can we go to their location?"

"I've already asked for the two helicopters on stand by, and they're on the way. I'll take a US medic with us in case we get there before the medevac choppers."

"I think they attacked while it was still dark, but the village has been secured. Can we stop and pick up the district chief at Hoi Duc?"

"Sure, I'll meet you at the helicopter pad in ten minutes," Pope said, and he headed out the door.

When Gomez and Pope arrived at the helipad, a lone chopper was settling down. While they waited for Dang, Pope ran to the chopper to talk with the pilot.

"Where is the gunship escort?"

"Sir, the gunship went on another mission last night, so we're on our own"

*   *   *

Dang arrived, and the chopper made the thirty-minute flight to Hoi Duc, picked up Captain Khoa, and headed for the village. Pope occupied the jump seat directly behind the Co-pilot on the left side of the aircraft. Dang was in the jump seat directly behind the pilot on the right side of the aircraft. Gomez and Khoa sat on the long bench seat between the two door gunners. Immediately after take off, Pope used his portable PRC 25 and contacted Captain Cox.

"What is your situation, over?"

"We've had some problems because we couldn't make very good time moving through the jungle. About half way here, the company commander removed your R & I scout from the point because he refused to get on the road, over."

"So, what happened? Over."

"We were all walking down the road, and our lead element stumbled onto the front gate in the dark. The enemy opened up on us and we took six WIA immediately. When taken under fire, we deployed and attacked, and the VC disappeared, over."

"What is the current situation? Over."

"We're about one hundred yards inside the East gate. We need a medevac, over."

"The Vietnamese medevac is on the way. It's important you get the company commander to attack through the village right away, over."

"I've tried to, but he's got a mind of his own, over."

Pope sensed the frustration in Cox voice and explained the situation to Dang. He frowned and said, "When we land, I will talk with the company commander."

Pope transmitted into the radio; "We need to land. Is the LZ secure? Over."

"That's affirmative. There hasn't been any shooting for about three hours. Land from the east. I throw smoke now. Please identify, over."

Seeing the cloud of yellow smoke in an open field just inside the gate of the village, Pope said, "I identify smoke as yellow. We're coming in, out."

The helicopter started it's descent. At 200 yards off the ground, small arms fire crackled from the woods to the north, followed by more small arms and heavy automatic weapons fire. The chopper shuddered as the bullets tore though the fuselage. Bullets whined by Pope. One hit the metal backrest and ricocheted out the door. The right door gunner returned fire and shouted over the intercom to Pope.

"Sir, your buddy has been hit."

Pope turned around in his seat to see Gomez standing over Dang who was slumped in his seat, blood pouring from a head wound. Gomez turned to Pope and shouted.

"He's dead sir. Took a fucken round right through the head."

Bullets continued to penetrate the skin of the Huey. Pope imagined this was probably what a whale felt like as his grandfather's men moved in for the kill. He saw the familiar green tracers from the RPD machine gun searching for the aircraft.

The helicopter was 100 yards off the ground and slowed slightly, nose up, as it continued it's descent. Blood splattered over Pope's leg and side as the door gunner next to him grabbed for his throat. Gomez went to his aid. Pope turned, poked the pilot and signaled him with his thumb to get out of the area. The pilot immediately pulled pitch and started a steep ascent. The right door gunner frantically fired at the hated green hell as bullets raked through the aircraft.

Pope got on the radio.

"What in the hell happened? Over."

A shaky voice on the other end said, "I don't know. The whole wooded area on the north side of the village opened up at the same time. Sorry about that, over."

"We have a couple casualties in the aircraft, and we don't know how long we can fly, but you have got to get that unit out of that village. There's an enemy unit there that's bigger than yours, over."

"Roger that! But I can't convince this commander. Can you put Dang on the radio and I'll put the commander on and maybe we can get moving, over?"

Pope explained the situation to Captain Khoa, and Khoa told the commander to take orders from the US advisor on the ground.

"Just to the south of the village is an open field. Move south into the clearing, then veer east into the woods while we cover you for as long as we can from here, over," Pope said.

"Will do. We'll mask our withdrawal with as many smoke grenades as we have. As soon as you see the smoke, we're out of here, out."

About ten minutes later, green, yellow, purple, and red smoke appeared on the ground below. The colors mixed and made a peculiar, almost surreal sight. The door gunner was shot in the throat—just above the collar of his flak jacket. Gomez and Pope moved him away from the door, and seated upright on the bench to keep him from choking on his own blood. Pope looked at Dang's lifeless body and noted how ironic it was that Dang was wearing a flack jacket and steel helmet. He was sitting on a flack jacket as well, yet he took one single bullet through his head.

Pope moved to the crew chief's seat and test fired the machine gun.

"Your door gunner is OK." Pope said to the pilot over the intercom. "The company is going to withdraw out the open field to the south, then swing to the east into the woodline, and back to district headquarters. I want to support their withdrawal with suppressing fire."

"We've got about an hour and a half of fuel. Forty five minutes to the hospital in Saigon and 30 minutes on-station here, fifteen minutes of reserve," the pilot answered.

"You'll have to fly parallel to the village, along the long axis, turn and fly back. On the first run, we'll fire the machine gun from the left side, and on the way back, fire the machine gun from the right side."

The RF Company ran through the broken fence, and Pope could see that some were in the open field.

"Let's rock and roll. The company has started its maneuver."

"Roger that, Captain. Let's, get some!" the pilot said. He swung the chopper for the run.

As the helicopter made its sweep from the west, Pope faced the hills. He looked down the barrel of the M-60 machine gun. Little black figures ran out of the woods and into the village. He fired short bursts of six rounds.

Pope was unaccustomed to shooting at moving targets from a moving weapon, but the red tracer bullets helped his aim.

Enemy fire went through the fuselage of the fast moving chopper. When the Huey reached the other end of the village, the pilot spun the aircraft around in a violent turn and started the run in the opposite direction.

Pope reloaded his weapon with a fresh ammo belt. Government soldiers exited the village into the open field, running and shooting wildly behind them. The helicopter made four more runs to protect retreating friendly forces and took more hits in the fuselage. It was strange to see holes appearing in the fuselage of the helicopter without seeing the bullets. When he could see the last of the little green figures disappear into the woods; he got on the radio to Cox.

"What is your situation? Over."

A panting voice came on and said, "We are in the jungle...are no longer receiving fire. We'll consolidate for about five minutes...head for home. We took more casualties, but we'll carry them with us, over."

"Roger. We'll have the medevac stop at district headquarters. When you arrive there, establish a perimeter defense, just in case the VC seize the initiative and attack you there. In the mean time, I'll radio for reinforcements, over."

"How much longer can you give us air cover? Over."

"We have a serious WIA on board and have to get him to Saigon. We don't know how long this ship can fly either. You're on your own. Good luck! Out."

Pope turned off the radio and over the intercom said, "You guys did a hell of a job bailing that unit out. Now let's head for the hospital and get your man taken care of."

"Thanks, sir. You don't have to tell me a second time. I hope the crew chief lasts till we get to Saigon. You can be my door gunner any time you want."

"Thanks, but I feel safer on the ground."

Pope radioed Special Zone headquarters requesting reinforcements to Hoi Duc before nightfall.

*   *   *

Forty minutes later, the helicopter landed on the roof of the hospital. While the wounded man was unloaded and the ship refueled, the pilot and Pope examined the battered Huey. They counted over 150 holes in the aircraft. The deck was slick with a mix of blood from the door gunner and Dang. The familiar stale-copper odor was sticking in Pope's nose.

"I'm amazed that they didn't hit anything critical. It's a miracle, considering the number of holes," the pilot said

"It's just as surprising only two of eight got hit. If it's OK with you, I'd like to take the body of Captain Dang back to province headquarters with me."

"I ain't getting in no more fucken aircraft with you, sir," Gomez said, as he looked at the slick and shook his head.

"Yeah. But ain't it great to be alive? The air even smells sweeter after a fight. Let's head back to the barn." Pope said and climbed back into the wounded aircraft.

*   *   *

When they landed at the helipad in Binh Tuy, Captain Bishop was waiting with an ambulance.

"It's good to see you, Johnny. When we heard the deputy province chief and an American were KIA, we thought your whale spirit let you down."

"Not so far," Pope said.

"The ambulance is for Captain Dang's body. The First Regional Force Company has been sent to the airstrip for air transport to Hoi Duc."

They loaded Captain Dang into the ambulance, and Pope waved to the chopper crew as it took off for its home base.

"Have you heard anything from Cox?"

"Negative. But Major Sullivan called, so I had to fill him in. He sounded pissed off, Johnny."

"Yeah, well, so am I. Let's go to sector headquarters and try to contact your district," Pope said to Captain Khoa as they piled into the jeep.

*   *   *

At the SOIC, the Chief of Staff told them that none of the company had returned to district headquarters yet. Pope got on the telephone to Special Zone headquarters for more helicopters to take him and Khoa back to district headquarters. There were no choppers available. Captain Trang told Pope the closest air strip was in Tanh Linh, about 15 kilometers from Tuy An, the village occupied by the VC. The First RF company would be transported this evening and attack the village from the south.

An incoming helicopter interrupted them. He patted the district chief on the back and said, "Come on, Captain Khoa, that's our ride."

The chopper touched down, a red-faced Major Sullivan and Major Nhia emerged from the chopper. Pope ran past them to the chopper pilot.

"Wait a minute. I have another mission for you."

He ran back to Sullivan and briefly and succinctly, briefed him on the debacle of the previous night and today—leaving out the reasons for Cox and Granger going on the operation together.

"God damn it, Captain. You know about my policy of not having two inexperienced men go on a combat mission. How the hell did you let this happen?"

Pope nodded his head.

"I'd like to discuss this with you, sir, but I have to get back to Hoi Duc and help Khoa organize his defenses in case of a counterattack. You can contact me by radio."

He turned and boarded the aircraft with Khoa and Gomez, leaving the Major with his mouth agape.

While airborne he shouted to the dozing medic, "Hey, Gomez, I thought you weren't going to get in any more aircraft with me!"

"Ah, shit, sir...I lie all the time. Besides, they still have the WIA's. And I don't think it's a good time to be around the Major."

Just as the helicopter got over the district headquarters, Pope made radio contact with Cox.

"What's your situation? Over."

"We're about one kilometer from the district and have eleven WIA's. Is there a medevac chopper available? Over."

Pope looked down. The helipad was empty.

"Negative, but maybe I can talk this chopper pilot into waiting here and transporting your wounded. See you soon. Out."

The pilot agreed to wait for the wounded. Khoa and Pope got two trucks and went to the west end of Hoi Duc to wait for the beleaguered company. Pope closed his eyes. The image of Dang's soft smile filled his mind. Pope wanted to destroy something to vent his anger and frustration.

Gomez moved to him and said, "Don't get down, sir. We've still got to get these fucken wounded out and defensive positions established."

"Thanks, Sarge, I'm OK," Pope said as he grimaced.

*   *   *

After a half-hour, the lead element of Second Company entered the village. Pope saw Cox and Granger laboring along, carrying a wounded soldier on a makeshift litter. He motioned them to the waiting truck, and Gomez ran to look after the wounded.

"Man, am I ever glad to see you, Johnny!" Cox panted, through a dirty, sweating face.

"Me, too. The district chief will take over with your company commander to set up the perimeter defense. Sit down and drink some water."

He handed a canteen to each of them. As the rifle company took up defensive positions, Gomez returned.

"I've done all I can for the WIA's, sir. I'll take them back to the helipad and meet you at district headquarters."

"OK. Thanks, Sarge. Good work," Pope said as he turned to Cox.

"Now that you've caught your breath, maybe you can fill me in on what went wrong, Bob."

"It was a real fuck up, Johnny. I owe you an apology. I should not have been on this operation. There's more to being an advisor than being shot at. You have to be able to convince the commander of what you want. I couldn't do that."

"Don't feel bad. The same thing happened to me at Tanh Linh. The only difference was my commander lost his life."

"Anyway, things started going bad as soon as we cleared the district headquarters. The CO wanted to get on the road immediately. I had to leave my machine gun crew to try to get them to get off the road."

"I couldn't stay with my machine gun crew either because I had to go with the lead platoon," Granger added.

"So, as you predicted, the ammo bearers threw away almost all their ammo," Cox said.

"Then we were going high diddle diddle, right down the middle of the road, when the lead platoon was taken under fire by VC guards at the gate. Six people were wounded with the initial burst of fire," Granger said.

"When we got inside the village, the commander told me the objective was secure. When I told him that we had to attack through the entire village, he refused, saying we had to take care of our casualties," Cox said.

"That's when you showed up, sir. And I'm sure glad you did. But who got hit in the chopper? Anyone from our team?" Granger asked.

"No. Captain Dang was killed and a door gunner seriously wounded," Pope said.

"I'm really sorry, Johnny. I was sure the LZ was secure. Damn!" Cox said, shaking his head in self-condemnation.

"Your covering fire sure saved our asses. Hey, sir, did you notice the smoke for concealment," Granger added with a grin.

"Nice touch, Larry. Good to know you keep your eyes and ears open," Pope said, smiling. "Well, we're in for a long night. We have to get in position for a possible counterattack. First company is scheduled to close into Tuy An tonight, but they may not make it until morning."

"You think First Company can handle them, Johnny?" Cox asked.

"Jesus Christ! That's a reinforced VC company in Tuy An, and If they decide to stay and fight, First Company will be chewed up! Lets get back to Binh Tuy fast—we've got to make some plans," Pope said and broke into a run for district headquarters.

Chapter Twenty Two

Pope burst into district headquarters and asked a startled Captain Khoa permission to use the radio.

As they walked toward the radio room, Pope said to Cox, "If First Company attacks Tuy An and the VC stay and fight, it'll be like a buzz saw."

"So how do we stop them?"

"Go to the chopper and tell the pilot to wait for me. I'll need a ride back to Binh Tuy tonight. You and Larry stay here and be prepared to attack Tuy An again with Second Company. This time you'll have help."

"I wonder what genius decided to send a company against a reinforced company?" Cox asked.

"I don't know, but I think it was Captain Trang. I'm pissed off at myself for not thinking of it before now. I was more worried about you guys getting back to Hoi Duc," Pope said, clearly disgusted with himself.

Pope set the proper frequency on the radio and transmitted.

"Binh Tuy, this is Hoi Duc, over."

"This is Binh Tuy, over."

"Binh Tuy, get your actual on the horn right away, over."

A minute passed and Sullivan said, "This is Binh Tuy actual, over."

"This is Hoi Duc. What is the location of reinforcing element? Over."

"Hoi Duc, it has just departed my location for its destination, over."

"Roger. Since this is not a secure line, I will give you the details when I reach your location, 30 minutes. In the meantime, request you contact your counterpart. Have the force remain in place and meet with me at his location, repeat, his location, immediately after my arrival, over."

"Roger, Hoi Duc, Will do, over."

"Hoi Duc, out."

Pope set the hand set down and turned to Khoa.

"First Company will not attack Tuy An until morning. Second Company will have to reinforce. Captain Cox and Lieutenant Granger will remain in Hoi Duc and move with Second Company."

"What is your plan, Captain Pope?"

"I would like to fly into Tanh Linh and move with First Company to attack Tuy An. Second Company will assault from this direction in a coordinated two pronged attack. Since Captain Dang is dead, and the Regional Force battalion commander is not a field soldier, will you agree to command the forces?"

"I think that it is a good plan, but it must be approved by Major Nhia."

"Of course. I'll meet with him right away and get back to you," Pope said. He shook hands with the district chief and ran out the door.

Pope stopped at the waiting helicopter and briefed Cox and Granger.

*   *   *

Sullivan was waiting by the helipad at Binh Tuy. Pope jumped into the jeep, and the Major drove to province headquarters. They walked into the dining room where Major Nhia was waiting.

"I knew you would be hungry after a busy day, Captain Pope. You can wash in the adjoining room, and we'll sit down to dinner."

"Thank you sir, I could use something to eat," Pope said, as he headed for the washroom.

Pope returned, and the three men sat down at the table. Nhia poured some beer into Sullivan's glass.

"Now, what is this plan you wanted to discuss, Captain Pope?"

"Sir, I don't know who made the plan to send a company to attack Tuy An. If the VC decide to stay and fight, it could be a disaster. I estimate that at least a reinforced company is holding the village. Since they aren't dug in, I believe we could make a two pronged attack from Tanh Linh and Hoi Duc and drive them out. We'll need help from ARVN as a delayed reserve."

"I can probably get a battalion from the 23rd Infantry division flown in to Tanh Linh air strip by tomorrow afternoon if you can hold that long. With Captain Dang dead, Captain Thanh will have to command the two companies."

"I don't know how to say this delicately, so I'll just say it with an advance apology. I think Captain Thanh's days as a field commander are behind him. I suggest that since the battle is in Hoi Duc, Captain Khoa command the force."

"It will take some establishing of special communications because two companies have never worked together on an operation. Especially if they attack from different directions," Sullivan added.

"I'd like to put together a written operations order for your approval, then fly to Hoi Duc tonight and brief Captain Khoa, Captain Cox, and Lt. Granger. After that fly to Tanh Linh and brief the commander of First Company. I'll stay there and go with First Company. I'll have direct communications with Captain Khoa. Once we converge on Tuy An, communications will no longer be a concern," Pope said.

"I agree with the concept of your plan, Captain Pope. Let's have our dinner before you go to work," Nhia said waving at the food on the table.

"Sir, I'm concerned about security in province headquarters. If you don't mind, can you contact 23rd Division headquarters from our radio at the advisory compound to get the ARVN battalion? I would like everyone in the SOIC to think we are going ahead with the original plan," Pope said.

"Yes, that's very easy to do. I'll even stay at the compound and watch the movie while you are writing the operations order. Now, please, let's enjoy the meal."

*   *   *

Pope wolfed down the food and excused himself, asking Sullivan if he could use his jeep. He suggested Sullivan could catch a ride with Nhia. Sullivan agreed, and Pope hurried back to the compound. He went into the dining room where the short-handed advisory team lounged around.

"I'm going on an operation and need a partner. I realize you haven't been on a combat operation before, but you'll have to go, Sergeant White."

A startled White looked up from his chess game with Bishop and said, "Yes sir, I'm ready."

"Sir, it sounds like a big operation with a shit pot of casualties. Maybe you could use a medic, too," Gomez said.

"Christ, Sarge, volunteering twice in one day. You're going to get a bad reputation. I can't take you both. You guys work it out."

"Shit, I hate waiting around here not knowing what's going on, and Whitey can get info from the SOIC about the operation. Besides, I'm already packed up from today," Gomez replied.

"OK, Gomez. You just got your ass in another jam. Go out to the airstrip and pick up a team from the R & I platoon. Tell Sgt. Ma that they'll be going with me for a couple days. They'll be flying to Hoi Duc tonight. Martin, get on the radio and have a helicopter here in three hours."

*   *   *

He spent the next two hours writing the operations order. He took it to the day room and had Sergeant White stop the movie projector.

Major Nhia read the order completely, and said, "Good job, Captain Pope. The 21st battalion of the 46th ARVN Infantry Regiment will be at Tanh Linh by tomorrow afternoon."

He signed the operations orders and handed them to Pope.

"I've got two choppers laid on for us at first light tomorrow morning, Major Nhia," Sullivan said.

"In the ops order, I'm including A1E Skyraider air support at first light to blast the hill side near Tuy An to soften it up and support our attack. I plan a night move for both companies, and a predawn attack from the south," Pope said to Sullivan.

"No problem. I'll get on requesting the TAC air right away," Sullivan said, and he left.

Gomez entered and said, "I left the team from the R & I platoon at the helipad, sir."

"Great, Sarge, lets get packed up and head for the pad. Our chopper should be here any minute. See you tomorrow, Major," Pope said.

Nhia waved them off.

Gomez and Pope went to the ammo bunker and picked up twice as much ammo as they usually carried. Pope figured that it would be a nature walk or a hell of a fight, depending on what Charlie chose to do. By the time they got to the helipad, the chopper was inbound. The R & I team boarded the chopper with the advisors, and it took off for Hoi Duc.

*   *   *

Pope briefed the chopper pilot on his mission for the night. By the time they touched down at Hoi Duc, Cox was waiting by the helicopter pad.

"We've given the warning order to Second Company commander, Johnny. Larry is waiting in Khoa's office."

"Thanks, Bobby. It's going to be a long night and a longer day," he said as the three converged on district headquarters.

In the district chief's office, Pope said, "I got permission from the province chief for you and me to work together on this operation, Captain Khoa. Here is the signed operation order."

Pope handed the order to the Vietnamese officer.

Then he turned to Cox and handed a copy to him.

"Please read the operations order and I'll answer any questions when you've both finished."

The two studied the plan. Pope sat near a coffee table and poured a cold soft drink for himself and Gomez. Both officers looked up from their papers and looked at each other.

"Just so I understand your English writing, let me tell you what I read in your plan. There is a reinforced communist company in and around the village of Tuy An. At 2400 hours, Second Company with a five man team from the R & I platoon in the lead will make a night move through the jungle to a point on the side of a hill about one kilometer this side of Tuy An. At that point, we will deploy our company in an attack formation from east to west. At daybreak, aircraft will bomb and strafe the hillside north of Tuy An for approximately thirty minutes. When the aircraft leave, we will attack and sweep past the village, but are not to pursue the enemy any farther," Khoa said.

"Right so far. Two of the scouts are from Tuy An and know those woods like the back of their hands. They should be very helpful to you during the move," Pope said.

"At the same time, you'll depart from Tanh Linh district with First Company and make a night move north across the open rice paddies and fields and deploy in battle formation. Then you'll wait until just before daybreak and make a predawn assault on the village of Tuy An," Cox said.

"Yeah. They will expect us to attack during daylight hours from Tanh Linh, so we'll hit them when it's still dark. In the middle of the firefight, Skyraiders will prep the hill to the north. Then you'll take the pressure off us by attacking the dug-in force on the side of the hill."

"How do we know there's only a reinforced company in the village? We originally thought there was only a platoon," Cox queried.

"I think that's why Captain Pope has requested an ARVN battalion for reinforcements to arrive the day of the attack," Khoa responded.

"Yeah. But we need to have special communications for this operation because it must be closely coordinated, and Charlie likes to listen in on our frequency. We'll stay off the radio unless it's an extreme emergency. When each of us have taken our objectives, we'll tell the other 'code green.' If the other has not taken the objective and expect to take more than 15 minutes, respond with 'code red.' Once we have both taken our objectives, Captain Khoa, give me 'code purple.' Then wait a few minutes until we get the word to our troops so you don't come under fire by friendly forces as you move down from the hill."

"Then we will establish a perimeter defense with Second Company on the north half of the village and First Company on the south half. We will consolidate our ammo and move wounded to the edge of town to the south for air evacuation, right?" Cox asked.

"The command post will be established in the first house from the market in the center of the village," Khoa said.

"Right, and we'll use the team from the R & I platoon and any Popular Force soldiers as the reserve platoon, and they will be located at the command post. Dig in deep and wait for reinforcements. Any other questions or comments?" Pope asked.

All of them looked at each other and shrugged their shoulders.

"I have 2205 hours. I better get to Tanh Linh, and you need to brief your platoon leaders. Good luck. I'll see you in Tuy An," Pope said as he shook hands with the four officers.

*   *   *

He and Gomez went back to the helipad, boarded the chopper, and sped off on the ten-minute ride to Tanh Linh. When they landed, Jutte and Waters met them.

"What are you two doing here?" Pope asked.

"We got a message to return to Tanh Linh district headquarters because Second Company was in deep shit in Tuy An." Jutte said. "What's going on sir?"

"I'm glad to see you guys. So I don't have to repeat myself, why don't you come with me while I give the operations order to the company commander of First Company at the air strip," Pope said and he started toward a waiting jeep.

The Vietnamese soldier drove them to the airstrip. The company commander was waiting. Pope approached the young lieutenant, introduced himself, and handed him the operations order.

As the officer read the plan, Pope sized him up. Lieutenant Kong was small, even by Vietnamese standards. To make matters worse, he looked like he was about 17 years old.

After studying the plan, Kong said, "This is very unusual, Captain Pope. The province chief says I am to take orders from you until we take the objective of Tuy An, then I take orders from Captain Khoa, at which time, you will become advisor to Captain Khoa. That's fine with me, sir. I have heard about your exploits with First Company and am proud to serve with you."

"I'm glad you understand that, Lieutenant. That is an important part of the plan."

"The plan is written in English. Just so I understand the order completely, will you be kind enough to tell me the plan verbally, sir?"

Pope squatted next to Kong and outlined the entire plan to the commander and the advisors.

"Lieutenant Kong, we should be on the road by 0100 hours to make the night move to Tuy An. Go ahead and give the attack order to your platoon leaders. Have them tell the men to leave their packs and rations here. Everything loose should be tied tight to their bodies. Fill canteens **completely** with water or keep them empty. Once on the move, we are to be quiet—no talking or smoking. We are going to get to our attack position without being discovered."

"Jutte, you and Duke remain in Tanh Linh until Third Company receives further orders. But under no circumstance do you come to our aid. I'm still worried about the enemy activity around the village of Bo Ninh. If you leave, Tanh Linh would be exposed."

"Roger that, sir. It sounds like you've had a bad day, and it could be worse tomorrow," Jutte said, looking solemn.

"This could be a nature walk, too. I'll see you guys when we get back," Pope said, and he and Gomez shook hands with the two advisors and walked to the infantry company.

As they sat at the airfield waiting for kick off time, Pope thought: *Well, here we go again, Grandfather. You were right. I dodged bullets today. The spirit of the whale is still with me. But what about tomorrow? Can this outfit make a night attack? The most difficult offensive tactical maneuver? At least there's some improvement. I'm commanding this company instead of going along for the exercise!*

Chapter Twenty Three

At 2400 hours, Second Company departed Hoi Duc with the Yard scouts in the lead. One was on point while two others took turns breaking trail with large machetes.

At exactly 0100 hours First Company departed the airstrip and crossed over the Dong Ba River Bridge into Hoi Duc district. Pope figured the walk would be easy because they would be crossing rice paddies and open fields. But the enemy could see for a great distance and sound traveled in the dark. The water in the rice paddies was not very deep, making walking easier, but the stink hung in Pope's nose.

By 0300, First Company was halfway to their assault positions. Pope halted the column and told the two assault platoons to deploy on line. If they were discovered prematurely, they would already be in an attack formation. He left the third platoon in reserve, then told the radio operator and Gomez to follow him forward. The half moon reflected off the paddy water and made them easy targets.

As they passed the sweating, waiting soldiers, Gomez thought, *Jesus Christ, now the Ice Man wants me to go with him while he leads the attack. When am I going to learn to keep my fuckin Mexican mouth shut!*

When Pope got to the front, the soldiers were spread out in battle formation 250 yards across the paddies. Pope squatted down and quietly cupped a handful of water. He poured it on his left shoulder, quietly cupped another handful, and poured it on his right shoulder. *Be with me whale spirit.* He stood, raised his arm and motioned the men forward behind him.

* * *

By 0500 hours, both attacking companies reached their assault positions. Khoa had his two lead platoons quietly deploy in a line assault formation in the thick jungle about one kilometer from the village of Tuy An. Pope was happy—his company was one kilometer from the edge of the village and had not been discovered by the enemy. He signaled with both arms for the men to lie in the wet, stinking paddies. They would wait until thirty minutes before dawn—0535, then attack. He lay in the muddy water, waiting, hoping Second Company was in position and the Skyraiders would appear as planned.

At precisely 0535, Pope and Kong got First Company on their feet and with a sweep of Pope's arm; the infantry unit crept quietly forward in a crouch. Three hundred yards from the edge of the village, a single shot rang out from the village, followed by machine gun fire and other small arms. The First Company machine gunners poured fire toward the muzzle blasts. The assault platoons held their fire as they staggered forward in the muck. Machineguns rattled and tracers streaked across the field in the predawn. For a few precious minutes it was a duel between the government machine guns and the communist automatic weapons.

Shots rang out from the fence surrounding the village. Bullets kicked up water around the assault force as the concern to keep quiet turned to a strong desire to stay alive. The muzzle flashes looked like a long string of blinking Christmas tree lights. Pope saw two soldiers fall to his right and yelled, "Fire!"

Pope opened fire with his Car 15. The entire attacking force fired its weapons and moved forward as one. The enemy machine guns' deadly green flames shifted toward the attacking force and more government soldiers fell, mortally wounded. Mortar rounds crunched and exploded with a white-orange color.

The sun peeked above the horizon. Four A1E Skyraiders screamed over Pope's head and bombed the hill north of the village. The enemy fire let up slightly, and Pope and Gomez ran for the lone VC machine gun still spitting deadly fire, 100 yards to their left front. Pope pulled a grenade from his pouch while he ran, pulled the pin and sprinted 30 yards closer. He slowed, got up on his tiptoes like he was back on the State U football field, and "passed" a grenade at the machine gun. It exploded in the lap of a startled assistant machine gunner and blew him and his two comrades into the next world.

When the machine gun was silenced, small arms fire from the enemy stopped and the government forces found the paths through the mine-field. They wriggled through the fence and into the village, yelling, screaming, and shooting.

Gomez panted up to Pope, "Son of a bitch, sir. You act like this is a foot-ball game. That VC was a tight end you hit with a spiral for a touchdown."

Pope smiled. "Football and war, they're not so different. Lets go!"

The Skyraiders pounded the hill, and the deadly explosions blocked the VC escape route to the jungle. Inside the fence, remnants of the communist force were in disarray and withdrawing west. Pope saw two guerrillas twenty yards away and fired at them on full automatic. One communist pitched forward as if hit in the back by a baseball bat. The other guerrilla's head snapped forward and his knees buckled. The attacking force swung to the left and pursued the retreating enemy.

Now it was a war of one on one—one soldier against another in a race to the end of the village. Enemy and friendly soldiers were intermixed, and confusion prevailed. The loud bomb explosions stopped. Pope quickly organized about ten soldiers close by and assaulted the few remaining VC, killing six. The remaining enemy withdrew out the gate at the edge of the village and melted into the jungle. He told the company commander to consolidate his force toward the northern edge of the village and support Second Company's assault.

The company got into position. Small arms and automatic weapons fire broke out from the jungle. They were pinned down and couldn't move in the village. The enemy commanded the heights and looked down the throats of First Company. Pope hoped Second Company would be able to accomplish their end of the plan.

∗   ∗   ∗

Before dawn, Cox and Granger heard the fight between Pope's unit and the VC, and the Skyraiders made their bomb runs on Second Company's objective. Captain Khoa signaled the assaulting platoons forward. The soldiers moved ahead, stumbling over bushes and logs as the jungle canopy hid them from the sun and daylight. It was easy to stay on a path toward their objective. All they had to do was follow the sounds of the exploding bombs. The explosions sounded so close that Granger hoped that the planes didn't stray in his direction.

Khoa stopped the advance and waited for the Skyraiders to finish their job. Daylight seeped through the canopy. He dressed up the lines of attacking troops and the planes withdrew. Cox heard small arms fire in the village. Khoa signaled the assault to continue. Small arms fire erupted to their front a hundred yards away and the assault line hesitated—but the fire wasn't directed at them. It was going toward the village.

Cox whispered to Khoa, "Hot damn, they're taking First Company under fire. We not only have them flanked, but their firing is giving away their positions!"

The RTO told Khoa First Company had just reported "code green." Khoa smiled and said, "Reply message to them, 'code red'."

The center of the assaulting force killed two guerrillas in a foxhole that were firing down into the village. They died without knowing what hit them. Cox ran by a dead VC soldier whose face was blackened and was oozing blood. The smell of exploded bombs and death was overpowering. Now the dug-in enemy was alert to government forces on their flank and fired wildly toward them. Jungle foliage made it difficult for the enemy to withdraw but slowed the government advance just as much.

As the assault moved forward, VC tried to escape north up the hill but ran into advancing troops and were killed instantly. The enemy commander recognized his flank had been turned, so he withdrew to the west along the side of the hill.

Cox got on the radio to Pope and said, "This is Second Company. Request you set up mortars and continue firing in the jungle north of the village near the west end of the village until I order cease fire."

"Roger. Will do."

Pope turned to Kong and repeated the fire mission. Mortar rounds rained down on the jungle north of Tuy An.

With his retreating troops' escape route to the west blocked by mortar fire, the VC commander fought his way up hill to the north. Second Company was in the middle of a "turkey shoot." The VC were completely disorganized and tried frantically to break out of the trap. Some of the enemy soldiers got away.

Second Company advanced close to the mortar fire. Cox radioed "Cease fire."

With all enemy resistance stopped, Khoa radioed "Code Purple."

* * *

Platoon leaders of Second Company organized their forces, moved out of the jungle, and into the village of Tuy An.

When Khoa entered the village, Pope was there to meet him.

They shook hands. Pope said, "Nice job, Captain Khoa. Now I turn command of First Company to you and the company commander."

"No, Captain Pope, we are a good team, and we'll work together."

"I love it when a plan comes together!" Cox said, slapping Pope on the back.

"Yeah, well, we don't know what Charlie is going to do now. He may crawl away and lick his wounds, or we may have a wounded, angry whale. We have to prepare for any eventuality. Let's organize our perimeter defense and move our wounded to the helipad."

"I'll call for the medevac," Granger volunteered.

"I'll organize and treat the wounded," Gomez said. Then he stopped, hesitated, and turned to Pope and said, "Sir, if you're planning on being a point man on the next assault, don't bother dialing this fuckin Mex's number." Before Pope could answer Gomez was gone.

"What was that all about?" Cox asked.

"Every time Gomez goes out with me, he ends up in the Lion's den," Pope said laughing.

He contacted Sullivan on the radio. "We have secured the objective, over"

"Roger that. Your friends have been delayed due to transportation problem, over."

"Understand delay. When can I expect them? Over."

"Sometime tomorrow. Can you hold? Over."

"I guess we'll have to, out.

"Well great, Cox said.

Pope said, "Every time we depend on higher headquarters, we get shit on. We pull off a text book night attack and the only thing Division had to do was get the reinforcements, and they blew it."

"Khoa is going to love this news." Cox replied.

Pope found Khoa. "I have just heard that the ARVN battalion won't be here until tomorrow."

"Maybe we should return to Hoi Duc headquarters then," Khoa said.

"I don't think that would be a good idea. Captain Dang always impressed on me that we have to show the civilians that we can protect them."

"Yes, but we are just turning this village into a battle ground."

"That may be true, but if we don't confront them here, we may have to fight them at Hoi Duc next week or next month."

"I guess you are right, Captain Pope. What do you suggest we do?"

"I think we should put half the unit digging fighting foxholes on the perimeter and the other half enlarging and improving the bomb shelters for the civilians. Just in case the communists decide to mortar the village."

"I'll give the order."

"In the meantime, I'm going to send one two-man team from the east and one from the west to sweep through your objective this morning, to count dead, and pick up weapons."

"Excellent. Maybe you could leave them there tonight as listening posts if the enemy returns."

"Great. I'll get them moving," Pope said.

He found the R& I team, gave them a radio and a frequency, and told them to report only to him. The two teams moved in opposite directions on their missions. Pope told Cox and Granger to dig deep bomb shelters, one for each advisor, in the house where Khoa and his command post were located.

*   *   *

In the afternoon, the scouts reported 48 dead VC soldiers and 12 AK 47s. Counting First Company's body count of 32 dead VC, they had 80 VC KIA and 37 captured weapons. Friendly casualties were only 5 KIA and 14 WIA. He ordered the teams back to the village with the weapons.

By 1500 hours, the wounded had been medevaced, and Gomez found the CP. Granger, and Cox, shirts off, were digging near a house.

"What's happening, sirs?"

"We're digging bomb shelters for us, you, and Captain Pope," Granger said. "Would it be asking too much for you to participate in a little manual labor, Sergeant?"

"Which hole is IceMan's?"

"The one I'm digging," Granger replied.

"With all due respect, sir, will you get your ass out of my hole so I can get to work?" Gomez asked, taking off his fatigue shirt.

"Why don't you make up your mind, Sarge? This morning you told Ice you didn't want anything to do with him. Now you want to be foxhole buddies."

"Listen, I said I didn't want to follow him leading the assault. The crazy bastard was twenty yards out in front of First Company and opening a bigger gap every minute. If that Whale spirit keeps a mortar round from his foxhole, I want to be in there with him. Now get your ass out of the Captain's hole, sir," Gomez said jumping into the pit to the laughter of Cox and Granger.

*   *   *

The scouts returned with the captured weapons and stored them in the house where the CP was located. Pope gave them each a claymore mine.

"What are those, Captain Pope?" Khoa asked?

"They are called claymore mines." Pope said, showing one of the small anti-personnel mines to Khoa. They are filled with little ball bearings. When they detonate, they spray the ball bearings in a thirty-five yard kill zone."

"How are they detonated?"

"They are rigged with a wire and the curved part is facing the enemy. Our scout attaches a wire to the back of the mine, let's the wire out twenty yards. When the enemy gets in the kill zone, he attaches the wire to this little battery."

"And the enemy is killed or wounded."

"That's right,"

To the scouts, Pope said, "You are to deploy as listening posts halfway up the hill at two separate locations. If enemy forces returns in strength, blow the claymore and get back here as soon as you can. Coordinate with foxholes that you will be returning through so you don't get killed by friendly fire."

He had an evening meal prepared for the scouts. They ate it in about five minutes, and by 1800 hours, they moved quietly into the jungle. The rest of the command group rested on the ground near their bomb shelters to wait out the night. The companies were put on fifty-percent alert, meaning one man in the foxhole slept while the other stayed alert.

Pope stayed awake while Gomez snored next to him. He thought: *Damn! I sure miss Kathryn. After this operation is over I'm going to call her and see if she will see me in Saigon. We caught Charlie with his pants down. They didn't expect the attack until daylight. That spy in our midst got the wrong information to them. I'm really going to miss Dang. Now I have to figure out another way to get things done without going through that son of a bitch, Sullivan.*

Chapter Twenty Four

An explosion at the west edge of the village interrupted Pope's pleasant thoughts about Kathryn. It was 0215. Another blast, and, as one, the command group rolled into their bomb shelters. Sporadic mortar rounds detonated throughout the night. No one was injured, but two homes burned to the ground.

At 0500 hours, Pope heard a large blast on the side of the hill. At 0545, one of the scout teams reported the enemy returned to the high ground in strength. They killed three VC with the claymore before withdrawing. Just before dawn, the other scout team reported they saw and heard many VC, but none got close enough to kill with the claymore, so they picked it up and returned.

As the morning sun brought the heat of the day, civilians moved about the village doing their routine activities. A few minutes later, soldiers got out of their shelters, warily watching the hillside. Rifle fire erupted from the jungle, wounding a corporal. Khoa ordered the troops not to move around.

"Why don't we put out the word to the hamlet chief to have the civilians evacuate the village and head for Tanh Linh. They don't seem to want to hurt them," Pope said.

"I'll tell him now," Khoa said. He got out of the hole and ran to the chief's house. Two bullets kicked up dirt behind him.

Two hours later a group of civilians, their worldly belongings piled on carts, exited the fence and walked down the road toward Tanh Linh. A machine gun fired on them. The ground around them erupted in puffs of dust and dull thuds. The civilians ran back into the village. No one else attempted to leave.

* * *

Meanwhile Sullivan got the message that the ARVN battalion was at the airstrip but the aircraft had been delayed for a higher priority mission. Major Nhia decided to move his headquarters to Tanh Linh to be closer to the action.

Before he left the compound, Sullivan answered a routine telephone call from Kathryn to Pope.

"I'm sorry, Kathryn. Pope is with a unit North of here that is under siege."

"How long have they been holed up?"

"A couple days. We're waiting for a battalion to be airlifted in but we can't get air transportation."

"That sounds ridiculous. There aren't that many major battles going on in Vietnam. You ought to be able to cut loose some transport."

"I've tried every way I can," Sullivan said, thinking, who the hell does she think she is? Telling me that I can't do my job.

"We'll see about that, major. I'll see you in a little while." The connection was broken.

* * *

"Binh Tuy, this is Tuy An. What is the status of my request, over?" Pope asked.

"This is Binh Tuy actual. My counter part says that your request has been delayed, over." Sullivan said.

"Binh Tuy, maybe you don't fully understand our situation, over."

"Why don't you enlighten me, over."

"This is Tuy An. We are under constant mortar fire, and are pinned down. We are taking casualties—both military and civilian. The longer we sit here, the more time the enemy has to mass for an attack. I estimate a battalion sized enemy force, over."

"Roger, understand battalion size enemy force. We have aircraft delay, but will request larger size reinforcements, over."

"This is Tuy An, I don't understand why aircraft would be a problem. How soon can we expect help, over?"

"Tuy An, There are no guarantees. I'll get it as soon as I can. Out."

Pope turned to Captain Khoa and the advisors and shouted over the mortar explosions. "I just got word that our reinforcements have been delayed. They can't get aircraft for transport."

"The village chief reported that the civilians have almost no food," Khoa said.

"Is there any way of transporting food from Hoi Duc?" Pope asked

"The road has been cut off by the enemy."

"I suggest that we take rations from the soldiers and give it to the civilians. We can survive on water for a couple days."

"I'll pass the word to the company commanders," Khoa said and he rose from the foxhole and sprinted down the street.

"Are we in as deep-shit as it appears, sir?" Gomez asked, between mortar explosions.

"It's pretty bad, Sarge, but we're pretty well dug in. We should be able to withstand one or two attacks," Pope said.

"The civilians will really get tore up, huh?"

"That's my biggest concern, right now, Gomez."

"It's almost dark—you think we'll get hit tonight?"

"We might, but I'm thinking tomorrow morning. Charlie needs time to get organized for the assault."

"Tuy An, this is Binh Tuy actual, over," Sullivan's words came from the radio handset near Pope.

Pope picked up the handset and took a deep breath. "This is Tuy An, over."

"Tuy An, what is your situation, over."

"This is Tuy An. We're holding our own. More importantly, what the hell are you doing, over?"

"This is Binh Tuy. A State Department plane and liaison officer just arrived. The State Department aid got the transportation released. Help will start arriving at first light in the morning, over."

"That may be too late, Binh Tuy. Especially if we are attacked tonight,"

Kathryn, standing next to Sullivan grabbed the handset. "Johnny, this is Kathryn. You just hold on. Help will be there."

"I'm really glad to hear your voice—Honey. I'm OK, but I need to talk to the boss, over."

Kathryn started to say something and Sullivan grabbed the handset.

"Can you hold out till morning, over?"

"This is Tuy An. We have plenty of ammo. We have been completely out of food for both military and civilians since this afternoon. I don't know how long the civilians can take this constant bombardment."

"This is Binh Tuy. I will request a food drop for noon tomorrow. Can you think of anything else?

"Roger, Binh Tuy, request air strikes at first light. Get help here soonest, out."

*   *   *

The government forces spent the second night in their bomb shelters as the mortar platoons exchanged H & I firing. Pope sent a scout team out with orders to capture a VC soldier. At 0100 hours, they returned with a prisoner bound and gagged. Pope turned the prisoner over to Khoa for interrogation.

The prisoner was a private in the 62nd VC battalion and said they were going to attack the village at dawn. Khoa got the word out to the commanders. Pope was glad he would have tactical air on station at dawn.

At 0430 hours, a salvo of mortar rounds fell on the village. The hellish rain of death continued until about 0500 hours. RPG 7 rounds ripped into the wooden fence on the Northern side of Tuy An. Pope immediately thought *they had either been had by false information, or the prisoner didn't get the right word. They were attacking early!* Machine guns fired from both flanks of the enemy-occupied hills into the village, riddling houses and setting three on fire with tracer rounds.

The firing shifted to the southern part of the village and five sappers approached the barbed wire about sixty yards from the outer fence to the north. Three VC were killed instantly by government fire. One blew a hole through the barbed wire with a satchel charge before he was killed. Pope fired illumination flares as fast as Gomez gave them to him.

Seventy black-clad communists, looking like ghosts in the eerie light of the parachute flares attacked in the direction of the hole in the barbed wire. Government forces fired mortar rounds on them, knocking several invaders down. Two machine guns opened up and cut down the advancing guerrillas like a scythe. Some of the VC got to the minefield, and four were blown up by land mines, but the attackers continued. Fifty more VC came out of the woodline heading for the break. They were stopped in their tracks by the withering fire of the automatic weapons. What was left of the attacking force pulled back into the tree line.

Mortar and RPG fire continued against the northern part of the fence. Pope moved the second platoon of First Company into bomb shelters with the command group. Four sappers, with two satchel charges blew a huge hole in the barbed wire at the other end of the village. The enemy fire shifted to the southern part of the village, and100 screaming enemy soldiers moved out of the woodline toward the defenses.

RF machine guns took them under fire, and more illumination rounds lit the battlefield. The assaulting force swept through the minefield, using their soldiers as human mine sweepers.

"The enemy has penetrated second platoon," Khoa shouted to Pope.

"I'm taking the reserves to counterattack," Pope said to Khoa in Vietnamese. Then to the reserve platoon, shouted, "We attack, follow me!"

* * *

As Pope leaped out of the bomb shelter, Gomez said, "Oh Shit!" jumped out of the hole, and followed his partner into the living hell.

They sprinted up the street as bullets kicked up dirt around them. The platoon of soldiers ran to keep up with him. The sun broke the horizon, and Pope saw VC had penetrated the village's defenses—ten black-clad devils were on a collision course with him. Gomez opened fire, and Pope took two hand grenades, pulled both pins, stopped, and threw them both at the same time—one from each hand.

Gomez cut down two VC with his M2 carbine, and the explosions sent four more sprawling. Pope waved the government soldiers to deploy. They formed an assault line and swept toward the break in the fence.

Two A1E Skyraiders swept in at tree top level and caught 40 VC in the open, just outside the fence. Pope could see the grim face of the pilot as he leaned forward in the cockpit, aiming his destruction on the guerrillas. The strafing chewed up several communists with 20-mm machine guns. Two more Skyraiders followed with a bombing run on the exposed attackers.

The VC in the village withdrew toward the hole in the fence, and Pope's attackers cut them down as fast as they could catch them. Within minutes, the perimeter was restored, and the mortar and RPG fire stopped. Pope gathered the reserves and returned them to their positions. The Skyraiders continued their attack on the enemy-held hill for thirty minutes, and the infantrymen in the village cheered them on. The respite was short lived: mortar rounds landed on the village a half-hour after the aircraft departed.

* * *

At noon the Skyraiders returned and rained 30 more minutes of death on the VC attackers in the hills. A half-hour after their departure, the enemy mortaring resumed. Constant fire from the hills meant no choppers could land for a medevac or food resupply. Pope was in radio communication with Sullivan in a helicopter, high above the fight.

"This is Binh Tuy actual, a force is about 2000 yards from your location, heading north. Another element is the same distance, heading west. They should converge on you within an hour, over."

"This is Tuy An. Roger, understand help in an hour. Situation here sporadic mortar rounds still falling on us. We have several wounded soldiers and civilians. We'll need a team of PsyOps/civil affairs people as soon as possible to deal with the civilians. Morale of troops and advisors better than it was last night. Over." He looked across the paddies and could barely make out the movement of ARVN troops plodding toward him.

"Roger, understand your message. Choppers are moving to airstrip. First priority is medevac, second priority is PsyOps/civil affairs, out."

Ten minutes after the transmission, enemy mortar rounds shifted from the village to the attacking 22nd ARVN battalion to the south. Pope heard small arms and automatic weapons fire in the hills northwest of Tuy An— the other ARVN battalion. As fast as the mortaring shifted, it stopped completely and the battle raged to the northwest. The village defenders became observers of a battle only a thousand yards away. Thirty minutes after the battle started, the firing stopped.

*   *   *

Cox and Pope went to the Village Square, where a makeshift aid station was established for the wounded soldiers and civilians. The wounded littered the stalls normally used to sell produce, and spread out onto the dirt streets. Some were in great pain, others near death, but most stared blankly, straight ahead. Hope was absent. Families of the sick and wounded leaned over their loved ones, some murmuring words of encouragement, others wailing in pain. Pope imagined how difficult it would be to witness his beautiful, peaceful home in Washington caught in such a battle. The stench of death and decaying bodies mixed together and permeated the village.

The team of advisors sat outside, eating bananas, shaded from the sun by a large palm tree.

"Damn! The silence is deafening, isn't it?" Cox said.

"Sir, it's Major Sullivan on the horn. He wants an LZ to land," Gomez said to Pope.

"OK, I'll head over there to meet him. Give him the landing instructions." *The shooting stops and the old man comes in to give advice,* Pope thought.

"Yes sir, but you ain't fuckin leaving me here. The Major probably has some C rats on the chopper," Gomez said as he picked up the pace to keep up.

The other two officers looked at each other, jumped to their feet, and fell in behind Gomez. When the chopper landed, Sullivan kicked out two cases of C rations then jumped down off the aircraft. The commander of the 46th ARVN Regiment and his senior advisor, an infantry major, followed him. Gomez and Granger grabbed the cases and carried them clear of the Huey. After introductions were made all around, the commander and senior advisor departed to coordinate the consolidation of their unit.

"The chopper is going back to Tanh Linh to Pick up a Civil Affairs advisor. It'll be right back," Sullivan said.

Four medevac choppers approached from the south.

"Gomez, coordinate the medevac, will you please?" Pope said.

*   *   *

The advisors took the rations two houses away and sat in the shade. Granger opened the cases, and the hungry advisors dug in. Granger excused himself and took some rations to Gomez.

"I thought it was bad, but not this bad." Sullivan said. "This has really been an eye opener for the division, Johnny. There will be some emphasis on Binh Tuy on the part of the government for a while now," and he shook his head.

"Yeah, but how long can we expect ARVN to stay here?" Pope said. He wanted to tell Sullivan there were more than a handful of VC in his "pacified province," but thought better.

"We can't expect the regiment to stay long, but I don't think it's unrealistic to expect a battalion to remain."

Pope peered down the dirt street and saw five men—two Americans and three smaller Vietnamese. The sun was at their backs but he recognized the taller American's familiar bow-legged gait.

"Well, I'll be damned! Bill McGuire!" He shouted as he jumped to his feet and dashed the thirty yards to the advisors.

McGuire ran about five yards and caught him in his arms as both men embraced. The combination of sleep loss, fatigue, and emotions caught Pope off balance, and he unashamedly hugged his friend and wept quietly.

"You're a sight for sore eyes, sir," McGuire said in Pope's ear.

"God. If I had known you were involved, I would have had more confidence that help would arrive. You have no idea how great it is to have my ass pulled out of the fire by you, Bill," he replied between sobs.

"I had a lot of help, sir. A beautiful woman in particular got State to go to MACV and get aircraft to transport my battalion."

"I'll be **double** damned! Kathryn?" He asked, stepping back and rubbing his face with both arms.

"Yes sir. I'm sure glad she's on our side. She tore some people some new assholes. Your boss included. You're a lucky man, Skipper."

"Don't I know it!"

"Sir, I want you to meet my assistant, Lieutenant Sam Purdey. Sam, shake hands with one of the finest officers in the army. He was my company commander in the eighty-deuce. I learned more from him in six months than I learned before or since."

Pope pumped the lieutenant's hand and said, "Glad to meet you. You've got a hell of a boss!"

"Tell me something I don't already know, sir."

"Come on over here, Bill, I want to introduce you to some friends."

* * *

Introductions were made, and the Vietnamese officers excused themselves and went to the command post of the regimental commander. As McGuire and his assistant sat with a can of C rats, Pope was engrossed in an animated conversation and didn't notice Kathryn approaching to his rear.

She put her hands over his eyes and said, "Don't shoot, I'm a friend."

Pope stopped in mid sentence as he recognized the soft hands and familiar scent of Chanel No. 5 perfume. Kathryn threw her arms around him and fell on top of him as he tried to stand. They lay on the ground and kissed for a half minute.

"I've waited too long to see you, Johnny." Kathryn said, breathless.

"What a great day this is. First Bill, and now you!" Pope said, getting to his feet, but keeping one arm around Kathryn's waist.

"You're lucky to have such a friend as Bill. I thought he was going to tear down division headquarters, then Tanh Linh CP, trying to get his battalion to you, Johnny." She said.

"Roger that. It's sure great to be alive!" Pope said.

"I hate to break up old home week, but someone needs a shower," Kathryn said moving away from Pope and holding her nose. Laughter erupted from the giddy advisors.

"Seriously sir, what's the game plan?" Pope asked.

"McGuire's battalion will occupy the high ground to the north for a few days. The 22nd battalion will stay in Tuy An. Tomorrow. C 123s will fly First Company back to Binh Tuy and bring in USAID supplies for the civilians. Kathryn will remain here to coordinate that effort with Granger. PsyOps teams will enter the village tomorrow with Bishop. I'm ordering you, Cox, Granger, and Gomez to return to the advisory compound before nightfall for a hot meal, a shower, and a good night's sleep. God knows, you've earned it."

"I'm sure I can speak for the others when I say that all three of us appreciate the chance to get back for a good nights sleep, but Sergeant Gomez would rather remain here and help the ARVN," Pope said, suppressing a smile.

"Bull shit!" Gomez said, and the others guffawed. "Um, excuse me, ma'am. I mean, heck no, I'm heading back to the compound with the rest of you."

*   *   *

Kathryn and Pope walked through the village together viewing the burned out houses and damaged souls. They saw the pallid faces of the civilians who survived the siege. The RF soldiers smiled at them and said hello.

"I've really got a lot of work to do here, Johnny," Kathryn said with a sigh.

"I don't understand why Charlie wouldn't let the civilians out of the village. I don't think he won any friends here."

"I hope you'll forget about that last conversation we had in Saigon. I'm sorry I was such a bitch."

Pope smiled through his filthy face and said, "It's already forgotten. Maybe we should have talked it through that night. I feel bad that I didn't contact you first.

"I'm worried about you, Johnny. Don't you think you're pushing the whale spirit thing to the edge?"

"Maybe so. I don't know. All I really know is that I've got a job to do."

"Yes, but do you have to be involved in everything?"

"It's my job, Honey. I'm good at it, and I like doing it. You saw the sad faces of the civilians. If you had been here when the encirclement was lifted, you would have seen them smiling and thankful. You should feel some measure of pride because you helped to make that possible."

"I know, but I've never spent such a long time worrying about you. We were only six miles apart, but it was like being a lifetime from you."

The couple returned to the lounging advisors, and Sullivan told Pope it was time to go. Pope kissed Kathryn and turned to McGuire. "I'm counting on you taking care of her until I get back tomorrow."

"Airborne, sir."

"I know, Bill. And stop calling me 'sir'. We're both captains now."

"Some habits are hard to change…Johnny."

On the chopper ride to Binh Tuy, he suddenly felt tired and sleepy. Three nights with no sleep and forty-eight hours under siege in Tuy An. With the thump-thump-thump of the helicopter engine, Pope was alone with his thoughts: *This is really a crazy war and it keeps getting crazier. It's hard to predict anything. Why is it that a female USAID worker has to go to State and they go to MACV to get aircraft to move troops? Military commanders should be able to take the responsibility to do it themselves. After what happened the last few days there is no doubt that there's a spy in our midst. I'm pretty sure I know who it is now.*

Chapter Twenty Five

The day after Pope and the other advisors returned to sector headquarters from Hoi Duc Sullivan met with him.

"I'm sorry I blew up at you in front of Major Nhia the other day. Captain Cox took responsibility for going on the operation without authority, and Captain Dang gave the attack plan to the chief of staff before he told you the details."

"No apology is necessary, sir. That seems like a long time ago."

"I'm still pissed off at you because the province is being over run with communists. Common sense tells me that you are not the cause, but I keep thinking how nice it was before you arrived."

"I don't know what to tell you, sir. Somehow we got off on the wrong foot. I hope we can work out our differences. Getting back to business, we have to do something about getting more responsive chopper support as well as close air support. If Charlie wanted to, they could have taken Hoi Duc headquarters that night after the Second Company debacle."

"I hate to tell you this, but I found out your gunship escort chopper was siphoned off for an administrative flight to Saigon for some staff officers. That will not happen again. Waters told me that you never sleep at night in the field. I let you sleep in today. Gomez, Granger, Bishop, White, and their Vietnamese counterparts have already gone back to Tuy An."

"What about the regional force units?"

"First Company arrived here this morning, and Second Company was trucked to Hoi Duc headquarters yesterday evening. The 23rd battalion of

46th Regiment was flown in to Tanh Linh yesterday and is on an operation sweeping the hill above the hamlet of Bo Ninh. The Regimental headquarters has been moved to Tanh Linh. Waters and Jutte have returned to the compound. Your Yard group choppered back this morning, and the team leader said you owed them some money."

I'll get the cash to him today. On another subject, I really think we have a spy in our midst. I wish I could smoke him out."

"For Christ sake. Are you still on that kick?"

"Yes, sir. I think that as a minimum, Captain Trang is the traitor. There could be more."

"The Chief of Staff? Now I know you've gone off the deep end. Listen, you God damn blanket-ass. You can't tell me a person of that rank and position is working for the Cong."

Pope felt the blood rush to his face and his jaws tighten. He clenched his fists at his side as he leaped to his feet.

"All right. There it is. Now we both know what the problem is. You're prejudiced against me because I'm an Indian."

"Bull shit. I lived near a reservation in Montana. Some of my best friends are Indians."

"They may be, but I'm not going to put up with you calling me names, sir."

"You don't have any choice in the matter, Captain.

"Why don't we just step outside and see whose is the master race?"

"You'd like that, wouldn't you. Legally kicking the shit out of an older man in front of his troops."

"Hell, I don't care where we do it. Let's rent a hall in downtown Saigon—I'm fed up with your racist bullshit."

"I suggest we continue this conversation at a later date, when we've both had a chance to cool off."

"I'll cool off, but I will not forget it, **sir**."

*   *   *

Pope joined the group in Tuy An. He spent his days working with White and Gomez treating civilians and contacting agents. His evenings were spent visiting with Kathryn and Bill McGuire. It was almost like a vacation, with no stress and a lot of laughing.

A few days after the debacle in Tuy An, one of Pope's intelligence agents reported the Viet Cong were planning to ambush the Second Company and shoot down any supporting helicopters. There were two companies of VC waiting in the wood line to attack the village as soon as his chopper landed. One trigger-happy VC soldier shot at the Huey prematurely, forcing others to fire as well. He was glad the South Vietnamese army didn't have **all** the undisciplined soldiers.

After occupying Tuy An for a week, the 46th Regiment pulled out, leaving the 22nd ARVN Battalion in Binh Tuy. Pope said his good byes to McGuire, and promised to meet sometime in the future and spend a couple days in Nha Trang on the beach. Kathryn caught a chopper back to Saigon the same day. All the advisors returned to Binh Tuy. Sullivan had a big feast prepared and bought the beer for a wild party that evening.

*   *   *

Two weeks later, Captain Dang's replacement arrived. Since the officer had very little combat experience, Pope concluded he got his rank through political connections. In addition, he was recently promoted, and young for a major. Major Phong was tall for a Vietnamese, about the same height as Pope, but much slimmer. With a handsome face and youthful enthusiasm, Phong cut a dashing figure as a leader. Pope was in the SOIC working with the Chief of Staff on MedCap missions when Phong entered the room.

He marched directly to Pope, grabbed his hand, shook it with both hands, patted him on the back, and said in perfect English, "You must be Captain Pope, the famous American Indian. I'm Major Phong, the new deputy province chief. We're going to kill many VC together."

Pope answered, "I'm pleased to meet you, Major Phong. I hope we will have a long and prosperous association."

Phong glanced around the room. The soldiers had stopped work and were watching them. He said, "Why don't we go to my office for some tea? We have a lot to discuss."

They entered Captain Dang's old office, and Pope could see a sharp contrast in furnishings. Dang had rather austere, plain furnishings: Phong's office was decorated with expensive furniture, paintings, and vases. Behind his desk, on the wall, were two pictures. He was in both of them, shaking hands with General Nguyen Cao Ky in one and with General "Big" Minh in the other.

"You'll notice I like to live comfortably. Just because there is a war on doesn't mean that we have to be deprived of simple comforts. Don't you agree, Captain Pope?"

"I never really gave it much thought, Major Phong. I'm just a simple Indian boy from a reservation in Washington State."

"You're much too modest. I've heard all about your humble beginnings, fame as a football player, and skill at finding and killing VC," Phong said, smiling.

"If you know all that, you also know the VC have a way of finding me, too."

With a laugh, Major Phong said, "I believe that you have made a very good start here, but the Viet Cong are building up in our area, and we need to be more aggressive. Do you agree?"

"Yes, but I think we need to take more time planning combat operations. We also have a spy in our midst who seems to know our plans. Our units have been ambushed far too many times for it to be a coincidence."

"Do you suspect anyone?"

"Yes." He thought, *I hope this boy wonder can keep his mouth shut. I hope he can be trusted.* "I suspect Captain Trang, the Chief of Staff. But I don't have any proof."

"Captain Trang! That is a very serious accusation. How did you come to such a conclusion?" Phong asked, clearly surprised by the accusation.

"Many things add up. Trang likes to report for work late in the morning, but then works late at night when there is only a skeleton crew on duty. He has access to empty offices that way. He insists we have map overlays of routes for patrols and search and destroy operations at least a week before the mission. If he is a 'mole' that would give him plenty of time to get the information to the VC, and have them plan and rehearse an ambush."

"Is there more substantive evidence available?"

"We were ambushed in Tanh Linh by a dug in force that had to know in advance we were going to be there. I found out from my own spies that the enemy was waiting for Second Company in Tuy An where Captain Dang was killed. Then Trang ordered an under-strength First Company to attack across open rice paddies to recapture Tuy An. A VC battalion defended the village. One of the reasons First Company was successful was because the night attack surprised the enemy. I think they expected us to assault during the day because that was Trang's original plan."

"That is very interesting. I read his service record, and he is originally from Hanoi. I don't know if he still has family there, but I will check. Do you have any other thoughts?"

"Yes. He is a very private person. Trang doesn't say much, and although he hasn't thrown roadblocks, he has never gone out of his way to help me either. He appeared disappointed when we ambushed and killed a VC colonel. Shortly after that, he asked me if he could be more involved in my agent network. Of course, I refused because I personally handle many of the agents."

"How can we prove he is a spy?"

"I've been toying with a plan for several days. We would give him information that no one else would have. I'd send a unit on a search and destroy operation and give Trang a copy of the plan, but I would have an additional plan for another unit to be in the area, and Trang would not know about that unit. If the VC ambush our unit, then our other unit ambush's the communists."

"That's excellent!" Phong exclaimed. "I approve, and I would like to participate with you on the operation," he added.

"Fine. I will get a copy of the plan for the search and destroy operation to you today with execution in one week. You will need to explain to Trang that you are very security conscious, and trust only him. He is not to tell anyone else the plan except the commander of the unit."

"Excellent. Trang should not suspect me because I am new, and he may just think that I am too cautious. That's it then. You will get the plan to me today. Now let's have some tea and discuss our families," Phong said, and he leaned back in his chair and lit a cigarette.

*　　*　　*

Pope returned to the compound and scheduled a meeting after lunch with Sullivan, Cox, Jutte, and Waters. Then he went to his room and made a map overlay of a search and destroy operation for a company-size unit. He added the written portion of the plan.

The meeting was conducted in his room. When Pope told them about his meeting with Major Phong and explained that he suspected Captain Trang, all of the other Americans looked at each other in surprise. Sullivan was clearly agitated, but said nothing.

"So how do we smoke him out, sir?" Asked Waters.

"Simple, Duke, we use the old 'tied up goat in the clearing' ruse. But don't worry, Duke, you won't be the goat. Captain Cox and Lt. Jutte will."

"I think I don't like the plan already," Jutte said with a halfhearted laugh.

"Before I tell you the strategy, this is a definite 'need to know' only. Those of us sitting here, plus Major Phong, will be the only people to know the entire plan."

"And that is?" Sullivan snapped.

Pope pulled out his map, overlay, and written plan and spread them on his desk. The others moved around in the cramped room so they could see.

"First Company will not be given the order until the day before departure. If there's a spy in the battalion, he will not have time to notify the enemy. They will have a search and destroy mission to move along this route," Pope said as he pointed at the map. "The route will be fairly close to and parallel to the coast. I picked this route for two reasons. First, there are only three logical points of ambush, here, here, and here. Second, there is a Navy junk fleet advisor that wants to test radio communication ship-to-shore. In fact, he says that he can get me naval gunfire support along the coast. This way we can get artillery support without going through Vietnamese channels."

"Good idea, but naval gunfire isn't going to help much in busting out of an ambush," Cox said.

"We don't really know until we try it. But that's where Waters, Major Phong, and I come in. The night before the operation kicks off, we'll move out with the R & I platoon and be ready to parallel the route of the RF Company. We will be in communication with Cox, and when the ambush is sprung, First Company will set up a base of fire, and we'll move in from the VC flank and attack them. No one but us will know about the R & I platoon's mission."

"Sounds good, sir, but what if the R & I platoon isn't big enough to handle the attack?" Waters asked.

"First, I think it's big enough. If our intelligence is correct, the enemy will plan for a company-size unit. They will probably ambush with a reinforced platoon—add a couple machine guns, like they did in Tanh Linh. Second, that's where Major Sullivan comes in. Right after First Company moves out, I'd like you to alert the 22nd ARVN battalion as a QRF in case we get into deep shit, sir." Pope said, staring at Sullivan.

"I can do that. You better be right, Captain. If you're wrong, and Trang finds out about this, your young ass is grass, and I'm a lawn mower," Sullivan said, frowning.

Pope ignored the threat and went on. "Just a reminder, Bob, there are only three places that look logical for ambushes. Be extra ready there, but also expect the unexpected. And trust no one!"

Late that afternoon, he took the plan to Phong who approved it and submitted the first half of it personally to Trang, with the planned air of secrecy. Trang assured him no one else would know.

*   *   *

Pope and Waters drove through Lai Gi to the waterfront where the Vietnamese junk fleet was located. Navy Lieutenant Horace Blackstone sat on the engine cover of a motorized Vietnamese junk reading a novel. His partner, Chief Petty Officer Warren Benning was sun bathing nearby. As they approached, Blackstone looked up from his reading.

"Hey, Johnny, what brings you down to the dregs of the waterfront?"

Blackstone was a large man. Almost as big as Waters, but a little heavier and softer. He had brown hair that was cut much too long to be close to regulation. He had a long, scraggly beard. He wore blue dungarees, cut off about eight inches from the crotch. He also had on an OD tee shirt that was dirty and soaked with sweat.

Benning was a smaller version of Blackstone with unkempt brown beard: long, brown hair: and a paunch. He wore a pair of cut off dungarees and no shoes. In Pope's opinion, neither would be nominated for soldier of the month at Fort Bragg. Blackstone and his partner were the two man advisory team to the five vessel Vietnamese junk fleet responsible for patrolling the coast of Binh Tuy. Their mission was to see that the VC didn't infiltrate supplies or men by ocean.

"Come down to give you your weekly lessons in 'couth'," Pope, said with a laugh. "How the hell did you ever get through Annapolis looking like that?" He added.

"I wasn't always this old and fat, my young Indian friend. But enough about me. What's new with you? Have you married that USAID babe yet?" Blackstone said, grinning through his beard.

"Not yet, but I'm here about business."

"You're about the most serious army officer I've ever met. Don't you ever relax, sir?" Benning chimed in.

"Hell, the Captain's just the opposite of you Chief—don't you ever get serious?" Waters challenged.

"Gentlemen, gentlemen. What you're really saying, Captain, is that you want something. Correct?"

"I can't hide anything from you, Horse. I want to use you, your radio, and your navy destroyer next week. Can do?"

"Perhaps. What's the plan?"

"Bob Cox and Jack Jutte are going out on a search and destroy operation with First Company a week from today, and I'd like you and your radio to go with them. I would also like you to bring the destroyer in close to the coast so they can fire on-call coastal artillery support if you guys run into Charlie."

"Sounds intriguing. I can find out how the other half lives, and I'm pretty sure the skipper of the ship would go for such a mission. Let me check it out through my channels and get back to you."

"Great. But don't tell anyone else. There are other things related to this mission that I'm doing, but can't tell you. I hope you understand—And I owe you a fifth of Jack Daniels if you pull it off."

"You Indians always seem to think you can buy us off with a few trinkets and fire water," Blackstone said, laughing. "But, seriously, Johnny you can count on me."

"Thanks, Horse, I knew I could."

*   *   *

Two days, later there was a big ceremony at sector headquarters. Major Nhia was promoted to Lieutenant Colonel. The high command in Saigon decided that a province chief's rank should be upgraded to Lieutenant Colonel to be commensurate with their responsibilities.

The same day, Blackstone showed up at the advisory compound and confirmed the destroyer would be available, and he would go on the operation with Cox. Pope thought: *Now the table is set. Will we have that son of a bitchen spy for dinner? Or will this be the answer to Sullivan's prayers?*

Chapter Twenty Six

The night before First Company moved off on their operation, Phong, Pope, and Waters rode out to the airstrip. Pope briefed Ma on the operation. At 2400 hours, the platoon moved out single file through the jungle, skirting the province town. Phong was surprised at how easily and gracefully the Yard soldiers moved during the night. When Phong mentioned it to Pope, he realized he had taken the little scouts for granted lately. They had much to be proud of. Pope was not surprised at how inexperienced Phong was at night movement.

After four hours of silent movement, Pope put the platoon in a tight perimeter around the command group. He sent a scout about three hundred yards away to let them know when the company reached their location. Pope thought how nice it was that he commanded the platoon of scouts. He would have control throughout the operation.

Half of the unit slept while the other half-stood guard. As usual, Waters slept, and Pope remained awake the entire night listening to the noises of the jungle. It gave him plenty of time to think about what he may have forgotten in his planning. The main thing, he cautioned himself, is to be prepared for what is not planned.

*   *   *

Just before departure, Cox briefed the First Company officers on the other part of the plan. Cox, Blackstone, and Jutte jumped off with First

Company at 0600 hours, marched to the beach, and followed it east for an hour. The company commander wanted to walk in the hard sand near the water because it was easier to walk on. Cox advised against it because it would leave their flank open to an ambush. They dispatched a two-man flank security about 100 yards off the beach, while the main body trudged through the soft sand weaving in and out of palm groves.

It was a tough, hot walk, and Cox was glad when they headed northeast into the jungle, and paralleled the beach. Blackstone had the destroyer off shore, and had plans for barrages in all three ambush positions. By 0800 hours, the scout returned to the R & I platoon and reported to Pope that First Company had crossed the designated location.

Knowing the VC liked to "sweep" the radio frequencies to pick up government transmissions, Pope and Cox agreed to a listening silence on the radios. They would listen but not transmit unless there was an emergency. The R & I platoon had already finished their rations and were moving parallel to the RF company.

Cox and First Company reached the first possible ambush position. It was an open rice paddy with jungle on two sides and thick elephant grass for about fifty yards, then the beach on the other. Lt. Kong sent a platoon across first. After they made it across the opening safely, the remainder of the company crossed.

*   *   *

Pope, Waters, and Phong waited west of the rice paddy in a position to counter attack. He noticed a woodline that would be the logical place to attack. *I hope I have thought of all the possible ambush sites, Pope thought.* By the time the "decoy" moved through the rice paddy, it was after noon, so both units stopped and had lunch. He sent a scout to watch the company eat, with orders to return and let him know when the unit moved again.

At 1400 hours, the scout returned, and the columns were on the move. As the company approached the second ambush site, the hair on the back of Captain Cox's neck stood up and his scalp itched.

He saw an open rice paddy about three hundred yards long with a labyrinth of dikes. There was a small-forested rise on the left side, thick underbrush. On the right side were trees but no underbrush and the ocean about a hundred yards on the other side of the trees. Cox lay near a fallen tree and scanned the area with his binoculars. He sighed, removed his black rimmed GI glasses, and rubbed his eyes.

"I figure that if this is the ambush spot, Charlie is dug in along that long knoll to the left. They probably have one or two machine guns on the other end of the paddy, looking right down our throats," Cox said to Jutte and Blackstone.

"We don't want the entire company in the paddy at the same time," Jutte added.

"Right, and we can't maneuver a platoon to the right because there isn't enough cover and concealment," Cox said.

"I'd like permission to radio the destroyer now and get two planned barrages, one along that knoll to the left and another on the woodline to our direct front. I can have a round on target within a minute after Charlie opens up on us," Blackstone whispered.

"Yeah, assuming we live though the mad minute," Jutte added.

"Great idea, Horace, go ahead," Cox said, and Blackstone rolled over and began transmitting. "This being bait for a trap doesn't do much for the nerves, does it, Jack?" he added.

The company commander crawled up next to Cox.

"Lieutenant, here is the plan. I expect an ambush here. I suggest we set up one machine gun to our left, pointed at the woodline at the other end of the paddy. The other machine gun should be set up to our right and aimed toward the long knoll on the left."

"First platoon will lead and cross the paddy with squads in skirmish lines and well spread out. Second platoon and the command group will wait until first platoon gets about fifty yards from the other end. We won't have many people in the open at the same time."

"What will we do if we are ambushed here?"

"Once the ambush is activated, we'll call in naval gunfire for five minutes, lift it, then attack both positions. The R & I platoon will attack the knoll to our left after the barrage lifts. Tell the machine gun crew on the right that they can shoot across the paddy over the heads of our troops lying in the water, but when the R & I platoon attacks the knoll, they will have to shift their fire to the other end of the paddy. What do you think?" Cox asked the young commander.

"I understand, Captain. I will pass the order to the platoon leaders," he said and turned and crawled to the rear.

*   *   *

Pope's scout returned and told him the company had stopped in front of the big rice paddy and appeared to be making plans. The scout gave a description of the open area. The R & I platoon was only 500 yards from First Company.

Pope sat with Waters, Phong, and Wa.

"The second ambush site is 500 yards ahead. We will move up 300 yards and get into position. If the ambush is activated, we will attack along the long axis of the knoll. First team on the left, second on the right, and third in reserve. Ma, you will be on the extreme right to tie in with First Company. Duke, you take the left flank. Major Phong and I will be in the center of the assault element. Does that sound OK, Major Phong?"

"Why don't we just attack the knoll and have First Company support our attack?"

"Because we have planned barrages on the knoll, and we could get under our own artillery. In addition, if the enemy isn't there, we have deployed for nothing."

"OK, Captain Pope, but let's get started before the VC get away," Phong said anxiously.

"Let's get the troops into position, Wa."

"Yes, sir," the little Yard answered with a smile, revealing the big gold cap on his front tooth.

*   *   *

First platoon started across the open as planned and maintained formation as they crossed the paddy. When they were fifty yards from the end, second platoon and command group moved into the open.

They moved twenty-five yards when mortar rounds fell amongst the troops in the open as well as those back in the trees. By the time Blackstone hit the ground in the smelly wet paddy, he was on the radio with his fire mission. As expected, enemy RPD fire opened up from the end of the paddy and wounded two members of the point squad in the initial burst. Flanking small arms fire and machine guns fired from the knoll to the left. The company RTO was hit in the initial burst of gunfire. Cox turned to look at him—half his face was gone. The unlucky bastard had been killed instantly.

Half-swimming and half-crawling, Cox inched his way to a two-foot dike ten yards ahead. The other members of the command group followed. The two supporting machine guns from First Company opened up, raking the woodline and knoll. Seconds later, naval gunfire screamed over their heads and blasted along the knoll. The rounds were so close Jutte was picked up and dropped by the explosions. The woodline ahead of them exploded in fire and dirt as the navy guns shifted. The air filled with explosions and screams.

Blackstone was on the radio, giving instructions and reports to the destroyer.

"I just hope to Christ I'm not killed by friendly fire!" Jutte screamed through clenched teeth.

"It's eerie to get such accurate shooting from a ship bobbing in the ocean," Cox yelled.

The naval gunfire continued. Sporadic fire came from the knoll on the left and nothing from the far end of the paddy.

"Cease fire! End of fire mission! Target destroyed!" Blackstone shouted into the radio.

The firing stopped, and the command group and the rest of the company rose to their feet as if one. They stumbled forward in the muck, firing weapons and shouting, advancing toward the knoll and the far end of the paddy.

*   *   *

When the ambush was activated, the firing sounded like it was coming only a few yards away from where Pope and the R & I platoon were lying in the jungle undergrowth. Phong started to get up and say something. Pope grabbed him and pulled him to his side.

"Wait, Major Phong. We don't want to get hit by our own artillery."

The naval gunfire hit seconds later. No one could hear anyone else speak. They could feel the shock waves of the explosions.

When the naval gunfire lifted, Phong was up and running ahead of the Yard platoon. They approached the knoll and continued the attack. A dazed enemy soldier sitting in a foxhole brought his AK 47 around, and Pope shot him with a three round burst. Charlie's head exploding.

Trees and tree limbs littered the ground, making it difficult for the attacking troops to go forward. What little resistance they had were dazed survivors of the barrage that didn't know what hit them. A minute after the attack began R & I platoon members on the right met up with the left flank of First Company and swept the objective together, screaming, running, and shooting. The attack was completed, and a dead silence hung over the battlefield.

*   *   *

First Company established a perimeter defense with both command groups and R & I platoon in the center as reserve. The dead and wounded were moved to a clear area near the beach. Jutte got on the radio.

"Binh Tuy, this is advisor, over."

"This is Binh Tuy actual, over."

"Mission accomplished. Objective secured. Request medevac at second ambush site, over."

"Roger, medevac at your location in two zero minutes, out."

Pope, Cox, and Phong walked the positions of the VC to collect weapons and get a body count. They collected two RPDs and 29 AK 47s, and counted 36 VC KIA. There was no wounded or captured enemy. Phong was elated.

"Today, we solved two problems. We know who the spy is and we killed many VC. We're going to be a lucky team, Captain Pope," he gushed, eyes flashing.

"That's called using a spy to our advantage," Pope said smiling.

"Son of a bitch, we only had one KIA and five WIA," Jutte said, clapping Cox on the back.

"Yeah, the KIA happened right next to me—kind of spooky," Cox said, shaking his head.

"That naval gunfire really tore Charlie a new asshole, Lieutenant Blackstone. I have a new respect for the swab jockeys," Waters said, looking at the navy officer.

"Yes, well, I hope you enjoyed it because you cannot expect me to go out in the woods and get my uniform dirty with you chaps **every** day," Blackstone said with a mock British accent.

They all laughed, and the sound of approaching choppers echoed from the distance.

"Sir, it's Major Sullivan and Colonel Nhia with medevac choppers," Jutte said.

"OK, tell them to land from the southeast."

*   *   *

As Phong and Pope briefed Nhia and Sullivan, the two senior men couldn't hide their joy at such a successful operation.

"You ought to see the landscape from the air. It looks like a hurricane hit this part of the jungle," Sullivan said.

"That naval gunfire is really deadly and accurate, sir," Pope said.

"I had Captain Trang placed under arrest before we left sector headquarters," Colonel Nhia said.

"Yeah, it's nice to get that son of a bitch out of the way. I was sure wrong about him," Sullivan added.

"I would like to talk with that traitor when we get back to headquarters—he has a lot to answer for," Phong said.

"I would like to be there when he is interrogated, too," Pope said.

"There will be some reporters here from Saigon in about an hour, so you will have to stay in the field over night," Colonel Nhia said.

Minutes later, helicopters approached from the east. By the time they landed, the R & I platoon had dragged all the VC bodies into the clearing and had them lined up neatly in a row. The captured weapons were lined up near the bodies.

There was a reporter from *The Stars and Stripes*, AP, UPI, and two reporters from the two Vietnamese newspapers. An overweight US army Lieutenant Colonel escorted them.

"Well, you folks had a real busy day," the rotund colonel said as he waddled up to the standing group of officers.

"Yeah, Major Phong and Captain Pope really planned and executed an excellent ambush operation here," Sullivan said. "The hunters became the hunted," he added.

The reporters took several pictures, interviewed a few soldiers and advisors, got in their helicopters, and flew away.

"We're leaving now. No one will question Trang until you return, Major Phong," Nhia said.

"Major, I can't think of any reason for me to play snuffy out here any longer. My work is done. Can I catch a lift back to sector headquarters with you?" Blackstone asked.

The assembled group laughed.

"Thanks again, Horse. I owe you a fifth of good booze," Pope said.

"Damn right you do!" The unorthodox Naval Academy graduate shouted over his shoulder as he made an exaggerated entrance to the chopper.

*   *   *

Early the next day, the two units started back to province headquarters, and closed in on the village at 1400 hours. Pope and Waters had lunch with the R & I platoon at the airstrip. He told them how proud he was of their work during the counter ambush operation—something that they had not been trained for. He gave them a 10,000 Piastres bonus for the dead VC and captured weapons.

*   *   *

On the way back to the advisory compound, Pope decided to stop and talk with Phong about the interrogation of Trang. They couldn't find Phong at his office so went to the SOIC. The intelligence sergeant told him Major Phong was interrogating Trang behind the SOIC building.

Pope and Waters went out the back door and saw Trang, stripped naked and tied to a tree. His face was swollen and he was bleeding from the nose and mouth. He had huge welts all over his body. Two armed Vietnamese guards stood by. Phong had his shirt off, and wore a sweat-soaked T-shirt. He was out of breath and had an 18" rubber hose in his left hand. He struck Trang in the chest with the hose and shouted in Vietnamese.

"You murdering scum. Who is your contact?"

Trang's head flew back against the tree as he was hit, but he didn't utter a sound.

Pope glanced at Waters, shook his head, and walked to Phong.

"Major Phong, can I speak to you in private in the SOIC for a minute?" Pope noticed that minus the bruises and blood, Phong didn't look much better off than Trang.

"Of course, Captain Pope," he replied, chest heaving.

The two officers went just inside the back door.

"What information have you received from Captain Trang?"

"I have only been interrogating him for about an hour. I have some interesting information. Trang admitted to being a spy for over two years. He said that prior to your arrival in Binh Tuy, the province was used as a rest area for Viet Cong soldiers. When the VC Colonel Khanh was killed, the communist commander decided to increase terrorism in Binh Tuy. He bragged about Captain Dang's death. Trang said his only regret is you weren't killed before he was caught. I haven't been able to find out who his contact is though. But I think he will break any minute now," Phong said, trying to catch his breath.

"That is all good information, but it is not **useful** intelligence information. I don't think it's a good idea to beat Trang any more. I have been trained that if you beat prisoners, eventually they will give you information. Unfortunately it's usually what they think you want to hear, and it's usually inaccurate."

"Let me guess. What you propose to do is keep asking Trang questions until his answers trip him up, and he will eventually tell everything?" Phong said sarcastically.

"Something like that. It's been successful before. What we found out from our own prisoners, captured in Korea during the war, was that their resolve to keep quiet increased with each beating."

"This is Vietnam, Captain Pope. And Trang is not an American. You don't know how my people think."

"I know **people**, and you can't beat intelligence information out of them."

Clearly irritated, Phong spouted, "This is my interrogation. If you don't like my methods, you can leave."

He spun on his heel and returned to the prisoner—Pope closely following.

For ten minutes, Phong hit Trang with the hose and his closed fist after asking him a question. Each time Trang said nothing. Pope tapped Phong on the shoulder.

"Major Phong, you're going to kill the prisoner before you get the information you want from him. Please let me talk with him."

Phong stared at Pope and shouted, "I'll get answers, or he will die!"

Phong pulled his pistol from his holster, jammed it under the chin of Trang and shouted in Vietnamese.

"You have two seconds to tell me how you communicated your messages, or I'll blow your traitorous head off!"

Trang spit at Phong and before the spittle hit his face, he pulled the trigger. The bullet splattered Trang's brains all over the tree trunk.

Pope and Waters were shocked. The two guards were startled initially by the sound of the pistol, but otherwise showed no reaction.

"I don't think you're going to get **any** information from Trang now," Pope said.

"I do not think Trang will betray his countrymen **again**," Phong exclaimed, and he holstered his pistol and stomped away.

*   *   *

By the time Pope was dressed after taking a shower, Martin knocked on his door.

"Sir, Miss Williams is on the phone calling from Saigon. If you would like a little privacy, you can take the call in my room."

"Thanks, Martin, I appreciate your letting me use your phone," Pope said as he followed the soldier into his room

Pope picked up the army field phone, pushed the button, and said, "Hello."

"Hello yourself. You knew who it was, you phony baloney. I just had to call you, darling," Kathryn said.

"I'm glad to hear your voice, sweetheart."

"Me too! I picked up *The Stars and Stripes* this morning, and who's handsome face is on the front page, but Captain John Pope's," She exclaimed happily. "Then one of the guys brought in a Vietnamese paper, and you were on the front page of that one as well," she added laughing.

"Well, it's no big deal. Most of the team was in on the operation."

"I know, but you can't blame me for busting with pride, can you?"

"No. I guess not. I'm proud of you, too, honey."

"It's so good to talk to you, Johnny. When will you be able to spend a week end in Saigon?"

"I don't know. Captain Dang's replacement is here, and I have to spend a lot of time with him the next couple weeks. I just don't know. I wish I could see you **today**."

"Yes, I understand. Captain Dang will be hard to replace."

"Yeah, Phong is a brave S.O.B. too. When is your next trip out here?"

"Not for a couple weeks, but maybe I can get some time off and just hitch a flight and come out. Would that be OK?"

"Yeah. That would be great. Well, I better get back to work. I have an after action report to write, and we can't tie up this operational phone too long."

"Sure, I know. I miss you, Johnny. I love you. Good-bye."

"Bye, Honey, I love you, too," Pope said and hung up the phone.

He sat in the radio operator's room for a few minutes thinking about Kathryn—how much he missed her, and how much he longed to hold her. *This is a peculiar kind of war. You don't know your friends from your enemies. I cannot believe any officer has received the kind of training to fight this kind of war. How can we expect to win a war like this?*

Then his thoughts turned to the combat operation just completed. *Well, at least we don't have a mole at as high a level as the chief of staff anymore. It's too bad all the operations aren't this easy. Then we could say with certainty that "The whale spirit is with us and no one will die."*

Chapter Twenty Seven

Lt.Col. Nhia decorated First and Second Company commanders and Captain Khoa for their performances at Tuy An. A US Brigadier General arrived in Binh Tuy a day later and decorated all the advisors in the Tuy An operation.

At the dinner after the awards ceremony, Gomez said, "I should have gotten the Congressional Medal of Honor for taking care of Captain Pope's ass all week."

That was only the beginning of the lighthearted banter at the table that evening. The consensus was the medals were nice but being alive was even better.

* * *

Pope spent almost every day with Phong touring the province and showing him MedCap team and intelligence gathering operations. Phong was impressed with the agent network Pope had developed through treatment of sick civilians. The RF battalion engaged in additional training. Jutte and Waters were impressed with Cox's method of working with the battalion leaders. They could see unit operation was improved.

Jutte saw Cox and Pope operated completely different with their Vietnamese counterparts—the former, used tact and diplomacy, and the latter, used a sledgehammer. Naturally, Waters went with the Pope approach.

* * *

The Regional Force unit had a successful search and destroy operation in Tanh Linh district. Cox and Jutte went with Third Company on a search and destroy operation east of Bo Ninh. They stumbled onto a VC base camp and killed 23 VC and captured 12 AK 47s.

Pope was especially proud of the operation because he had suspected VC activity in that area. There were indications Trang didn't have an accomplice because there were no more ambushes, but Pope thought if there were an accomplice, he might be laying low until things cooled off. Pope maintained a close hold on agent handling.

*   *   *

Saturday morning Pope got an unexpected surprise: Kathryn showed up for a three-day weekend. That afternoon, he talked Martin, Bannister, Cox, and Granger into going swimming in the South China Sea with them. Since Kathryn was the guest, it didn't take much coaxing. The ocean area was considered relatively secure, but the Major had a policy that enough of them had to go so that half could provide local security while the others swam. Kathryn had brought her swimming suit. It was a yellow two-piece that showed more of her exceptional figure.

They took two jeeps, drove through the village of Lai Gi, and out over the sand dunes to the beach.

They passed a couple palm trees and looked out over the uninhabited beach. Kathryn said, "This beach is so beautiful. It hasn't been touched by the war."

"The war seems a long way from here," Pope said.

"And so are people," Kathryn mused.

"I brought a football, sir. Can we play some catch?" Martin asked.

"Sure, Jim, that sounds great," Pope replied.

Bannister parked his jeep next to a palm tree. The three men dismounted and took up positions about twenty-five yards apart. They took off their shirts and lay on towels facing away from the beach—weapons close at hand.

Pope, Kathryn, and Martin had the first shift playing. They decided to play catch with the football. Both men carefully set their weapons near the waters edge so that they could get to them in a hurry if necessary. The war wasn't really very far away.

Kathryn was included in the ball toss while they stood about five yards apart. She showed remarkable ability not only catching but also throwing the ball. As the men backed further apart, Kathryn decided to sit down in the shallow water and watch while the waves lapped over her. They were throwing the ball about forty yards. The football felt good in Pope's hands. Martin had a strong arm.

Martin puffed up with pride when Pope yelled, "Hey, Jim, when you get out of the army, let me know, and I'll talk to my coach at State U. you've got a Division I arm!"

Pope playfully threw the football about 35 yards toward Granger and accidentally hit him in the butt.

"Hey, watch it, guys, I've got my weapon on full automatic," Granger yelled, laughing.

Martin turned and ran into the waves yelling, "Man, the surf is great today. Too bad we don't have surf boards."

Pope and Kathryn walked into the warm water holding hands.

"This is really nice, Johnny."

"It's almost like a Saturday afternoon at the beach in the States. I'm really glad you came."

"So am I," she said, and she put her arms around his neck and kissed him on the mouth.

"Hey, not in front of the enlisted man," Martin yelled, laughing. "Just kidding. Pretend that I'm not here," he added before being knocked over by a wave.

"Did you hear someone say something?" Pope said laughing. The lovers walked hand in hand in the shallow water as small waves lapped against their legs.

"I can't imagine a beach being more beautiful than this."

"Whenever I come here, I look across the horizon and imagine that if I had supernatural eyes, I could see the coast where my village is. The ocean must be a terrific place for whales to live. They have so many obstacles to overcome. Things that help them be strong warriors."

"I've never considered the whale as a warrior."

"Oh, yes. That's one of the reasons we have so much respect for them."

After cavorting in the water for about a half-hour Pope, Kathryn, and Martin picked up their weapons and walked up the beach to replace the security. The three other advisors walked to the water's edge for their swim.

Kathryn took Pope's pistol from his holster and said, "Is this gun hard to shoot, Johnny?"

Surprised, Pope said, "You mean you've never had any weapons training?"

"No. During our orientation, I asked, and the instructor said we were noncombatants, and besides, the 'rules of engagement' are complicated."

Both men laughed. "Yeah, we're army issue automatic pop-up targets," Pope said. "We have one rule here, shoot first or you go home in a body bag," he added.

"Will you teach me how to shoot, sometime, Johnny?" Kathryn asked.

"There's no time like the present," Pope said.

He took the pistol from Kathryn and removed the clip and ejected the round from the chamber. Martin picked up the bullet and blew the sand from it and handed it to Pope.

"The pistol is used for short range—about twenty-five yards. Your target is that palm tree." Pope pointed at a tree with a trunk about the width of a man. "Hold the weapon with both hands. Take a deep breath and let some of it out. Line up the front sight with the rear sight. Squeeze the trigger." Pope demonstrated.

"That looks easy enough," she said.

"OK, you try it," Pope said. He handed the unloaded weapon to Kathryn.

Kathryn held the weapon in both hands, aimed it at the tree, while Pope stood behind her, looking down the barrel.

"That's good. Now we'll try it with ammo. To load the weapon you hold the 45 in your right hand, clip in your left. With your right thumb, push the lever on the side of the weapon, and with your left hand pull the slide to the rear and release the lever with your right thumb. The slide locks to the rear. To load, take the clip, and with the lead part of the bul lets facing toward the front end of the barrel, insert the clip into the butt, and pop the clip into position with the heel of your left hand. Then with your right thumb push the lever on the side of the weapon again, and the slide will go forward, chambering a round."

After showing Kathryn how to use the safety, she practiced loading and unloading the weapon. Satisfied, Pope told Martin to go down to the water and tell the men they were going to do some target practice. He took the weapon, aimed at the tree trunk and fired two rounds. Kathryn jumped backward from the noise of the explosions. Both rounds hit the tree.

"I didn't realize the gun was so noisy. Did it jump up like that, or did you make it?" Kathryn asked.

"It is noisy," Pope laughed. "There is a severe recoil upwards, so you have to hold the gun-butt firm," he added, handing the weapon to her.

Kathryn held the pistol, aimed at the tree and pulled the trigger twice. The recoil forced both her hands and the weapon above her head. Only pope's bullet holes were in the tree.

Martin and Pope laughed at Kathryn's surprised expression. The other advisors, hearing the shooting and laughter, ran up from the water.

"I forgot to tell you each time you pull the trigger, a bullet goes out the end of the weapon," Pope said. "As you hold the weapon, aim with both eyes open—last time you didn't have either eye open," he added, to the laughter of the men.

"All right, smarty. If you can do it, so can I," she said. She held the pistol up, aimed and fired. The round hit the edge of the tree trunk.

"You didn't kill him, but you sure scared the hell out of him," Martin said to more guffaws from the other men.

"What do you guys do for laughs when I'm not around?" Kathryn said smiling. Turning serious, she crouched slightly, aimed, and fired. The round hit just right of the center of the tree. The men cheered and clapped as Kathryn jumped and smiled.

Kathryn fired three magazines of ammo, practicing. The last eight rounds hit the tree. Pope pronounced her an "expert-markswoman" and they returned to the advisory compound.

Kathryn showered first, Pope on guard. The other swimmers took their showers. Kathryn napped, and Pope and Jutte sat in the dining room talking, while he cleaned his pistol.

*   *   *

Phong entered the dining room, excited and said, "Captain Pope, something important has come up. Can I talk with you?"

"Yes, of course. Lt. Jutte, will you excuse us?"

Jutte left, and Phong said, "I have just received information that a VC platoon attacked the village of Hoi Cao in Ham Tan district. The Popular Force platoon fought bravely, but many were killed. Three of them came to province headquarters to tell the story."

Pope walked to the map and put his finger on the village.

"Hoi Cao is a small fishing village about 18 kilometers from our location. There is one road that runs directly from here to there. It is only a few kilometers from the adjoining province of Phuoc Tuy."

Phong interrupted him and said, "We have to recapture the village right away. I have alerted 22nd Battalion to send a reinforced company down the road and attack them."

"Wait a minute, sir. Let's think about this a minute. Remember our lesson from Hoi Duc. They sent in a platoon of VC to occupy the village to lure a government unit into an ambush. If we send a force down that road, they could be waylaid, too."

"What do you suggest we do?"

"If it is a planned ambush, the VC will set the trap between here and the village. I suggest we fly to Phuoc Tuy and ask them to deploy troops across the province border and attack the VC. The enemy would not expect it. We could support the attack from here."

"No. It is too difficult to coordinate. Phuoc Tuy might have higher priority missions, and they would not want to commit their troops to our province. We would need to coordinate with III Corps because it is on the Corps boundary," Phong argued. "There are too many political problems," he added.

"OK. You know more about political problems than I do. I have some friends who are advisors to the Airborne Brigade in Saigon. Maybe I could call them and see if they would commit a battalion to make the attack across the Corps boundary into Hoi Cao. How about that?"

"No!" Phong said, raising his voice. "All those things take too much time, and it is our problem. We have the troops to do it. If you do not want to make the plan, I will have my staff make it."

"All right. You're right about one thing—it is our problem. I'll make the plan. Can you come back in two hours?"

"Yes, but I would like to attack tomorrow. We can kill many VC's."

Christ, Pope thought. *This guy is out to make a name for himself and get another quick promotion. I guess I can't blame him. He's anxious to get on with the fight. How can you argue with that? Now I have to make a plan that will keep our asses out of the fire.*

Pope and Cox went to work and follow with devising the plan. They had just completed it when Phong returned.

Pope and Phong stood next to the wall map, as Pope pointed at the map and spoke.

"This will have to be a coordinated attack because 22nd Battalion has only two infantry companies here now. We will truck both companies about eight kilometers down the road they will dismount, Second Company will move through the jungle on the north side of the road, and Third Company on the south side of the road. They are to keep off the hard surface. Since it is a coordinated attack, they will not stop or eat a meal until they have secured the objective."

"We will move down the road to a location ten kilometers from province headquarters. The weapons and scout platoons will provide security for the 105-millimeter artillery howitzer, armored car, and command group. The artillery fire will support the attack. I will try to get air support, but on such short notice, I wouldn't count on it. You should have the soldiers from the artillery section bring sand bags to protect the crew."

"It looks like a good plan, Captain Pope. Let's put it in writing and brief the commanders at 1700 hours today."

"Roger that, Major Phong."

*   *   *

That evening, the commanders received the attack order. The two US advisors to the ARVN battalion were also present: Captain Roger McAllister, a short, stocky, 30 year old career officer from Maine: and SFC Anthony Washington, a medium sized, muscular, black career NCO from Detroit. The two advisors had been in Vietnam over six months and were seasoned combat veterans.

*   *   *

After the briefing, Pope went to Kathryn's room and found her reading. She stood, and he took her in his arms and kissed her.

"I'm really sorry, Honey. Major Phong came to me with an unexpected important operation."

"I'm sure it is. And I know it's your job. Maybe we can spend some more time together on Monday."

"I've been doing a lot of thinking since we were together in Saigon and since Tuy An. I know it might be asking a lot. Especially since we haven't known each other for very long. But I know I love you more than I could ever imagine I could love anyone. Will you marry me?" Pope said, gazing into her eyes while holding his breath.

"Oh, Johnny, I can't think of anyone I would rather spend the rest of my life with. Yes! Yes! Yes!"

She threw her arms around him and kissed him on the mouth. He could feel her body get warm and her breathing get deeper.

Pope pulled back and said, "I'm sorry, Darling, I'd really like to make love, but I just don't think it's the right place."

"To hell with your sense of duty and honor," Kathryn said, unbuttoning her blouse. "We're in a war, and we don't ever know what tomorrow will bring us," she added.

"When your right, you're right," he said, smiling, and bent over to unlace his boots.

"Last one in bed naked is a communist sympathizer," Kathryn said pulling her shorts and panties off together.

Ten minutes later, Pope held Kathryn in his arms, smiled, and whispered in her ear, "Thanks. I'm glad you seduced me."

"Well, someone had to!" Kathryn said, looking into Pope's eyes and smiling.

"Say, I'm due for a mid-tour R & R in less than two months. Could you get away for a week?"

"That's wonderful! I'm due for one, too!"

"Maybe we could go to Hawaii together and get married. I want to hurry up and marry you before you find out I'm not good enough for you and dump me."

Kathryn laughed and said, "I've always wanted a big wedding, and I know my mother will be disappointed, but I'm pretty sure my parents could meet us there for the wedding. I've written them and told them all about you. They're dying to meet you, Johnny. I'd love to get married in Hawaii."

"Let's tell everybody the good news at the dinner table."

* * *

Even though there was a combat operation the following day, there was a great deal of good-natured kidding and an atmosphere of celebration around the table. Maybe it was false bravado. Or maybe it was giddy nervousness.

After dessert, Pope stood and said, "At ease, everybody. I have a little ceremony to perform. Miss Williams, will you please stand here?"

As Kathryn moved to the head of the table with a bewildered expression, Cox stood, pulled a piece of paper from his pocket, and began reading. "Attention to orders!"

The other advisors rose to their feet and stood at attention.

"For Gallantry in action, the Silver Star medal is hereby awarded to Miss Kathryn Williams for actions against a hostile force, which included an armed enemy **and** an armed friendly, namely the VC **and** *MACV*."

Cox waited while laughter filled the room and stopped.

He continued, "In the Republic of Vietnam. When friendly forces were completely surrounded and under siege in the village of Tuy An, no aircraft was available to move reinforcing troops. Miss Williams immediately recognized the problem and took necessary action. With no regard for her own personal safety or career, Miss Williams went to State Department and convinced her boss to go to MACV and persuade them to get off their fat asses and allocate the required transports. Her actions resulted in adequate transportation for troops to be deployed, which resulted in our butts being saved. This medal is a symbol from a grateful nation—and an even **more thankful** advisory team."

Pope stepped to Kathryn, took a Silver Star medal from his pocket, pinned it on her blouse above her left breast, and kissed her on the mouth. The rest of the advisors clapped, cheered, and yelled, "speech, speech, speech."

Kathryn stood with Pope, wiped tears from her eyes, thought for a few seconds, and took a deep breath.

"This is really wonderful and certainly unexpected. I can't tell you how much I appreciate the thought and gesture. Before I came to Vietnam, I read about the 'Brotherhood of Warriors.' Now I understand it. You **all** will always be a part of my life. Every time I look at the medal, I'll think of you boys."

That brought more clapping and cheering from the advisors. Kathryn raised her hand for silence.

"I want everyone to know that I'm the happiest woman in the world. Johnny Pope has asked me to be Mrs. Pope!" She shouted.

The room erupted in cheering, whistles, and applause as the advisors rushed to the couple, shaking Pope's hand and hugging Kathryn.

Granger was the first one there and said, "Well, do I get to kiss the bride?"

"Yes, Larry, but that's after the wedding. A hug is appropriate now," Kathryn said as she spread her arms.

The group stayed up late talking and drinking beer and sodas. Pope told Bannister that he would stand his 2400-0200 hours guard duty because he was so wound up he couldn't sleep anyway. Kathryn stayed up and kept him company.

"This has to be the best day of my entire life, Johnny," Kathryn said as she sat on Pope's lap holding her medal.

"I can't think of a better day either—unless you count the Rose Bowl," Pope said, and she poked him in the ribs. He laughed, and the two lovers spent the two hours talking about their families and plans for the wedding and their future together.

*   *   *

At 0800, the convoy formed near the open field where the ARVN battalion was bivouacked. Since not enough trucks were available to make one trip, they shuttled the troops to the drop off point. Pope decided to take along two boxes of fragmentation grenades and loaded them into his jeep. Pope, Captain McAllister, SFC Washington, and Waters followed the armored car as it led the first part of 22nd Battalion to the drop off point.

They stopped at an open, flat field, 300 yards square. Trees had been removed and defoliant used on the vegetation. It looked to Pope like the moon. The soldiers dismounted the trucks and milled around, smoking and talking while they waited for the remainder of the troops. After two more trips, all the soldiers were in the assembly area.

The 105 was towed into position 300 yards from the woodline. Artillerymen set in the weapon and piled sandbags around it. The two infantry companies walked in single lines into the jungle to the west.

Pope recognized a ticklish command situation caused by Phong's enthusiasm. The bulk of the force was the 22nd Battalion, and the battalion commander normally commanded the operation. But they were operating in Binh Tuy province under the operational control of Phong, the deputy province chief, who was present in the field. After giving it some thought, Pope decided that the troops belonged to Phong and he would act accordingly until an argument ensued.

He told the platoon leaders to form a perimeter defense around the command group and the howitzer. The scout platoon of about 30 men formed the circle of the clock facing the enemy from 9 o'clock to 3 o'clock, and the 40-man weapons platoon from 3 o'clock to 9 o'clock. The mortar section was formed to the rear of the howitzer.

He told the platoon leaders to dig in. Neither of them was accustomed to digging foxholes, and they reluctantly followed orders. After Pope and Phong made two tours of the digging, giving instructions to dig their fighting positions deeper, they were satisfied with the defenses.

Shortly after noon a jeep and a trailer arrived at the command group position, followed by a two and a half-ton truck. Cooks and orderlies from province headquarters unloaded two long tables, complete with white tablecloths and set up an elaborate sit-down lunch for the command group. They had even brought out tableware and china. Phong strolled up to Pope, who was talking to the other advisors.

"You gentlemen are invited to lunch. We have a delicious meal prepared."

The advisors looked at each other, waiting for someone to make a move. It went against almost all of their military training: while in the field, eat what and where the troops eat. In Vietnam, there was a wide gap between officers and enlisted men, and to turn down the invitation would result in the Vietnamese officer losing face.

"We accept your kind invitation, Major Phong," Pope said.

The advisors and the officers from the ARVN battalion and regional force unit sat at the two tables. The Vietnamese officers sensed the discomfort of the advisors. There was very little table talk. As soon as he thought he could, Pope excused himself to walk the perimeter defense again. The other advisors took his cue and excused themselves as well, finding weapons to clean and ammo to check.

As he inspected the positions Pope thought, *this is a very different war and certainly not the kind he expected to fight.* He thought *it might even be called a "gentleman's war." We get out of bed in the morning, take a shower, get dressed, and go out and fight a battle. Then we return to our bed for a good night's sleep and do the same thing the next day. Is this what I can expect until my tour of duty is over in Vietnam? Or am I always being lulled into a false sense of security?*

Chapter Twenty Eight

Pope opened the cases of hand grenades in the back seat of the jeep. Captain McAllister approached him, half-running, from the command post.

"We've just lost radio contact with both attacking rifle companies. We're going to send a jeep down the road a few kilometers and try to contact them."

The armored car came careening down the road, out of the jungle and into the open, the machine gun firing to the rear. It was 200 yards from the artillery piece when an RPG 7 round blasted into the back of it, knocking the turret off. The little car spun off the road in flames. It was clear that there were no survivors. Government machine guns hosed down the woodline using short bursts of six rounds, even though they couldn't see any targets.

Pope ran to the officer in charge of the artillery piece and said in Vietnamese, "Lower the muzzle of the gun and use it as a direct fire weapon. Fire it into the woodline and try to get tree bursts."

The Vietnamese lieutenant nodded his head, screamed instructions to the crew, and the muzzle dropped. An RPG round came from the left front of the jungle and exploded harmlessly 20 yards from the artillery piece. It got the gun crew's attention, and, within seconds, they fired in the direction the RPG 7 round had come from. No sooner did it explode than small arms and machine gun fire came from the left front of the woods. Pope recognized the familiar green tracer rounds of the RPD machine gun, reaching out its deadly breath. His ears were ringing from the artillery piece firing so close by.

The perimeter defense force returned fire immediately. Fifty VC ran out of the woodline firing wildly. They were all wearing different kinds and colors of uniforms. Pope identified the regular black pajamas worn by most. Others wore the green uniforms of the regular ARVN infantry and "Tiger suits" and "Cammies" of the elite ARVN Ranger and Airborne units. The uniforms were taken from dead government soldiers in previous battles. The defense hesitated, and he yelled at them in Vietnamese to take them under fire. The delay cost the defenders, because it let the enemy get closer before friendly fire thinned their ranks.

The command group was located in a three-foot deep ditch along side the road 40 yards from the artillery piece. Waters had already carried the two boxes of hand grenades to the ditch and placed some on the ground. The crew fired the artillery piece at the woodline as fast as they could reload. Branches of trees flew up into the air and fell like confetti.

The VC blew a high pitched bugle, and the attacking troops withdrew into the woodline. As soon as they disappeared into the jungle, ARVN soldiers stopped shooting. Women appeared from the jungle, went into the clearing, picked up weapons, and helped wounded soldiers back to the shelter of the woods. The government forces stood in their foxholes and watched the women clean the battlefield.

"I know that neither of us want to, but you must order the troops to shoot the women," Pope told Phong.

"We can't fire—they are women," Phong replied, voice rising, clearly rattled.

"You have no choice."

Just as the last woman reached the woodline helping a wounded comrade, the bugle was blown again. Fifty more attacking soldiers charged out of the woodline. This time the ARVN scout platoon returned fire immediately, cutting the screaming warriors down in stride. Mortar rounds fell among the enemy soldiers killing still more of them. The howitzer continued to hammer the woodline, scattering the VC. The bugle sounded again, and the enemy withdrew. As the last shot was fired by the scout platoon, the women reappeared and repeated their mission, while the government forces sat and watched.

Clearly angry, Pope grabbed Phong by the arm and looked him in the eye.

"Those women serve the same purpose as a man fighting us. We're allowing them to take weapons back to their unarmed comrades. If you don't order the men to kill them, they'll take the weapon off your dead ass before night fall."

Phong hesitated for a second and said to the ARVN battalion commander, "I have never faced this situation. What do you think we should do?"

The commander nodded his head at Pope and said, "The Captain is right. We have no choice but to kill the women."

"Kill the women!" Phong yelled at the howitzer leader.

The Battalion commander yelled the same command to the ARVN soldiers. Hearing them, the women dropped their wounded and turned to run back into the relative safety of the jungle. The howitzer spit out its heavy-duty death, and the government infantrymen fired at the retreating women. Several of the scavengers fell on the battlefield while the rest scampered into the woodline as fast as they could. The bugle sounded and a hundred enemy troops poured out of the jungle. Fire from the artillery piece dropped them in their tracks, but the attack continued relentlessly.

If the enemy troops closed within 200 yards of the command group, the artillery piece was ineffective. Pope grabbed a box of grenades and ran toward the edge of the perimeter defense, bullets hitting all around him. When he jumped into one of the foxholes, he found two dead government soldiers. He pitched the corpses out like they were store mannequins and set them in front of the foxhole for protection.

Waters shouted to the other advisors, "cover Pope!"

The three men shot six enemy soldiers within twenty yards of Pope's foxhole. Pope picked up some grenades and threw them toward the enemy. He looked to his right and saw Waters in a foxhole 25 yards away.

Waters piled dead soldiers in front of the foxhole, copying Pope. Duke was strong: he picked the dead soldiers up, one with each hand, and threw them in front of the foxhole like they were rag dolls.

McAllister and Washington ran to Pope from his rear. Pope cut down three charging guerrillas with his CAR 15 and yelled, "Hey, Duke, drop what you're doing and give covering fire. Help's on the way."

Waters dropped the last body, picked up his weapon, and shot a VC 20 yards in front of his foxhole. The VC's head snapped back and a piece of it flew off as he pitched forward. McAllister dove into Waters's foxhole headfirst. Pope dropped a spent magazine from his weapon and inserted a fresh one. An enemy soldier, ran by the foxhole, slipped on the edge, and fell on top of Pope. Pope wrestled with the startled soldier and felt a heavy weight fall on top of him. He lost his breath. A loud explosion sounded right next to his ear. The side of the VC's head turned into a bloody ooze of bone and brains.

Washington had jumped into the foxhole and shot the soldier with his pistol. Pope took in a deep, ragged breath and gagged on the familiar smell of open fire smoke and fermented fish sauce coming from the dead soldier. Washington changed his pistol from his right hand to left, picked up the unrecognizable, butchered meat with his right hand, and flung him high out of the hole.

"Glad to see you, Sarge. If you'll try to keep that machine gun occupied to the left front, maybe I can get my grenades out a bit further," Pope shouted, ears still ringing.

"Can do, sir," Washington said. He holstered his pistol, picked up his M-14 rifle, and took the enemy under fire.

Pope tossed grenades 70 yards out as fast as he could pull the pins. Bullets cracked by his ear.

Waters, shouted to McAllister, "Cover me, sir. I'm taking these grenades over to Captain Pope. He can throw them a hell of a lot farther than I can—and more accurately!"

"Roger that, and keep your big butt down," McAllister said, as he shot a fast charging guerrilla ten yards to his front. The burst hit him full in the chest, knocking him on his back. The big slugs punctured a lung and pinkish bubbles oozed out of the wound. He was gasping for air.

Waters crawled to Pope's foxhole, dragging a half-full box of grenades. Bullets pounded into the dirt around him. He dropped them into Pope's foxhole, turned, and began crawling back toward McAllister. Ten yards along, Waters was hit in the thigh by small arms fire and screamed out in pain. Washington dropped his rifle and jumped out of the foxhole. He ran, grabbed the wounded sergeant by the pack harness, turned, and pulled him back toward Pope.

Almost to the foxhole, Washington was shot through the chest and head and fell next to the hole, dead before he hit the ground. Waters looked at Washington lying next to him. A bullet had taken off the top part of his head and his eyes were locked open in surprise. Waters grimaced and rolled into the cavity next to Pope.

"I'm kind of busy. Can you take care of your wound, Duke?" Pope said as he fired his CAR 15.

"Fuck the wound," Waters said as he fired Washington's rifle at the attacking VC.

The all-too familiar bugle sounded again, and the enemy retreated into the woods. The women didn't return to the battlefield and fallen wounded enemy soldiers moaned and cried out for help. Pope took the first aid bandage from Waters's pouch, while Duke tore his fatigue pants above the wound.

When it was exposed, Pope examined it and said, "You're lucky. It missed the bone."

He wrapped the bandage around the bleeding leg and tied it off.

"No, if I was lucky, the fucken round would have missed me completely." He nodded toward Sgt. Washington's lifeless body, and added, "But luckier than him." Waters shook Washington's dead, outstretched hand. "Thanks, Sarge."

"Don't get any dumb ideas about that deal of ours, Duke. We're a long way from being over run."

"Oh hell, sir, this is just a scratch. If we get over run, Charlie will have to hit me in the ass because I'll be going that-a-way!"

"Washington's dead, isn't he?" McAllister yelled at Pope between howitzer shots at the woodline.

"Yeah. How are you fixed for ammo?"

"I've got three more magazines for my Thompson, some M-1s, and eight clips from the dead ARVN soldiers. Good bye, Sergeant Washington," McAllister said in a whisper.

"I've got about a half box of grenades, but we won't be able to hold out much longer. Damn. I never heard of Charlie maintaining contact this long."

"Neither have I. I just hope the RF Company from sector is on the way. I guess our two attacking companies must have been ambushed," McAllister said.

Pope started to say something to McAllister when the dreadful bugle was blown again, and a hundred VC ran out of the woodline. He fired his CAR 15 until the enemy got within 90 yards, then chucked hand grenades. Waters stood on one leg firing Washington's M-14 at the machine gun.

McAllister emptied the last magazine from his Thompson, knocking a charging guerrilla flat on his back. He picked up an M-1, and saw another enemy soldier running right at him. Without aiming, the captain pointed the unfamiliar rifle and pulled the trigger. The VC clutched his stomach, dropped his weapon, and pitched forward on his face. Pope tossed his last grenade. A large volume of fire sounded from the rear.

*   *   *

Pope spun around and saw First RF Company and another ARVN unit counterattacking through the perimeter defense. Phong, pistol in his right hand, firing and yelling in Vietnamese, led them. Jutte and Cox were to the rear and headed right for Pope. Every man was firing in a wild, feverish haste.

The enemy, startled by the sudden turn of events, wheeled and tried to fight an organized withdrawal. Within seconds, the communists sprinted for the woodline. As the counterattackers approached the outer perimeter defense, scout and weapons platoon soldiers rose from their foxholes and joined the attack. They hit the Viet Cong like a shock wave.

When Cox and Jutte passed him, Pope said, "You wait here for the medevac, Duke, I'll be right back," and jumped out of the hole.

The government force was completely out of control as it continued into the woods shooting and yelling. They smelled blood and wanted some of it. They ran for 1000 yards and came to a sudden stop.

"I haven't run for some time, sir, and my stomach is saying 'screw you'," Jutte said as he leaned against a tree, trying to catch his breath.

"It's nice to see you, Jack. Thanks!" Pope said as he smiled at the pudgy soldier and patted him on the back.

"Well, shit, sir, I had to do my part keeping your whale spirit alive," the still-panting Jutte said between deep breaths, hands on knees.

The advisors all laughed, and Pope led them forward to find out the reason for the sudden stop. They walked past some government soldiers resting stone-faced.

Lying on the trail was the entire ARVN assault company. They were all dead. All of their weapons and some of their uniforms were stripped from them. It was apparent from their positions and the food scattered near the bodies that, against orders, they had stopped for lunch.

"Look, Johnny, there are spider holes dug six feet off both sides of the trail," Cox said.

"Yeah, the unlucky bastards stopped right in the middle of the kill zone. They couldn't have picked a worse place."

Holding up a round, man-hole-shaped mass of branches and vegetation, Jutte said, "Look at this. It looks like the VC had overhead cover.

They just hunkered down in their holes and, on signal, all popped up at the same time."

"Yeah, this guy even has powder burns on his face and neck," Cox said, pointing at the head of a dead ARVN soldier.

"Now we know where the guerrillas got their ARVN uniforms," McAllister said.

"We don't know what Charlie is going to do next, so we better establish a perimeter, take care of our wounded, and get a VC body and weapons count," Pope said.

"Good idea. Jutte, why don't you come with me, and we'll try to get the perimeter defense established with the remnants of the battalion," McAllister said.

"That leaves you and me with the lovely job of counting corpses, Bobby," Pope said and turned to accomplish the macabre task.

*   *   *

The first figure Pope and Cox had was 101 ARVN soldiers from 22nd Battalion KIA. As they retraced their steps to the open field, they found a few VC bodies, but there were many blood trails heading north. Two hundred yards from the clearing, they found VC bodies and equipment strewn everywhere among the debris from the fallen trees and branches. They were sprawled around on the ground in rag doll positions. Arms and legs askew— some missing. The smell of death and cordite permeated the battlefield.

They counted 127 enemy KIA and found 6 severely wounded VC but no weapons in the jungle area. When they got to the clearing, Vietnamese civilian medical personnel had already arrived and were working feverishly on friendly and enemy wounded.

They counted 162 dead and 16 wounded VC. They found 48 US carbines, two RPDs, and 201 AK 47s among the VC bodies. The body count totals were 289 confirmed VC KIA, and 22 VC WIA—over 300 casualties.

Cox saw his first dead VC woman in the clearing and said, "Hey, Johnny, this one's a woman. How do we count her?"

"She was picking up weapons and pulling wounded VC to safety. She's just as communist as the men," Pope said through a tight jaw. *Grandfather would not approve of this. He would say there is no honor in killing women,* Pope thought.

They would not be able to figure the total friendly casualties for a couple days because there were so many different government units involved. There was no doubt in Pope's mind that it was not a **great** victory. But they were able to make adjustments and turn defeat into victory.

* * *

It was late afternoon when medevac choppers flew in and hauled out the wounded. Trucks moved in from town to pick up all the bodies from the 22nd Battalion unit that had been ambushed. As Pope and Cox finished helping load some wounded into a chopper, Jutte and McAllister arrived and said the perimeter defense was completed.

"When we came down the road to reinforce you, we ran into Third Company of 22nd Battalion, who was heading back to sector headquarters," Cox said. "The company commander said that right after shooting started on the opposite side of the road where Second Company was, VC attacked them and drove them back. They couldn't communicate with battalion headquarters. He had light casualties," Cox added.

"It's a good thing you caught them and were able to talk them into coming with you," Pope said.

"You guys put up a hell of a fight. That 105 really brought some serious smoke on Charlie. Those woods look like someone chopped off the limbs for toothpicks. I'm really sorry about Sergeant Washington, sir." Jutte said to McAllister.

"Yeah, me too, Mac." Pope added. "Washington greased a guerrilla that I was wrestling with in my foxhole,"

"Thanks. He was a good soldier. He pulled Waters to safety just before he was killed."

"Damn. I didn't know that. By the way, where **is** Duke?" Jutte asked.

"He took a round in the leg and must have been medevaced before we got back from taking the body count," Pope said. "I think he'll be OK."

Phong ran up to the group and was clearly excited.

"I have just finished interrogating three wounded VC prisoners, one a battalion commander. We fought the 42nd VC Regiment, reinforced with the 17th VC battalion today. Their plans are to attack province headquarters tonight!" Phong shouted.

"Well, we bloodied their noses today. Maybe they'll head back into the woods and lick their wounds," McAllister said, realizing it was wishful thinking as soon as the words left his mouth.

"Yeah, but once Charlie makes a plan, they stick with it. Just like they did in Tuy An. They figure their battle plans are so good, regardless of what happens, they stick to it. We have to forget the dead now and use the trucks to get the troops back to sector headquarters to take up defensive positions," Pope advised.

"Yes. I'll get the soldiers into defensive positions now," Phong said over his shoulder as he ran down the road to the trucks.

"Bob, you and Jutte take your jeep, go to the airstrip, get the R & I platoon, take them to the advisory compound. They're pretty exposed out there all by themselves. We can use them to bolster our defense," Pope said.

"Will do," Cox said, turning toward the parked jeep.

"Roger, you and I need to head back to the advisory compound and establish defensive positions."

"I'll get on the jeep radio and see if I can get air from Special Zone or division," McAllister said as he slid into the jeep next to Pope.

As he drove the jeep back through the province town at break neck speed, Pope tried to think of a way to get Kathryn out. With the withdrawal of the R & I platoon from the airstrip, a fixed wing plane couldn't land there. Anyway, it would be dark soon, and no planes could land on the tiny field at night. The only hope was a chopper, but it would be dark in another half-hour.

"I've got Zone and division working on air support tonight, Johnny."

"Good. Now see if you can get a chopper in here to get Kathryn out before dark!"

*   *   *

Pope jumped out of the jeep at the compound and met Sullivan coming out of the dining hall. He briefed Sullivan on the results of the afternoon battle and the current intelligence that put the advisory team in peril.

Sullivan nodded and said, "We've got to get Kathryn out of here right away."

McAllister heard the Major as he arrived, shook his head slowly, and said, "Sorry, Johnny—there are no choppers available."

"Well, we better start positioning ammo, food, and water. I doubt if we'll be hit before midnight, so we have a little time," Pope said.

"Let's get moving then. We'll send two jeeps to the airstrip to transport the rest of the R & I platoon in here. McAllister, will you take care of that please?" Sullivan said.

"Yes sir," McAllister said, and he opened the door to the dining room to get another driver.

Pope followed him into the dining room to look for Kathryn. She stood by the door, hands on hips.

"Johnny Pope, I heard the whole thing from in here. I knew people got hurt in Vietnam before I came here. I can't think of any place I would rather be than right here. Captain McAllister, I can drive a jeep, let's go."

McAllister looked at Pope and said, "She's a hell of a lot of woman, man."

Pope was speechless as Kathryn kissed him lightly on the cheek. She followed the McAllister out the door, leaving him alone. *Yeah, she has the courage of a warrior,* Pope thought.

*   *   *

White and Gomez were in the command bunker testing the generator. Pope hauled bottled water into the bunker. Sullivan went into the command bunker to make a communications check. Granger and Bishop were carrying ammo to the foxhole positions.

Pope got with the squad leader of the compound security and told him what was expected. He ordered the squad leader to put his men under Sgt. Ma when he arrived with the R & I platoon. He went to the top of the sand dune where the advisors fighting positions were located and looked at the last fading glimmer of the sun as it slid behind the hills.

Pope thought: We'll have to get tied in with the government forces on the left and right flanks as soon as possible. With the woodline more than 300 yards away, Charlie will be exposed for a long time before he reaches our position. The minefield will slow him down, but we'll have to be alert initially for sappers trying to blow a hole in our barbed wire. I sure wish we could get Kathryn out before the fighting starts. Will the spirit of the whale be with me through this long night?

Chapter Twenty Nine

Darkness enveloped the defenders. By 2000 hours all the positions had been manned in the advisory compound. Cox, Jutte, and Martin occupied the left flank machine gun emplacement. Bishop, Granger, and White were in the right flank machine gun position. Both guns were set so that they had interlocking fire to cover the entire front.

In the center McAllister and Gomez occupied a third machine gun nest. Their mission was to pick up targets of opportunity. The R & I platoon and security squad occupied the site on the other side of the barracks, near the road. Sullivan and Bannister stayed in the command bunker. They had communication with province headquarters and Binh Lam Special Zone.

Pope's foxhole was about twenty yards behind Gomez and McAllister. He had a single strand "hot" telephone line to Ma to use if and when the reserve needed to be committed. But he thought when he felt it was necessary to commit the reserve, he would go back and get them and lead the counterattack. He didn't plan to spend much time in his foxhole because he would be checking the other positions, the reserves, and the command bunker throughout the night.

The team had built a wooden arrow about 12 feet long out of two inch by twelve-inch planks. On top of the planks were eight cans of fuel oil containing rags. When air strikes were needed at night, someone would light the fuel oil. The arrow is pointed toward the enemy, and air strikes could be made within two hundred yards in the direction the arrow was pointed, and friendly forces wouldn't be bombed during the fight.

The First RF Company was tied in on the right flank and provided security for sector headquarters. Third Company of the 22nd ARVN Battalion was on the left flank and connected. They were stretched pretty thin but had better defensible ground than they had earlier in the day. Pope estimated that the advisory team occupied the most likely avenue of approach for the VC attack. Having the additional firepower of three machine guns made the teams' defensive position more tenable. He wished they had enough men to occupy listening posts to let them know when Charlie moved closer. As long as he was wishing, he might as well wish for an ARVN division.

Then he remembered what his grandfather had told him when he was younger. "Wish in one hand and spit in the other. Then see which one fills first. You can't just wish for something. You have to work hard and make it happen. *Oh Grandfather, I sure miss your pearls of wisdom,* Pope thought.

*   *   *

Pope went to the command bunker, occupied by Sullivan, Bannister, and Kathryn. She was seated in the far corner, and Pope sat next to her and put his arm around her. "Do you remember how to shoot my pistol?" He asked, trying to sound cheerful.

"Yes, but do you think I'll need it?" She asked.

"Probably not, but it may give you some comfort."

She took the pistol, looked at it and pushed the safety off, then on. "I'm more worried about you, Johnny. You'll be out there in the middle of the fight."

Pope looked at her, started to say something, kissed her, and smiled. "Remember, Honey, the spirit of the whale is with me." He winked, and patted Bannister on the shoulder, as he left the bunker.

He checked the left flank machine gun position manned by Cox, Jutte and Martin.

The young clerk breathed deeply to control his shaking.

"Captain Pope, do you ever get scared?"

He was taken by surprise—not because of the question, but by the lack of response from Cox and Jutte.

"Of course I get scared, Jim. Any man going into combat that says he isn't scared is either a fool or a liar."

"But you Indians are supposed to love this shit, and combat is second nature to you. Besides, you've got that whale spirit protecting you."

Cox and Jutte both laughed, and Cox said, "Martin, you make the same mistake that most non-Indians make. You believe in the Hollywood stereotype given the Indians in the films about the west. Some Indians grow up in the city and know nothing about the forest or war until they go in the army."

"I understand that, Sir, but I know all about Captain Pope's exploits since he's been here. And besides, explain to me why the three of us are sitting in this hole sweating like a French poodle shitting peach seeds, and Captain Pope is wandering around as cool as a cucumber—like there ain't no VC regiment coming after us."

All three officers laughed, and Pope said, "I don't know what I can say to convince you I'm frightened—but that doesn't really matter. We're all alarmed, but how we handle ourselves in spite of being scared separates the soldiers from the cowards."

Jutte shrugged, his expression philosophical in the dark of night. "But if we all die here tonight, will we have died for anything?"

"I really can't answer that question, Jack. I wish I could. I can only say that when we volunteered to come to Vietnam, we believed that we were not only helping this tiny nation but were stemming the flow of communism toward our country," Pope said, as he shook his head. "But I can tell you that my world has gotten smaller. I'm fighting for something a lot simpler tonight. I'm fighting to stay alive and help the rest of the team stay alive."

"There you are, Johnny," Cox said, firmly.

"I'm convinced everyone will do their share tonight, and we'll do fine. Now let's keep our eyes on the wire and beyond," Pope said, and he turned to move toward his own foxhole.

*   *   *

The small advisory team stood in their fighting positions. Each in their own thoughts: Some about their homes and loved ones; some about their return home; and some about the attacking enemy. All of them wondered if they would live through the night.

Pope stood alone and thought about Martin's questions. This is what drew his grandfather into combat. It drew his father into the Second World War. All the blood of past warriors coursed through his veins. He could feel his grandfather and his father and all the Makah warriors around his foxhole. They loved being warriors, and he understood why: it was what he was meant to do.

*   *   *

At 2300 hours, Pope checked the defensive positions for the sixth time. He stopped by McAllister and Gomez foxhole.

"Hey, Gomez, if you see fire coming out of the sky, don't get shook—we've got 'Puff' on thirty minute alert," Pope said.

"What the fuck's Puff, sir."

"It's an old WW II, C47 aircraft called 'Puff the Magic Dragon'." McAllister offered.

"Jesus Christ! Here I am, putting my young Meskin ass on the line and Uncle Sugar can't get a newer plane than WW II!" Gomez said.

Both officers laughed. "Puff carries three machine guns. Each gun is like a gattling gun, with six barrels electrically rotated," Pope said.

"The weapon fires 6,000 rounds per minute. When all weapons are fired, it dispenses 18,000 rounds per minute. The guns are fixed in the aircraft, so they are aimed by the direction that the plane flies," McAllister added.

"All them numbers don't mean shit to me, sir. Will it rattle Charlie's shit?" Gomez asked.

"I've seen it in action in the highlands. They call it Puff because with all the tracer rounds being fired, at night it looks like a dragon breathing fire—hence, Puff the Magic Dragon," McAllister said.

"Well, I hope Charlie is in his fart sack early tonight and we don't need no Puff," Gomez sniffed.

* * *

Pope had just returned to his foxhole from the command bunker. It was exactly 2400 hours. The first rocket exploded 300 yards to his rear and blew up a house. A steady hail of rockets exploded to the left and right rear, hitting housing areas. Charlie walked the rocket fire toward the perimeter defense. The inexperienced Jim Martin pressed himself against the wall of his foxhole and clenched his teeth—waiting for the explosion that would end his young life. The rocketing continued for about an hour, with a few landing in the compound. No casualties.

Mortar rounds landed all around the town. Part of one wing of sector headquarters was on fire. An RPG round flew over the compound and exploded harmlessly on the helipad to the rear. There were five explosions in the minefield, and Pope crawled to McAllister and Gomez for a better view.

Gomez said, "Fuck, sir, I'm a non-combatant. I shouldn't even be here."

"Well, I'm glad you're here. We need you. But if you got a complaint see the chaplain tomorrow."

"Yeah, if I live that long."

An explosion in the minefield, and two trip flares went screaming into the sky: six VC sappers crawled in the wire. Both machine guns opened up and killed them instantly. Two fell over the barbed wire when they were hit. Sappers crawled up to the wire several more times and tried to cut a path. The machine guns took them under fire. Enemy machine gun fire came in from the woodline, 300 yards away.

"Don't try to return fire on the machine guns just yet." Pope shouted to the advisors. "You'll not only expose yourself, but also give away your positions. Toss grenades."

From the right came a scream, "medic."

Gomez ran in the direction of the scream. The medic was surprised he was not shot as he made the move. He jumped into the fighting position and landed on top of Granger.

"Ow! Damn, you trying to kill me?" the wounded officer said.

"Where are you hit, sir?" The medic asked, opening his medical kit.

"Left shoulder. I'm losing some blood, and it hurts like hell."

"OK. I can't see shit, but I'll bandage it and give you some pain pills. I can't give you any morphine 'cause you might pass out."

The medic bandaged the wound and returned to his foxhole. Enemy firing intensified.

A bugle sounded, and a hundred black, shadowy figures ran out of the jungle across the open field, headed straight for the barbed wire. Some of them were carrying wooden ladders.

"Damn. Of all the places around here to attack, Charlie picks my fucken foxhole to disrupt," Gomez shouted to no one in particular.

He picked up the CAR 15 Pope gave him and shot a sapper in the head and the enemy soldier slumped forward as if asleep. McAllister fired his 30-caliber machine gun, and, as fast as the enemy fell, more replaced them. Pope fired flares as fast as he could, illuminating the battlefield. Enemy ghosts moved toward them.

Pope got on the landline telephone and informed Sullivan, "We are under heavy fire by enemy mortars and are under attack by a VC battalion. You better call for Puff."

"You got it. Keep your head down," Sullivan, said and hung up the phone.

Enemy soldiers put the ladders across the barbed wire and crawled toward the hot death of the US machine guns. As fast as one VC was knocked off the ladder, another replaced him. All three machine guns were firing and cut down the exposed enemy soldiers.

The attack was broken, and the VC faded into the woodline. They carried dead and wounded on the assault ladders. Mortars and 105 rounds fired from ARVN positions hastened the enemy's retreat. Mortar fire fell in the compound. The small compound guardhouse disintegrated in a ball of flame.

*   *   *

In the command bunker Sullivan talked on the radio to Phan Thiet.

"This is Binh Tuy actual, get Puff to my location immediately, over."

"This is Phan Thiet, understand that you want Puff. What is your situation? Over."

"Get them in the air, call me back and I'll give you my God damn situation, out."

Bannister called Phong at sector headquarters and reported they were under heavy attack by a VC battalion.

Kathryn sat on the ground in the far corner of the bunker, looking at the pistol and absently shifting it from hand to hand. *What was it Johnny said? Put the safety off. Aim the pistol, using both eyes, hold it steady, and squeeze the trigger*, she thought. *It seems pretty easy, but can I point it at a man and pull the trigger? I sure wish Johnny was here—but he's busy doing his job. Safety off, point the pistol using both eyes to aim, hold it steady, squeeze the trigger…*

"Don't be alarmed, Kathryn. This bunker will withstand a direct hit from an enemy rocket," Sullivan yelled.

"Binh Tuy, this is Phan Thiet. Puff is enroute to your location. Estimated ETA three zero minutes. What is your situation? Over."

"This is Binh Tuy actual. We are under heavy mortar and rocket attack from at least a reinforced VC battalion. They have not penetrated our defenses yet, over."

"Roger, Binh Tuy, this is Phan Thiet. Good luck, out."

The three sat quietly in the dimly lit bunker, each in their own thoughts. They could hear the fighting getting closer.

*   *   *

A bugle sounded and 300 figures emerged from the woodline and hit the government defenses like a tidal wave. They attacked both flanks of the US advisors, but the main attack was once again right at the Americans. ARVN soldiers on both flanks opened fire on the enemy. It seemed like as fast as one was killed, two more appeared to replace him. The guerrillas reached the minefield. Several mines detonated, picked soldiers up and dropped them like rag dolls—and on they came. Charlie used his own men as human minesweepers. Under heavy fire from all three US positions, the VC still got through and over the barbed wire. Pope threw hand grenades as fast as he could, as far as he could.

"I'm going for reinforcements. We'll be right back," Pope yelled, as he sprinted around the corner of the dining hall and billets to the R & I platoon positions.

*   *   *

Cox fired at the enemy with his machine gun when a grenade exploded near the position, knocking him away from the gun.

Martin looked at Cox and said, "Half his face is gone L Tee, I'm sure he's dead."

"Keep up the fire Jim while I get this gun back into action," Jutte said. He picked up the weapon and stood in the foxhole and fired long bursts from the hip.

"Oh shit, they're really breaking through, sir. We can't hold them," Martin said, and he crouched in the hole and reloaded his weapon.

This must be what it's like to die, Jutte thought. *Everything seems to be happening so slowly, and I can see, smell, and hear better. I just hope the pain will not be bad. Well, I'll take some of these little bastards with me.* "Come on you sons of bitches! Jutte screamed. He fired the red-hot machine gun on full automatic.

Another grenade exploded next to the foxhole and Jutte fell sideways and landed on top of Martin, with a shell fragment wound to his stomach. Martin, thinking Jutte was dead, pulled the body of his fallen comrade over him. Intestines and blood from the open stomach wound saturated the Californian. He took off his hat and held it against the lieutenant's wound.

* * *

McAllister, saw the enemy pouring over the US position to his left and more VC five yards in front of him shouted, "Get down in the foxhole and play dead, Sarge. It's our only chance."

He grabbed Gomez and pulled him down, shielding him with his own body. Gomez looked up from the bottom of the foxhole and watched enemy soldiers run by. *He wondered why none stopped to finish them off.*

* * *

Bishop and his group fought their own little war with communists to their left. Granger yelled, "They've overrun both positions to our left. If we stay here we're dead. White, grab the ammo. Let's pull back to the supplementary positions."

All three continued to fire at the onrushing enemy as they crept back toward the command bunker. Bishop noticed that mortar rounds fell all around them, even though the enemy had penetrated the defenses. *What kind of people kills their own soldiers*, he thought?

* * *

In the bunker a shot rang out and Bannister slumped over, mortally wounded. Two guerrillas entered the room and one shot Sullivan, hitting him four times with AK 47 rounds. Kathryn calmly switched the safety to the off position aimed and shot both VC, killing them instantly. She saw another rifle muzzle by the doorway, behind the blanket door, and fired twice killing a third enemy soldier. Two more VC crept into the bunker. Kathryn aimed and kept pulling the trigger until the pistol was empty. Both communists fell face forward. Only one of them was dead. The other had been shot in the stomach, looked at her through half-glazed eyes and slowly brought his AK 47 up to a firing position.

*   *   *

The dining hall was on fire. Pope could hear small arms fire on the other side of the billets.

"Wa, they've broken through. You take your teams around the building to the right and I'll go to the left."

Pope lobbed two fragmentation grenades over the billets between the two buildings and ran to the left, 15 Yard scouts following. Three figures to his left crossed the volleyball court. He fired from the hip, and they went flying in the air before falling in separate clumps on the athletic court.

The Yards caught 15 VC between the burning dining room and the bunker and killed them instantly. Ma's Yard team swept past the bunker. Pope took another team left of the dining room and killed six VC near the silenced machine gun position. He threw two more grenades just past the machine gun emplacement. A mortar round landed near Pope, lifting him off his feet.

*   *   *

Pope regained consciousness, wondered how long he'd been out. His head ached, ears were ringing, and left arm hurt so badly he wanted to scream. Pope tried to flex the hand and couldn't. In the darkness, he felt the arm and found it wet with his own blood. No time to cover it with a bandage. He rose to his feet and ran to the left machine gun position. His R & I teams were lying next to the position, firing at the retreating enemy soldiers. Martin was crouched in the bottom of the foxhole next to Jutte. Pope picked up the machine gun and set it up again.

"Come on, Jim, get some ammo into this gun, and let's kick some ass."

"God! You have no idea how glad I am to see you, sir," Martin said. He loaded an ammo belt into the gun. Pope fired at the fleeing enemy. Martin felt something move by his foot and looked down. Jutte gasped for air.

"Christ, the L Tee is still alive. Medic!"

Wa met less resistance to the right, and his Yards swept up to the right machine gun position and fired at the retreating enemy soldiers. Bishop, Granger, and White were overrun, had retreated, then joined the Yards' counterattack. They carried their machine gun back into position.

McAllister and Gomez had crouched in the bottom of their hole until Charlie retreated, got up and joined the firing. A Yard took over Pope's machine gun, and Pope lobbed grenades at the enemy.

*   *   *

Pope fired his last illuminating flare and saw what looked like hundreds of advancing enemy. Others had left the woodline, joined the retreating soldiers, and turned them around.

"Christ. Here they come again," Bishop shouted.

Pope looked skyward and saw the lights of a lone airplane, circling the carnage below. He ran to the signal arrow, pointed it toward the enemy, and lit the fuel oil. Mortar rounds fell in the compound as he ran back to the center foxhole position to engage the advancing force.

The VC assault group hit the wire. "Puff" circled slowly, firing illumination rounds into the sky. Americans and Yards fired on the charging enemy and stopped them in their tracks. Puff turned slowly, lining up left-to-right across Charlie's charge.

A bright red streak erupted, like a dragon breathing fire. It cut the enemy down like a burning scythe and tore them into pieces.

"Come on, Puff, get some!" Gomez shouted. He looked up from bandaging Jutte's wounds.

The defensive force continued firing. Puff began a second run right-to-left. The dying attackers screamed and some were literally vaporized as they were blown to bits. The second run sent the remnants of the attackers in retreat. The US machine gunners knocked down black figures as the race against death continued. Puff made two more runs, attacking the woodline as he followed the beaten enemy.

Pope yelled at the soldiers, "Consolidate your ammo and be ready for the next attack."

Suddenly he thought, *Oh no, the VC got as far as the command bunker. Kathryn!*

He leaped out of the foxhole, ran around the still smoldering dining room building and burst into the darkened bunker yelling, "Kathryn! Major! Bannister!"

The familiar smell of death was overpowering in the small bunker. He stumbled over three bodies in the doorway, fell, and landed on a dead man. As Pope's face landed on the dead man's chest, he could tell by the smell that it was a VC. Feeling around near the radio, he found a candle and lit it. In the dim light of the candle, he saw Bannister hunched over the radio, dead. Beside him was the body of Sullivan with the radio hand set near him. In a split second, Pope thought: *It looks like the bunker didn't save you, sir.* He looked to his right and saw two more dead VC.

In the far right corner of the bunker, Kathryn sat on the ground in an upright position, legs sprawled apart. Her eyes were closed, and it looked like she was peacefully asleep. Pope's pistol was lying near her open hand. He could see that the weapon was empty, and she had put up a hell of a fight. The front of Kathryn's blouse was covered with blood. He rushed across the bunker, but he knew she was dead before he got to her. He sat down on the sandy floor and pulled her onto his lap. Pope cradled her lifeless body in his arms, stroked her hair, rocked back and forth, and wept.

"What kind of war is this? US soldiers put out in the middle of no-where to advise foreign soldiers in their war. Spies in our midst who assassinate their relatives! Commanders kill their own soldiers with mortar fire! Women on both sides, locked in mortal combat. I didn't sign up for this! This isn't a warrior's war! Oh, Grandfather! You said the Whale spirit would be with me and no one would die! But you didn't tell me that you can die a little bit at a time by losing the woman you love."

End

About the Author

1-595-12148-9

Charles A. Hall is a full-blood Native American—registered Makah, who was born near Neah Bay, WA. He spent his first few years and several later years on the Indian reservation. Dr. Hall completed a twenty-year career in the US Army as an infantry and intelligence officer, and retired as a Lieutenant Colonel—one of the highest-ranking full blood Native Americans to serve. The author recently completed a twenty-year career as a public school teacher, coach, high school principal, and superintendent of schools. Degrees were earned at Eastern Michigan University (BS), Antioch University (MA), and Century University (Ph.D.). Other books include: ABC's of School leadership, and So You Want To Be A School Administrator? The Sure fire Way to Land that Principal Or superintendent Job. He and his wife, Katherine move between their homes in Yelm, Washington and Mazatlan, Mexico.

Glossary

Actual	The unit commander. Used to differentiate between the radio operator and the actual commander.
Advisor	A US citizen sent to Vietnam to provide advice to Vietnamese military and civilian officials.
Agent	Someone hired by a government to provide enemy intelligence.
Agent Handler	An individual that recruits, pays, and obtains intelligence from an agent. He or she usually handles more than one agent.
AK-47	7.62mm Soviet-bloc assault rifle.
Ao Dai	Traditional Vietnamese female dress.
Airborne	Paratroopers. Soldiers and equipment dropped from an airplane by parachute.
Air Cover	Aircraft overflying a ground combat unit on a search and destroy mission.
Ambush	A tactical maneuver where one force surprises another.
A1E Skyraider.	Propeller-driven fixed wing fighter/bomber. Slower than a jet, but can carry larger payload and stay over the target longer.
ARVN	The Army of the Republic of Vietnam. Vietnamese government soldiers advised by US soldiers.
ATT	Army Training Test. Tests given annually to army units to test their level of combat readiness.

AWOL	Absent without leave.
Battalion	A military unit of 300-500 soldiers. There are usually three companies in a battalion.
BOQ	Bachelors Officer Quarters'. Where officers without families resided.
Boonie rat	An infantryman, grunt, dog face soldier, snuffy.
Cammies	Camouflage uniforms, unique to ARVN airborne, ranger and special forces units.
CAR 15	Similar to M-16 rifle but has a shorter barrel and folding stock. It is lightweight and can be fired on automatic as well as semi-automatic.
Charlie	Short for Victor Charlie, the phonetic representation of VC, and the abbreviation for Viet Cong.
Cherry	A soldier who has never been shot at or gone on a search and destroy mission.
Chieu Hoi	Vietnamese words for "Open Arms." A program where enemy soldiers could surrender. Also Viet Cong sympathizers and civilians with no identification cards. They were sent to a retraining program, given identification cards, and released.
Chopper	Helicopter.
Chopper pad	Designated location for helicopters to land.
Chow	Food or a meal.
CIB	Combat Infantryman's Badge. Awarded to officer and enlisted personnel in an infantry occupational specialty, in combat for 30 days and shot at by a hostile force.
Claymore	A fan shaped anti-personnel mine. Has a plastic case and contains steel ball bearings. It is electrically detonated.
Commo	Communication. Either a radio or telephone.
Company	A military unit usually composed of 100-150 soldiers. There are usually three platoons in a company.

COMUSMACV	Commander, United States Military Assistance Command, Vietnam. Highest ranking US officer in Vietnam.
Concertina	Coiled, barbed wire used around the perimeter of a defense force.
Cordon and Search	A military operation to surround a village at night, then call the villagers together to check identification.
C Rats	US produced combat rations. Mostly canned food that had a long shelf life. Considered tastier than Vietnamese food. Higher in nutrition.
Counterpart	Vietnamese officer that a US army officer is assigned to advise.
Dai Uy	Vietnamese for Captain.
DEROS	Date Estimated Return from Overseas Service. The date that all advisors kept track of as the day they leave Vietnam for home.
Division	A military unit consisting of 7,000 soldiers. There are usually three regiments in a division.
Double agent	An individual that works for both opposing forces. Sometimes neither force is aware of the employment by the other. At other times an agent handler can recruit an agent to be a double agent. In either case, the double agent is dangerous.
EIB	Expert Infantryman Badge. Awarded to enlisted men and officers of infantry that passed a grueling series of tests. Not many soldiers qualified for the badge. El Tee Spelling of Lt. The abbreviation for lieutenant.
EM	US Army enlisted men.
Escort	Armed helicopter escorting another helicopter.
Get Some	Slang for killing the enemy.
GVN	Government of Vietnam. Government US supports.

Hamlet	A village where civilians lived. Usually a fenced in housing area guarded by popular force soldiers.
H & I	Harassment and Interdiction. Artillery fire. Targets were usually places enemy is expected to be. Used at night to harass the enemy.
Horn	Radio.
Hump	To walk or carry a rucksack or backpack.
Infrastructure	The organization and/or leadership of an organization or group.
Info	Information concerning friendly or enemy activities.
J-2	Joint intelligence section for MACV. This organization gathers intelligence on the enemy forces.
K-Bar	A military multipurpose knife.
KIA	Killed In Action. Used to report enemy or friendly casualties.
Killing zones	The area in an ambush where enemy soldiers are expected to be under most fire from an ambushing unit.
Latrine	Toilet.
LT	Lieutenant. An officers rank. Also called El Tee.
LZ	Landing Zone for a helicopter.
MACV	Military Assistance Command Vietnam. The command in which all military personnel in Vietnam were assigned.
Mas 36 rifle	An old rifle that was used by the French in the Indochinese War.
MedCap	A team of medics that go into villages and treat sick and injured civilians.
Medevac	Medical evacuation by chopper.
M14	Standard 7.62mm rifle issued to US advisors.
M60	US army machine gun. Used on Huey choppers. Fires 7.62mm rounds.
Mole	A spy that has been working among the government forces for several years.

Montagnard	Indigenous mountain people from the Central Highlands of Vietnam.
OD	Olive Drab. Army color. A dull dark green.
PF	Popular Forces soldiers. They were home guards for local villages.
Platoon	A military unit traditionally composed of 40 soldiers.
Point or Point Man	The first man in line of a squad or platoon as they walk on a trail or through the jungle.
POW	Prisoner of War.
PRC 25	radio used by US advisors.
PSP	Perforated Steel Panels used to build airstrips and bridge surfaces. Also used for the top of fortifications to absorb the impact of enemy rockets and mortars.
PSYOPS	Psychological Operations. Propaganda operations against the enemy.
Pull pitch	Military term for a helicopter quickly gaining altitude.
PX	Post Exchange. The store where US personnel bought personal goods shipped from the United States.
QRF	Quick Reaction force. A unit on stand by to reinforce a smaller unit engaged in a fight they couldn't handle themselves.
Recon	Reconnaissance. To go out and look around for the enemy or check out an area on the ground.
RF	Regional force unit. Soldiers under the control of the Province chief.
Regiment	A military unit of 1,000 soldiers. There are usually three battalions in a regiment.
ROTC	Reserve Officers Training Corp. Officers take this training in college for a commission in the army.
RPD	Soviet-bloc machine gun. Similar to US M-60 except tracer rounds fired are green.

RPG 7	A communist-made anti tank rocket used by the Viet Cong.
RTO	Radio Telephone Operator.
R & R	Rest and Recreation. US soldiers usually had an out of country R & R of about five days in Hawaii or Thailand.
Ruff Puff	regional force unit.
Satchel Charge	An explosive device usually carried in a canvas bag. Used by VC sappers to blow openings in barbed wire or government buildings.
Search and Destroy	A military mission to seek out the enemy and destroy him, but not to hold ground.
Sector	Province.
Short	An advisor that has less than 90 days before he goes home.
Sub Sector	District.
SFC	Sergeant First Class. A senior non-commissioned officer in the US army.
SOIC	Sector Operations and Intelligence Center. Vietnamese headquarters and nerve center for the province. Most of the military planning is conducted in this office.
Special Zone	Binh Lam Special Zone. An Intermediate support headquarters between province and division headquarters.
Spider hole	A fighting foxhole usually used by the Viet Cong.
Smoke grenade	A canister about twice the size of a hand grenade. Used to signal aircraft, but used in larger numbers, can be used to mask friendly forces.
Sp4	Specialist Fourth Class. A rank for an enlisted person.
Stars and Stripes	A US military newspaper.

II Corps	A tactical zone. The country of Vietnam was divided into four tactical zones. Binh Tuy was part of II Corps and on the boundary of III Corps.
USAID	United States Aid to International Development. A State Department organization.
VC	Viet Cong. The guerrillas—the enemy.
WIA	Wounded in Action. Term used in reporting of friendly and enemy casualties.
Yards	Shortening of Montagnard name for Montagnard hill people.

Order Information

The author has written two other books:

So You Want to Be A School administrator? The sure Fire Way to Land that principal or Superintendent Job: A simple, step-by-step method for you to land that dream job!

ABCs of School Leadership: Valuable tips from a practitioner that will help you be a successful school principal or superintendent.

Tear out this sheet and give it to a friend so that he/she may order a book (s):

Telephone Orders:

To order, please contact customer service at 1-877-823-9235, Monday through Friday, 9:00 AM to 6:00 PM, Central Standard Time

On Line order:

Visit our web site at www.iuniverse.com, 24 hours a day, seven days a week, to order on line or generate a printable order form that can be faxed to 1-402-323-7824.

Please note that we accept Visa, MasterCard, American Express, and cashier's checks or money orders.

Printed in the United States
21530LVS00002B/136

9 780595 121489